Books Belong To:
Ridgeview Assisted Living
872 Golf View Drive
Medford, OR 97504

Peter Tremayn̲... well-known authorit... his knowledge of t... ...tury Irish society t... ...ctive fiction.

Sister Fidelma made her first appearance in October 1993 when she appeared in no less than four short stories in different detective anthologies: 'Murder in Repose' (*Great Irish Detective Stories*, ed. Peter Haining), 'The High King's Sword' (*Chronicles of Historical Crime*, ed. Mike Ashley), 'Hemlock at Vespers' (*Midwinter Mysteries 3*, ed. Hilary Hale) and 'Murder by Miracle' (*New Constable Crime*, ed. Maxim Jakobowski). The *Book and Magazine Collector* has already predicted that 'Sister Fidelma ... promises to be one of the most intriguing new characters in 1990s detective fiction'. ABSOLUTION BY MURDER, Peter Tremayne's first Sister Fidelma Mystery, is also available from Headline.

Also by Peter Tremayne from Headline

Absolution By Murder
Suffer Little Children
The Subtle Serpent
The Spider's Web
Valley of the Shadow
The Monk Who Vanished

Shroud for the Archbishop

Peter Tremayne

HEADLINE

Copyright © 1995 Peter Tremayne

The right of Peter Tremayne to be identified as the Author of
the Work has been asserted by him in accordance with the
Copyright, Designs and Patents Act 1988.

First published in 1995
by HEADLINE BOOK PUBLISHING

First published in paperback in 1995
by HEADLINE BOOK PUBLISHING

10 9 8 7 6

All rights reserved. No part of this publication may be
reproduced, stored in a retrieval system, or transmitted,
in any form or by any means without the prior written
permission of the publisher, nor be otherwise circulated
in any form of binding or cover other than that in which
it is published and without a similar condition being
imposed on the subsequent purchaser.

All characters in this publication, other than the historical
personages, are fictitious and any resemblance to real persons,
living or dead, is purely coincidental.

ISBN 0 7472 4848 6

Printed and bound in Great Britain by
Caledonian International Book Manufacturing Ltd, Glasgow

HEADLINE BOOK PUBLISHING
A division of Hodder Headline PLC
338 Euston Road
London NW1 3BH

For Peter Haining; who advised at the christening, also for Mike Ashley; the first 'converts' of Sister Fidelma.

Everywhere there is one principle of justice, that is the interest of the stronger.

The Republic
Plato (427–347 BC)

HISTORICAL NOTE

The setting of this tale is Rome during the late summer of 664 AD.

Readers unfamiliar with the so-called 'Dark Ages' should be aware that the concept of celibacy among the Christian religious, both in the Roman Catholic and in what is now called the Celtic church, was not universal. While there were always ascetics who sublimated physical love in a dedication to a deity, it was not until the Council of Nicea, in 325 AD, that clerical marriages were condemned but not banned. The concept of celibacy in the Roman Church arose from the customs practised by the pagan priestesses of Vesta and the priests of Diana. By the fifth century Rome had forbidden clerics from the rank of abbot and bishop to sleep with their wives and, shortly after, even to marry at all. The general clergy were discouraged from marrying by Rome but not forbidden to do so. Indeed, it was not until the reforming papacy of Leo IX (1049–54 AD) that a serious attempt was made to enforce the western clergy to accept universal celibacy.

In the Eastern Orthodox Church, priests below the rank of abbot and bishop have retained their right to marry until this day.

The condemnation of the 'sin of the flesh' remained alien to Celtic Church concepts for a long time after Rome's attitude became a dogma. Both sexes inhabited abbeys and monasteries which were known as *conhospitae*, or double houses, where men and women lived raising children in Christ's service. A knowledge of this fact is essential to an understanding of some of the tensions of this story.

Chapter One

The night was warm and fragrant; but as oppressively scented as only a Roman summer's night can frequently be. The gloom-shrouded courtyard of the Lateran Palace was filled with the bitter-sweet scents of the herbs that grew in the well-tended beds around its borders; the muskiness of basil and the pungent smell of rosemary ascended, almost overpoweringly, in the stifling air. The young officer-of-the-watch of the palace *custodes* raised his hand to wipe the perspiration from his brow where it gathered in droplets on his forehead beneath the bronze visor of his helmet. Although the atmosphere was sultry now, he reflected that in a few hours he would be glad of the warmth of the tough woollen *sagus*, hanging loosely from his shoulders, for the temperature would sink into a sudden pre-dawn chill.

The single bell from the nearby basilica of St John chimed the midnight hour, the hour of the Angelus. As the bell chimed, the young officer dutifully mumbled the ritual prayer: '*Angelus Domini nuntiavit Mariae* . . . The angels of the Lord announced unto Mary . . .' He muttered the prayer automatically, with neither feeling for the words nor the meaning of the sentences. Perhaps it was because his mind was not concentrating on the formula that he heard the noise.

Above the tenor chiming of the single bell and the gushing of the small fountain in the centre of the courtyard, there came another sound to the young man's ears. The sound of leather scraping on paving stone. The youthful *custos* frowned, holding his head to one side to identify the direction of the noise.

He was sure that he had heard a heavy footfall in the dark shadows of the far side of the courtyard.

'Who's there?' he demanded.

No answer came back.

The officer-of-the-watch eased his short sword from its leather sheath, the broad-bladed *gladius* with which the famed legions of Rome had once imposed their imperial will on the peoples of the world. He frowned at his inconsequential thought. Now this same short sword defended the safety of the palace of the Bishop of Rome, the Holy Father of the Universal Church of Christ – *Sacroscancta Laternensis ecclesia, omnium urbis et orbis ecclesiarum mater et caput.*

'Who is there? Show yourself' he called again, his voice raising harshly with the command.

No answer again but . . . yes; the officer heard a shuffling, hurried step now. Someone was moving away from the shrouded courtyard and down one of the darkened alleyways. The *custos* silently cursed the darkness of the courtyard but, with swift strides, he moved over its paved stones and reached the entrance to the alley. In the gloom he could see a figure, with hunched shoulders, moving rapidly along it.

'Halt!'

The young officer summoned as much force as he could into his voice.

The figure broke into a run, the leather of its flat-soled

sandals slapping noisily on the stone.

Letting dignity go to the wind, the *custos* began to run down the alley. While he was young and agile, his quarry seemed more nimble for when the officer reached the end of the alley there was no sign of the object of his pursuit. The alley opened out into a larger courtyard. This courtyard, unlike the smaller courtyard from where he had come, was well lit with several blazing torches. The reason for this was simple; this courtyard was surrounded by the chambers of the administrators of the papal palace while the smaller courtyard gave entrance only to the guests' sleeping quarters.

The young officer halted, eyes narrowed, and stared around the large rectangle. On the far side, against the entrance to one of the main buildings he could see two of his fellow *custodes* standing guard. If he called to them for assistance, he might warn his quarry. He compressed his lips and continued his narrow-eyed examination. But he could see no one else. He began to walk across the courtyard with the purpose of asking the other *custodes* if they had seen anyone exit from the alleyway when he was halted by a slight noise behind him to his left.

He swung round peering into the gloom.

A dark figure stood before one of the doors facing onto the courtyard.

'Identify yourself' he commanded harshly.

The figure stiffened and then took a few paces forward but made no reply.

'Come forward and be identified!' snapped the officer, sword held ready across his breastplate.

'In the name of God,' wheezed a voice unctuously, 'you identify yourself first!'

Surprised by the answer, the young man replied:

'I am the *tesserarius* Licinius of the *custodes*. Now identify yourself!' Licinius could not help a sense of pride in his rank for he had been newly promoted. In the ancient imperial army the rank signified the officer who received from his general the ticket, or *tessera*, on which the password of the day was written. For the *custodes* of the Lateran Palace, it was the rank of the officer-of-the-watch.

'I am Brother Aon Duine,' came the reply in the lisping accent of a foreigner. The man made a further step forward so that the flickering light of a nearby torch fell on his features. Licinius observed that the man was slightly rotund and spoke with the wheeze of someone with respiratory problems, or someone who might have been running shortly before.

Licinius examined the man suspiciously and motioned him forward another pace so that the light might fully illuminate him. The brother had a full, moon face and wore the outlandish tonsure of an Irish monk whereby the front of the head was shaved from a line from ear to ear with the hair worn long behind.

'Brother "Ayn-dina"?' He tried to repeat the name given to him by the monk.

The man smiled a pleasant affirmation of the name.

'What are you doing here at this hour?' the young officer demanded.

The rotund, middle-aged monk spread his hands.

'That is my office, *tesserarius*,' he said in explanation, motioning to the building behind him.

'Have you been in the small courtyard yonder?' Licinius asked, pointing with his short sword up the dark alleyway.

The moon-faced monk blinked and looked surprised.

'Why should I have been there?'

4

Licinius sighed in exasperation.

'I chased someone down that alley but a moment ago. Do you say that it was not you?'

The monk shook his head vigorously.

'I have been at my desk until I left my office just now. I came into the courtyard and was accosted by you as I stepped beyond the door.'

Licinius sheathed his sword and passed a hand across his forehead in perplexity.

'And you saw no one else, someone who had been running?'

Again the monk shook his head emphatically.

'None before you called on me to identify myself.'

'Then forgive me, brother, and be about your business.'

The rotund monk paused only a moment to bow his head in gratitude before scurrying away across the courtyard, the leather of his sandals slapping as he made his way through the arched entrance to the streets of the city beyond.

One of the guards from the main gate, a *decurion*, had crossed the courtyard to see what the disturbance was about.

'Ah, Licinius! It's you. What is happening?'

The *tesserarius* grimaced in his annoyance.

'Someone was skulking up in the small courtyard yonder, Marcus. I challenged him and chased him down here. Now he seems to have eluded me.'

The *decurion* named Marcus chuckled softly.

'Why should you be pursuing anyone, Licinius? What's so improper about anyone being in the small courtyard at this hour or any hour?'

Licinius looked sourly at his colleague, feeling bitter at the world and, in particular, the guard duty he had landed that night.

'Don't you know? The *domus hospitale*, the guest chambers, are situated there. And His Holiness has special guests; bishops and abbots from the outlandish Saxon kingdoms. I was told to mount a special guard on them, for the Saxons are said to have enemies in Rome. I have been told to question anyone behaving suspiciously in the vicinity of the guest chambers.'

The other *custos* gave a dismissive sniff.

'I thought the Saxons were still pagans?' He paused and then nodded in the direction in which the monk had vanished. 'Who were you questioning just now if that was not your suspicious character?'

'An Irish monk. Brother "Ayn-dina", he called himself. He happened to come out of his office there and I thought he might have been the man whom I was pursuing. Anyway, he hadn't seen anyone.'

The *decurion* grinned crookedly.

'That door leads to no office but to the storehouse of the *sacellarius*, His Holiness' treasurer. It has been padlocked for years, certainly ever since I have been a guard here.'

With a startled look at his comrade, Licinius grabbed the nearby brand torch from its metal holder and took it to the door from which the monk had claimed to emerge. The rusted bolts and padlock confirmed the *decurion*'s statement. The *tesserarius* Licinius swore in a language totally unfitted for a member of His Holiness' palace guard.

The man sat hunched over the wooden table, head bent over a sheet of vellum, his mouth compressed in a thin line of concentration. In spite of the position of his body, it was obvious that he was a tall man. His head was uncovered showing the distinctive tonsure of the religious on the crown of his head, surrounded by tufts of jet-black hair which balanced his swarthy skin and dark eyes. His features spoke of a life lived constantly in a warm climate. They were thin, the nose aquiline and prominent; the nose of a Roman patrician. The cheekbones were conspicuous under the sunken flesh. The face was scarred somewhat, perhaps from the ravages of smallpox contracted in his childhood. The narrow lips were red almost as if their colour was artificially heightened.

He was quiet and still as he bent to his task.

Even if the tonsure had not marked his religious calling, his clothing did so for he wore the *mappula*, a white fringed cloth, the *campagi*, flat, black slippers and *udones*, white stockings, all inherited from the imperial magistrature of the Roman Senate, which now marked him as a senior member of the Roman clergy. Even more distinctive was the thin scarlet silk *tunica* and the ornate crucifix of gold inlaid with precious stones which also proclaimed him to be more than a simple cleric.

The soft tinkle of a bell interrupted his concentration and he glanced up with an expression of irritation.

A door opened at one end of the large cool marble hall to allow a young monk in a rough brown homespun habit to enter. The newcomer carefully shut the door behind him; then, folding his arms in his broad sleeves, he hurried to the table at which the man sat, his flat-soled slippers slapping hollowly on the mosaic floor of the hall as he seemed to waddle, almost duck fashion.

'*Beneficio tuo*,' the monk bowed his head and uttered the ritual opening.

The older man sat back and sighed, not returning the ritual but simply waving his hand for the monk to state his business.

7

'By your leave, Venerable Gelasius, there is a young sister in the outer chamber who demands to be received.'

Gelasius raised a dark eyebrow threateningly.

'*Demands*? A young sister, you say?'

'From Ireland. She has brought the rule of her monastery to be received and blessed by the Holy Father and bears some personal messages from Ultan of Armagh to His Holiness.'

Gelasius smiled thinly.

'So the Irish still seek the blessing of Rome even when they argue against the practices of Rome? Is that not a curious contradiction, Brother Donus?'

The monk contrived to shrug with his arms still folded in his voluminous sleeves.

'I know little of these outlandish places, save that I believe the people follow the heresy of Pelagius.'

Gelasius pursed his lips.

'And the young sister *demands* . . .?' He accented the word for the second time.

'She has been waiting to be received these five days, Venerable Gelasius. Some bureaucratic muddle, no doubt.'

'Well, as this sister brings us word from the archbishop of Armagh we should receive her at once, especially as our young sister has journeyed all this way to Rome. Yes, let us see her and the rule she brings and hear her arguments as to whether the Holy Father should receive her. Does this young sister have a name, Brother Donus?'

'Indeed,' replied the young monk. 'But it is some peculiar name which I cannot quite pronounce. It is similar to either Felicity or Fidelia.'

A wan smile spread over Gelasius' thin lips.

'Either may be a portent, for Felicitas was the goddess of

good fortune in Rome, while Fidelia means one that can be trusted – faithful and steadfast. Bid her enter.'

The young monk bowed and slapped his way across the expanse of the echoing hall to the door.

Gelasius set his papers aside and sat back in his carved wooden chair to watch the entrance of the young foreigner announced by his factotum, Brother Donus.

The door opened and a tall figure in the robes of a religieuse entered. The dress was obviously foreign to Rome, Gelasius observed; the undyed wool *camilla* and white linen *tunica* placed the wearer as someone newly arrived in Rome's warmer climate. The woman crossed the mosaic floor of the hall with a youthful spring to her step that seemed at odds with the demure posture required by the religious habit. But her manner of approach was not ungraceful. Gelasius noted that while she was tall, her figure was well proportioned. Rebellious strands of red hair streaked from under her head-dress. His dark eyes alighted on the young, attractive features of her face and stayed fascinated by the bright green of her eyes.

She halted before him, frowning slightly. Gelasius remained seated in his chair and stretched out his left hand, on whose third finger was a large gold band inset with an emerald stone. The young woman hesitated and then stretched forth her right hand to grip Gelasius' hand gently, jerking her head forward stiffly from the neck.

Gelasius controlled his surprised features. In Rome a member of the religious would have knelt before him and kissed his ring in token of recognition of his high office. This strange young foreigner had merely bowed her head in acknowledgment of his office and not in obsequiousness. Her expression was slightly fixed as if to disguise her irritation.

'Welcome, Sister . . . Fidelia . . .?' Gelasius hesitated over the name.

The young woman's expression did not change.

'I am Fidelma of Kildare in the kingdom of Ireland.'

Gelasius noted her voice was firm and not awed by the tapestried splendour of her surroundings. Strange, he reflected, how these foreigners seemed unaffected by the might, wealth and sanctity of Rome. Britons and Irish reminded him of the stiff-necked Gauls he had read about in Caesar and Tacitus. Wasn't there a king of the Britons, brought by Claudius as a captive to Rome, who, looking on the mighty splendour, had not been struck with dread but merely said: 'And when you have all this, do you still envy us our hovels in Britain?' Gelasius was a man proud of his Roman patrician past and often wished he had been born in the golden days of the empire of the early Caesars. He stirred uncomfortably at the thought which was at odds with the humble ambition of his faith and brought his mind back to the figure before him.

'Sister Fidelma?' he repeated the name carefully.

The young woman gestured gracefully in acknowledgement of his pronunciation.

'I have come here at the request of the archbishop Ultan of Armagh to bring . . .'

Gelasius held up his hand to still the tide of words that came rushing out.

'Is this your first visit to Rome, sister?' he asked softly.

She paused and then nodded, wondering if she had made some error of protocol in address to this senior figure of the church whose name the factotum had not even informed her of.

'How long have you been in our beautiful city?'

Gelasius wondered if he had heard that young woman repress a sigh? There was a slight movement, an exaggerated rise and fall of her bosom.

'I have been seeking audience with the Bishop of Rome for five days . . . I regret that I have not been informed of your name or position.'

Gelasius' thin lips trembled with the hint of a smile. He admired the young woman's directness.

'I am Bishop Gelasius,' he replied. 'I hold the office of *nomenclator* to His Holiness. My function is to receive all petitions to the Holy Father, assess whether he is to see them and offer my advice to him.'

Sister Fidelma's eyes lightened.

'Ah, now I see why I have been sent before you,' she commented, the square set of her shoulders dropping slightly as she relaxed a little. 'It is difficult to respond adequately when no one tells you of the rituals of office here. You will forgive me if I make mistakes and blame it merely on my foreign birth and upbringing?'

Gelasius inclined his head in humorous solemnity.

'Nicely said, sister. You speak an excellent Latin for one whose first visit it is to our city.'

'I am also versed in Greek and have a little Hebrew. I have a small facility with languages and even speak some of the tongue of the Saxons.'

Gelasius stared hard at her in case she was gently mocking him. There was no boast to the woman's tone and Gelasius was impressed by her continued directness.

'And where did you achieve these accomplishments?'

'I studied as a noviate at Kildare, in the house established

11

by the Blessed Brigid, and later with Morann at Tara.'

Gelasius frowned in surprise.

'You studied and learnt your languages only in Ireland? Well, I have heard of your schools but now I have proof of their excellence. Be seated, sister, and let us discuss the reason for your visit here. The journey from Ireland must have been long and tiring and fraught with dangers? Surely you did not make it alone?'

Fidelma glanced round in the direction Gelasius had indicated, saw a small wooden chair nearby and moved it into position facing the bishop. She sat down and settled herself before replying.

'I journeyed here in the company of Brother Eadulf of Canterbury who is *scriba* to Wighard, the archbishop-designate of Canterbury in the Saxon kingdom of Kent.'

Gelasius raised a quizzical brow.

'Surely I am told that you Irish have little in common with Canterbury or are you one of the few Irish brethren who has accepted the rule of Rome rather than that of Columba?'

Fidelma smiled faintly.

'I hold to the rule of Palladius and Patrick who converted our small island to the faith,' she said quietly. 'I had been attending the synod at Witebia and came to know the Saxon delegates. It was at the end of the synod that Deusdedit, the archbishop of Canterbury, fell sick and died of the Yellow Plague. Wighard, as archbishop-designate, announced his intention to journey here, to Rome, for the papal blessing of his office, and, as Ultan had instructed me to bring the *Regula coenobialis Cill Dara* here, I decided to journey in the company of Brother Eadulf, whom I had come to know and respect.'

'And what were you doing in attendance at the council at

Witebia, sister? I have already had news of that argument between the advocates for usage of the customs of Rome and those of your own Irish churches. Did not our Roman representatives win the argument and cause the withdrawal of your Irish delegates?'

Fidelma ignored the mocking tone in Gelasius' voice.

'I attended the synod to give legal advice to the delegates of our church.'

The bishop's eyebrow shot up in astonishment.

'You were there to give legal advice?' he asked in bemusement.

'I am not only a religieuse but a *dálaigh* of the Brehon Court of Ireland ... that is, I am an advocate tutored in both the code of the civil law of the *Senchus Mór* and of the criminal law of the *Leabhar Acaill* by which our country is governed in justice.'

Gelasius' face was a mask of incredulity.

'Is it then the custom for the kings of Ireland to allow women to be advocates in their courts of law?'

Fidelma shrugged indifferently.

'Among my people, woman can fulfil any profession including kingship and the leadership of their people in battle. Who has not heard of Macha of the Red Tresses, our greatest warrior queen? Yet I have heard that women are not so equally regarded in Rome.'

'You may be assured of it,' Gelasius replied vehemently.

'Is it true that no women can then aspire to any of the learned professions for public practice in Rome?'

'Indeed not.'

'Then it is a strange society that denies itself the use of the talents of half of its population.'

'No stranger, good sister, than a society that allows women an equal place. In Rome you will observe that the father or husband has complete control over the women of his family.'

Fidelma grimaced sarcastically.

'It is a wonder that I am allowed to tread the streets of this city without being accosted for my effrontery.'

'Your habit is recognised in place of the *stola matronalis* and you may not only visit public places of worship, but theatres, shops and law courts. However, these privileges are not open to one who does not wear the habit of a religieuse or who is unmarried. Maidens must remain in the proximity of their own homes. However, women of our upper classes can even take an influential part in affairs of business provided it is done in the privacy of their own palaces and conducted through their husbands or fathers.'

Fidelma shook her head sombrely.

'Then this is a sad city for women.'

'It is the city of the Blessed Peter and of Paul who brought us light in the darkness of our paganism and it was given to Rome to spread that light throughout the world.'

Gelasius spoke proudly, perhaps too proudly, as he sat back and studied the young woman. He was a man of his nation, his city and his class.

Fidelma made no reply. She was diplomat enough to realise when words led only to bolted doors. After a moment or two it was Gelasius who prompted the conversation.

'Your journey, then, was without incident?'

'The journey from Massilia was quiet except for one point when a sail appeared on the southern horizon and the captain nearly ran the ship on to some rocks for fear.'

Gelasius' expression was serious.

'It might have been a ship of some of the fanatical Arabian followers of Mahomet who have been raiding throughout the Mediterranean against all the ships and ports of our Emperor Constans. They continually ravage our southern ports. Thanks be to God, that your ship was safely delivered from their hands.' Gelasius paused to reflect a moment before continuing: 'And do you have good accommodation in the city?'

'Thank you, I have. I am lodging in a small hostel not far from here next to the oratory of the Blessed Prassede by the Via Merulana.'

'Ah, the hostel administered by the deacon Arsenius and his good wife Epiphania?'

'Exactly so.'

'Good. I shall know where to contact you. Now let us examine the messages you have brought from Ultan of Armagh.'

Fidelma's well-shaped chin raised a little pugnaciously.

'Those are for the eyes of His Holiness alone.'

Gelasius' brows drew together in annoyance, he stared at the bold green eyes confronting him and then he seemed to change his mind and nodded with a broad smile.

'You are quite right, sister. But it is the rule here that they pass through my office as *nomenclator*. I must also examine the rule that you have brought for the Holy Father to bless. That is in my jurisdiction to examine,' he added with mocking emphasis.

Sister Fidelma reached within her robes and drew forth the rolls of vellum. She handed them across to the bishop. He unrolled them, glancing through their contents before setting them aside on his table.

'I will read them at my leisure and then ask my *scriptor* to examine them. If all is well, we can arrange an audience with His Holiness seven days from now.'

He saw the corners of her mouth turn down.

'No sooner?' she asked in disappointment.

'Are you, then, in such a hurry to leave our beautiful city?' Gelasius asked mockingly.

'My heart yearns for my own country, lord bishop, that is all. I have been away from her shores for many months now.'

'Then, my child, a few days more will not matter. There is much to see here before you return, especially as it is your first pilgrimage to this place. Doubtless you will wish to visit the Vatican Hill where the basilica of the Blessed Peter stands over the tomb of that saintly man, that saintly rock upon which Christ ordained that his church should be built. On that very hill we are told that our blessed Lord appeared to Peter as he was leaving the city where Nero was persecuting his brethren. There Peter turned and retraced his footsteps to the city to be crucified with his flock and there he was taken for burial.'

Fidelma lowered her head to hide her irritation that the Bishop presumed her so lacking in knowledge.

'I will await your summons then, Gelasius,' she said, rising from her seat and standing as if waiting for his dismissal. Indeed, Gelasius had to hide his astonishment again that this young girl seemed to be effortlessly in control when he was so used to being in charge.

'Tell me, Fidelma of Kildare, are there many like you in that country of yours?'

Fidelma frowned, trying to understand his meaning.

'I have met many men from your country, we even have some working here in the Lateran Palace, but my experiences with the women of your land are limited. Are they all as forthright as you?'

Fidelma smiled evenly.

'I can only speak for myself, Gelasius. But, as I have told you, in my land a woman is not subservient to a man. We believe that our creator made us equal. Perhaps, one day, you should journey to the land of Ireland and see its beauty and its treasures.'

Gelasius chuckled.

'I may well do so. I may well, though I am afraid the passing of my years have been too many to contemplate arduous journeys now. In the meantime I hope you will enjoy our city. You may go. *Deus vobiscum.*'

Satisfied that he had finally managed to take control of the ending of the interview he reached forward and rang a tiny silver handbell.

He held out his left hand and once more, to his irritation, Fidelma simply took the hand and inclined her head rather than kissing his ring of office as was the custom in Rome.

The tall sister turned and walked across the chamber to where Brother Donus stood holding the door open.

Chapter Two

Sister Fidelma exited with some relief through the ornately carved oak doors into the main hall of the Lateran Palace, where every Bishop of Rome had been crowned for the last three hundred and fifty years. The *atrium*, or public hall, was a magnificent structure, of that there was no doubt. Tall marble columns towered skywards to an arched roof. The floor was an ever-stretching carpet of mosaic, the walls were festooned with colourful tapestries and the vaulted canopies above were of polished darkened oak. It was a fitting palace for a temporal prince.

The palace guards, the *custodes*, stood at every entrance, each guard in ceremonial military dress with burnished breast-plates and plumed helmets, short swords drawn and held across their breast; an impressive show of worldly splendour. Clerics moved hither and thither about mysterious tasks, their homespun robes making a curious contrast to the dignitaries and potentates from every conceivable country in the world.

Sister Fidelma paused to take in the spectacle again; for several hours she had been made to wait among the noisy throng before Brother Donus had summoned her to the presence of Bishop Gelasius. There could be little doubt, indeed, that this was the meeting place of all the peoples in the world. The royal court at Tara, the seat of the High Kings of the five kingdoms of Ireland, seemed a quaint backwater compared with this magnificence. But, Fidelma reflected as she began to ease her way through the groups of chattering people, she preferred the quiet dignity of Tara, its homely atmosphere amidst the serene beauty of the royal province of Midhe.

A young religieuse, pushing her way forward in the opposite direction, collided with Fidelma.

'Oh, forgive me . . .'

The girl raised her head and broke off with a look of flustered recognition.

'Sister Fidelma! I have not seen you since we arrived in Rome.'

The young Saxon religieuse was about twenty-five years of age, thin with slightly melancholy features and mousy, untidy hair poking out from beneath her headpiece. Her eyes were dark brown but seemed to hold little expression and, although slight, her hands were strong and sinewy, calloused from hard work. It had come as no surprise to Fidelma to find that Sister Eafa had worked on a farm before entering the religious life. Fidelma smiled down at her. She had been in Sister Eafa's company during most of the voyage from the port of Massilia to Ostia. The young sister was one of a small party of pilgrims from the kingdom of Kent who had come to witness Wighard of Canterbury ordained by the Holy Father. Fidelma felt a sympathy for the young girl. A simple, drab but amenable girl who seemed scared of her own shadow. The way she carried herself, the slightly stooping, awkward posture, and the way that she always wreathed her head and shoulders in her head-dress, seemed to indicate a wish to make herself inconspicuous in the world.

'Good day, Sister Eafa. How goes it with you?'

The young religieuse grimaced nervously.

'Truly, I shall be glad to return to Kent. To be in the city where Peter, who walked and spoke with the Christ, and who was martyred here, is a truly moving experience. However . . .' she gave a restless jerk of her head, 'I have no liking for the city. In truth, sister, I find it rather threatening. There are too many people, too many strange people. I would rather be at home.'

'I share your wish, sister,' Fidelma's sympathy was heartfelt. Like Eafa, she, too, was more used to rural life.

An anxious look suddenly passed across the lustreless features of Sister Eafa as she glanced beyond Fidelma's shoulder.

'Here comes Abbess Wulfrun. I must join her. I am accompanying her to the Oratory of the Forty Martyrs. We have already been to the tomb of the blessed Helena, mother of Constantine, this morning. Everywhere we go people see that we are foreign pilgrims and try to sell us holy relics and mementos. They are like beggars who will not be turned aside. Look at this, sister.'

She gestured to a small, cheap copper brooch with which she had fastened her headpiece. Fidelma peered at it closely. It displayed a piece of coloured glass mounted in the copper.

'I was told that it contained a hair of the blessed Helena's head and parted with two *sestertius* . . . I have no head for such coins. Do you think it was too much?'

Fidelma peered closely at the brooch and grimaced. She could just see a strand of hair embedded in the glass.

'If, indeed, that was the hair of the blessed Helena, then it is worth the money, but . . .' she left the sentence hanging with a shrug.

The young Saxon religieuse looked crestfallen.

'You doubt that it is genuine?'

'There are many pilgrims in Rome and, as you have already said, many people who earn their living by selling them all manner of things claimed as holy relics.'

Fidelma had the feeling that Eafa would have liked to talk more but she gave another quick glance over Fidelma's shoulder and gestured apologetically.

'I must go. Abbess Wulfrun has seen me.'

The young Kentish anchoress turned, anxiety still on her features, and pushed her way through the people to where a tall woman in religious robes stood waiting with an austere and disapproving expression on her beak-like countenance. Fidelma felt a pang of sorrow for the young sister. Eafa was making this pilgrimage in the company of Abbess Wulfrun. They were both from the abbey of Sheppey but, as Eafa had confessed to Fidelma, Wulfrun was a royal princess, the sister to Seaxburgh, Queen of Kent, and she made sure everyone knew of her rank.

That was probably why Fidelma had sought to befriend the young girl during the voyage from Massilia to Ostia, for Wulfrun treated the girl as little more than a slave. Yet Eafa had seemed more apprehensive of Fidelma's offer of friendship than her own loneliness. She was reluctant to be friendly with anyone and made no complaints about the autocratic way Abbess Wulfrun ordered her to do this or that. A strange, lonely girl, reflected Fidelma. Introspective, not anti-social but simply unsociable. Above the hubbub of those around her Fidelma could hear the piercing tones of Abbess Wulfrun ordering Eafa to carry something for her. The Abbess' imperious figure pushed its way through the crowds towards the palace gates, like the prow of a warship cleaving through stormy water, with the thin, bobbing figure of Eafa in her wake.

Sister Fidelma halted a moment or two in order to let them vanish in the throng before, with a soft sigh, she passed through the palace doors and out on to the sunbaked marble steps before the great façade. The Roman sun enveloped her in its warmth causing her to pause and catch her breath. From the cool of the interior of the great palace, the emergence into the heat of the Roman day was like plunging from a cold shower into a hot one. She blinked and took a deep breath.

'Sister Fidelma!'

She turned towards the crowd pushing their way up the steps and narrowed her eyes trying to identify the owner of the familiar deep baritone voice. A young man wearing rough brown woollen homespun, his dark brown hair capped by the *corona spina* of the Roman tonsure, detached himself from the group and waved to her. He was muscular, more like a warrior in build than a monk; a handsome man of her own age and height. She found herself smiling broadly in greeting, at the same time mentally questioning why she should feel such a surge of pleasure at seeing him again.

'Brother Eadulf!'

Eadulf had been her companion on the long and tedious journey from the kingdom of Northumbria. He was secretary and interpreter to Wighard, the archbishop-designate of Canterbury. They had become friends during the council at Hilda's monastery at Streoneshalh, by the coastal town of Witebia where, together, they had solved the dark mystery of the murder of the Abbess Étain of Kildare. Their abilities had complemented one another, for Eadulf had once been heredi- tary *gerefa*, the magistrate, of Seaxmund's Ham before he had been converted to the Faith by an Irish monk named Fursa and taken to Durrow in Ireland for his religious education. Eadulf also possessed a physician's knowledge having also studied at the great medical school of Tuaim Brecain. Then Eadulf had spent two years in Rome and had chosen to follow Rome's teaching, rejecting the rules of the Columban order, before returning to his native land. He had been at Hilda's abbey in support of Canterbury and Rome while Fidelma had travelled there to support her fellow Irish clerics from Lindisfarne and Iona.

The two youthful religious stood facing each other for a moment, smiling happily at their chance encounter, on the sunbaked white marble steps of the Lateran Palace.

'How goes your mission to Rome, Fidelma?' Eadulf asked. 'Have you seen the Holy Father yet?'

Fidelma shook her head.

'No. I have only seen a bishop. One who calls himself the *nomenclator*, who has to assess my petition from Kildare and ascertain whether the Holy Father should be bothered by it. The bureaucrats who surround the Bishop of Rome do not even seem interested that I bear personal letters to him from Ultan of Armagh.'

'You sound disapproving.'

Fidelma sniffed in agreement.

'I am a simple person, Eadulf. I dislike all this temporal pomp and ceremony.' She gestured with hand outstretched to the rich ecclesiastical buildings surrounding them. 'Do you remember the words of Matthew? The Lord instructed: "Lay not up for yourselves treasures upon earth where moth and rust doth corrupt, and where thieves break through and steal . . ." These temporal treasures are blinding to the simplicity of our faith.'

Brother Eadulf pursed his lips and shook his head in mock censure. Although his expression was serious there was no disguising the quiet humour in his eyes. He was aware that Fidelma had a keen scholastic mind and could readily quote scripture to enforce her arguments.

'It is their history, the sense of their past, that causes the Romans to keep such treasures, not their financial worth nor their faith,' he replied in defence. 'If the church has to exist in this world to prepare people for the next then surely it must be of this world with all its pomp and circumstance?'

Fidelma disagreed immediately.

'It was clear, as Matthew said, no man can serve two masters, for either he will hate the one and love the other or else he will hold to the one and despise the other. You cannot serve God and Mammon. Those that live in this fine palace and parade in temporal aggrandisement must surely be placing Mammon before God.'

Brother Eadulf looked slightly shocked.

'You are speaking of the household of the Holy Father. No, Fidelma; it is part of Rome's heritage as well as the Christian heritage to be in this beautiful palace. Everywhere you go in Rome you will stand in history.'

Fidelma grinned derisively at his enthusiasm.

'Anywhere in the world you would stand on a spot that has an historic memory to someone,' she replied dryly. 'I have stood on the poor bare hill of Ben Edair where the battle-torn, bleeding body of Oscar, son of Oisín, was taken for burial after the catastrophic battle of Gabhra. I have seen the cairn which was raised over the grave of Oscar's widow, Aidín, after she had died of grief on seeing the body of her husband. A small cairn of grey stone can encompass as heart-rending a history as this big edifice.'

'But look at this . . .' Eadulf waved enthusiastically to encompass the great Lateran Palace and the adjoining basilica of St John. 'This is the very heart of Christendom. The home of its temporal leader for the last three hundred years. It has such history in every brick and piece of mosaic.'

'A marvellous set of buildings, I will accept that.'

Eadulf shook his head at her lack of reverence.

'Even when the emperor Constantine gave the palace and its lands to Melchiades, three hundred and fifty years ago, so that he, as Bishop of Rome, could erect a cathedral for the city, it already had a history.'

Fidelma silently resigned herself to the monk's animation.

'It was the palace of a great patrician family of ancient Rome, the Laterani. At the time when the evil emperor Nero was persecuting the Christians there was a conspiracy to assassinate him. Gaius Calpurnius Piso, who was a consul, a great orator as well as a rich and popular figure, led the plot. But it was discovered and the conspirators were arrested and condemned to death, others were forced to commit suicide rather than face execution as respect and deference to their patrician rank.

'Among them were Petronius Arbiter who wrote the *Satyricon*; the poet Lucan and the philosopher Seneca, as well as Piso. In addition to those intellectuals was Plautius Lateranus who owned this palace. He was deprived of his property and put to death.'

Fidelma eyed the rich façade of the Lateran Palace, still disapproving of its opulence.

'It is a beautiful building,' she said softly, 'but not as beautiful as a pleasant valley or great mountain or windswept cliff.

26

That is true beauty, the beauty of nature untrammelled by man's temporary constructions.'

Eadulf looked at her in sorrow.

'I would not have marked you for a Philistine, sister.'

Fidelma raised a contradictory eyebrow and gave a shake of her head.

'Not so. You have put those two years of your life here in Rome to good use by attaining knowledge. But in your praise of these buildings you neglected to mention that the original Lateran palace was destroyed and that Melchiades constructed his buildings on their ruin. You forgot to say that those buildings have been rebuilt twice during the last two hundred years, especially after their destruction by Vandals two centuries ago. So where is the continuity with history of which you speak? These are but temporary monuments.'

Eadulf gazed at her in chagrined surprise.

'So you knew its history all the time?' he demanded accusingly, ignoring the point she had made.

Fidelma shrugged eloquently.

'I asked one of the keepers at the basilica. But as you were so eager to impart your knowledge . . .' She grimaced and then smiled apologetically at his petulant expression, reaching forward and laying a hand on his arm. A sudden urchin grin of mischief spread over her features.

'Come, Brother Eadulf. I merely make the point that buildings are temporary cathedrals to the greater cathedral of nature, which man often destroys with his own miserable constructions. I have recently wondered what the seven hills of this remarkable city looked like before they were submerged by buildings.'

The Saxon monk's face remained a study of petulance.

'Don't be angry, Eadulf,' Fidelma cajoled contritely, regretting that she had pricked his ego. 'I must be true to myself, but I am interested in all that you have to tell me about Rome. I am sure there is much more in this city that you can usefully instruct me about. Come, walk with me a while and show me what you may.'

She turned down the broad steps and made her way through the beggars clustered at the bottom, held back by grim-faced *custodes*. Dark haunted eyes in skeletal faces followed them, thin, bony hands were held out in mute supplication. It had taken Fidelma several days to get used to the sight as she passed from her lodging to the ornate palace of the Bishop of Rome.

'That is a scene that you would not see in Ireland,' she remarked, nodding to the beggars. 'Our laws provide for the relief of the poor without their recourse to such straits to provide for themselves and their families.'

Eadulf was silent knowing, from his years in Ireland, that she spoke truthfully. The ancient laws of the *Fenechus* administrated by the Brehons, or judges of Ireland, were, he knew, a code by which the sick did not fear illness nor did the destitute fear starvation. The law provided for all.

'It is sad that so many have to beg to live in the shade of such affluence, especially when the opulence is dedicated to a god of the poor,' Fidelma continued. 'Those bishops and clerics who dwell in such splendour ought to read more closely John's epistle in which he said: "But whoso hath this world's riches and sees his brother has need, and closes his heart and his ears to him, having no compassion, how can he say that he loves God?" Do you know this passage, Eadulf?'

Eadulf bit his lip. He glanced around, worried for the outspoken Irish religieuse.

'Careful, Fidelma,' he whispered, 'lest you be accused of following the Pelagian heresy.'

Fidelma snorted in annoyance.

'Rome considers Pelagius a heretic not because he forsook the words of Christ but because he criticised Rome for disregarding them. I simply quote from the first epistle of John, chapter three, verse seventeen. If that is heresy then I am indeed a heretic, Eadulf.'

She paused to rummage in her pocket, dropping a coin in the outstretched hand of a small boy who stood apart from the other beggars, gazing into space with sightless eyes. The hand closed over the coin and a small grin split the pock-marked and ravaged face of the child.

'*Do et des,*' Fidelma smiled, uttering the ancient formula. 'I give that you may give.' She walked on, glancing at Eadulf who fell in step beside her. They were passing through a quarter of slum dwellings, which lay at the bottom of the Esquiline Hill, the highest and most extensive of the seven hills of Rome with its four summits. Fidelma crossed the Via Labicana and turned along the broad thoroughfare of the Via Merulana which led up to the summit known as the Cispius. ' "Give to the person that begs from you, and do not refuse a person who would borrow," ' she quoted solemnly at Eadulf who had watched disapprovingly as she had given to the beggar.

'Pelagius?' Eadulf asked, troubled.

'The Gospel of St Matthew,' replied Fidelma seriously. 'Chapter five, verse forty-two.'

Eadulf gave a deep and restive sigh.

'Here, my good Saxon friend,' Fidelma halted in mid-stride and laid a hand on his arm, 'you see the fundamental nature of our argument between the rule of Rome and the rule which

29

we in Ireland and, indeed, the kingdoms of the Britons, follow?'

'The decision to follow the rule of Rome has been taken by the Saxon kingdoms, Fidelma. You will not convert me. I am but a simple cleric and no theologian. So far as I am concerned, when Oswy of Northumbria made his decision at Streoneshalh to follow Rome, that was the end to any argument. Don't forget I am now the archbishop's secretary and interpreter.'

Fidelma regard him in silent amusement.

'Have no fear, Eadulf. I am simply amusing myself for I have not yet agreed that Rome is correct in all its arguments. But, for friendship's sake, we will discuss the subject no more.'

She continued her walk down the wide road with Eadulf falling in step beside her. In spite of their differences of attitude, Fidelma had to admit that she felt some comfort in being with Eadulf. She could tease him over their contrasting opinions and he would always rise good-naturedly to the bait but there was no enmity between them.

'I understand that Wighard has been well received by the Holy Father,' she commented after a while.

Since arriving in Rome seven days ago Fidelma had hardly seen Eadulf. She had heard that Wighard and his main entourage had already arrived a few day's previously in the city and had been invited to lodge at the Lateran Palace as personal guests of the Holy Father, Vitalian. Fidelma suspected that the Bishop of Rome had been overjoyed at the news of Canterbury's success over the Irish faction at Streoneshalh.

Having parted company with Eadulf on arriving in Rome, Fidelma had been recommended to a small hostel in a side street off the Via Merulana next to the oratory erected by Pius I to the Blessed Prassede. The community in the hostel was transitory for it consisted mainly of pilgrims whose periods of stay in the city varied. The household was run by a Gaulish priest, a deacon of the church, Arsenius, and his wife, the deaconess, Epiphania. They were an elderly couple without children but were as a father and mother to the foreign visitors, mainly Irish *peregrinatio pro Christo*, who sought lodging with them.

For over a week now all Fidelma had seen of the great city of Rome was the modest house of Arsenius and Epiphania and the magnificence of the Lateran Palace with the varying poverty of the streets that separated them.

'The Holy Father has treated us well,' Eadulf confirmed. 'We have been given excellent chambers in the Lateran Palace and have already been received in audience. Tomorrow there is going to be a formal exchange of gifts followed by a banquet. In fourteen days, the Holy Father will officially ordain Wighard as archbishop of Canterbury.'

'And then you will commence the journey back to the kingdom of Kent?'

Eadulf nodded. 'And will you be returning to Ireland soon?' he asked, quickly glancing sideways at her.

Fidelma grimaced.

'Just as soon as I can deliver the letters from Ultan of Armagh and have the rule of my house of Kildare blessed. I have been too long away from Ireland.'

For a while they walked in silence. The street was hot and dusty in spite of the shelter of fragrant, resinous cypress trees under whose shade traders gathered to buy and sell their wares. The traffic up and down the thoroughfare, one of the main streets of the city, was continuous. Yet still, above the bustle of its traffic, Fidelma could hear the chirping noise of the *gryllus*, the grasshoppers, as they tried to keep cool in the stifling heat. Only when a cloud passed across the sun did the strange noise abruptly cease. It had taken Fidelma some time to discover the meaning of the sounds.

The slopes of the Esquiline beyond was a region of few inhabitants, an area of rich houses, vineyards and gardens. Servus Tullius had built his ornamental oak grove here, Fagutalis had planted a beech grove, it was home to the poet Virgil, Nero had built his 'Golden House' and Pompey had planned his campaign against Julius Caesar. Eadulf, in his two years of Rome, had come to know it well.

'Have you seen much of Rome yet?' Eadulf suddenly asked, breaking their companionable silence.

'Since I am here I should try to understand why a church of the poor bedecks itself with such riches . . . no,' she laughed as she saw his brows draw together, 'no, I will not speak of that anymore. What would you have me see?'

'Well, there is the basilica of Peter on the Vatican Hill, where the great fisherman himself is buried, the keyholder to the kingdom of heaven. Nearby lies the body of the Blessed Paul as well. But one has to approach the tombs in great penitence for it is said terrible things befall men and women who approach without humility.'

'What terrible things?' demanded Fidelma suspiciously.

'It was said that when the Bishop Pelagius – not he of the heresy who was never a Bishop of Rome, but the second Holy Father to bear the name – wished to change the coverings of silver which are placed over the bodies of Peter and Paul, he received an apparition of considerable terror as he approached them. The foreman in charge of the improvements died on the spot, and all the monks and servants of the

32

church who saw the bodies died within ten days. They say it was because the Holy Father bore the name of a heretic and therefore it has been decreed that no pope will ever bear the name Pelagius in future.'

Fidelma's eyes narrowed as she examined the complacent features of the monk.

Was he subtly repaying her by the introduction of this story?

'Pelagius . . .' she began, the tone of her voice dangerous, but Eadulf suddenly guffawed, unable to keep his face solemn.

'Let us quit, Fidelma. Though I swear the tale is true. Let there be a peace between us.'

Fidelma pursed her lips in annoyance, and then let her features relax into a smile.

'We will save the pilgrimage to the tomb of the Blessed Peter for another day,' she replied. 'The deaconess of the house where I am lodged did take me and some others to a place where it is said that Peter was imprisoned. It was astounding. In the cell were a pile of chains and a priest stood by ready with a file which, for some incredible price, he would make filings from – assuring us that these were the chains worn by Peter. Holy pilgrimage to Rome seems to have become a business in which great sums of money are made.'

She had been aware of the Saxon monk casting glances over his shoulder for a short while now.

'Sister, there is a round-faced monk with a tonsure which might make him Irish or a Briton following us. If you glance quickly behind to your right, you will see him standing under the shade of a cypress tree on the opposite side of the road. Do you know him?'

Fidelma gazed at Eadulf for a moment in surprise and then turned quickly in the direction he had indicated.

For a moment her eyes met the astonished widened dark eyes of a middle-aged man. He was, as Eadulf had described him, bearing a tonsure which placed his origin as either from Ireland or Britain, shaved at the front of his head on a line from ear to ear. He wore poor homespuns and his face was round and moon-like. He froze at Fidelma's gaze and then turned quickly away, the colour on his face deepening, and vanished suddenly into the crowds behind the line of cypress trees at the far side of the street.

Fidelma turned back with a puzzled frown.

'I do not know him. Yet he certainly seemed interested in me. You say that he was following us?'

Eadulf nodded quickly. 'I was aware of him on the steps of the Lateran Palace. As we began to walk up the Via Merulana, he followed. I thought at first it was coincidence. Then I noticed that when we stopped a moment ago, he also stopped. Are you sure that you do not know him?'

'No. Perhaps he is of Ireland and heard my speech. Maybe he wanted to speak with me of home and had not the courage?'

'Perhaps.' Eadulf was not convinced.

'Well, he is gone now,' Fidelma said. 'Let us walk on. What were we speaking of?'

Reluctantly, Eadulf followed her example.

'I think you were being disapproving of Rome again, sister.'

Fidelma's eyes sparkled.

'Yes, I was,' she admitted. 'I even find, at our community where I lodge, that there are books to guide pilgrims to the places of interest where shrines and catacombs may be found and at which pilgrims are persuaded to part with what money they have to take away relics and remembrances. There is such a guide book kept at the community entitled *Notitia Ecclesiarum Urbis Romae . . .*'

'But it is necessary that a memorial is kept of where the shrines are and who is buried in them,' interrupted Eadulf in protest.

'Is it also necessary that great sums be charged to pilgrims to supply them with *ampullae* or phials which purport to come from the oil of lamps in catacombs and shrines?' snapped Fidelma. 'I hardly think that the oil from the lamps of the shrines of saints can be deemed to have miraculous powers?'

Eadulf heaved a sigh and shook his head in resignation.

'Perhaps we should abandon the seeing of such sights.'

Fidelma was immediately contrite again.

'Once more I have let my tongue run away with my thoughts, Eadulf. Forgive me . . . please?'

The Saxon tried to look disapproving. He wanted to continue his annoyance but when Fidelma smiled that urchin grin of hers . . .

'Very well. Let us find something that we can both agree upon, Fidelma. I know . . . a little way from here is the church of St Mary of the Snow.'

'Of the Snow?'

'I am told that one August night the Blessed Virgin appeared to Liberius, then Bishop of Rome, and to a patrician named John, telling them to build a church on the Esquiline on the spot where they would find a patch of snow on the following morning. They found a patch of snow covering the exact area where the church was to be built.'

'Such tales are told of many churches, Eadulf, why should this one be of particular interest?'

'There will be a special mass held there tonight for the

memory of the Blessed Aidan of Lindisfarne who died on this day thirteen years ago. Many Irish and Saxon pilgrims will be attending.'

'Then so shall I,' affirmed Fidelma, 'but first I would like to visit the Colosseum, Eadulf, so that I may see where the martyrs of the Faith met their end.'

'Very well. And we will talk no more of the differences between Rome, Canterbury and Armagh.'

'It is agreed,' affirmed Fidelma.

Some way behind them, the moon-faced monk, carefully concealing himself among the cypress trees, followed their progress along the Via Merulana with narrowed eyes.

Chapter Three

It seemed to Fidelma that she had only just fallen asleep when her slumber was disturbed by a bell clanging urgently. She moaned softly in protest, turned and tried to chase the elusive comfort of her dream. But she was woken by the continuous clamour of the bell followed by the sound of a caustic voice in the stillness of the night. Already she heard the agitated movements of the brethren awakening and voices raised demanding to know what disrupted their sleep. Fidelma was fully awake now, noticing the darkness of the night. She slipped from her bed, drew on her robe and was about to feel for a candle when there came a timid tapping on the door of her small chamber. Before she had time to open her mouth in reply it swung open to reveal, in the glow of the lamp kept permanently alight in the corridor, the agitated figure of the deaconess, Epiphania. She wrung her hands, twisting them as if to suppress her apparent distress.

'Sister Fidelma!' Epiphania's voice was a fearful wail.

Fidelma stood quietly, examining her apprehensive features.

'Calm yourself, Epiphania,' she instructed softly. 'What is the matter?'

'It is an officer of the Lateran Guard, the *custodes*. He demands that you go with him.'

Several thoughts went through Fidelma's mind at that moment; panic-stricken thoughts; thoughts of regret that she had agreed to Ultan's request to come to Rome at all; guilty thoughts of her criticism of the Holy Father and the trumpery of Roman clerics in making small fortunes from pilgrims. Had someone heard and denounced her? Then she made an effort to inwardly control herself. Her facial expression and outward demeanour had not changed.

'Where does he wish me to go?' she asked quietly. 'And for what purpose?'

The deaconess was abruptly pushed aside and in the doorway of her *cubiculum* stood a good-looking youthful soldier in the ceremonial uniform of the *custodes*. He stared arrogantly over her head, avoiding eye contact. She had been in Rome long enough to recognise the emblems of a *tesserarius* or junior officer of the guard.

'We have orders to take you to the Lateran Palace. At once, sister.'

The young man's voice was brusque.

Fidelma managed a wan smile.

'For what purpose?'

The young man's expression remained wooden.

'I have not been informed. I follow orders.'

'Will your orders then allow me to bathe my face and dress?' she asked innocently.

The guard's eyes suddenly focused on her and his wooden expression relaxed for a moment. He looked embarrassed, hesitating only a moment.

'We will await you outside, sister,' he agreed, withdrawing as abruptly as he had entered.

Epiphania let forth a low moan.

'What does it mean, sister? Oh, what does it mean?'

'I won't know until I have dressed and accompanied the *custodes* to the palace,' Fidelma replied, trying to sound nonchalant in order to disguise her own apprehension.

The deaconess looked confused, hesitated and then also withdrew.

Fidelma stood for a moment feeling cold and very lonely. Then she turned and forced herself to pour water into a basin. Mechanically, she began her toilet, each movement made with a slow deliberation to calm her inner turmoil.

Ten minutes later, serenely calm on the outside, Fidelma went into the courtyard. The deaconess stood by the gate and Fidelma was aware that the brethren of the house were peering nervously from their rooms. As well as the young officer who had come to her *cubiculum*, there were two members of the Lateran Guard standing in the courtyard.

The young man nodded approval at her appearance and took a step forward.

'Before we proceed, I have to ask you formally whether you are Fidelma of Kildare from the kingdom of Ireland?'

'I am,' Fidelma bowed her head slightly.

'I am the *tesserarius* Licinius of the Lateran Guard, acting under orders of the *Superista*, the military governor of the Lateran. I have been ordered to accompany you immediately into the presence of the *Superista*.'

'I understand,' Fidelma said, not really understanding at all. 'Am I accused of some crime?'

The young officer frowned and contrived to raise a shoulder and let it fall as an indication of his ignorance.

'Once again, I can only say that I am following my orders, sister.'

39

'I will come,' sighed Fidelma, there being nothing else for her to do in the circumstances.

The deaconess opened the gate, her face pale and lips trembling.

Fidelma, walking side by side with the officer, passed through it followed by the two guards, one of whom had now lit a brand torch to light their way through the dark night streets of the city.

Apart from the distant yelp of a dog, the city was amazingly silent. There was a crisp stillness to the air, a chill that Fidelma had not noticed before. It was cold, though not as icy as mornings in ' er native land, but enough for her to be glad of the warmth of her woollen robe. It still lacked an hour before the first streaks of dawn light would thrust their probing fingers into the eastern sky beyond the distant hills. Only the rhythmic hollow slap of the leather soles of her sandals and the heavier soldiers' studded *caligulae* on the paved street made any noise.

They proceeded without speaking down the broad thoroughfare of the Via Merulana, south towards the tall dominating dome of the Basilica of St John, which dwarfed the complex of the Lateran Palace. It was not far, no more than a thousand metres, or so Fidelma had worked out in her daily passage to and from the palace. The gates to the palace were lit by flickering torches and *custodes* stood ready, swords drawn and held across their breasts in the traditional stance.

The officer led his charge up the steps and through the *atrium* where Fidelma had waited for so long in her attempt to see the Holy Father. They immediately crossed the hall and exited through a side door, moving along a bare, stone-paved passageway, whose gauntness seemed at odds with the rich-

ness of the preceding hall. They turned across a small courtyard, in the centre of which an ornate fountain gushed water,
and then came to a chamber where two more guards stood.
The officer halted and knocked gently on the door.

At a called instruction from beyond the door, the young
man opened it and motioned Fidelma to go inside.

'Fidelma of Kildare!' he announced, then withdrew, shut-
ting the door behind her.

Fidelma halted by the door and peered round.

She was in a large room hung with tapestries, but not so
richly furnished as the chamber in which she had met Gelasius.
The furnishings were minimal and spoke of utility rather than
decorative opulence. This was clearly a room which was purely
functional. The *officium* was well lit and a thickset man with
close-cropped steel-grey hair and a pugnacious jaw came forward to greet her. He was obviously a military man though he
wore no armour nor carried a weapon.

'Fidelma of Kildare?' There was no aggression in his voice,
in fact the man sounded anxious. When Fidelma suspiciously
nodded confirmation, the man continued. 'I am Marinus, the
Superista, that is the military governor, of the Lateran Palace.'

With a motion of his hand he drew her to a large hearth in
which a fire crackled, warming the chill early morning air.
There were two chairs set before it and he indicated for her to
be seated in one while he settled himself in the other.

'You are obviously wondering why you have been summoned?' He made the statement seem like a question and
Fidelma responded with a slight smile.

'I am a human being, *Superista*, with natural curiosity. But
you will doubtless tell me what that reason is in your own
good time.'

Marinus stared at her as if in momentary mild amusement at the reply and then abruptly grimaced in seriousness. There was no mistaking the anxiety on his features.

'Truly spoken. A problem has arisen which affects the Lateran Palace, indeed, the Holy See of Rome.'

Fidelma sat back waiting.

'It is an event in which there may be much at stake, including the dignity of the office of the Holy Father, the security of the Saxon kingdoms and the possibility of conflict and warfare between your own country of Ireland, the Saxons and the Britons.'

Fidelma gazed at the military governor with some astonishment mixed with bewilderment.

Marinus gestured with his hand, as if seeking explanation in the air.

'There is one thing that I must do before I can explain further . . .'

He hesitated and there was a silence.

'Which is?' prompted Fidelma after a while.

'Can you tell me where you were around the hour of midnight?'

'Certainly,' Fidelma replied at once, suppressing her surprise. 'I accompanied Brother Eadulf, *scriptor* of the archbishop-designate Wighard of Canterbury, to attend the celebratory mass for the life and work of the Blessed Aidan of Lindisfarne. Yesterday was the anniversary of the death of Aidan. The mass was held in the church of Saint Mary of the Snow on the Esquiline.'

Marinus was nodding as if he knew the answer beforehand.

'You answer with great precision, Fidelma of Kildare.'

'In my own land, I am an advocate of the court of the

Fenechus. Precision is part of my profession.'

The *Superista* again nodded absently, as if he already knew that this would be the reply to his implied question.

'And why would Irish and Saxon be attending the mass for Aidan of Lindisfarne, sister?'

'Simply because Aidan was an Irish monk who converted the kingdom of Northumbria to the Faith and is thereby venerated by Irish and Saxon alike.'

'The mass started at what hour . . . ?'

'At the stroke of midnight.'

'But before that, sister, where were you and Brother Eadulf?' Marinus leant forward abruptly, his face thrust towards her, his eyes searching.

Fidelma blinked.

'Brother Eadulf and I had accompanied a group of pilgrims to view the Colosseum where so many died for the Faith in the days of the pagan emperors of Rome. We examined some of the Holy Shrines and then went to the church were the mass was being celebrated. There were a dozen of us in all. Three monks from Northumbria, including Brother Eadulf, and two sisters and four brothers from the monastery of Columban at Bobbio. There were also two guides from the hostel of Prassede where I lodge.'

Marinus was nodding impatiently.

'And were you together with Brother Eadulf until after midnight?'

'I have said as much, *Superista*.'

'And are you acquainted with an Irish monk named Ronan Ragallach?'

Fidelma shook her head.

'I have not heard of that name. Why do you ask? Perhaps,

you will now tell me what has happened to cause my being brought hither?'

Marinus gave a deep sigh, pausing as if to gather his thoughts.

'Wighard, the archbishop-designate of Canterbury, who was to have authority over all the abbots and bishops of the Saxon kingdoms, was found dead at midnight by a *decurion* of the palace guards. Not only that, but his chamber was robbed of the priceless gifts which he was to present to the Holy Father at his official audience later today.'

Chapter Four

'Am I suspected of some involvement in the death of Wighard of Canterbury?' Fidelma demanded coldly, after she realised the gravity of the *Superista*'s news.

Marinus looked unhappy and spread his hands, an odd gesture which implied some apology.

'I had to ask the questions. Many people might wish Wighard dead, especially those who opposed Canterbury's support of Roman rule among the Saxon kingdoms.'

'Then we are talking of countless thousands who would wish that Canterbury had not been successful at the council at Witebia,' replied Fidelma icily.

'But not that many in Rome who have an opportunity,' Marinus said slyly.

'Are you saying that Wighard was slain by someone who was angered by the success of Canterbury during the recent synod at Hilda's monastery?'

'No such conclusions have yet been reached.'

'Then why am I here?'

'To help us, Sister Fidelma,' replied a new voice. 'That is, if you would.'

Fidelma looked round and found the tall, thin figure of

Bishop Gelasius shuffling forward from a side door which had
been shielded by a curtain. He had obviously been standing
there listening to Marinus' interrogation of her.

Fidelma rose uncertainly in deference to the bishop's rank.

Gelasius held out his left hand. This time Fidelma did not
even bother to take it but folded her arms before her and
inclined her head in a brief bow of acknowledgment. Her lips
were compressed into a thin, determined line. If these
Romans were going to accuse her of some responsibility with
Wighard's death then she felt no obligation to make any token
of obeisant observation. Gelasius sighed and took the chair
which Marinus had now vacated. The military governor of
the Lateran stood respectfully to one side, slightly behind
the chair.

'Bring the monk in, Marinus,' Gelasius instructed, 'and be
you seated, Fidelma of Kildare.'

Fidelma was now faintly bewildered as she sank back into
her seat. Gelasius seemed to share Marinus' anxiety and it
was reflected on his gaunt features.

Marinus strode across the room to the door and signalled
someone beyond.

There was a pause. Gelasius sat staring at the fire a while
before he raised his eyes towards the newcomer who had
entered the *officium* and stood waiting patiently.

Fidelma turned around on her chair. Her eyes widened
in surprise.

'Brother Eadulf!'

Eadulf smiled, a little tiredly, as he crossed with the *Superista* and stood hesitantly before Bishop Gelasius.

'Be seated, Eadulf of Canterbury.'

Marinus had brought forward two more wooden chairs,

scraping the stone floor as he did so, and seated himself on one while Eadulf took the other.

Fidelma turned back to Gelasius with a look of inter-rogation.

The bishop spread his hands and smiled in placation.

'You have merely confirmed what our Saxon brother Eadulf has told us . . .'

'Then . . .?' began Fidelma, her perplexity showing.

The bishop raised a hand to command silence.

'This death of Wighard is a serious matter. No one is above suspicion. You freely admitted that you were one of the dele-gates who were in conflict with Canterbury at the synod held at Hilda's monastery. You might easily have sought vengeance on Wighard who, as archbishop-designate of Canterbury, had emerged victorious from the argument.'

As Fidelma exhaled deeply in annoyance he continued hurriedly: 'But, Brother Eadulf has informed us of the singular service you performed during the debate at Witebia by solving the murder of the Abbess Étain.'

Fidelma glanced towards Eadulf who was sitting with his eyes downcast, his face expressionless.

'The service was achieved in cooperation with Brother Eadulf, for without his assistance there might not have been a positive resolution to the matter,' she replied icily.

'Just so,' Gelasius agreed. 'But even with such fulsome recommendation as has been given of your character by Brother Eadulf one had to be sure . . .'

Again Fidelma frowned.

'Sure of what? Where is this interrogation leading?'

'Sister Fidelma, when we met the other day you mentioned that you were a qualified advocate of the law courts of your native land. Brother Eadulf confirms this. You apparently have a singular ability at solving puzzles.'

Fidelma was exasperated by Gelasius' pedantic approach. Why didn't he get to the heart of what he wanted to say?

The bishop went on carefully: 'The fact is that you have the talent of which the Lateran Palace is sorely in need. We wish that you, Sister Fidelma, together with Brother Eadulf here, make inquiries to ascertain the cause of Wighard's death and discover who has stolen the gifts that he brought with him.'

There was a silence while Fidelma absorbed what Gelasius was saying. An immediate thought came into her mind.

'Does the Lateran Palace have no law officer to conduct such an investigation?' she asked with a meaningful glance at the military governor.

'Indeed. Rome was, still is, the *communis patria* of the legal and political world,' replied Marinus, his voice torn between resentment and pride. Fidelma nearly replied that Rome's law had never extended to her own land whose ancient legal system was equally as old for it had been collected together in the time of the High King Ollamh Fódhla, eight centuries before the birth of the Christ. Yet Fidelma put a curb on her tongue.

'Law in this city of Rome,' Gelasius explained more temperately than the *Superista*, 'is administered by the *Praetor Urbanus* and his staff who upholds the rule of existing law. Because there are foreigners involved, this case comes under the jurisdiction of the *Praetor Peregrinus* who is responsible for all legal matters in which those involved are foreigners.'

'Then why do you need any help from myself, whose knowledge is limited to Irish law, and to Brother Eadulf, who was once a *gerefa* – a magistrate of the Saxons?'

Gelasius pursed his lips trying to frame a careful reply.

'We, in Rome, are sensitive to the differences between the churches of the Irish, the Britons and the Saxons. We are aware of our own perceived role in this matter. It is a matter of politics, Sister Fidelma. Since the Irish bishop Cummian tried to unite the churches of the Irish and Britons with Rome thirty years ago, we have tried to promote just such a reconciliation. I am old enough to remember how Bishop Honorious and his successor John both wrote to the Irish abbots and bishops begging them not to widen the schism which had developed between us . . .'

'I am aware of the differences between those who hold to Roman rule, Gelasius, and those who remain steadfast to the original council decisions which we in Ireland maintain,' interrupted Fidelma. 'But where does this lead us?'

Gelasius bit his lip, clearly unhappy at being checked in the flow of his argument.

'Where?' He paused almost as if expecting an answer. 'The Holy Father is sensitive of these differences, as I have said, and hopes to reunite our factions. The death of the archbishop-designate of Canterbury, so soon after Canterbury's success at persuading the Saxon kingdoms to turn from the Irish Church to Rome and while the archbishop-designate was staying in the Bishop of Rome's own palace, may ignite a torch of war that will ravage the lands of the Saxons and the Irish. That conflict will inevitably draw Rome into it.'

Fidelma sniffed deprecatingly.

'I fail to see why.'

It was Marinus, having been silent for a while, who now answered her.

'I asked you if you knew a monk named Ronan Ragallach.'

'I have not forgotten,' Fidelma replied.

'It was he who killed Wighard.'

Fidelma's eyebrow raised slightly.

'Then,' her voice was still even, 'why, if this fact is known, do you ask me and Brother Eadulf to investigate? You already have your culprit.'

Gelasius raised his hands helplessly. It was clear that he was far from happy with the situation.

'For politics,' he answered earnestly. 'To avoid war. That is why we seek your assistance, Fidelma of Kildare. Wighard was Rome's man. Wighard is murdered in the very palace of the Holy Father. Questions will be asked among the Saxon kingdoms who have agreed to accept Rome's rule and look to Canterbury as their ecclesiastical centre, rejecting the missionaries of Ireland. In reply to those questions, Rome will claim that an Irish monk slew Wighard. The Saxons will be angered. And will not Ireland say that this was too convenient an explanation coming in the wake of their defeat, perhaps another move to discredit them? Perhaps the Saxons will react against all the Irish clerics still in their kingdoms. At best they might drive them from the land or, at worst . . .' He left the sentence unfinished. 'Perhaps outright warfare will ensue. There are many possibilities, none of them pleasant.'

Sister Fidelma gazed at the troubled face of Gelasius.

For the first time she found herself examining the face of Bishop Gelasius carefully. Previously, she had mentally registered Gelasius as a man of age, not old but certainly of the age when a person looks on all change as a worsening of life. But now she was aware of his vitality, the energy and emotion which she expected only in youth; a determined man lacking the meekness, patience and humility which one usually assumed with venerable age.

'Your hypotheses are reasonable ones, but possibilities only,' she observed.

'Rome is concerned to stop them even becoming possibilities. We have had too many internecine wars between Christian factions. We need allies throughout Christendom, especially now the followers of Mahomet are raiding through the Mediterranean, devastating our trade and ports.'

'I still follow your logic, Gelasius,' Fidelma replied as Gelasius looked to her expecting an answer.

'Good. What better way to defuse the animosities that will inevitably arise than if you, Sister Fidelma, a law expert from Ireland, and Brother Eadulf here, a Saxon learned in his own law, both with the reputation brought from Witebia, examine this case? If you both came to an agreement as to the culprit, who could accuse either of you of bias? Yet if we of Rome make an assertion as to guilt or innocence, it would be argued that we had much to gain by pointing the finger of guilt to those who disagree with us.'

Fidelma began to see the subtleness of Gelasius' thinking. Here was the sharp mind of a politician as well as churchman.

'Has this Ronan Ragallach admitted that he killed Wighard?'

'No,' Gelasius was dismissive. 'But the evidence against him is overwhelming.'

'So you want to be able to announce that this crime was resolved by Eadulf of Canterbury and Fidelma of Kildare agreeing in unison in order to prevent a possible conflict arising?'

'You have understood perfectly,' Gelasius said.

Fidelma looked at Eadulf and the monk grimaced faintly at her.

'Are you agreed on this matter, Eadulf?' she asked.

'I was witness to how you resolved the murder of the Abbess Étain. I have agreed to assist you in any way I can in the resolution of Wighard's death to prevent the spilling of blood between our peoples.'

'Will you undertake the task, Fidelma of Kildare?' pressed Gelasius.

Fidelma turned back to gaze at his thin, hawk-like features and again noticed anxiety in the dark eyes of the bishop. She pursed her lips reflectively wondering if it was merely fear of a conflict on the north-western edge of the world that made him so anxious. There was no decision to make. She inclined her head.

'Very well, but there are conditions.'

'Conditions?' Marinus caught the word and frowned suspiciously.

'Which are?' Gelasius invited.

'Simple enough. The first you have agreed to, that Brother Eadulf is my equal partner in this investigation and our decisions must be unanimous. The second condition is that we will have full authority in the conduct of the inquiry. We will be able to question everyone who we need to question and go where we need to go. Even if we need ask a question of the Holy Father himself. There can be no limitations on either of us.'

Gelasius thin features relaxed into a smile.

'You are aware that some parts of the city, areas connected with the Holy See of Rome, are closed to any foreign-born *clericos*?'

'That is why I make the conditions, Gelasius,' replied Fidelma. 'If I am to conduct such an inquiry and my path takes me here or there, I must be sure that I have such authority as to tread that path.'

'Surely there is little need? We already have the culprit. All you have to do is confirm his guilt,' interrupted Marinus.

'Your culprit pleads his innocence,' Fidelma pointed out. 'Under the law of the *Fenechus* of Éireann, a man or woman is considered innocent until it has been demonstrated beyond all doubt that he or she be guilty. I, too, will proceed from the viewpoint that Ronan Ragallach is innocent until I have proved his guilt. If you wish me merely to state that he is guilty now then I cannot undertake this investigation.'

Gelasius hesitated and exchanged an unhappy glance with Marinus. The *Superista* of the *custodes* was frowning in annoyance.

'You will have what authority you need, Fidelma,' Gelasius conceded after a moment or two. 'You and Brother Eadulf may conduct your inquiry in whatever way you see fit. I will ensure that the *Praetor Peregrinus* is informed. But you must remember that you may only inquire and may not take the law into your own hands. In the administration of the law you are subject to the judicial procedures of this city under the immediate jurisdiction of the *Praetor Peregrinus*. Marinus will draw up that authority and I will ensure it is signed by the *Praetor*.'

'That is well,' Fidelma accepted.

'When do you wish to start?'

Fidelma stood up abruptly. 'There is no better time than the present.'

They came almost reluctantly to their feet.

'How will you proceed?' asked Marinus gruffly. 'Presumably you will wish to see this monk Ronan Ragallach?'

'I will take matters step by step,' Fidelma replied, glancing at Eadulf. 'First we would see the *domus hospitale* and the chambers of Wighard. Has his body been examined by a physician?'

It was Gelasius who answered.

'By the Holy Father's own physician, Cornelius of Alexandria.'

'Then Cornelius of Alexandria shall be the first whom we shall question.'

She began to stride towards the door, hesitated and turned back to Gelasius.

'By your leave, lord bishop?'

Gelasius was uncertain whether her voice held a mocking tone but he waved a hand in a helpless gesture of dismissal. While Eadulf turned and bowed low over the bemused bishop's hand, brushing the man's ring with his lips, Fidelma was already at the door.

'Come, Eadulf, there is much to do now,' she urged softly.

'I will take you to Wighard's chambers,' offered Marinus, going to accompany them.

'That will not be necessary, Eadulf will conduct me. I would be obliged, however, if you made out our authority as soon as possible and ensure we have the written approval of the *Praetor Peregrinus* before the midday Angelus.'

She had opened the door and was aware of the young officer of the *custodes* who had escorted her from her lodging. He was still standing outside waiting for orders.

'Also,' Fidelma went on turning to Marinus, 'I would be indebted if I could have the services of one of your palace guard as a symbol of my authority. It is always better to have an immediately recognisable symbol of authority. This young man might do.'

Marinus pursed his lips wondering whether he ought to protest but then he slowly nodded.

'*Tesserarius*!'

The young guard sprang to attention.

'At your service, *Superista*!'

'You will take your orders from Sister Fidelma or from Brother Eadulf until I personally relieve you of that duty. They act with the authority of myself, Bishop Gelasius and the *Praetor Peregrinus*.'

The young man's face was a picture of astonishment.

'*Superista*?' he stammered as if he doubted that he had heard correctly.

'Have I made myself clear?'

The *tesserarius* coloured hotly and swallowed hard.

'By your command, *Superista*!'

'Good. I will send the authority after you, Sister Fidelma,' Marinus assured her. 'Do not hesitate to call upon me if I am needed.'

Fidelma, followed by Eadulf, swept from the room, followed by a bewildered young officer of the guards.

'What are your orders, sister?' the young man asked as they entered the courtyard. The sky was light now with the pale grey shades of dawn and the birds were beginning to make a noisy chorus which offset the gushing of the central fountain.

Fidelma paused in mid-stride and examined the young man who had brought her so rudely from her bed. In the light of day he still looked slightly arrogant and in the richness of his attire, even though it was the ceremonial of the Lateran

Guard, he was every inch a Roman noble. Fidelma suddenly smiled broadly.

'What is your name, *tesserarius*?'

'Furius Licinius.'

'Of an old patrician family of Rome, no doubt?'

'Of course ... yes,' the young man frowned, missing her sarcasm.

Fidelma sighed softly.

'That is good. I may need someone who will advise me closely on the customs of this city and of the Lateran. We are charged with investigating the death of the archbishop-designate Wighard.'

'But an Irish monk did it.' The young man seemed perplexed.

'That is for us to ascertain,' Fidelma said sharply. 'But you obviously know about the death?'

The young man cast a long and curious glance at Fidelma and then shrugged.

'Most of the guards do, sister! But *I* know that the Irish monk is guilty.'

'You seem very certain, Furius Licinius. Why?'

'I was on duty in the guard room when my comrade, the *decurion* Marcus Narses, came in with the Irish monk, Ronan Ragallach. The body of Wighard had just been discovered and this Ronan was arrested in the vicinity of his chamber.'

'That would be called an evidence of circumstance,' replied Fidelma. 'Yet you say you are certain. How so?'

'Two nights ago, I was on guard duty in the courtyard where Wighard's chambers are situated. Someone was skulking there about midnight. I chased the person and came upon this same Irish monk who denied being the person I had chased.

In doing so he lied to me. He gave me a false name – Brother "Ayn-dina" . . .'

'Brother Aon Duine?' Fidelma queried, gently correcting the pronunciation and when the *tesserarius* nodded his assent she turned slightly to hide the grin which split her features. Even Eadulf, having a good knowledge of Irish, could share the joke hidden to the young officer.

'I see,' she said solemnly, having composed herself. 'He told you then that he was "Brother No-one", for that is what it means in my tongue. What then?'

'He claimed that he had come from some chambers which I later knew to be as false . . .'

'. . . as his name?' Eadulf asked with an air of innocence.

'By the time I realised his lies, he had fled. This is why I am convinced he is guilty.'

'But guilty of what?' Fidelma observed. 'Whether it proves him guilty of the murder has yet to be seen. We will discuss this later with the monk, Ronan Ragallach. Come, Furius Licinius, conduct me to this physician who examined the body of Wighard.'

Chapter Five

Cornelius of Alexandria, the personal physician to His Holiness, Vitalian, Bishop of Rome, was a short, swarthy man. A black-haired Alexandrian Greek, with a prominent, bulbous nose and thin lips. While clean shaven, a blue-black stubble gave the impression that he would need to scrape his facial hair three times daily to remain without a beard. His eyes were dark and penetrating. He rose uncertainly as Furius Licinius entered his chamber, followed by Fidelma and Eadulf.

'Well, *tesserarius*?' His tone demonstrated his annoyance at being disturbed.

'Are you Cornelius the physician?' It was Fidelma who asked, falling easily into Greek. Then she realised that Brother Eadulf was not fluent in the language and so repeated her question in colloquial Latin.

The Alexandrian examined her with a speculative look.

'I am personal physician to the Holy Father,' he confirmed. 'Who are you?'

'I am Fidelma of Kildare and this is Brother Eadulf of Canterbury. We are charged by the Bishop Gelasius to investigate the death of Wighard.'

The physician snorted derisively.

'There is little to investigate, sister. There are no mysteries about the facts of Wighard's death.'

'Then you may tell us, how did he die?'

'Strangulation,' came the prompt reply.

Fidelma recalled her meeting with Wighard at Witebia when he was *scriba*, secretary to the archbishop Deusdedit.

'Wighard was a big man, as I remember. It would take a powerful person to strangle him.'

Cornelius sniffed. He had, it seemed, an annoying habit of making sounds through his nose by way of comment and punctuation.

'You would be surprised, sister, how little effort it takes to strangle even a powerful man. A mere compression of the carotid arteries and the jugular veins in the neck cuts off the supply of blood to the brain and produces unconsciousness almost immediately, perhaps three seconds at the most.'

'Provided the subject allows that pressure to be exerted on his neck,' replied Fidelma thoughtfully. 'Where is Wighard's body now? Still in his chamber?'

Cornelius shook his head.

'I have had it removed to the *mortuarium*.'

'A pity.'

Cornelius compressed his lips in annoyance at the implied criticism.

'There is nothing about his death that I cannot tell you, sister,' he said distantly.

'Perhaps,' Fidelma's reply was softly said. 'Show us the body of Wighard and then you may explain to us how you came by your findings.'

Cornelius hesitated and then gave an elaborate shrug combining with it a mocking half-bow.

'Follow me,' he said, turning and leading the way from his chamber through a small door which opened on to a small spiral stone staircase. They descended after him, down into a gloomy passageway and thence into a large cold marble-flagged room. There were several table-like slabs, also of marble, which immediately proclaimed their usage by their shrouded contents. The slabs held what were obviously bodies covered by stained linen cloths.

Cornelius went to one of them and removed the cloth casually, tossing it to one side.

'The body of Wighard,' he sniffed, nodding towards the pale, waxy-faced corpse.

Fidelma and Eadulf moved to the slab and peered down while Licinius hovered dutifully in the background. In life, Wighard of Canterbury had been a large, jovial-looking man with greying hair, and rotund features. Although, as Fidelma recalled from their meeting at Witebia, his cherubic-like features had hidden a coldly calculating mind and an ambition sharpened like a sword. The eyes in the rotund face had been those of a cunning fox. Without muscle tension to control his features, the pale, waxy flesh sagged causing a change of expression that made him almost unrecognisable to those who had known him in life.

Fidelma's eyes narrowed as she saw the traces of lesions around his neck.

Cornelius saw her examination and moved forward with a grim smile.

'As you see, sister, strangulation.'

'Not by use of the hands, though.'

Cornelius raised his eyebrows at Fidelma's observation, doubtless surprised at her attention to the detail.

'No, that is true. He was garrotted by his own prayer cord.'

The religious wore knotted cords around their habits which doubled as a belt and as a guide for their prayers, each knot marking the number of prayers to be said daily.

'The facial expression seems one of tranquillity, as if he were merely asleep,' Fidelma said. 'There seems little sign of his violent end to life.'

The Alexandrian physician shrugged.

'He was probably dead before he knew it. As I have said, it does not take long to achieve an unconscious state once the carotid arteries are compressed . . . here and here,' he indicated on the neck. 'You see,' he began to warm to his theme as a teacher imparting knowledge to bright students, 'it was the great physician Galen of Pergamum who identified these arteries and showed that they carried blood and not air as had been commonly supposed before. He named them carotid from the Greek word to stupefy, showing that a compression of these arteries produces stupor . . .'

Brother Eadulf shot an amused glance at Fidelma.

'I had heard,' he intervened, 'that Herophilus, who founded your own great school of medicine at Alexandria three centuries before the birth of the Christ, argued that blood not air passed through the arteries and that was four centuries before Galen.'

Cornelius stared at the Saxon monk in some astonishment.

'You know something of a physician's lore, Saxon?'

Eadulf grimaced disarmingly.

'I studied for a few years at Tuaim Brecain, the premier school of medicine in Ireland.'

'Ah,' Cornelius nodded, satisfied with the explanation. 'Then you may have a little knowledge. The great Herophilus certainly did reach that conclusion, but it was left to Galen to clearly identify it as fact and name the function of the carotid arteries. Additionally, the *jugulum*, that which we call the collarbone, gives its name to several veins here. These convey blood from the head while the arteries send blood to the head. All were compressed in the case of Wighard. Death, I believe, was within seconds.'

As he was speaking, Fidelma was examining the limbs and hands of the corpse, paying particular attention to the fingers and the nails. Finally she straightened.

'Was there any sign of a struggle, Cornelius?'

The physician shook his head.

'How was the body lying?'

'Face down on the bed, as I recall. Rather, the torso was on the bed while the lower legs were on the floor as if he had been kneeling by the side of the bed.'

Fidelma exhaled gently in thought.

'Then let us remove ourselves to Wighard's chambers. It is essential I know the exact position of the body.'

Furius Licinius interrupted by clearing his throat.

'Shall I ask the *decurion* Marcus Narses to attend us, sister? It was he who found the body, as well as apprehended the murderer.'

A brief expression of vexation crossed Fidelma's features.

'You mean, he apprehended Brother Ronan?' she corrected softly. 'Yes, by all means have this Marcus Narses meet us in Wighard's chamber. Go and find him. Cornelius will conduct us to the chamber.'

The physician stared a little resentfully at Fidelma's assumption that he would obey her orders but he made no protest.

'This way, then.'

They left the *mortuarium* and crossed a small courtyard, following a maze of passages until they came out into a pleasant courtyard, dominated by a fountain. Cornelius led Fidelma and Eadulf across the yard and into a building of three storeys in height, ascending a marble staircase. This was clearly the *domus hospitale* of the Lateran Palace, the guest quarters where the special guests of the Bishop of Rome were given hospitality. On the third floor Cornelius halted in a corridor. A single *custos* stood on guard before the door but he deferred to the authority of Cornelius who pushed open the tall, carved door into the rooms beyond.

There was a pleasant-looking reception room while beyond was the bed chamber of the late archbishop. It was a fine suite of rooms with tall windows opening on to the sun-filled quadrangle.

Cornelius led the way into the bed chamber.

Fidelma observed that the room was in keeping with the opulence of the other chambers of the Lateran Palace, hung with rich tapestries and with rugs spread over the tiled floor. These were no mere narrow *cubicula* of the type she had been used to. The bed was large, of a wooden frame, carefully carved with a myriad of religious symbolism. Apart from a rumpled bed cover, it appeared that the bed had not been slept in nor even prepared for the night. The bed cover was still firmly in place though it looked dishevelled as if someone had lain on the bottom half of the bed.

Cornelius pointed to the end of the bed.

'Wighard lay face downward across the lower part of the bed.'

'Can you show us exactly his position?' Fidelma asked.

Cornelius looked far from happy but he moved forward and

bent across the bed. From the waist upwards he laid his torso on the bed itself but his legs were bent almost in a kneeling position at the side of the bed and on the floor.

Fidelma stood for a while in thought.

Eadulf was also examining the position.

'Could it have been that Wighard was kneeling in prayer when his killer entered and garrotted him with his own prayer cord?'

'A possibility,' mused Fidelma. 'But, if he knelt at prayer, his prayer cord would be in his hands, and, if not, around his waist. The killer must have struck at once, so swiftly as not to have alarmed Wighard. Therefore, the killer had the prayer cord in his own hands . . . there could have been no struggle for its possession to alarm the archbishop.'

Eadulf agreed reluctantly.

'Can I get up now?' demanded Cornelius almost petulantly from his uncomfortable position.

'Of course,' Fidelma agreed contritely. 'You have been most helpful. I do not think we need trouble you further.'

Cornelius rose with a loud sniff.

'And the body? His Holiness expects to offer a requiem mass in the basilica at midday. After which the body is to be taken to the Metronia Gate of the city and buried in the Christian cemetery outside the Aurelian Wall.'

'A burial so soon?'

'It is the custom in this land.'

Eadulf said: 'The heat of the day makes burial at the earliest moment advantageous to public health.'

Fidelma half nodded absently as she studied the rumpled bed covers. Then she raised her eyes and smiled quickly at Cornelius.

'I have no further need to view the body. Let its disposal be as the Holy Father wishes.'

Cornelius hesitated at the door, almost reluctant to leave now.

'Is there anything further . . .?'

'Nothing,' Fidelma replied firmly, turning back to the bed.

The Alexandrian physician sniffed again, then turned and left the apartment.

Eadulf was watching Fidelma's examination of the bed with curiosity.

'Have you seen something, Fidelma?'

Fidelma shook her head.

'But there is something here I do not yet understand. Something which . . .' She caught herself and shook her head. 'My old master, Morann of Tara, used to say, do not speculate before you have acquired as much information as is available.'

'A wise man,' observed Eadulf.

'It was such that made him chief of the judges of Ireland,' agreed Fidelma. She pointed to the position which Cornelius had taken at the end of the bed. 'Here we have Wighard, standing or kneeling by his bed, presumably, in view of the hours, about to prepare for his night's repose. Was he about to draw off the bed cover and prepare for bed, or was he kneeling in prayer?'

She stood staring thoughtfully at the spot as if seeking inspiration from it.

'Either way, we must presume his back was to the door. His murderer enters, so quietly that Wighard does not even turn, is not even suspicious, and then, we must believe that this murderer is able to seize Wighard's prayer cord and garrote him so swiftly that he does not struggle and is dead before he even realises it.'

'That is according to the information so far,' Eadulf grim-aced. 'Perhaps we should now see this Brother Ronan and see what light he has to shed on the matter.'

'Brother Ronan can wait a moment more,' Fidelma said, her intent gaze wandering around the room. 'Bishop Gelasius said that the gifts that Wighard brought for the Holy Father were stolen. As Wighard's secretary, Eadulf, you would know where they were kept.'

Eadulf pointed into the other room.

'They were kept in a trunk in Wighard's reception room.'

Fidelma turned back into the first room. It also reflected the affluence and elegance of the palace, with its furnishings and tapestries. As Eadulf had indicated, a large wooden trunk, bound with iron, stood in one corner. Its lid was already opened and she could see that there was nothing left inside.

'What was kept in the trunk, Eadulf? Do you know?'

Eadulf smiled a little vainly.

'That was my duty as *scriba*, secretary to the archbishop. As soon as I arrived in Rome, I was called upon to take up my duties, so I know all about the matter. Every kingdom in the Saxon lands had sent gifts to His Holiness through Canterbury to show that they all submitted to the decision at Witebia; to demonstrate by those gifts that the rule of Rome was accepted among them and that Canterbury was to be the principal bishopric of the kingdoms. There was a tapestry woven by the ladies-in-waiting to the saintly Seaxburgh. She is wife to Eorcenberht of Kent and has endowed a great monastery on the Isle of Sheppey.'

'So? A tapestry. What else?'

'Oswy of Northumbria sent a book, a Gospel of Luke, illuminated by the monks of Lindisfarne. Eadulf of East Anglia sent a jewelled casket. Wulfhere of Mercia sent a bell, worked in gold and silver, while Cenewealh of the West Saxons sent two silver chalices wrought by craftsmen of his kingdom. Then, of course, there was the gift of Canterbury itself.'

'Which was?'

'The sandals and staff of Canterbury's first bishop, Augustine.'

'I see. And all these objects were placed in this trunk?'

'Exactly. Along with five gold and silver chalices to be blessed by His Holiness and distributed to the cathedrals of the five kingdoms of the Saxons together with a sack of gold and silver coins for votary offerings. And none of these precious objects is there now.'

'Such a treasure,' reflected Fidelma slowly, 'such a treasure would take some moving.'

'The objects taken were worth the ransom of a king,' Eadulf said.

'So, at this time,' mused Fidelma, 'we are asked to consider two motives for the murder of Wighard. The first motive, which Bishop Gelasius suspects on the evidence of the arrest of Brother Ronan, is that Wighard was slain by a malcontent of the Columban church angered by Canterbury's victory at Witebia. The second motive is that Wighard was slain during the course of a robbery.'

'The two motives might well be one,' argued Eadulf. 'The artifacts of Augustine were beyond price. If a malcontent of the Columban church killed Wighard then what a blow it would be to Canterbury to have the relics of Augustine go missing!'

'An excellent point, Eadulf. Those artifacts were only beyond price to someone who knew what they were and of the Faith. Other than that, they were worthless.'

There was a discreet knock on the door of the apartment and Furius Licinius entered. Another member of the *custodes* followed him in. Fidelma had the impression of a rather pleasant-looking man. He was of medium height with broad, powerful shoulders, a strong face and dark, well-tended wavy hair. His appearance, Fidelma noted, was meticulous, the hands scrubbed and fingernails clean. In her native Ireland, clean fingernails were considered a mark of rank and beauty.

'The *decurion* Marcus Narses, sister,' Licinius announced.

'You have been informed of our authority and our intention?' Fidelma asked.

The *custos* nodded. His movements seemed vigorous and his expression a hearty one.

'I am told that it was you who discovered Wighard's body and later arrested Brother Ronan.'

'That is so, sister,' agreed the *decurion*.

'Then tell us in your own words how this came about.'

Marcus Narses glanced from Fidelma to Eadulf, paused a moment as if to collect his thoughts, and then turned his gaze back to Fidelma.

'It happened last night, or rather in the early part of this morning. My watch was to end during the first hour. The duty of my *decuria* . . .'

'A company of ten men of the *custodes*, sister,' interrupted Licinius, eager to explain. 'The *custodes* of the Lateran Guard are so divided.'

'Thank you,' Fidelma, who knew quite well, replied solemnly. 'Continue, Marcus Narses.'

'My *decuria* were to guard the grounds of the *domus*

hospitale, the guest quarters where the foreign dignitaries, who were personal guests of His Holiness, were assigned.'

'I had the same guard duty on the previous night,' interposed Licinius again. 'The *Superista*, the military governor, was especially concerned for the welfare of the Saxon archbishop and his entourage.'

Fidelma gazed thoughtfully at the young man.

'Was he now?' she asked softly. Then to the impatient *decurion*: 'Go on, Marcus Narses.'

'The watch was very boring. Nothing untoward had occurred. It was the hour for the Angelus. I heard the bell chiming in the basilica. I was walking across the courtyard . . .' he pointed down through the tall window of the chamber, '. . . that same courtyard as you see below . . . when I thought that I heard a noise coming from this building.'

'What sort of noise?'

'I am not sure,' frowned the *decurion*. 'It sounded like a piece of metal dropping on a hard surface. I was not even sure which direction it came from.'

'Very well. What then?'

'I knew the archbishop-designate to be quartered here, so I entered and ascended the stairs to the corridor outside. I wished to check that all was well.'

The young *custos* paused and swallowed, as if moistening a drying throat.

'I had reached the head of the stairs and was staring along the corridor outside when I saw a figure, dressed in the habit of a religious, hurrying away from me towards the stairs at the far end. There are two flights of stairs that ascend to the corridor, one from this end of the building, from that courtyard, and the other from the far end into a smaller courtyard and garden.'

'Was the corridor in darkness or was it lit when you reached it?' asked Eadulf.

'It was lit by three torches in their holders. I . . .' Marcus Narses paused and then smiled. 'Ah, I see what you mean, brother. Yes; the corridor was lit well enough for me to recognise Brother Ronan Ragallach.'

Fidelma raised a surprised eyebrow.

'Recognise?' she repeated with emphasis. 'You knew Brother Ronan Ragallach?'

The *custos* flushed and shook his head immediately with embarrassment and corrected himself.

'What I meant was that the person I saw hurrying away from me down the corridor, I later saw again and arrested. At that point I knew him to be Brother Ronan Ragallach.'

Licinius nodded in melancholy agreement.

'He was the same person who called himself Brother "Ayndina" when . . .'

His voice trailed away at Fidelma's slim upraised hand.

'We are, at this moment, hearing testimony from Marcus Narses,' she chided softly. 'Continue, *decurion*. Did this Brother Ronan Ragallach give you his correct name when you apprehended him?'

'Not at first,' answered the *custos*. 'He tried to give me the name Brother "Ayn-dina". But one of my men recognised him as a *scriptor* working in the *Munera Peregrinitatis* . . .'

'The Foreign Secretariat,' supplied Furius Licinius quickly.

'The guard recalled his name . . . Ronan Ragallach. It was then that the brother admitted his identity.'

'We seem to have raced ahead,' Fidelma said. 'Let us return to where you first saw the man who later you knew to be Brother Ronan. You say that you saw him at the far end of the corridor in which Wighard's chamber was situated? Is that so?'

The *decurion* nodded agreement.

'Did you call upon the brother to stop?' prompted Eadulf. 'Did you think he was behaving suspiciously?'

The *decurion* took the cue eagerly.

'Not at first. As I reached the corridor and noticed the brother at the far end, I simultaneously saw that the door to the archbishop-designate's apartment was slightly ajar. I called out to the archbishop-designate and when there was no reply I pushed it open, calling again. On receiving no reply, I entered.'

'Was the apartment lit?' Fidelma asked.

'Well lit, sister. Candles were burning in both rooms.'

'And what did you see?'

'On entering I detected no disturbance but saw that the lid of the chest was raised,' he gestured towards the chest which had contained the treasure. 'There was nothing in the chest, nor sign of anything in the vicinity which looked as if it had been removed from it.'

'Very well. And then?' prompted Fidelma again, when he paused.

'Again I called to the archbishop-designate. I moved to his bed chamber. Then I saw his body.'

'Describe how the body was lying?'

'I will show you, if I may?'

Fidelma nodded and the *decurion* led the way into the bed chamber and knelt down, towards the foot of the bed, in almost the same posture as demonstrated by Cornelius of Alexandria.

'The archbishop-designate was sprawled with his torso on the bed, face downwards. I saw a knotted cord around his neck. I reached forward to check for a pulse. The skin was cold to the touch and I knew him to be dead.'

'Cold, you say?' Fidelma demanded eagerly. 'The skin was *cold* to the touch?'

'It was,' confirmed Marcus Narses rising to his feet. As he rose, the point of his scabbard snagged on the coverlet and dragged it a little. Fidelma's eyes caught sight of something under the bed but she allowed her features to remain composed and her face turned attentively to the young *decurion*.

'Go on,' she invited, for he had paused once more.

'It was obvious that the archbishop had been strangled with the cord. Murdered.'

'What was your immediate thought?' Fidelma was interested. 'Your immediate thought when you knew Wighard to be dead?'

Marcus Narses stood for a moment, pursing his lips as he reflected upon the question. 'That the person I had seen hurrying along the corridor might be the murderer, naturally.'

'Quite so. And what of the empty chest? What was your thought about that?'

'I thought that perhaps a robbery had been committed in which the archbishop had disturbed the thief and been slain for his pains.'

'Perhaps. The figure you saw hurrying away, was it carrying a sack or other means of transporting bulky objects such as those that were stored in this chest?'

The *custos* reluctantly shook his head.

'I do not recall.'

'Come. You have been fairly specific until now,' snapped Fidelma. 'You can surely continue to be specific?'

The *decurion* blinked at the sudden, unexpected belligerence in her voice.

'Then I have to say that I did not observe any sack or bag being carried.'

'Just so. And the body was cold when you touched it. Did you deduce anything from that?'

'Simply that the man was dead.'

'I see. Go on. What did you do?'

'I shouted to raise the alarm and ran in pursuit of the figure which by then had disappeared down the stairway.'

'Where did you say that this stairway at the far end of the passageway led to?'

'To a second quadrangle at the back of this building. As luck would have it, two of the *decuria* were passing through the courtyard and had observed the figure of the brother making his hurried exit from the building. They called on him to halt. He did so.'

'He did so?' Fidelma was surprised.

'There was little else he could do when faced by two armed *custodes*,' smiled the *decurion* cynically. 'They asked him to identify himself and his business. He gave this name of "Ayndina" and he was almost persuading them to let him go when they heard my voice raising the alarm. Then they held on to the man until I arrived. There is little else to say.'

'They held on to him?' queried Eadulf. 'Do you mean he tried to escape?'

'At first, yes.'

'Ah,' Eadulf smiled triumphantly. 'Not the action of an innocent man.'

Fidelma ignored him and asked: 'Did you ask the brother what he was doing in the vicinity of the archbishop-designate's chambers?'

The *decurion* grinned sardonically.

'As if he would confess that he had murdered the archbishop-designate!'

'But did you ask?' pressed Fidelma.

'I told him that I had seen him fleeing from the chambers where the archbishop-designate had been murdered. He denied having anything to do with the murder. I marched him off to the cells in the guard house and reported the matter immediately to Marinus, the military governor. Marinus came and questioned Brother Ronan who simply denied everything. That is all I have to say.'

Fidelma rubbed the bridge of her nose thoughtfully with her slender finger.

'Yet what you told him was inaccurate, wasn't it?' she asked almost sweetly.

The *decurion* frowned.

'I mean,' went on Fidelma, 'that you had not seen him fleeing from the archbishop-designate's chamber. You say that you first saw him only at the end of the corridor in which the archbishop-designate's chambers were situated. Is that not so?'

'If one wishes to be precise, but it is obvious . . .'

'A witness must be precise and not draw conclusions. That is the task of the judge,' Fidelma admonished. 'Now, you say your men arrested him as he ran out of the *domus hospitale*?'

'That is correct,' Marcus Narses replied with pique in his voice.

'And was he carrying anything?'

'No, he was not carrying anything.'

'Has a search been instigated for the missing items from Wighard's trunk? We know that many precious items have been stolen from these chambers. The supposition is that whoever killed the archbishop-designate stole these items. But you did not observe Brother Ronan Ragallach carrying anything in the corridor and now you confirm that he was not carrying anything when he was arrested.'

Fidelma smiled thinly at the *decurion*.

'So has a search been made for the lost treasures?' she spelt out her question carefully and with patience.

'A search was made, of course,' replied Marcus Narses. 'A search of the vicinity; anywhere that he might have dumped them during his flight.'

'But nothing was found?'

'Nothing. Marinus ordered that we search Brother Ronan's chambers at the *Munera Peregrinitatis* and also his lodgings.'

'And still nothing was found, of course?' Fidelma asked, assuming the answer.

'Nothing,' confirmed Marcus Narses, with growing irritation at Fidelma's prescience.

'And was this chamber searched?' Fidelma asked innocently.

Both Licinius and Marcus Narses exchanged a derisive grin with each other.

'If the treasures were stolen from here then the thief would hardly be likely to hide them in the very room he was taking them from,' the *decurion* sneered.

Without a word, Fidelma crossed to the bed and knelt down to where she had seen Marcus Narses' sword scabbard drag the coverlet away. She reached forward before their astounded gaze and drew forth a stick and a pair of leather sandals, together with a heavy leather-bound book. Beyond these was a rolled up tapestry which she also dragged out. Then she rose turning a bland gaze on them.

Eadulf was smiling broadly behind his hand at their sudden chagrin.

'I would presume that these are some of the missing items. The staff and sandals of Augustine and the book from Lindisfarne and the tapestry made by the ladies attending the Queen of Kent.'

Eadulf moved forward and eagerly examined them.

'There is no doubt that these are the items from the treasure,' he confirmed.

Licinius was shaking his head like a pugilist recovering from a blow.

'How . . .?' he began.

'Because no one searched thoroughly,' Fidelma replied evenly, enjoying their discomfiture. 'It seems whoever took the treasure was only interested in the items of immediate mercenary value. The thief wanted nothing that could not be quickly converted into exchangeable currency.' Fidelma could not help a sly dig at Eadulf. 'It somehow weakens the point you made that these artifacts were what the thief wanted as a means of hurting the authority of Canterbury.'

Eadulf pulled a face. He was far from convinced. Instead he turned to Marcus Narses and asked in tones of innocence: 'Perhaps, the *decurion* Marcus Narses should make another and more thorough search of all the chambers on this floor?'

Marcus Narses mumbled something which Fidelma was charitable enough to accept as assent.

'Good. Now while you do that, Furius Licinius can conduct us to see Brother Ronan Ragallach.'

'I think it would be the next logical step,' Eadulf agreed solemnly.

'And at least,' Fidelma smiled mischievously, 'we can report to the Bishop Gelasius that not all of Wighard's treasures have been stolen.'

They were turning towards the door when it burst abruptly open. The agitated figure of the *Superista*, Marinus, stood framed in the portal. His face was flushed and his breath came quickly from the exertion of running. His eyes moved rapidly over the group until they came to rest on Sister Fidelma.

'I have just heard from the guard house . . . Brother Ronan Ragallach has escaped from his cell and is nowhere to be found. He has vanished.'

Chapter Six

The last notes of the chant echoed into silence against the great vaulted roof of the austere round basilica of St. John of Lateran. Massive oriental granite columns towered upwards on either side of the short nave, above which brightly coloured frescoes depicted scenes from both Old and New Testaments. The smell of incense and the fragrance of beeswax candles, in their opulent gold and silver stands, mixed into a heavily scented aroma which created a stifling atmosphere. Marble was omnipresent, blending in with the stones and granite which supported a tower above the ostentatious high altar approached by a variegated pavement of semi-precious stones inserted into mosaic form. Little chapels led off from the main domed area of the basilica; unobtrusive little chapels compared with the splendour of the area of the high altar. Here were some of the remarkably modest sarcophagi of the Holy Fathers of the Roman Church, although the custom now was, whenever possible, to have their remains interred in the basilica of St Peter to the north-west of the city.

Before the richly endowed high altar, resting on trestles, was the opened wooden coffin of Wighard, the late archbishop-designate of Canterbury. A dozen bishops and their attendants sat to one side and behind them a score or more of abbots and abbesses, while on the other side of the altar sat the official mourners from the band of Saxon religious, who had followed the Kentish priest to Rome for his ordination. Now they were witnesses to his funeral rites.

Sister Fidelma had positioned herself behind Brother Eadulf who had taken a prominent place as the *scriba* of Wighard. Next to Eadulf sat an austere-looking abbot whose features were remarkably handsome, she thought, although they seemed to lack something. Compassion, perhaps? There was something callous about the set of his mouth and expression in his pale eyes. She wondered who this abbot was as he sat in a place of prominence among the mourners. She would ask Eadulf later, but she could not help notice the side glances the man kept giving towards the prim-featured Abbess Wulfrun sitting at his side. The dowdy figure of Sister Eafa sat next to her while two more brothers were ranged at Eafa's other side.

From her position Fidelma could also see across the apse and down into the short darkened nave of the crowded basilica. The vast throng of people, people of all the Christian nations, judging by the variety of their styles of dress, filled the nave and clustered between the niches of the massive columns which supported the roof. Fidelma knew well that it was not the requiem mass for the Saxon archbishop-designate which had brought the vast concourse crowding into the church. The attendance was due only to the fact that the Holy Father himself was conducting the mass for the departed soul of Wighard. It was Vitalian, incumbent of the throne of St Peter, whom they thronged to see.

She glanced across to the high altar where the Bishop of

Rome, supported by his attendant, was rising from his ornately worked throne.

Vitalian, the 76th successor to the throne of Peter the Apostle – according to the chroniclers – was tall with a large but flat nose and strands of long, wiry black hair spilling from under his tall white *phrygium*, a tiara-like crown of his office. His lips were thin, almost cruel, observed Fidelma, and the eyes black and impenetrable. Although he was a native of Segni, not far south of Rome, it was said that his ancestry was Greek and Fidelma had already heard talk in Rome that Vitalian had, in contrast to his papal predecessors, embarked on a policy of the restoration of religious unity, openly wooing the patriarchs of the eastern churches to repair the break with Rome which had begun two centuries before.

As the voices of the choristers fell silent, the Bishop of Rome stood with raised hand for the blessing. There was a shuffle as everyone knelt before him. At his side, his *mansionarius*, the head verger, presented the thurible, containing the incense, to the acolyte whose duty it was to dispense the perfume around the coffin.

After the blessing was intoned, the pall bearers, with bowed heads, moved slowly forward to transport the earthly remains of Wighard to the cart that waited outside the basilica. Wighard would begin his last journey from the basilica to the Gate of Metronia and thence to the Christian cemetery under the bleak southern city wall of Aurelian.

The Bishop of Rome followed the coffin first. But before the funeral cart itself went a detachment of the *custodes* of the Lateran Palace with the *primicerius*, or papal chancellor, and his deacons. After His Holiness came Gelasius, as *nomenclator*, together with the other two main dignitaries, the *vestararius*, in charge of the papal household, and the *sacellarius*, the papal treasurer.

The chief mourners were marshalled by an officious young cenobite, in charge of ceremonies, to a position immediately behind the bishops.

After them would come the rest of the congregation, walking solemnly in procession to the place of burial. As the cortège began to move slowly away from the basilica, the choristers began a hearty chant.

> *Benedic nobis, Domine, et omnibus donis Tuis . . .*
> Bless us, O Lord, and all thy gifts . . .

It was said that Vitalian was vigorous in encouraging the use of music in all aspects of religious worship, contrary to the policy of his predecessors in office.

Unlike the others in the procession, Fidelma did not walk with head bowed. She was too busy gazing around her, taking in the sights and sounds of the ceremony and especially the faces of those accompanying the funeral. Somewhere, she reasoned, in those solemn faces might be the murderer of Wighard.

As she examined her fellow mourners she contemplated the facts of Wighard's death as she saw them. There was something about them that did not seem right; in spite of Brother Ronan Ragallach's curious, and seemingly guilty, behaviour. In fact, she suddenly realised, it was because of that behaviour. No murderer would draw such attention to himself as the Irishman had done. And the exact manner of Wighard's death, the missing gold and silver artifacts, did not seem to fit to the pattern which Bishop Gelasius and the military governor, Marinus, offered as a solution.

As the procession wound its way under the shadow of Mons Caelius and the remnants of the ancient Tullian Wall of Rome, the choristers started a new chant, a soft sorrowful dirge.

> *Nos miseri homines et egeni . . .*
> We miserable men and needy . . .

They turned through the impressive portals of the Gate of Metronia, outside the ancient city.

The Christian cemetery, in the shadow of the remains of the third-century Aurelian walls which encircled the seven hills of Rome, was surprisingly large, with its monuments and mausoleums, crypts and cenotaphs. Fidelma was amazed by the vastly differing styles of entombment.

Noticing her surprise, Eadulf unbent a little from his grim-faced mourning.

'The ancient law of Rome prohibited burials taking place within the city, within the confines set up by Servius Tullius, the sixth king of Rome. As the population increased, the boundary was extended for a mile. Thus, sister, you will find many cemeteries outside the city limits, such as this one.'

'But I have heard that because of persecution, those of the Faith in Rome would bury their dead in vast subterranean caverns,' Fidelma said with a frown.

Eadulf shook his head and smiled.

'Not because of persecution. It was simply that the early members of the Faith followed their own customs. Mostly, Greeks, Jews and Romans, the earliest members of the Faith, would either burn or bury their dead. The remains would be put into urns or laid in sarcophagi and, in turn, these would be located in chambers under the ground. The practice to open up these chambers grew from the second century after Christ's birth and only just ended during the last century. It was more custom than persecution.'

The final blessing had been given and the procession re-formed to be led away by the choristers with a dramatic paen of triumph, the *Gloria Patri*, Glory be to the Father, symbolising thanks for the passing of Wighard's soul into heavenly repose. It was appropriate, thought Fidelma. The lament to the grave and the rejoicing at the return.

She moved closer to Eadulf.

'We must discuss the case,' she insisted.

'There is plenty of time, surely, especially now we know that Ronan Ragallach is guilty,' Eadulf replied easily.

'We know nothing of the sort,' snapped Fidelma, annoyed by Eadulf's presumption.

Heads turned from the departing mourners in surprise at her sharp tone.

She coloured and lowered her gaze.

'We know nothing of the sort,' she repeated in a whisper.

'But it is obvious,' Eadulf responded, with a frown of equal annoyance. 'What other evidence do you want than Ronan's flight? His escape from custody is an admission of his guilt by itself.'

Fidelma shook her head vigorously.

'Not so.'

'Well, so far as I am concerned, Ronan is clearly guilty,' replied Eadulf stubbornly.

Fidelma's lips compressed. A dangerous sign.

'Let me remind you of our agreement; the decision on this matter of culpability was to be unanimous. I will continue my investigation . . . alone, if need be.'

Eadulf's face was a mask of frustration. The matter seemed clear to him. But he knew that Bishop Gelasius would find a divided opinion worse than no opinion at all. At the same time he felt disquiet. There was no denying that Sister Fidelma had shown a remarkable aptitude at delving into a puzzle and reaching a solution where he thought there was none. He had been more than impressed by the affair at Witebia, in Northumbria. But surely this case was so simple. Why didn't she see that?

'Very well, Fidelma. I believe Ronan is guilty. His actions proclaimed it. I am prepared to report as much to Gelasius. However, I am willing to listen to any arguments you may have against that conclusion . . .'

He became aware of some of the lingering mourners examining them curiously, watching the animated faces of their disagreement.

Brother Eadulf took Fidelma's arm and guided her through the cemetery towards a tall mausoleum with a marble edifice.

'I know a place where we may get some peace to exchange our views on the matter,' he grunted.

To her surprise, Fidelma saw a young boy squatting outside the entrance to the mausoleum with a basket of candles before him. Eadulf placed a coin into the bowl which the lad held out and selected a candle. The boy had flint and tinder and struck a light for the candle.

Without a word, Eadulf led Fidelma inside. She found herself in a small stairwell in the crypt leading down into the darkness.

'What is this place, Eadulf?' Fidelma asked, as the Saxon monk began to descend a series of carved stone stairs.

'This is one of the catacombs where the early members of the Faith were buried,' he explained, holding the candle aloft as he guided her downward some twenty feet or more into a large corridor which had been carved through the stone. 'There are sixty of these cemeteries within the immediate vicinity of Rome which were used until the end of the last century. It is said that some six million Christians were buried in these places during the last four or five centuries.'

The tunnel, Fidelma could see, led into a network of subterranean galleries, generally intersecting each other at right angles, though sometimes taking on a very sinuous course. They were six feet wide and rose sometimes as high as ten feet.

'These tunnels seem to be cut through solid rock,' she observed, pausing to run her hand over the walls.

Eadulf smiled and nodded assent.

'The countryside about Rome consists of volcanic rocks, sometimes used as building stone. The stone is dry and porous and can be easily worked. The galleries which our brethren made were not unsuitable for living in and were often used as retreats during the great persecutions.'

'But how could people breathe underground?'

Eadulf pointed to a small aperture above their heads.

'See? The builders ensured that openings were made at distances of two or three hundred feet.'

'They must be immense constructions if this is but one of sixty.'

'Indeed,' Eadulf agreed. 'They were greatly extended during the reigns of the emperors Aurelius Antoninus and Alexander Severus.'

They suddenly came upon a wider space with long recesses cut into the walls. Several were empty but more than a few were blocked in by carved stone.

'Here we have the vaults of the dead ones,' Eadulf explained. 'The niche is called a *loculus* in which the body is placed. Each family had such a chamber called an *arcosolia* where they buried their dead.'

Fidelma gazed with some admiration at the beautifully coloured frescoes that were painted on the outside of some of the tombs. There was some writing on the archway above.

'*Hic congesta jacet quaeris si turba Piorum,*
'*Corpora Sanctorum retinent venereanda sepulcra . . .* '

'If you would know,' echoed Eadulf, translating to Irish, 'here are piled together a host of holy ones, these venerated sepulchres enshrine the bodies of the saints.'

Fidelma was impressed.

'It is very fascinating, Eadulf. I thank you for showing me this.'

'There are even more interesting catacombs elsewhere in Rome, such as the one under Vatican Hill itself, where Peter and Paul repose. But the largest of all is the tomb of the blessed Calixtus, pope and martyr, on the Appian Way.'

'I would be enthusiastic in any other circumstances, Eadulf,' Fidelma sighed, 'but we still have to talk about the manner of Wighard's death.'

Eadulf exhaled deeply, halted, and set the candle down on a nearby slab of stone, leaning back against the wall with folded arms.

'Why are you so sure that Ronan Ragallach is innocent?' he demand. 'Is it simply because he is Irish?'

Fidelma's eyes seemed to flash dangerously in the flickering light of the candle. Eadulf saw the sharp intake of her breath and mentally prepared himself for a blast of her anger. It did not come. Instead, she exhaled slowly.

'That is unworthy of you, Eadulf. You know me better than that,' she said softly.

Eadulf had regretted his words as soon as he had uttered them.

'I'm sorry,' he said simply. The words were offered as no mere empty formula.

There was an uncomfortable silence. Then Eadulf said: 'Surely you must concede that Ronan Ragallach's behaviour points to his guilt?'

'Of course,' conceded Fidelma. 'It is obvious . . . perhaps too obvious.'

'Not all killings are as complicated as that of the Abbess Étain at Witebia.'

'Agreed. Nor do I argue that Ronan Ragallach is innocent. What I say is that there are questions that need to be answered before we can say with assurance he is guilty. Let us examine these questions.'

She held up a hand to strike off the points on her fingers.

'Wighard, according to the evidence, is kneeling by his bed and is garrotted with his own prayer cord. Why was he kneeling?'

'Because he was at his prayers?'

'Allowing his murderer to enter his chambers and come up behind him, take his prayer cord and strangle him before he could even attempt to rise from his kneeling position? Surely this is curious? And it relies on Ronan Ragallach being so stealthy that one must be entirely credulous. We know that Ronan Ragallach is a heavy man. Rotund and given to wheezy, noisy breathing.'

'Perhaps Ronan Ragallach had been invited in by Wighard and . . .' began Eadulf.

'And asked to wait while Wighard knelt with his back to him and said his prayers? Hardly likely.'

'All right. But this much we can ask when Ronan Ragallach is recaptured.'

'In the meantime we should question whether Wighard might have known his murderer so well as to feel no fear in praying in such a manner,' Fidelma pointed out. 'As his secretary, could you say that Wighard knew Brother Ronan Ragallach at all, let alone well enough to trust him in such circumstances?'

Eadulf raised one shoulder slightly before letting it fall.

'I cannot say that Wighard knew Brother Ronan at all,' he confessed.

'Very well. There is another aspect that is worrying me. We are told that Ronan Ragallach was seen leaving Wighard's chambers. The gold, silver and coins are missing. This has also been put forward as a possible motive for the killing.'

Eadulf inclined his head in reluctant agreement.

'We are also told,' Fidelma went on, 'that Brother Ronan was not carrying anything when he was seen in the corridor outside Wighard's rooms. Nor was he carrying anything when he was stopped and arrested in the courtyard outside. Nor has the search by the *custodes* discovered where Wighard's gold and silver has been hidden. If Ronan is the culprit, seen within moments of leaving Wighard's chamber after killing him, why was he not seen with these precious items, which are bulky to say the least?'

Eadulf's eyes narrowed. Inwardly he was annoyed with himself for not seeing the logic of the point made by Fidelma. His mind worked rapidly.

'Because Ronan killed Wighard earlier and took the treasure,' he began, after a moment or two's thought. 'That is why the body was cold when Marcus Narses found it. Because Ronan had killed him earlier but then returned to the chamber to retrieve something and then was caught. Or because he was working with someone else.'

Fidelma smiled solemnly.

'Three possible alternatives. But there is a fourth. He might simply have been in the wrong place at the wrong time.'

Eadulf was silent.

'These questions can only be answered when Brother Ronan Ragallach has been recaptured,' he said again.

Fidelma put her head to one side quizzically.

'So you still think there are no questions to be asked before that time?'

'I agree that there are several mysteries here that need to be sorted out. But surely only Brother Ronan . . .'

'Well, at least we are agreed on the first part of your statement, Eadulf,' she interrupted. 'However, would you agree, in the absence of Brother Ronan, that we continue our investigation in another direction by asking questions of the other members of Wighard's entourage and those who attended him while in Rome?'

'I don't see . . .' the Saxon monk hesitated. 'Very well,' he went on after a pause. 'There can be no harm in it, I suppose.'

Fidelma smiled.

'Good. Then let us assess who we shall question when we return to the Lateran Palace. Who was in his entourage?'

'Well, for a start, I was his *scriptor*,' Eadulf grinned sourly. 'You know me well enough.'

Fidelma was not amused.

'Idiot! I mean the others. There are more in your party,

including Sister Eafa and the overbearing Abbess Wulfrun who it was our great joy to travel with on the ship from Massilia.'

Eadulf grimaced at her sarcasm.

'Abbess Wulfrun is, as you may have gathered, a royal princess. She is sister to Seaxburgh, queen of Kent, who is wife to Eorcenberht the king.'

Fidelma raised an eyebrow in displeasure at the respectful tone in his voice.

'Once you have taken the cloth you are one with the church and have no rank other than that which is bestowed upon you by the church.'

Eadulf flushed slightly in the candle light. He shifted his weight against the stone wall.

'Nevertheless, a Saxon princess has . . .'

'No more recognition than any other of temporal rank who enters among the holy orders. Abbess Wulfrun has the unfortunate attitude of believing that she is still a princess of Kent. I feel sorry for Sister Eafa, whom she bosses so arrogantly.'

Inwardly Eadulf, too, had felt a sympathy for the young sister. Yet in the lands of the Saxons, birth and rank mattered greatly.

'Who comprised Wighard's party apart from yourself?' prompted Fidelma.

'Well,' he continued after a moment, 'as well as Wulfrun and Eafa, there is Brother Ine, who is the personal servant of Wighard and who serves him in all the menial tasks. He wears a face as if he is in permanent mourning and is hard to get close to. Then there is Abbot Puttoc from the Abbey of Stanggrund.'

'Ah,' Fidelma interposed, 'the handsome man with the cruel mouth?'

Eadulf snorted in disgust.

'Handsome? That is a woman's perception. He thinks a lot of himself and rumour has it that he is equally ambitious. He is personal envoy of King Oswy of Northumbria. I am told he is a close friend of Wilfred of Ripon.'

'I see. He is in Rome as a representative of Oswy?'

'He is, for Oswy is now regarded in Rome as *bretwalda*, or, as you would call it, high king over the Saxon kingdoms.'

Wilfred of Ripon, as Fidelma knew from her time at Witebia, was the main enemy of the Irish missionaries in Northumbria who had been the leading advocate of Rome during the recent synod.

'Then Brother Eanred serves as Puttoc's servant. A placid man but somewhat simple. I am told that Puttoc bought him as a slave and freed him in accordance with the teachings of the Faith.'

Fidelma had long been aware that the Saxons still practised slavery. She could not help the jib: 'Puttoc freed Eanred from slavery in the outside world so that he might be his slave in his abbey?'

Eadulf stirred uncomfortably and decided not to comment.

'Then there is Brother Sebbi,' he went on hurriedly. 'He is also from Stanggrund Abbey and journeys here as an adviser to Abbot Puttoc.'

'Tell me of him,' invited Fidelma.

'I have never learnt much about him in the time I have been in Rome,' Eadulf confessed. 'I believe him to have an excellent mind but also that he is as ambitious as he is astute.'

'Ambition yet again?' sniffed Fidelma in disgust. 'And all Wighard's party had their rooms within the same building, the *domus hospitale*, as Wighard?'

'Yes. In fact, my room was the nearest, for it was on the opposite side of the corridor facing Wighard's chamber.'

'Who was in the next apartment to Wighard? His servant Ine?'

'No. That was empty as are the other rooms on that side of the building. I believe they are merely storerooms.'

'So where was Ine?'

'He had the room next to mine. Opposite to Wighard's room. Next to him was Brother Sebbi's room; then the room of Abbot Puttoc and next to him, at the far end of the corridor, was Brother Eanred, his servant.'

'I see. And where were Abbess Wulfran and Sister Eafa lodged?'

'On the floor immediately below. The second floor of the *domus hospitale*.'

'I see,' reflected Fidelma. 'So, in fact, your room is the closest to Wighard's chamber?'

Eadulf smiled mockingly.

'Therefore it is lucky that I have an alibi being with you at the basilica of Saint Maria.'

'I had not forgotten,' Fidelma replied as if serious. For a moment Eadulf looked at her closely but Fidelma's face was a mask. Yet the eyes were twinkling with mischief.

'There now,' Fidelma suddenly stretched herself, 'if you will lead us back to the Lateran Palace, I suggest we occupy ourselves with questioning some of your brethren and hope the *custodes* have managed to pick up Brother Ronan Ragallach.' She suddenly shivered. 'I hadn't realised how cold it is in this place.'

Eadulf turned to pick up the candle and gave an abrupt exclamation.

'We'd better move swiftly, sister. I had no idea that the candle was burning so low.'

Fidelma saw the wax of the candle had almost burnt away and the remaining piece of wick had already begun to splutter.

Eadulf seized her hand and began to hurry along the passageway, through the various twists and right-angled turns. Then, with only a faint hiss to warn them, they were plunged into darkness.

'Don't let go of my hand,' instructed Eadulf's hoarse voice out of the darkness.

'That I won't,' Fidelma reassured him with some forcefulness. 'Do you know which way from here?'

'Straight on . . . I think.'

'Then let us move cautiously.'

There was not even a hint of light in the blackness of the man-made tunnels as they slowly felt their way forward.

'I was an idiot,' came Eadulf's tone of self-rebuke. 'I should have watched the candle.'

'Well, self-recrimination is of no use to us now,' Fidelma said regretfully. 'Let's get . . .'

She suddenly halted and exclaimed softly as she felt about with her free hand.

'What is it?'

'The passageway divides here. Left and right . . . which way? Can you remember?'

Eadulf closed his eyes in the darkness. His mind raced as he tried to make a decision. He felt helpless and as he realised that he did not know which way to turn, his thoughts were a vacillating stream of panic-stricken images and his sweat felt cold on his brow.

He felt Fidelma abruptly squeeze his hand.

'Look!' came her sibilant whisper. 'To the left. I think it is a light . . .'

Eadulf turned and stared into the blackness. He could see nothing.

'I was sure it was a light,' came Fidelma's baffled tone. 'Just for a minute . . .'

Eadulf was about to disillusion her when he caught a glimpse of a brief flicker of light. Were his eyes trying to create what his mind wanted to see? He stared longingly into the darkness. No; she was right! There was definitely a flicker in the blackness. He let out a bark of relief.

'Yes, there it is. You are right! Quickly!' He began to pull her in the direction of a flickering glow and at the same time calling at the top of his lungs. 'Hey! Hey!'

There was a silence before a gruff voice could be heard calling, echoing back along the tunnelways.

'*Heia*!'

The light grew in strength and then they saw an elderly man moving in their direction, holding up a lantern.

He halted as they came hurrying along the passageway towards him.

'*Heia vero*!' his voice was gruff as he stared from one to the other.

They halted before him slightly breathlessly, feeling like children caught at some foolish prank by an elderly but benign paternal figure. For a moment they could do no more than smile and gasp with relief. The run along the tunnel had deprived them of the breath to speak. The old man shook his head as he gravely regarded them.

'H'mm. The boy said that you had been down a long time

with only one candle. You were silly to tarry.'

'We didn't realise the passing of time,' gasped Eadulf, recovering his voice and feeling foolish at the elderly man's scornful chastisement.

'More people perish by such foolishness,' the old one grunted in reply. 'Are you both fit to follow me now? I will lead you back to the entrance.'

He turned as they both nodded silently, feeling ridiculously embarrassed at their behaviour. The old man led the way talking over his shoulder.

'Yes, yes; we have had many deaths in these catacombs. Death among the dead!' He laughed coarsely. 'Ironic, isn't it? People wander off to see the bones of the saints and martyrs and lose themselves. Others, like yourselves, allow themselves to be caught in the darkness and are doomed to wander for eternity unless they are lucky. Lucky, indeed! Why, do you know how far all the catacombs of Rome would stretch if placed as one long tunnel? It is computed that they would stretch nearly six hundred miles. Six hundred miles of tunnel! Some who have disappeared in those passages have never been found. Perhaps their souls still wander down there, down among the dead, among . . .'

Thankfully they came to the steps which led up into the mausoleum from which they had descended and emerged into the sunlight of the Christian cemetery with blinking eyes.

The small boy sat in front of his basket of candles and gazed at them without expression.

The old man paused to blow out his lamp and set it down by the side of the mausoleum entrance.

He spat reflectively to one side.

'Had the boy not told me . . .' he shrugged.

Fidelma fumbled in her *marsupium*, the money pouch in the folds of her robes, and handed the boy a silver coin. The boy took it and dropped it in his bowl without a change of expression. Eadulf, meantime, had produced a coin and proffered it to the old man but he shook his head.

'The coin for the boy is enough,' he said gruffly. 'But if you religious value your temporal existence, next time you are in that splendid basilica yonder,' he gestured to the distant tower of St John of Lateran, rising behind the Aurelian Wall, 'you might light a candle and say a prayer for the boy.'

Fidelma turned with an expression of interest.

'You asked nothing for yourself, old man. Why?'

'The boy needs prayers more than I do,' grunted the old man, defensively.

'Why is that?'

'He will be alone in this world when my time comes. I am old and my course has been navigated these long years. But the boy's father, who was my son, has already gone ahead of me with his wife. The boy has no one and perhaps a prayer might ensure him a better life than being condemned to sit here and sell candles.'

Fidelma examined the impassive face of the child. The quiet, blank eyes of the boy returned her stare without expression.

'What would you like to do in this world?' she asked quietly.

'It matters little. For all I can do is sit here and dream,' muttered the boy.

'But what is your dream?'

For a brief moment the boy's eyes sparkled.

'I would like to be able to read and write and serve in some great monastery. But I cannot.'

The child's eyes fell again and his face became a mask.

'Because you cannot afford to be tutored,' sighed the old man. 'I have no schooling, you see,' he turned to them apologetically. 'And I have no money. Selling candles to pilgrims is no more than a means of subsistence. There is none to spare for luxuries.'

'What is your name, boy?' asked Fidelma with a kindly expression.

'Antonio, son of Nereus,' the boy said with a quiet pride.

'We will pray for you, Antonio,' Fidelma assured him. She turned to his grandfather and inclined her head. 'And for you, old one. Thank you for your timely rescue.'

Chapter Seven

It was still warm and humid although it was late afternoon.
Sister Fidelma had returned to the hostel run by the deacon
Arsenius and his wife Epiphania, following her return from
the cemetery. She was exhausted for she had been up since
before dawn. Not only had she wanted to eat but to take a
siesta, as it was called locally from *sexta*, the sixth hour of the
day, the hottest period when most citizens of Rome took a rest
from the oppressive heat. Now bathed and refreshed by her
nap she found the *tesserarius*, Furius Licinius, waiting to escort
her once again to the Lateran Palace where she had promised
to meet Brother Eadulf to begin the questioning of
Wighard's entourage.

Her first question of the young palace guard was of the news
of the missing Brother Ronan Ragallach.

Licinius shook his head.

'Not a sign of him since he escaped the cells this morning,
sister. Just as likely he is hiding somewhere in the city, though
I would have thought he would have been easily noticed
with that outlandish tonsure which the male Irish and British
religious wear.'

Fidelma inclined her head thoughtfully.

'You are confident that he is still in the city, then?'

Licinius shrugged as they returned from the oratory of St Prassede and began to walk down the Via Merulana towards the Lateran Palace at the bottom of the hill.

'We have notified all the gates of the city which are watched by members of the *custodes* day and night. But Rome is a big city and there are several quarters in which a man might hide for years or even slip out. Along the Tiber, for example, to Ostia or Porto on the coast and from there one can secure passage to the four corners of the earth.'

'I have a feeling that he has not left the city. He will be found sooner or later.'

'*Deo Volente*,' echoed Licinius piously. 'God willing.'

'Do you know this city well, Licinius?' Fidelma changed the direction of the conversation.

Licinius blinked.

'As well as anyone. I was born and raised on the hill of Aventinus. My ancestors were nobles of Rome at its very foundation, tribunes who brought in the Licinian Laws nine centuries ago.' Fidelma noticed the proud flush which had come to his youthful features. 'I might have been a general of the imperial armies in the days of the mighty Caesars and not . . .'

He caught himself, glancing in annoyance at Fidelma as if blaming her for the unleashing of his suppressed frustration at his role in the *custodes*, and fell silent.

'Then perhaps you may clear up something which has puzzled me,' Fidelma pretended to be oblivious to his outburst of ancestral pride. 'So many people have told me what a beautiful and rich city this Rome is and yet I find the buildings curiously scarred as if by war. Some buildings are almost falling down while others are open to the weather. They give the impression of recent vandalism as though the city had been threatened by barbarians. I know it is many years since Genseric and his Vandals sacked the city. But surely this damage is new?'

Licinius, to her surprise, gave a snort of laughter.

'You are perceptive, sister. Except that the barbarian that did this thing was none other than our own emperor.'

Fidelma was bewildered.

'Tell me about it,' she invited.

'You know that the empire has been at war with the Arabians for over twenty years. They have been sending raiding fleets into our seas. They have conquered most of the areas of the former empire in north Africa which they use as bases to attack us. Constans the emperor decided to move from Constantinople to create a strong fortress in Sicily from which to organise the defence against these fanatics . . .'

'Fanatics?' queried Fidelma.

'Since they have adopted a new religion as followers of a prophet named Mahomet, the Arabians have expanded rapidly westward. They named their faith Islam, submission to God, and those who profess this faith are called Muslims.'

'Ah,' Fidelma nodded. 'I have heard of these people but don't they accept the tenets of both the faith of the Jews and our own Faith?

'Yes; but they say that this Mahomet embodied in his person the definitive expression of the divine word of God. They are fanatics,' Licinius said dismissively. 'They are causing death and destruction throughout Christendom.' He paused for a moment before continuing. 'Well, earlier this year, the Emperor Constans arrived with a large fleet and twenty thousand soldiers from the Asiatic armies of the empire. He came to Taranto and fought several campaigns in the south before paying a state visit to Rome last month. He was here but twelve days and I doubt if even the Muslim army could have inflicted as much damage on the city as our brave emperor of Rome in that time.'

Fidelma frowned at his vehemence. 'I don't understand.'

'Constans was greeted in his first visit to this mother city of the empire with all deference. His Holiness took his entire household to the sixth milestone to greet him with all proper solemnity. Feasts were prepared. The emperor then went to the basilica of St Peter's on the Vatican Hill and then, with his army, which had accompanied him, he went to the basilica of St Maria Maggiore.'

Fidelma suppressed a sigh.

'I don't see . . .' she began.

The young *tesserarius* waved his arms around at the surrounding buildings.

'While the Emperor was praying, his soldiers, at his orders, began to strip the buildings of Rome of all metal parts; the bronze tiles, clamps and ties with which they were bonded; the great statues and artifacts which had stood since the days of the great Roman Republic. Never had there been such savagery which has reduced the city to the pitiful state you see today.'

'But why?'

'Why? Because Constans wanted that great mass of metal, riches in antiquary, to melt down for armaments for his army. He had them sent to Ostia and shipped for the port of Syracuse. From there it was said that the metal would be taken to Constantinople.'

He laughed bitterly but stopped when he saw Fidelma staring curiously at him.

'It is just the irony of the thing,' he explained with a shrug.

'Irony?'

'Yes. The metal never even reached Syracuse. An Arabian raiding fleet intercepted the stolen metal of Rome before Constans' ships could make the port and the metal was taken to Alexandria.'

'Alexandria?'

Licinius nodded.

'It has been in the hands of the Muslims these last twenty years.' He gave a shrug. 'That is the answer to your question, sister.'

Fidelma considered the matter thoughtfully.

'And the Emperor of Rome is now in the south of the country?'

'Four weeks ago, he left for the south. I understand there is still fighting there with the Muslims.'

'So that is why there is a nervousness about this place; why the captain of my vessel, on my journey here, leapt at the merest hint of sails on the southern horizon?'

They had come to the steps of the Lateran Palace.

'The *Superista* has made a chamber available to serve you by way of an *officium* in which you and the Saxon brother may conduct your examinations,' the *tesserarius* informed her, assuming that Fidelma had answered her own questions. He led the way along the corridor to an apartment near that of the one used by the military governor of the papal household. Fidelma noted that its furnishings were sparse but functional. Brother Eadulf was already inside, rising from his seat as they entered. He looked rested and refreshed.

'I have warned the brethren to be ready to be called for examination,' he greeted, as Fidelma entered and seated herself in one of the several wooden chairs that were in the room.

'Excellent. Licinius here will act as our *dispensator* and bring them to us when we require their presence.'

The young *tesserarius* nodded his head stiffly, all official business now.

'By your command, sister.'

Eadulf scratched the tip of his nose. He had gathered some clay writing tablets and a *stylus* and placed them on a small table.

'I will make notes as required,' he said, 'but, in truth, Fidelma, I see little of worth coming from this exercise. I believe . . .'

Fidelma held up her hand to silence him.

'I know. Brother Ronan Ragallach is the guilty person. So indulge my curiosity, Eadulf, and we may get through this more easily.'

Eadulf tightened his jaw and was silent.

Fidelma was unhappy. She wished Eadulf was more open on the subject, for she appreciated his keen mind and perceptive assessment of people. But she could not go against her intuition and she was sure that there was a hidden mystery to be delved.

'Let us start with Brother Ine, Wighard's personal servant,' she announced firmly.

Eadulf glanced to Licinius.

'Fetch Brother Ine to us. I have asked those we may wish to see to make themselves available in the great hall. You will probably find him waiting there.'

The young *tesserarius* inclined his head and left.

Eadulf returned his gaze to Fidelma and grinned wryly.

'Our patrician friend seems to have little liking for our investigation.'

'I think he would prefer to be fighting in the ancient imperial armies of Rome than simply acting the custodian and body-guard to a group of religious,' replied Fidelma solemnly. 'He wears his patrician's ancestry with all the impatience and arrogance of an immature youth. Yet in that he has time on his side, for he will grow and mature.'

It seemed that Licinius had gone but a moment when the door opened.

A short, thin man with mournful features entered. He was about forty years of age, so Fidelma judged. Behind him came the young *tesserarius*.

'Brother Ine,' announced Licinius, almost propelling the monk unwillingly into the room and closing the door behind him.

'Come in, Brother Ine,' Eadulf motioned to a seat. 'This is Sister Fidelma of Kildare who has been commissioned with me by Bishop Gelasius to investigate the death of Wighard.'

The monk looked with dark solemn eyes at Fidelma without a change of his melancholy expression.

'*Deus vobiscum*,' he mumbled, sinking into the chair.

'Brother Ine,' Fidelma thought she should ensure the monk understood clearly. 'You do understand that we are investigating the murder of Wighard of Canterbury with the authority of the papal household?'

Brother Ine nodded, a swift, nervous jerk of his head.

'You were the personal servant to Wighard?'

'*Requiscat in pace!*' intoned Brother Ine piously, genuflecting. 'I served the late archbishop-designate. Indeed, I was more of his confidant.'

'You are from the kingdom of Kent?'

Eadulf decided to sit back and let Fidelma ask all the questions she wished.

'I am,' the monk seemed to let an expression of pride cross his doleful features, but only momentarily. 'My father was a churl in the house of Eadbald the king, and my brother remains in the house of Eorcenberht who now sits upon the throne.'

'A labourer,' explained Eadulf, in case Fidelma's knowledge of Saxon failed her. 'A churl is a servant who does menial tasks.'

'And how long have you served Christ?' Fidelma asked, turning back to Brother Ine.

'My father gave me to the abbey at Canterbury when Honorius was archbishop. I was ten years of age and was raised in the service of Our Lord.'

Fidelma had heard of this curious Saxon custom of giving their children away to the service of a monastery of abbey.

'And how long have you been in service to Wighard?'

'Twenty years. I became his servant when he was appointed secretary to Bishop Ithamar of Rochester.'

'Ithamar was the first Kentish man to be consecrated a bishop, nearly fifty years after Augustine brought Christianity to Kent,' intervened Eadulf in explanation.

Fidelma did not acknowledge his amplification but Brother Ine nodded in agreement.

'It was the same year that Wighard's family were slaughtered in a Pictish raid on the north Kent coast. When he was only a lowly priest, the archbishop-designate was married with young children. After their slaughter Wighard threw himself into the work of the church and served Ithamar for ten years. When Honorius died and Deusdedit became first Saxon archbishop of Canterbury, Deusdedit chose Wighard as his secretary and so we went to Canterbury from Rochester. I have been with Wighard ever since.'

'Indeed; so you have known Wighard a long time?'

Brother Ine grimaced affirmatively.

'In your experience, did Wighard have any enemies?'

Ine frowned and gave a furtive glance at Eadulf before dropping his eyes. He seemed to have difficulty framing his words.

'Wighard was an advocate of Roman Rule and, as such, encountered much hostility . . .'

When he did not finish, Fidelma smiled tiredly.

'You were going to say from those who advocate the Rule of Colmcille, such as myself?'

Brother Ine shrugged helplessly.

'No other enemies?' pressed Fidelma.

The gloomy monk raised his dark eyes and shrugged.

'None who would resort to murder.'

She ignored the implication and continued, 'Let us go to the night of that murder, Brother Ine. As personal servant to Wighard, would you normally help the archbishop-designate prepare for bed?'

'I would.'

'But not that night?'

Brother Ine frowned, a hint of suspicion spreading over his features.

'How did . . .?' he began.

Fidelma made an impatient gesture with her hand.

'The bed chamber was unprepared, the coverlets not turned back. An elementary deduction. Tell me, when did you last see Wighard alive?'

Brother Ine sat back and sighed, gathering his thoughts together.

'I went to Wighard's chambers at two hours before the midnight Angelus tolled.'

'And where was your own chamber?' asked Fidelma.

'Next to Brother Eadulf's chamber which was directly opposite the archbishop-designate's rooms.'

This confirmed what Eadulf had told her but it was best to leave nothing to hearsay.

'So you had merely to cross the corridor to Wighard's chamber?'

'Yes, that is so.'

'Continue.' Fidelma sat back watching the Saxon monk carefully.

Brother Ine hesitated again.

'I went to Wighard's chambers as I normally did at that hour. As you suggest, it was part of my duties to prepare the bed and see whether the archbishop-designate had everything he wanted for his night's repose.'

'Two hours before the midnight Angelus is surely an early hour to retire? Did Wighard always go to bed so early?'

'He found the climate uncomfortable and would prefer to rise early before the sun came up and work then. It has been his custom, since coming to this land, to go to bed early and rise early.'

Fidelma glanced to Eadulf who, having been Wighard's secretary, nodded confirmation of what Ine said.

'And so you went to prepare his bed?' prompted Fidelma.

'The archbishop-designate seemed . . .' Brother Ine hesitated and thought about the word he was to use, '. . . preoccupied. He told me that he would dispense with my services for that evening.'

'Did he offer an explanation?'

'Only that . . .' Ine hesitated again and he blinked rapidly for a moment, as some distant memory was recalled. 'He said that he had things to do, someone to see. He would turn down his own bed when the time came.'

Sister Fidelma raised her eyes interrogatively.

'Someone to see? Did you find this odd, if, as you say, he was in the habit of retiring early?'

'No. I simply presumed that he had some extra work to do with his secretary, Brother Eadulf here, in preparation for today's audience with His Holiness. Wighard was a man of simplicity and he would often perform menial tasks for himself.'

'So, what you are saying, is that Wighard was expecting a visitor in spite of the lateness of the hour? In spite of his usual routine of retiring early?'

Brother Ine again looked to Eadulf.

'Surely he spoke of this to you, brother?'

Eadulf shook his head negatively.

'I knew nothing of Wighard's expected visitor. It was certainly not I. That evening I did not return to the palace until after Wighard was found dead.'

'And after Wighard had informed you that you were not needed, you then returned to your own chamber?' went on Fidelma, addressing Ine.

'I did. I left Wighard, closing his chamber door and returned to my own. It was after midnight that I was awakened by a commotion to find the palace *custodes* thronging the corridor and learn that Wighard had been killed.'

'You went to sleep immediately after you left Wighard?' Eadulf asked.

'I did. And soundly.'

'It would seem that you were the last person to see and

speak to Wighard before his death,' Eadulf observed thoughtfully.

Brother Ine's chin raised sharply.

'Apart from his killer,' he said with emphasis.

Fidelma gave a placatory smile.

'Of course. Apart from Wighard's killer. And we have no idea as to who this late-night caller was?'

Brother Ine raised his shoulders in an expressive shrug.

'I have said as much,' he grunted. Then he frowned and looked from one to the other in bewilderment. 'But I thought the *custodes* had arrested an Irishman who was seen leaving Wighard's chambers? So it would follow that it was this Irish religious who was the visitor that he expected.'

'Tell me, Ine,' Fidelma went on, ignoring his point, 'as servant to Wighard, was it your job to look after the valuable gifts from the Saxon kingdoms which he had brought to give to His Holiness?'

Again the fleeting look of suspicion crossed Ine's face.

'It was. Why?'

'When did you last see those treasures?'

Ine frowned and gently chewed his lip thoughtfully for a moment.

'Earlier that day. Wighard asked me to ensure that everything was polished and cleaned in readiness for the presentation to His Holiness today.'

'Ah!' Fidelma breathed quickly. 'So Wighard's audience with His Holiness was to present him with the gifts which he had brought?'

'And also to get His Holiness to bless the chalices from the seven kingdoms,' Eadulf pointed out in intervention. 'That was known by a great many.'

Fidelma turned to Eadulf.

'So if robbery were a motive in this, many people would know that the valuables would be handed over to His Holiness' treasury today and from which it would be hard to extricate them?'

'Also,' Eadulf was diffident, 'it was known that the chalices would be blessed and returned to Wighard for restoring to Canterbury.'

'But the main part of the treasure would be gone? It would be in the safe keeping of the palace treasury?'

'That is true,' agreed Eadulf.

Brother Ine was looking at them with a slight frown of bewilderment.

'Are you saying that the treasure is gone?' he asked.

'You have not heard?' Fidelma was interested. The expression of surprise on Ine's face was absolutely genuine.

'No. No one has told me this.'

The melancholy Saxon monk looked unusually outraged. Fidelma thought the news had come as a blow to his pride, since he regarded himself as confidant to Wighard. The outrage left his face quickly and once more the woeful countenance formed.

'Is that all?' he asked.

'No,' answered Fidelma. 'You cleaned or made sure the treasure was in Wighard's trunk . . . at what hour?'

'Just before the evening meal.'

'And everything was there then?'

The chin came up slightly and then fell back. Whatever protest died.

'Yes. It was all there,' he answered sullenly.

'When you went in to see Wighard, to prepare his bed,'

Eadulf intervened, 'was the trunk open or shut?'

'Shut,' came the immediate reply.

'How can you be so sure?' demanded Fidelma quickly.

'The trunk was not hidden from view when you entered the archbishop-designate's chambers.'

'Was there any guard on this so valuable treasure?'

'Only the palace *custodes* ordered there by the military governor. One was always patrolling the stairways to the corridor.'

Fidelma thought a moment.

'Patrolling . . . but not permanently in the corridor?'

'That is so. There were guards always around the entrance to the guest quarters. The chambers were on the third floor of the building and so only the stairways gave access to them.'

'But the guards were not permanently stationed in the corridor itself so that the treasure could well be removed without anyone observing?'

'Truly. But anyone from outside the building could not come and leave without encountering the *custodes*.' Ine's face lightened. 'But, of course, that was how they caught the Irish monk! So the treasure must have been recovered.'

Fidelma glanced at Eadulf at the simple, significance of the comment.

'But you can confirm that there was no permanent guard to the treasure? No one was on duty outside Wighard's rooms all the time?'

'No, there was not.'

Fidelma gave a long sigh and leant back.

'That is all. We may want to speak with you later.'

Ine, with as much reluctance as he had shown on entering the room, rose and left. When he had done so, Fidelma turned to Eadulf.

'So. The stolen treasure was last seen just after the evening meal and Wighard was alive and well two hours before midnight but dead just after midnight. We know that he was expecting someone within two hours of his death and that just after midnight Brother Ronan Ragallach was seen coming from his room and arrested. This Brother Ronan was not carrying any of the treasure which, with the exception of the relics which have no commercial value, has now disappeared entirely.'

'That is little more than we know already.'

'Licinius!' Fidelma rose from her seat and called to the *tesserarius*.

The young guard opened the door and came in.

'Whom do you wish to speak with now, sister?' he asked formally.

'You, just for a moment.'

The *tesserarius* looked surprised but he came in and stood before her, self-consciously in a soldier's easy stance.

'Tell me, Furius Licinius, how long have you been a guard in the Lateran Palace?'

Licinius frowned slightly.

'I have been of the *custodes* for four years, of which I commanded a *decuria* for two years and am now newly appointed officer of the watch or *tesserarius*.'

'So you know the palace well?'

'As well as anyone, I would say,' the young man replied, trying to forget how easily he had been deceived by the Irish religious two nights before over the matter of the *sacellerius*' storeroom.

'The *decurion* Marcus Narses has, I believe, carried out another search of the rooms in the guests' quarters following our conversation this morning.'

Licinius smiled softly, remembering his fellow officer's mortification at the discovery of some of the missing relics from Wighard's treasure under Wighard's own bed.

'He did, sister, and found nothing more.'

'Let us hypothesise; say you went to rob Wighard's chamber. Say you killed Wighard and then had to remove a large treasure, what would amount to two large sacks of heavy metal objects. How would you do it?'

The *tesserarius*'s eyes were wide but he thought carefully before replying.

'If I were in that position, I would know that there were patrols. I would know that the stairs, of which there are two flights leading up to the third floor apartments, were guarded. So I would have to hide it on the same floor and return for it later. It would then be impossible to attempt to leave and avoid the guards. But Marcus Narses has already searched the rooms on that floor, and it should be remembered that they were all occupied apart from two storerooms. There are no hidden chambers or alcoves in the vicinity.'

Fidelma's mouth drooped.

'Yet we are being asked to believe that somehow Brother Ronan Ragallach killed Wighard and escaped with this bulky treasure . . . while at the same time being spotted by your friend, the *decurion* Marcus Narses, and arrested as he attempted to flee from the scene of the crime. Is Ronan Ragallach then a wizard that he could make the treasure disappear? There was, according to *decurion* Narses, nothing on his person. Explain this to me, Furius Licinius.'

To her surprise the *tesserarius* did not hesitate.

'It is simple, sister. Either Brother Ronan had already hidden the treasure when Marcus spied him and gave chase, or he had an accomplice who carried the treasure away unseen while Ronan was caught.'

Fidelma shook her head dubiously.

'An accomplice. An excellent thought. An accomplice who was able to avoid the guards? It does not sound quite right, Furius Licinius. You have killed someone and then wait in their chamber while your accomplice makes at least two journeys back and forth to take away the valuables and hide them whilst avoiding the guards. Then you wait further until the accomplice is well clear before you make your own empty-handed exit from the murder room and ... and are then caught.'

'Then it must be the first solution. That Ronan had already hidden the treasure when he was caught,' Eadulf said. Thinking aloud, he added: 'But if Ronan was in the process of hiding the treasure he would not have gone back to Wighard's chamber after removing the last load. The quicker he removed himself from the scene of the crime the better.'

'Who said that Ronan Ragallach was coming from Wighard's chambers when the *decurion* Marcus saw him?' Fidelma suddenly asked.

'What do you mean?' demanded Eadulf, as he and Licinius turned to her with frowns on their faces.

'It was something which Furius Licinius said earlier that made me think . . .'

'Me?' asked the young officer, puzzled.

Fidelma nodded thoughtfully. 'Say Ronan did kill Wighard for the treasure. Wighard is dead. Ronan has to put the treasure into at least two sacks. How can he hide them? He has to make two journeys. And it is after having completed his last journey that Marcus Narses sees him, not coming from

Wighard's chamber but from the very place in which he has hidden the treasure on the same floor.'

'Well?' prompted Eadulf, when Fidelma paused again.

'But where could he hide it?' demanded Licinius, interrupting. 'I told you there are no secret rooms or alcoves or cupboards anywhere in the vicinity where the treasure could be hidden. Marcus Narses has twice searched the rooms that were unoccupied that night.'

'You said so, indeed. And the *custodes* looked in all possible places . . .' Fidelma suddenly broke off, staring pensively at Licinius.

'Marcus Narses has . . . *what*?' Her voice was like a whiplash.

The young *custodes* tried to remember what he had said to provoke such a reaction.

'I simply said that Marcus Narses has obeyed your instruction and twice searched the rooms what were unoccupied that night.'

'I thought *all* the rooms had been searched?'

Licinius made a puzzled gesture.

'Surely Brother Ronan Ragallach would not have attempted to hide the stolen treasure in any of the rooms occupied by Wighard's entourage? We naturally thought that . . .'

Fidelma groaned softly.

'All the rooms, occupied or unoccupied, should have been searched.'

'But . . .'

'For example, did Marcus Narses search Brother Eadulf's room?' demanded Fidelma.

Licinius looked from her to Brother Eadulf as if they were both mad.

'Of course not,' he replied.

'My room was unoccupied that night,' Eadulf observed slowly, trying to keep his voice calm.

'Let's go!' Fidelma snapped her fingers causing the *tesserarius* to start in surprise as she rose quickly to her feet.

Licinius looked bewildered.

'I don't understand. Go where?'

Fidelma gave him a scornful glance.

'Eadulf's room was unoccupied because he was at the basilica of Santa Maria at the midnight mass for the Blessed Aidan of Lindisfarne.'

Chapter Eight

The search of Eadulf's *cubiculum*, for it was far less grand than Wighard's palatial rooms, proved disappointing. Fidelma had not really expected to find the missing valuables. Nevertheless, she had hoped that there might have been some sign of their passing, of their being temporarily hidden, in order to explain the conundrum which had annoyed her from the start. But there was no sign of anything which ought not to have been there, in spite of a detailed examination of every aspect of the chamber.

Furius Licinius pulled a face.

'Then it is as I said – this Brother Ronan Ragallach had an accomplice. When the *custodes* seized him, the accomplice simply went off with the treasure.'

Sister Fidelma was not satisfied although she was beginning to accept the logic of the young man's argument.

'I presume Brother Ronan Ragallach's lodgings were also thoroughly searched?' she asked.

Furius Licinius nodded vigorously.

'Marcus Narses himself searched them but there was no sign of Wighard's treasure.'

'I would like to examine Ronan's lodgings myself.'

Licinius' eyes were disapproving.

'Now?'

'Why not?'

As they turned to the door there was a figure standing framed within it. The figure was tall, so tall that it seemed it would be unable to pass under the wooden lintel. The face was darkly personable yet, at the same time, Fidelma felt it was somehow repulsive. It was that lack of compassion which she had noticed before on the face of the Abbot Puttoc of Stanggrund. His was a swarthy face, with a cruel mouth and ice-blue eyes set well back under black cavernous brows. No, the Abbot Puttoc was not a man Fidelma would find immediately attractive, although she would conceive him handsome to some. He seemed to have a speculative gaze as he examined her, the intense look of a cat observing its prey before pouncing.

'I hear that you wish to question me, Fidelma of Kildare,' the abbot said in a soft, modulated voice though with little warmth in it. He seemed to ignore Brother Eadulf entirely. 'There is no time like the present.'

His tall figure pushed into the chamber, towering over everyone. Behind him came another, a comparatively more diminutive figure; Puttoc's *scriptor* and servant, Eanred. He was a self-composed and gentle man who was easily passed by in a crowd as he was unassuming and not particularly memorable in features. Fidelma noticed that he appeared like a faithful shadow, always hovering behind Abbot Puttic's shoulder.

Fidelma frowned. She disliked Puttoc's assured manner and attitude that everyone must dance to his tune.

'I was going to call upon you later, Puttoc . . .' she began, but the abbot made an impatient wave of his hand.

'We will conclude this matter now, for I am busy later. I have an appointment with the Bishop Gelasius.'

He paused to raise a hand and wipe it across his forehead.

'Now,' the abbot crossed to Eadulf's bed and slumped down heavily on it, staring up at them with his chill-blue eyes, while Eanred, arms folded in his habit, stood dutifully by the door. 'What are these questions which you must ask me?'

Furius Licinius' expression was impassive as Fidelma exchanged a glance with Eadulf. The Saxon monk was clearly suppressing his mirth at the way the abbot seemed to propel his will without argument. But Eadulf, under Fidelma's look, swiftly composed his features into a more serious expression. He knew what the tight lines around Fidelma's mouth could portend.

'Speak now!' Puttoc ordered, oblivious to the anger his attitude caused, 'my time is precious.'

'So is our time, Puttoc of Northumbria.' Fidelma's tone was coldly studied, as she suppressed the more irritable answer which had initially sprang to her lips.

The dark-featured abbot merely smiled thinly. The smile made him appear more sinister.

'I doubt that,' he replied, missing her anger entirely. 'Now that Wighard is dead, I have to take charge. It is obvious that we cannot return to Canterbury without an archbishop and who among we Saxons is qualified to receive the Holy Father's blessing?'

Fidelma stared at the complacent tall man in surprise.

'Have you been nominated in Wighard's stead?' she asked. 'I am sure Brother Eadulf here would have told me if he had known this.'

'I have no knowledge . . .' Eadulf had begun but Puttoc was not perturbed, smiling in self-satisfaction.

'I have yet to put my arguments to the Holy Father but the selection is obvious.'

Eadulf's face became serious.

'But the bishops and abbots of the Saxon kingdoms elected Wighard . . .'

The ice-blue eyes turned on Eadulf. The expression was withering.

'And Wighard is dead. Who else is here, in Rome, qualified to take his place? Name the man!'

Eadulf swallowed, at a loss for words.

The abbot turned, still confidently, back to Fidelma.

'Now, as to these questions . . .?'

Fidelma hesitated and shrugged. Now was as good a time as later, even if it meant giving in to the man's bombast.

'I wish to know where you were at the time of Wighard's death.'

Puttoc stared at her. Only the eyes seemed to carry any emotion. Those pale eyes shone with a strange malignancy.

'What are you implying, sister?' his soft voice became sibilant.

Fidelma's jaw tightened.

'Implying? I have asked a question which is plain enough. I have the authority of the papal household to ask these questions of everyone who occupied this floor with Wighard of Canterbury. Is this quite clear?'

The abbot blinked, the only sign of his surprise that this young Irish girl could speak so bluntly to him. Yet he was not cowed by her authority.

'I think that you forgot your position, sister. As a member

of the community of St Brigid of Kildare . . .'

'I do not forget my position, Puttoc. I speak, not as a member of the community of Kildare, but as an advocate of the Brehon courts of Ireland, empowered by Bishop Gelasius and the military governor of the Lateran Palace, together with Brother Eadulf here, to investigate the death of Wighard. I have asked you a question and wish it answered.'

The abbot stared back again, his mouth opened but words did not come. Finally, his mouth closed. The chill eyes blinked again.

'That being so,' he began huffily, 'there is no need for discourtesy on your part. I will bring this behaviour to the attention of Bishop Gelasius.'

As he turned for the door, Fidelma called sharply: 'You have not answered my question, Puttoc of Northumbria. Do you wish me to inform Bishop Gelasius that you refuse to cooperate with the inquiry he, as *nomenclator* of the Lateran household, has commissioned?'

The tall abbot froze. There was an uncomfortable silence at the clash of wills.

'I was fast asleep in my chamber,' the abbot replied eventually, turning his head to stare at Fidelma, the eyes like gimlets, boring hatred.

'At what time did you go to bed?'

'Early. Not long after the evening meal.'

'That is early, indeed. Why did you go to bed at that hour?'

Again there was a pause and Fidelma wondered if Puttoc would continued to indulge in a verbal duel. But the abbot, after a moment or so's hesitation, seemed to shrug his shoulders.

'One thing I shared with Wighard was that this climate does

123

not agree with me and neither does the food. I did not feel well last night. The sooner I sail again for the shores of Northumbria or Kent the better.'

'So you fell asleep immediately? When did you wake?'

'I had a restless night. I thought I heard some disturbance at one point but I was too fatigued to investigate. It was at two o'clock that my servant awoke me and told me the sad news of Wighard's death. May he rest in eternal peace.'

There was no feeling in the pious expression.

Fidelma had the impression that the news was not sad at all to Puttoc. His ambitions were obvious. He was excited by the prospect of stepping into Wighard's shoes.

'You heard and saw nothing?'

'Nothing,' affirmed Puttoc. 'And now I will go to see Bishop Gelasius. Come, Eanred.'

The abbot made to push his way beyond Brother Eanred and into the corridor.

'Wait!'

The abbot turned abruptly at Fidelma's command, his jaw dropping at her continued defiance of him. Never had anyone confronted him thus, and for a mere woman and a mere Irish woman at that . . .! Words were beyond him. Eadulf was hiding his mouth behind his hand, as he pretended to wipe something from his face.

'I have not questioned Brother Eanred,' smiled Fidelma evenly, ignoring the outraged face of the abbot and turning to the quiet, unassuming monk.

'He will tell you no more than I,' snapped Puttoc angrily before she could start her questioning.

'Then let him speak,' came Fidelma's uncompromising tone. 'I have finished with you, Puttoc of Northumbria. You may go or stay as you wish.'

Puttoc swallowed at the air for a few moments and then turned sharply to Eanred, like a master commanding a dog.

'You will attend me in my chamber as soon as you have finished,' he snapped, thrusting his way from the room and stomping off along the corridor.

Brother Eanred stood, hands still folded, looking at Fidelma with an expression of docility on his features. He seemed unruffled by what had passed, as if the tensions of the last few moments meant nothing him.

'Now, Brother Eanred . . .' began Fidelma.

The monk waited, an almost vacant smile on his lips. His eyes were pale, but almost expressionless.

'Where were you last evening? Describe what you did after the evening meal.'

'Did, sister?' The man continued to smile. 'I went to bed, sister.'

'Immediately after the meal?'

'No, sister. After the meal I went for a walk.'

Fidelma raised an eyebrow. She had already assumed that Eanred's placidity disguised a simple mind. The monk was a willing servant but had to be directed the whole time.

'Where did you go for a walk?'

'To see the great arena, sister.'

Eadulf interrupted. He had not spoken for a long time.

'Do you mean the Colosseum?'

Eanred nodded calmly.

'That is what it is called. The place where so many people were slaughtered. I had a mind to see such a place.' He smiled contentedly. 'There was a torchlight procession to the arena last night.'

It had been the same procession that Eadulf and Fidelma had participated in before going on to the midnight mass for the soul of Aidan of Lindisfarne.

'When did you return here?'

Eanred frowned momentarily before the vacant smile returned.

'I am not sure. There were many people about by then and soldiers thronging the rooms.'

'Are you saying that you arrived back after Wighard had been killed? But that would be after midnight. Did anyone see you when you arrived back?'

'The soldiers, I suppose. Oh, and Brother Sebbi. He was in the corridor and asked me to wake and inform Abbot Puttoc that Wighard was dead. I did so.'

'You must have spent hours at the Colosseum to return here so late,' intervened Eadulf.

'I was not there the whole time.'

'Then where did you go?'

'I was invited for a glass of wine at a fine villa not far from here.'

Eadulf exchanged an exasperated look with Fidelma.

'And who invited you to this fine villa, Eanred?'

'The Greek physician that I have seen here so often.'

Fidelma raised her eyebrows in surprise.

'Cornelius? Do you mean Cornelius of Alexandria?'

Eanred smiled happily and nodded.

'That is his name, sister. Yes, Cornelius. Cornelius invited me back to his villa nearby to show me some ancient works of art he has and invited me to drink with him. I love to hear him speak of tales of far away places, even though my Latin is poor, for I am not a scholar, you know.'

'So you spent the evening with Cornelius and he will undoubtedly confirm this?'

'I was with him,' frowned Eanred, apparently not understanding what Eadulf meant.

'I see. And when you returned and discovered what was happening, you say that Brother Sebbi told you to wake the Abbot Puttoc. Did you do so?'

'I did.'

'Abbot Puttoc was in his chamber asleep?'

'He was in his chamber fast asleep,' agreed the man.

'And what happened?'

'The abbot became excited and he donned a robe and went to Wighard's chamber where many people were.'

'And what did you do?'

'I went to my own chamber, next door to the abbot's room, and fell asleep for I was tired and had drank a great deal of the Greek physician's wine.'

'Were you not interested in how Wighard had come by his death?'

Brother Eanred shrugged indifferently.

'We all die sometime.'

'But Wighard had been murdered.'

The man's face was expressionless.

'Brother Sebbi told me to tell the abbot that Wighard was dead. That's all.'

'You did not know that he was murdered?'

'I know now, sister. Since you say so. May I go now? The abbot wanted me to go to his chamber.'

Fidelma looked long and hard at Brother Eanred and then sighed softly.

'Very well. You may go.'

The monk inclined his head and left the room.

Fidelma turned to Licinius and Eadulf. Eadulf was smiling and shaking his head.

'Well, now . . . A simple man, indeed. Yet it strikes me as odd that Cornelius would seek out his company for an evening's drinking, let alone to discuss art.'

'It sounds as though the conversation was all one-sided,' agreed Fidelma. 'But there are many people who love to talk and are not concerned whether it is in dialogue or monologue. Perhaps our friend Cornelius is one of those. He merely wanted someone to talk at and not with.'

'It is Abbot Puttoc who does not inspire the Faith,' observed Furius Licinius sourly.

'That is truly said. Ambitious, officious . . .' Fidelma paused. 'I wonder how ambitious?'

Eadulf suddenly frowned, looking at the Irish religieuse with a speculative gaze.

'Come, Fidelma. You are forgetting Brother Ronan Ragallach. You are not surely suspecting the abbot of Wighard's murder?'

Fidelma smiled briefly.

'I am not forgetting, Eadulf. But I am still keeping an open mind about Ronan Ragallach. There is still something unresolved here.'

Furius Licinius had been standing with a look of growing impatience on his aristocratic young features.

'Do you still want to go to Brother Ronan Ragallach's lodgings?' he demanded.

'In a moment, Licinius. I want to examine all the chambers on this floor. Simply because we found nothing here does not mean to say we should ignore the other chambers.'

'But they were occupied at the time of Wighard's death.' Licinius was clearly uncomfortable.

'Not so,' replied Fidelma. 'We now hear from Eanred that his chamber was not occupied for he did not return until after the murder.'

'You wish to search all the chambers?' queried Eadulf, with

humour. 'Puttoc's chamber for example?'

Furius Licinius grimaced unhappily.

'The abbot's chamber is at the far end of the corridor but no one would suspect the abbot . . .'

Fidelma let out an exhalation of exasperation.

'If I am to function in this matter, I must be told all the facts,' she snapped at the young officer. 'I am firstly told that a search was made. I find that no search was made of Wighard's apartment and then you tell me that not all the rooms on this floor were searched. Only those you thought unoccupied that night were searched.'

The face of the young *tesserarius* blanched slightly at her vehemence.

'I'm sorry, but it was the responsibility of the *decurion* . . .' He paused unhappily, realising that it seemed he was shifting blame. 'I simply thought . . .'

'Let me do the thinking,' Fidelma interrupted. 'Just tell me the truth, actually and specifically, no more and no less.'

Furius Licinius moved uncomfortably.

'But surely you cannot search Abbot Puttoc's chamber. He is . . . well, he is an abbot . . .'

The unfeminine snort which Fidelma gave expressed what she thought of the reason and induced Furius Licinius to search for another excuse.

'But he was in his chamber at the time. The murderer could not have hidden anything there without disturbing the abbot . . .'

Fidelma turned to Eadulf.

'Check to see if Puttoc and Eanred have left for their meeting with Bishop Gelasius. If they have, we will examine his chamber now.'

Furius Licinius looked scandalised.

'But . . .'

'We have the authority, *tesserarius*,' Fidelma cut him short. 'Need I remind you of that?'

Eadulf moved down the corridor and returned a moment later.

'They've gone,' he reported.

Fidelma led the way to the chambers of the abbot and his servant. It did not take long to examine Abbot Puttoc's room. The only thing that became clear was that Puttoc believed in pampering himself, for his was not the sparse simple chamber which Fidelma associated with a man proclaiming frugal piety. It was obvious that Puttoc had gathered many little luxuries to take back to his monastery. But there was no indication that anything had been secreted in his rooms which could be associated with the missing hoard from Wighard's treasure trunk.

There was a window, similar to that in Eadulf's room, which gave a view into an enclosed courtyard three floors below. Below the window was a narrow ledge which ran the entire length of the building. While it was several inches in width, Fidelma noted there was no way in which anyone could have hidden anything beyond the chamber.

'And Eanred's room is next door?' Fidelma asked in irritation as she turned from the room.

Licinius quietly gestured assent. He had no wish to further incur the woman's ire by saying the wrong thing. He had never encountered a woman who could command and snap at men as this Irish woman did.

Fidelma turned into the religieux' room. It was bare and simple. There was, indeed, scarcely anything of personal value excepting a *sacculus* in which the Brother Eanred carried his belongings. Only a second pair of sandals, some underwear and shaving gear were stored there.

Fidelma stood, hands folded before her, and examined the room. Then she crossed to the window and peered out. The room was situated at right angles to the next block of buildings which formed the square courtyard but into which there was no entrance from the *domus hospitale*. Her discerning eye saw that the building seemed of more pristine plaster and tiles and therefore of newer origin than the one in which she stood. This probably accounted for the rooms not being one unit. She noticed, however, that the small ledge under the window had been reproduced on the other building but with the architect being more generous in the width. The ledge was a whole foot in width and, with this chamber window being so close into the angle of the two buildings, it was easy to step across to that ledge.

'You see?' Eadulf was saying behind her. 'I think Furius Licinius is right. We are pursuing the wrong path.'

'Eanred's chamber is rather spartan, isn't it?' she commented, turning back into the room.

'Eanred seems to like austerity,' Eadulf agreed. He turned and followed Furius Licinius back into the corridor. Fidelma paused a moment before giving an inward shrug. Eadulf was probably right. Maybe she was imagining more than the facts were telling her. It was just that she could not shake this odd feeling that she was missing something.

'We have yet to search the chamber occupied by Ine and Sebbi,' she said.

She turned out into the corridor and was closing the door when her eyes dropped to the door frame. The wood of the frame had splintered about three feet above the floor and a tiny piece of material had caught on it, a small jagged strip torn away and left hanging on the frame.

She bent down and reached out a hand to unsnarl it.

Eadulf was watching her with a frown.

'What is it?'

She shook her head negatively.

'I am not sure. A piece of sackcloth, I think.'

She took it between thumb and finger and drew herself up holding the object up in the light.

'Yes, a piece of sackcloth.'

Eadulf nodded agreement as he peered at it.

'What does that mean?' Furius Licinius asked, watching them.

'I don't know yet,' Fidelma replied. 'Perhaps someone was taking something into Eanred's room and the splinter snagged the material tearing a piece off.'

Eadulf was staring at her, trying to read her thoughts.

'Are you saying that the treasure was carried into Eanred's room?'

Eadulf always had the ability to make a quick deduction along the lines Fidelma was speculating on.

'I said that I don't know,' Fidelma replied softly with a shrug of her shoulders. 'It is a bad judge who forms conclusions before all the evidence is before them.'

'But it could have happened,' insisted Furius Licinius, eager to contribute something. He felt he had to retrieve something of the honour of the *custodes* which had been lost by not making a proper search. 'Eanred, by his own statement, did not come back until after Wighard's body was discovered and, therefore, after Ronan Ragallach was arrested. Perhaps Ronan stashed the loot in Eanred's room when he was away?'

Fidelma grinned quickly.

'Yes? Ronan Ragallach concealed two sacks of gold and silver objects in Eanred's room. Then he came out and was arrested by the *custodes*. And what happened to the sacks?'

Licinius compressed his lips.

'I have already suggested an accomplice,' he muttered.

'So you have. We will discuss this matter later. Let us examine Brother Sebbi's room,' suggested Fidelma.

'But the sackcloth?' demanded Eadulf, watching her place it in her *marsupium*, the large bag which she carried.

'The wise judge gathers the evidence, piece by piece,' smiled Fidelma. 'And when all the pieces are gathered, the wise judge will consider them and, like a craftsman making a mosaic, the judge will try to form patterns before the eyes, so that, by inserting a piece here and there until it fits, it will gradually form an entire picture. It is the bad judge who seizes one piece of evidence and tries to conjure a picture from it. Who knows? That piece may not even be part of the picture the judge seeks.'

She looked up at him with a mischievous grin and then turned down the corridor.

The searches of the chambers occupied by Brother Sebbi and by Brother Ine revealed no more than they should have done. After that Fidelma suggested that they continue the original plan to examine Ronan Ragallach's lodgings.

Eadulf exchanged a glance with the frustrated young *tesserarius* and let his shoulders droop in a shrug before following her. So far as he was concerned the matter was fairly clear and there was little need for the fatigue of searches. Ronan Ragallach had obviously killed Wighard for the treasure and had been able to hide it before he had been caught. Now that he had escaped, he had probably retrieved the booty and, if sensible, had placed a considerable distance between himself and the city.

As they came down the foot of the stairway into the main

courtyard at the front of the *domus hospitale* they saw Abbot Puttoc's tall figure by the fountain. But it was the second figure that arrested Fidelma's attention and caused her to halt in the doorway, forcing Eadulf and Furius Licinius to stop behind her. It was the slight figure of Sister Eafa who seemed to be shaking as she stood before him, her voice raised in tearful distress. From this distance it looked as if the cruel-faced abbot was attempting to placate and calm her with his thin sneering smile and gestures. Then Eafa turned abruptly and went running towards one of the exits to the courtyard. She never even noticed their presence.

Abbot Puttoc stood a moment looking after Eafa with an odd expression. Then he turned and saw Fidelma, with Eadulf and Furius Licinius behind her. He did not acknowledge them but turned and strode rapidly away towards a door in the far building.

'It seems our narcissistic abbot has upset poor Sister Eafa,' mused Fidelma. 'I wonder what that was about?'

'It is not for the first time,' Eadulf commented grimly.

Fidelma turned to him with a look of surprise.

'What do you mean, Eadulf?'

'Yesterday morning, when returning from the refectory to my room, I heard voices raised from Puttoc's chamber. I was just going into my chamber. In fact, I was in the act of closing the door, when I heard Puttoc's door bang open. Curiosity became the better of me and I reopened my door a crack to see what the matter was. Sister Eafa, her headdress askew, and appearance dishevelled, came running out as if she had seen Lucifer herself. She ran down the corridor and down the stairs.'

'Did you ask Puttoc what was wrong?'

Eadulf compressed his lips for a moment and a faint red hue tinged his cheeks.

'I came to my own conclusion. I am afraid that I have been given to understand that Puttoc has a reputation among women. The rule of Rome might teach celibacy for abbots and bishops but I fear that Puttoc would probably prefer the easy way of Columba where such celibacy is not the rule.'

Fidelma's eyes narrowed.

'That is hardly a reputation for someone to have if they have an ambition to follow in the footsteps of Augustine of Canterbury. Are you saying that Puttoc has been known to force his attentions on women who were unwilling?'

Eadulf's expression was acknowledgement enough but he said: 'That is what I have heard.'

'Are there no laws against rape among the Saxon kingdoms?' Fidelma demanded, horrified at what she was hearing.

'None for the poor,' Eadulf replied.

'Not only does our law of the *Fenechus* protect all women from rape by force but even if a drunken woman is made to have intercourse then the offence is as serious. Our law protects all women. If a man dare kiss, or even touch a woman against her will, by the law of the *Fenechus* he çan be fined two hundred and forty silver *screpall*.'

Eadulf knew that the *screpall* was one of the main Irish coins that were circulated.

'Perhaps I speak too freely and merely repeat gossip,' he said, feeling uneasy at Fidelma's vehemence on the subject. 'I heard the story only from Sebbi.'

'And I would not trust the ambitions of Brother Sebbi,' admonished Fidelma. She seemed about to make some further comment but then changed her mind. She said: 'Come, Furius

Licinius, show us the way to Ronan Ragallach's lodgings.'

'It is a lodging house by one of the arches of the Aqua Claudia.' Licinius was clearly intrigued by the conversation that had passed.

'Where is that?' frowned Fidelma.

'A place not far from here, sister,' Licinius explained. 'You must have seen the aqueduct. It is a prominent construction that was begun by the notorious emperor Caligula over six hundred years ago. It brings water from a spring near Subla-quea, sixty-eight kilometres from the city.'

Fidelma had, indeed, seen the aqueduct and admired its engineering. There was nothing like it in Ireland but, then, the kingdoms of Ireland were replete with water and there was no need to alter the course of the rivers or site of springs to water such dry, arid areas as occurred in this land.

'The lodging is in the house of the deacon Bieda,' Furius Licinius went on. 'I would warn you, sister, it is a very shoddy and cheap accommodation. It is not run under supervision of the religious. It is a place where the sensitivities of female religieuse are not catered for, if you understand my meaning.'

Fidelma regarded the young man solemnly.

'I think we understand your meaning, Furius Licinius,' she replied gravely. 'But if Bieda is a deacon of the church I fail to see how it can be the sort of place you described.'

Licinius shrugged.

'It is easy to buy favours in Rome. Easy to purchase a deaconship.'

'Then I will do my best not to be offended by any lewdness that I observe. Now, I think we should be on our way for I am in no mood to miss the evening meal which,' she glanced up at the sky, 'will soon be served.'

Chapter Nine

Furius Licinius led the way through the many courtyards and gardens of the Lateran Palace until they emerged through a side gate in the walls on to the slopes of the Hill of Caelius. Even Fidelma was impressed at the extensive grounds of the palace. For once Licinius was pleased to display his knowledge, pointing to a building which could just be seen from the spot where they stood.

'That is the *Sancta Sanctorum*,' he said, indicating a dominating chapel. He caught sight of Fidelma's frown and allowed himself to explain. 'The *sanctorum* is the Holy Father's private chapel which now houses the *Scala Santa*, the very staircase that the Holy Christ descended from governor Pilate's house after He was condemned.'

Fidelma raised a sceptical eyebrow.

'But that house stood in Jerusalem,' she pointed out.

Licinius's features broke into a smirk as he perceived that he had knowledge Fidelma did not possess.

'The Blessed Helena, mother of the great Constantine, brought the staircase from Jerusalem – twenty-eight Tyrian marble steps – which even the Holy Father must ascend only on his knees. She found the staircase at the same time as she found the true cross, buried on the hill of Calvary, the very cross on which the Saviour suffered.'

Fidelma had heard the story of the finding, some three centuries before, of the true cross by the aging mother of the Emperor Constantine. She was dubious that such a wooden artifact could have been so positively identified but felt a pang of guilt at daring to question the matter.

'I have heard that the pious Helena forwarded whole ship-loads of relics from the Holy Land even to pieces of wood from the Ark of the Covenant,' she allowed herself to comment dubiously.

Licinius' face was serious.

'Let me show you, sister, for we are very proud of the sacred relics we have here in the Lateran.'

He would have forgotten their original quest and turned back, in his eagerness to show her. Fidelma put a restraining hand on his shoulder.

'Perhaps later, Furius Licinius. First things first. Now we must examine Ronan Ragallach's lodgings.'

Licinius coloured furiously as he realised how he had been carried away by his boyish enthusiasm. He immediately pointed towards the towering aqueduct across the square in which they stood on the eastern edge of palace grounds.

'That building there is the hostel run by Bieda.'

Brother Ronan Ragallach's lodgings were in a small dilapidated house by the Aqua Claudia, as Furius Licinius had described them. The impressive stone arches of the aqueduct rose many metres in height so that even Fidelma was forced to admire their immensity.

The lodging house was built beneath the shadow of the aqueduct, almost under one of the great arches.

There was a solitary member of the palace *custodes* on duty outside Bieda's house.

'He is stationed here in case Brother Ronan Ragallach attempts to return,' explained the young *tesserarius* as he led the way into the dingy building.

Fidelma sniffed scornfully.

'I doubt whether Brother Ronan Ragallach is so unintelligent as to do that, knowing that this is the first place where he will be sought.'

Licinius' jaw hardened. He was still unused to a woman's criticism or to one who gave him orders. He had heard about the women of Ireland, of Britain and Gaul, who had positions in society so unlike the women of Rome. They knew their place and stayed mainly at home. It was so undignified that a woman, a foreign woman at that, could give him orders. Nevertheless, he kept reminding himself that the military governor, the *Superista* Marinus, had made his position clear. He was to serve and obey this woman, and the mild and almost unassertive Saxon religieux.

As they began to ascend the stairs in the darkened house, a short, middle-aged woman appeared from a ground-floor room, saw Licinius' uniform and led forth a torrent of abuse in the curious rolling dialect of the Roman streets. Fidelma could scarcely understand a word although she detected that what the woman was saying to the young *tesserarius* was not flattering. She caught the end of the sentence which invited Licinius *'ad malam crucem'*!

'Why is this woman displeased?' she demanded.

Licinius was unable to answer before the woman pushed forward and addressed herself to Fidelma, slowing her rate of delivery so that she could be understood.

'Who is going to pay for this empty room? The foreign brother won't return now nor pay me what he owed. A whole month, it is, since he paid any rent. And now, with all the pilgrims in Rome and me with an empty room, I cannot rent it to others, all because of the orders of this *catalus vulpinus*!'

Fidelma smiled somewhat cynically.

'Calm yourself. I am sure you will be compensated, for when we have done, if Brother Ronan does not return, you will be able to sell what belongings he has left, won't you?'

The woman did not seem to appreciate the cynicism in Fidelma's voice.

'That one!' her voice was a sneer. 'Never have I let a room to an Irish pilgrim who has possessed more than the clothes they stood up in. He has no money. Nor are there any belongings in his room worthy to sell for rent. I shall be made a pauper!'

'Doubtless, you have already made sure there is nothing of value?' asked Fidelma dryly.

'Of course I have . . .'

The woman suddenly snapped her mouth shut.

Furius Licinius frowned with anger.

'You were ordered not to enter his room until you were told,' he said threateningly.

The woman brought her chin up aggressively.

'All very well for you to give orders. I'll warrant that you have never gone short of a meal.'

'Did you remove anything from Brother Ronan Ragallach's room?' Fidelma asked sharply. 'Tell the truth or you will regret it.'

The woman brought a startled gaze back to Fidelma.

'No, I have not touched . . .'

Her voice died away under Fidelma's penetrating scrutiny and she dropped her eyes.

'One must live, sister. These are hard times. One must live.'

'Brother Eadulf, go with this woman and find out what she has removed from Ronan Ragallach's room. If you are not honest, woman, you will be discovered and lies are not only rewarded by punishment in this world.'

The woman hung her head sullenly.

Brother Eadulf glanced with a suppressed smile to Fidelma, knowing that her harsh tone was often feigned. He nodded briefly and turned to the woman.

'Come now,' he said sternly. 'Show me what you have taken and be sharp about it.'

Furius Licinius turned back and continued his ascent of the stairs in response to Fidelma's gesture to continue.

'These damned peasants!' he muttered. 'They would rob you if you lay ill and dying. I have no time for them.'

Fidelma decided not to reply but followed him silently to a small room on the next floor. It was dark and dismal with a smell of stale sweat and cooking odours.

'I wonder how much they demanded for this hovel?' mused Licinius, swinging back the door and motioning Fidelma to enter. 'There are too many of these thieves who rent rooms to pilgrims to Rome and acquire great fortunes by overpricing them.'

'You did tell me that this hostel was not under the control of the church,' Fidelma said. 'But surely the church has some say about rents in the city?'

Licinius smiled thinly.

'Bieda is a fat little businessman who makes a fortune from

various properties. In each he hires a *quae res domestic dispensat . . .*'

'A what?' demanded Fidelma.

'Someone to run the house for him, like the woman downstairs. The good Bieda is probably deducting the cost of this empty room from her salary.'

'Well, it is wrong of the woman to take things from this room but I would not like to see her suffer if her income depends on keeping the room occupied.'

Furius Licinius sniffed deprecatingly.

'The likes of her will survive anyway. What did you wish to see?'

Fidelma looked into the shadowy darkness of the room. Even though the shutters were not closed, the tiny window let little light into the room, the sky being blotted out by the towering aqueduct outside.

'Simply to be able to see would be my first priority,' she complained. 'Is there a candle here?'

Licinius managed to locate a stub of a candle by the bed and lit it.

There was scarcely a thing in the room apart from a rough wooden bed, with a sweat-stinking blanket and a pillow, and a small table and chair by its side. A large *sacculus* was slung on a hook hammered into one wall. Fidelma took it down and poured the contents on to the bed. There was nothing of interest but Brother Ronan's spare clothes and sandals. His shaving tackle was placed on the table by the bed.

'He lived a frugal life, eh?' grinned Licinius, allowing himself some pleasure at the disappointment on Fidelma's face.

Fidelma did not reply but stuffed the clothes back into the *sacculus* and rehung it on the hook. Then she examined the

142

room carefully. There certainly was nothing to show that someone had lived for some months in this place. She went to the bed and began to strip it with care. Ten minutes later there was still nothing to show for her labours.

Furius Licinius stood leaning against the door post, watching her with interest.

'I told you that nothing had been found,' he said. However, the relief in his voice was obvious after the humiliation in Wighard's chambers.

'So I understood.'

She bent down and peered round the floor. Nothing but dust. She started as she saw black beetles scurrying this way and that. What were they? Large, ugly creatures!

'*Scarabaeus*,' Furius Licinius identified laconically, as he saw the object of her consternation. 'Cockroaches. These old houses are riddled with them.'

Fidelma was about to rise to her feet in disgust when she saw something half hidden by the bed. She bent forward, trying to ignore the scurrying beetles. It was a small scrap of papyrus. She knew from the texture that it was not vellum. It had been well trodden on so that it was covered in dirt and scarcely discernible against the grime of the floor.

She raised the stub of candle and peered closely at it.

The papyrus was clearly torn from a larger piece. It was a jagged piece not more than a few inches square. There were some strange hieroglyphics on it which she was unable to recognise. The characters were neither Greek nor Latin or even the ancient Ogham script of her own land.

She handed it to the mortified Furius Licinius with a tight smile.

'What do you make of these characters? Can they be identified?'

Furius Licinius peered at the torn papyrus and then shook his head.

'I have not seen this sort of writing before,' he said slowly. Then he added, lest the *custodes* be humiliated by this woman yet again, 'Do you think it matters?'

'Who knows?' Fidelma shrugged and put the slip of papyrus into her *marsupium*. 'We shall see. But you were right, Furius Licinius; there is nothing which seems immediately of help to us in this room.'

There came the sound of footsteps on the stair. Eadulf came in with a smile and carried a small pile of objects.

'I'm afraid it took some time to retrieve everything. At least, I think this is everything. We were just in time to prevent these items being sold by the good lady downstairs,' he grinned.

One by one he placed the items on the bed: a string of prayer beads; a crucifix of red Irish gold, not very well worked but certainly of some value; an empty *crumena* or purse without anything in it; several objects of veneration presumably purchased from local shrines, and two small testaments, one of Matthew and one of Luke.

Furius Licinius gave a cynical chuckle.

'A month's rent, eh? This would have covered three months or more in this hovel. Not to mention the coins that must have gone missing from the *crumena*.'

Fidelma was examining the two testaments very carefully, turning them page by page as if expecting something to fall out of them. They were in Greek but not of good workmanship. There was nothing compressed within their leaves. She gave up with a sigh as she finished her task.

'You found nothing?' Eadulf asked, glancing round the room.

Fidelma shook her head, thinking he meant between the pages of the testaments.

'Hidden panels?'

Fidelma realised that he was referring to their search of Brother Ronan's room.

Furius Licinius smiled tolerantly.

'The *decurion* Marcus Narses has already looked for any place where things could have been hidden.'

'Nevertheless . . .' Eadulf returned the smile and began to examine the walls carefully, tapping gently on them with his knuckles and listening to the sound of the knocking. They waited until he had covered the walls and the floor and returned with a sheepish smile.

'The *decurion* Marcus Narses was right,' he grinned at Licinius. 'There are no places where Brother Ronan Ragallach could hide the stolen valuables from Wighard's trunk.'

Fidelma had collected Brother Ronan Ragallach's belongings and put them in the *sacullus*, which she had taken from the wall.

'We will take these with us for safe keeping, Furius Licinius. You may tell the woman that when we are satisfied, they will be returned in default of any outstanding payment. But the deacon Bieda must come to claim them and present his accounts for the room at the same time.'

The young *tesserarius* smiled approvingly.

'It shall be as you say, sister.'

'Good. I was hoping to question Brother Sebbi before the evening meal and, hopefully, Abbess Wulfrun and Sister Eafa afterwards. But I think the hour grows too late.'

'Would it not be a good idea to find out more about this Ronan Ragallach?' queried Eadulf. 'We have been concentrating on those close to Wighard but information about the very man accused of killing him has not been examined at all.'

'Since Ronan Ragallach has fled his prison, this would be hard to achieve,' replied Fidelma dryly.

'I did not mean the questioning of Ronan,' Eadulf said. 'I thought, perhaps, the time had come to see the place where Ronan Ragallach worked and question his companions.'

Fidelma realised that Eadulf was absolutely correct. She had been overlooking matters.

'He was employed in a minor role in the *Munera Peregrinitatis* – the Foreign Secretariat,' interposed Licinius.

Fidelma silently rebuked herself. She should have examined Ronan Ragallach's place of work before now.

'Then,' she said with studied tone, 'we must by all means examine this Foreign Secretariat next.'

In the chamber which the military governor had set aside for them, Eadulf had taken up his clay tablets and stylus and was jotting down the notes concerning the salient points of the Abbot Puttoc's interview and the questioning of Brother Eanred. On returning to the palace they learnt that the department of the *Munera Peregrinitatis*, in which Ronan Ragallach had been employed as a *scriptor*, was closed and its superior was at *cena*, the evening meal.

To her annoyance, Fidelma discovered that no arrangements had been made for them to eat in the main refectory of the palace and so Furius Licinius was sent to secure something for them to eat and drink while they returned to the chamber.

While Eadulf busied himself with his note taking, Fidelma stored the items gathered from the lodging house. Having done so, she returned to the table and, sitting down, placed two items on it and examined them with curiosity. The piece of sackcloth picked up from the splinter on Eanred's door and the torn piece of papyrus.

Eadulf looked up from his writing and paused with a frown.

'What are those?' he demanded.

'I wish I were sure,' replied Fidelma frankly. 'They probably have nothing to do with this inquiry.'

'Oh, the sackcloth,' Eadulf made a dismissive grimace as he recognised it. 'And the other?'

Fidelma was apologetic.

'Sorry, I forgot to mention it. A piece of papyrus found on the floor of Ronan's room. I can make nothing of it.'

She slid it across to Eadulf.

'It has writing on it,' he observed.

'Strange hieroglyphics,' Fidelma sighed. 'I have no idea of what they are.'

Eadulf smiled broadly.

'Easily answered. It is the language of the Arabians. Those who follow the prophet Mahomet.'

Fidelma stared at him in almost speechless surprise.

'How do you know this?' she demanded. 'Can it be that you are proficient in this tongue?'

Eadulf's face wore a smug expression.

'I cannot pretend that much. Alas, no. I will not deceive you. But I have seen such writing before, when I was pre-viously living in Rome. The hieroglyphics are distinctive and I have not forgotten their shape. It may be another language entirely using the same form of lettering but I would say that it is probably the writing used by the Arabians.'

Fidelma looked at the papyrus and pursed her lips thoughtfully.

'Where in Rome would we be able to find someone able to decipher what is written here?'

'There should be someone, perhaps in the *Munera Peregrinitatis . . .*'

Fidelma gave him a quick glance. Eadulf abruptly realised what he said.

'The very office in which our friend Ronan Ragallach worked,' he mused. Then he shrugged. 'But is that significant?'

There was a discreet knock on the door.

Fidelma took up the pieces of papyrus and sackcloth and put them back into her *marsupium*.

'That we shall see,' she said, before calling, 'enter!'

A thin, wiry man, with dark hair and a sallow complexion entered. One of his dark eyes was slightly cast, so that Fidelma felt, at times, an embarrassment as to which eye she should focus on. The face was familiar but Fidelma could not place him.

Eadulf recognised the religieux immediately.

'Brother Sebbi!'

The wiry man smiled.

'I heard from a *custodes* that you wished to speak with me and, as I had finished my evening meal, I asked where you might be found.'

'Come in and be seated, Brother Sebbi,' invited Fidelma. 'You have saved us the task of sending for you. I am Fidelma . . .'

Brother Sebbi nodded as he seated himself.

'Fidelma of Kildare. I know. I was at Witebia when you and

Brother Eadulf cleared up the mystery of the death of the Abbess Étain.' He paused and grimaced awkwardly. 'This is a bad business, very bad.'

'Then you know what we are about, Sebbi?' Fidelma asked.

Sebbi drew his thin lips back in a grin.

'It is common talk all over the Lateran Palace, sister. The Bishop Gelasius has empowered you and Brother Eadulf to investigate the circumstances of Wighard's death, just as Oswy commanded you to find the murderer of Abbess Étain at Witebia.'

'We would like to know your whereabouts at the time of Wighard's death,' Eadulf added.

Sebbi's smile seemed to broaden.

'Asleep, if I had sense.'

Fidelma gazed thoughtfully at him.

'And did you have sense, Brother Sebbi?'

Sebbi's face was serious a moment and then the grin came back.

'I see you have a sense of humour, sister. I was in bed asleep. I was awakened by some noise in the corridor. I went to the door to see several *custodes* around the door of Wighard's chamber. I asked what was wrong and was told.'

'Was there anyone else about? I mean Puttoc, for example?'

Sebbi shook his head.

'But the noise woke you?'

'Yes.'

'So it was loud?'

'Of course. There was shouting and stamping feet.'

'Did it not surprise you that the Abbot Puttoc, whose chamber is next to your *cubiculum*, was sleeping through all this?'

Eadulf cast a worried glance at Fidelma, clearly concerned

that she was still casting doubts on Puttoc's statement in retaliation for the abbot's treatment of her.

'No,' Sebbi leant closer across the table. 'The Abbot is known to take sleeping draughts, for he suffers from insomnia. He takes medications as another takes food.'

'Is this hearsay, Sebbi, or do you know it as a fact?' demanded Fidelma.

Sebbi made a small gesture with his hand.

'I have served under the abbot at Stanggrund for fifteen years. I should know. But ask Eanred, his servant. It is a fact. Eanred always carries a bag of medications. Each evening Eanred has to mix a concoction of mulberry leaves, cowslip and mullein into a wine which Puttoc drinks.'

Fidelma glanced at Eadulf who nodded understanding.

'A sleeping draught not uncommonly used.'

Sebbi continued.

'Puttoc lives on his medicines. That is probably why he bought Eanred here in the first place. Only Eanred is capable of producing cures for Puttoc's insomnia. Puttoc never wanders far without his servant.'

Fidelma was curious.

'A servant?'

'Eanred was a slave before Abbot Puttoc bought and freed him in keeping with the Faith of the Holy Church. But Eanred still considers himself as Puttoc's man, even though he is a freeman.'

'How did this come about, Sebbi?' prompted Fidelma.

'Well, during the days of Swithhelm, who ruled the East Saxons, few in the kingdom kept the Faith. Seven years ago, Puttoc decided to journey to that land in an attempt to recall the lost sheep back to the one true God. Because I was raised there . . . in fact, I was named after the prince Sebbi who now rules that land . . . the Abbot Puttoc chose me to accompany him. It was when we arrived at Swithhelm's court that we found Eanred as a slave awaiting execution.'

Sebbi paused for a moment and when they made no comment he went on:

'It arose in conversation with Swithhelm that the king regretted the forthcoming death of this slave for Eanred had a reputation as a herbalist and healer. But if a slave kills a master, there is an end to it. He must forfeit his life unless someone else compensate the kin of the slain master by paying them his *wergild* and then buying the slave. But who wants to buy a slave who has already killed his master?'

'So Eanred was Swithhelm's slave?' Fidelma queried.

'Oh no. Eanred belonged to a farmer named Fobba near the northern banks of the River Tamesis.'

'How did this Eanred become a slave?' asked Eadulf. 'Was he captured or was he born to it?'

'His parents sold him into slavery when he was a child during a time of great famine so that they might have the means to live,' Sebbi replied. 'In our lands a slave is a piece of property, like a horse or other livestock, which can be bought and sold for profit.' He grinned wryly at Fidelma's disgusted expression. 'The Faith abhors this practice but the law of the Saxons is older than their conversion to the Faith and so the Church has to tolerate . . .'

Fidelma made an impatient gesture with her hand. She knew as much from her own experiences of the problems which Irish missionaries faced in the conversion of the heathen Saxons. It was scarcely seventy years since the Saxons had begun to give up their gods of war and bloodshed and converted to Christianity. Many still clung to their old beliefs while even the Christians intermixed the new faith with old customs.

'So Eanred was sold into slavery and grew up to kill his master?'

'Indeed. Puttoc, who was ever sensitive about his health, and always looking for potions to arrest his ailments, was intrigued. Eanred, though apparently simple and slow-witted, was, so we were told, a genius when it came to searching for herbs and plants with healing properties. People from all over the kingdom would go to Fobba's *tun* to pay Fobba for the cures which Eanred provided.

'After some thought, Puttoc put a proposal to Swithhelm. He asked the king to delay the execution for a further day. He told the king that he suffered from sleeplessness at night. If that evening, Eanred could concoct a potion which would cause him drowsiness then he, Puttoc, would be prepared to buy Eanred and pay the *wergild*.'

'This *wergild* you speak of, what is that?' asked Fidelma.

'It is the means by which a man's social position is defined,' interposed Eadulf, who had once been a hereditary *gerefa* or magistrate of his people. 'It is the means by which a *gerefa* can fix the size of compensation to be paid to the kinsmen of a slain man or fix other means of legal recompense. For example, a noble *eorlcund* has a *wergild* of three hundred shillings.'

'I see. We have the same method of measurement in Ireland where the fine is called an *eric* fine, in which a *eneclann* or "honour price" is fixed on the rank of all citizens. In our society the "honour price" decreases, as a punishment, if anyone is found guilty of a crime or misdemeanour. Yes, I understand this *wergild* now. Continue.' She sat back in satisfaction at her new knowledge.

'Well,' Sebbi continued, 'the king was happy with the idea for doubtless he would take a commission from this transaction if completed. Eanred was summoned from the cells and asked to prepare a sleeping potion for the abbot. This he did. The next morning Puttoc came before the king full of enthusiasm. The sleeping potion had worked. The kin of the slain slave-master were summoned and a *wergild* of one hundred shillings was asked for, plus fifty shillings for the person of Eanred.'

Eadulf sat back with a soft whistle.

'One hundred and fifty shillings is a large sum,' he observed. 'Where did the Abbot Puttoc get such a sum?'

Sebbi leant forward with a wink.

'The church encourages the freeing of slaves and suppressing the trade in them. Slaves are required by the church to be manumitted as an act of charity. That charity was paid for by the abbey and the transaction was duly noted among the manumissions of the abbey.'

'It is still a large sum.'

'The sum is that as set forth in law,' replied Sebbi. 'Both *wergild* are established.'

'But a slave has no *wergild*,' Eadulf pointed out.

'Nevertheless, a slave has his value set.'

'So Eanred was bought and freed by Puttoc,' Fidelma summed up. 'But not because of Christian charity but because of Eanred's talent as a healer to help the abbot sleep at nights?'

'You understand it well, sister,' Sebbi affirmed in a rather patronising tone.

'When was this?'

'As I have said, some seven years ago.'

'So Eanred was freed and was so grateful to Puttoc that he converted and returned to the abbey in Northumbria with you both?' Fidelma's voice was cynical.

Again Sebbi grinned in appreciation of her scornful tone.

'That's not exactly how it happened, sister. As you know, Eanred is a simple man. He had been a slave since he was a small child. Puttoc did not explain the niceties of freedom to Eanred until after we had returned to the monastery. He made Eanred believe that the price of saving him from the gallows was that he was to serve Puttoc. As for Eanred's conversion to Christianity, I am not sure that the poor man understands it deeply. For him it may be that Christ is just another deity like Woden, or Thunor or Freya. Who knows what passes in his mind?'

Fidelma tried to keep her bewilderment at Sebbi's open criticism of Puttoc behind a mask.

'It would seem that you are no friend of the abbot?' she observed dryly.

Sebbi threw back his head and roared with laughter.

'Can you name me one friend of Puttoc?' he asked. 'Other than certain women, that is.'

'Are you saying that the abbot has relationships with women?' Fidelma tried to encourage directness.

'Puttoc believes wholly in the kingdom of the spirit but that does not mean that he wishes to reject the kingdom of the flesh. Not for Puttoc the self-denial of the ascetics.'

'Although an abbot is supposed to remain chaste, are you saying that Puttoc ignores this rule?' Eadulf was scandalised.

Sebbi chuckled softly.

'Didn't the blessed Augustine of Hippo write somewhat

154

cynically about chastity? I believe the abbot subscribes to that philosophy.'

'So the abbot enjoys the company of women, even though he would profess the celibacy which Rome requires to ordain him as both abbot and bishop?'

'Puttoc argues that he is not old. It is easy to be an abbot or a bishop when one is old but too chaste a youth makes for a dissolute old age.' Sebbi added hurriedly: 'That, of course is his argument. Not that I would agree with him.'

'Then why do you follow him?' demanded Eadulf, the sneer in his voice clearly showing he had no time for Sebbi.

'One should always follow the rising star,' grinned Sebbi cynically.

'And you feel Puttoc is a rising star?' Fidelma queried with interest. 'Why so?'

'Puttoc has his eyes on Canterbury. I have my eyes on Stanggrund Abbey. If he goes to one, I can claim the other.'

Fidelma pursed her lips for a moment at Sebbi's candour.

'And how long has Puttoc had his eye on Canterbury?'

'He has thought of nothing else but the archbishop's throne at Canterbury since Stanggrund Abbey declared for Rome and allied itself with Wilfrid of Ripon years ago. Puttoc is an ambitious man.'

Fidelma's eyes narrowed slightly.

'Are you saying that Puttoc is ambitious enough to remove any obstacle in his path?'

Sebbi gave that curiously knowing smile of his and made no further comment other than a shrug.

'Very well, Sebbi,' Fidelma said, after a silence, glancing to Eadulf. 'Let us return to the other evening. When did you last see Wighard alive?'

'Shortly after the evening meal which we had together in the main refectory of the guest house. The Bishop Gelasius had joined all those visitors to the Lateran Palace who were being lodged within the palace itself. Everyone then went into the chapel for the evening devotion and then each retired to their own chambers.'

'Apart from Wighard, who else was there?'

'Everyone in our party, except Brother Eadulf here.'

'And you returned to your own room then?'

'No. It was a hot evening and so I wandered in the gardens. It was in the gardens that I last saw the archbishop-designate.'

Fidelma started forward. This was new information. It began to fill in the gaps of what Wighard had done on his last evening.

'At what time was this?'

'An hour after the evening meal, say three hours before midnight.'

'And we are placing midnight as the time of the discovery of his death,' interposed Eadulf, speaking to Fidelma.

Fidelma cast him a warning look.

'Just tell me what you saw,' she invited Sebbi.

'I was in one of the larger gardens near the southern wall of the palace, behind the basilica itself. I recognised Wighard, for he had made it a routine to take a walk in the gardens before retiring at night. I believe he hated the heat of the day and would prefer to walk in the evening when the sun had vanished. I was about to go towards him when I saw someone detach themselves from the shadows and accost him.'

'That is an interesting word – "accost",' observed Fidelma.

Sebbi shrugged indifferently.

'I meant simply that Wighard was walking as if deep in

thought when the person stepped in his path. They started talking. I was going to continue my approach when the person talking to Wighard become angry, the voice rose to a high pitch. Then the person turned and vanished abruptly. I think they must have gone into the cloisters at the back of the basilica.'

'Did you recognise this person?'

'No. It was just someone in the clothes of a religious with a hood over their head. I would not recognise them.'

'In what language did they speak?' asked Eadulf.

'Language?' Sebbi thought a moment. 'That I cannot say. All I know is that after an exchange or so the voice was raised almost like a dog howling.'

'Did you go up to Wighard?'

'After that, no. I did not want to embarrass him in case it was something personal. I turned and left the garden and went to my room. I did not see him again.'

'Did you speak of this encounter when you heard that Wighard had been killed?'

Sebbi's eyes widened.

'Why should I? Wighard was killed later in his own chamber not in the garden. And everyone knows that some mad Irish religieux killed him and stole the precious gifts he was going to present to the Holy Father. Why would this encounter in the garden mean anything?'

'That is what we are here to decide, Brother Sebbi,' Fidelma replied gravely.

'If you had been able to identify the Irish religieux in this encounter in the garden . . .' Eadulf begun.

The sharp exhalation of breath from Fidelma halted him and he looked sheepish before her angry gaze of condemnation. It was not her way to make suggestions to witnesses.

'Well,' Sebbi went on, ignoring their by-play, 'I could not identify the person. And it was only this morning at the breaking of the fast that I heard others speak of this Brother Ronan Ragallach.'

'Very well,' Fidelma said, 'I think that is all for the time being, Sebbi. We may need to speak with you again.'

'I shall not be far away,' Sebbi smiled, as he rose and turned towards the door.

He was opening it when Fidelma raised her head as a sudden thought came into it.

'By the way, as a point of interest, why did Eanred kill his former master?'

Sebbi turned back.

'Why? As far as I recall Eanred had been sold into slavery by his parents, together with a younger sister. The sister was bought by the same master. It seems that at the time of puberty the master forced the young girl into his bed. It was the day afterwards that Eanred killed him.'

After a moment Fidelma prompted: 'How did he kill him?'

Sebbi paused a moment as if trying to dredge the memory from his mind.

'I believe he strangled the man.' He paused again and then smiled broadly, nodding. 'Yes, that's it. He garrotted the man with his own belt.'

Chapter Ten

'Well, one thing is clear,' remarked Brother Eadulf, after Brother Sebbi had left the room.

Fidelma raised her eyes which sparkled in amusement at her companion, for there was humour in his voice.

'And what is that?' she asked gravely.

'Brother Sebbi has no love for Abbot Puttoc. He seemed intent on sewing seeds of suspicion about Puttoc and his servant, Eanred.'

Fidelma inclined her head in thoughtful agreement at this statement of the obvious.

'Too eagerly intent?' she queried thoughtfully. 'Perhaps we should be careful of reading anything into Brother Sebbi's statements. He is clearly as ambitious as his abbot. Remove Puttoc and he believes that he will be abbot of Stanggrund. Now how much does his own ambition guide his attitudes?'

Eadulf made a small gesture of agreement.

'Yes, but perhaps we might do well to speak with Brother Eanred again.'

Fidelma grinned mischievously.

'Aren't you forgetting about Brother Ronan? Surely you have no doubts about his guilt?'

The Saxon monk stirred and blinked uncomfortably. He realised that he had become so intent on the by-play provided by the questioning of Sebbi that he had forgotten the main purpose of the enquiry.

'Of course I have no doubt,' he replied almost defensively. 'The facts speak for themselves. But it is curious . . .'

'Curious?' prompted Fidelma, after he had paused for some time.

Eadulf gave a soft sigh. He was about to continue but he went no further for Furius Licinius returned carrying, to their surprise, a tray bearing a jug of wine, some bread, cold meats and some fruit. Licinius smiled cheerfully as he set the tray down.

'All I could forage,' he announced, as they eyed the contents with hunger. 'I have already eaten, so go ahead. Oh, and on my way back, I happened to fall in with the very man you seek . . . the superior of the department of the *Munera Peregrinitatis* in which Ronan Ragallach worked.'

Fidelma turned regretfully to Eadulf.

'We will eat after we have seen this brother,' she announced firmly.

Eadulf pulled a face but did not protest otherwise.

Licinius went to the door and ushered in a slender young man. He looked scarcely out of adolescence with pale olive skin, thick red lips and large dark eyes which he had a habit of narrowing as if to focus better. The young man's head was entirely shaven.

'This is the sub-praetor of the *Munera Peregrinitatis*,' announced Licinius.

Fidelma was confounded for a moment. She had been expecting an older man to aspire to such an office. This youth was scarcely in his twenties.

The young man stepped forward a pace and halted, peering short-sightedly from Eadulf to Fidelma and back again.

'What is your name?' asked Fidelma.

'Osimo Lando,' the youth replied, with an odd lisping accent to his voice.

'You are not a Roman?' Fidelma asked.

'I am a Greek, born in Alexandria,' Osimo Lando replied. 'Though I was raised in Syracuse.'

'Be seated, Brother Osimo,' invited Fidelma. 'Has the *tesserarius*, Furius Licinius, told you our purpose?'

Brother Osimo moved forward slowly and seated himself before the table, adjusting his robe with an unexpected delicate gesture.

'He has.'

'We are told that Brother Ronan Ragallach works in your department?'

The sub-praetor nodded.

'Perhaps you can tell me what the *Munera Peregrinitatis* does?' suggested Fidelma.

Brother Osimo's eyes narrowed a fraction and then he shrugged with an oddly dainty motion.

'We are the means by which the Holy Father can communicate with all our missions throughout the world.'

'And Brother Ronan Ragallach works under you?'

'That is correct. I am the *sub-praetor* in charge of all matters relating to our churches in Africa. There is only Brother Ronan, together with myself, working at this task.'

'How long has he worked in the secretariat?'

'He came as a pilgrim to Rome a year ago, to my knowledge, sister. He had a gift for languages and so he remained and for the last nine months or more has worked under my direction.'

'What kind of man is he, brother?'

Brother Osimo pursed his lips and stared thoughtfully into space. A faint redness spread over the pale cheeks and his expression seemed to be one of embarrassment.

'A quiet man, not given to displays of irritation or of temper. Placid, I would say. Conscientious in his work. He never expresses any problems.'

'Does he have strong views?' interposed Brother Eadulf.

Osimo looked at Eadulf in bewilderment.

'Strong views? On what subjects?'

'He is Irish. We are told that he wore the tonsure of the Irish rather than our Roman *corona spinea*. That means that he rejected the Roman rule and maintained that of Colmcille.'

Brother Osimo shook his head vehemently.

'Brother Ronan is merely a man of habit. He wore his tonsure, like many others from Ireland and from among the Britons because that is their custom. It made little difference to us. It is what is in a man's heart that matters, not what is on his head.'

Fidelma lowered her face, raising a hand to cover her smile at Eadulf's flush of mortification.

'And what is in Ronan's heart?' Eadulf demanded, not succeeding in covering his annoyance at being so publicly rebuked on prejudice.

Brother Osimo pouted.

'As I have told you, brother, he is a man of easy and placid temperament.'

'You never heard him speak ill of Rome?'

'Why would he be in Rome if he thought ill of Rome?'

'You never heard him speak ill of Canterbury? How, for example, did he treat the news of the decision at Witebia, when the Saxon kingdoms opted for the rule of Rome and rejected that of the Irish monks of Colmcille?'

Osimo's smile indicated that he thought the question was a silly one.

'He never uttered an opinion. He was concerned with matters of the African churches rather than those of the extreme west. He is an excellent Greek and Aramaic scholar and so his function was to deal with our missions to north Africa. This task grows hard as the Arabians, with their new fanatical belief in the prophecies of Mahomet, sweep westward along the Africa shore.'

Eadulf suppressed a breath of annoyance.

'Does it not come as a shock to you, Brother Osimo, that Brother Ronan Ragallach stands accused of the murder of the archbishop-designate of Canterbury and that it has been postulated that the cause of this was because of the news of Witebia?' he demanded.

To their surprise, Osimo threw back his head and laughed; a gentle soprano laugh.

'I have heard as much and give no creed to such an argument.' His face became abruptly serious. 'When I heard the news of the archbishop-designate's murder,' he paused to piously genuflect, 'and that Brother Ronan had been arrested for it, I could not believe it. I will not believe it. I would look elsewhere if you want to find the real murderer.'

Fidelma examined his intense face with some interest.

'Why so?' she demanded. 'What makes you so sure that Ronan Ragallach did not kill Wighard?'

'Because . . .' Osimo looked around the room as if seeking an answer. 'Because it is simply not in his character, sister. Tell me that . . .' he searched for an analogy, '. . . that the Holy Father has attended the feast of Bacchanalia and, God forgive me, danced naked in the Temple of Bacchus on the Sacra Via and I will believe you sooner than I will believe that Brother Ronan is capable of murder.'

Fidelma smiled thinly.

'That is testimonial, indeed, Brother Osimo.'

'One not lightly given,' added the *sub-praetor* firmly.

'Yet Ronan was arrested fleeing from the archbishop-designate's chamber at the time the murder was discovered. He tried to give a false name and he later escaped from custody,' interposed Eadulf, somewhat maliciously. 'That is hardly the action of an innocent man, is it, Brother Osimo?'

Osimo hung his head unhappily but his voice was full of passionate defence.

'It may have been the action of a desperate man, a man who sees the world rise up against him in his innocence. Desperate to prove his honesty, he seeks freedom in order to prove that virtue.'

Fidelma gazed at the youth for a moment in silence and then she asked quietly, 'Has Brother Ronan told you this much?'

Osimo flushed immediately.

'Of course not.' His voice trembled with indignation.

Fidelma felt there was little conviction in his voice. She decided to press the matter.

'So, you have not seen Brother Ronan since his escape? Yet you seem to speak with some authority on his behalf.'

'I have worked with him closely these last nine months and we have become as . . . as friends. Close friends.'

Osimo did not meet her eye but stuck out his chin with an unusual expression of stubbornness.

Fidelma leant confidingly forward.

'You realise that if you see Ronan Ragallach it is your duty, under law, to advise the *custodes*?'

'I realise it,' Osimo replied quietly.

Fidelma sat back and examined the young man for a while.

'So long as you do, Brother Osimo. Believe me, it is my intention to get to the bottom of the murder of the archbishop-designate of Canterbury. If Brother Ronan is innocent, I shall prove it. If he is guilty, then he will not escape.'

Her confident, rather than boastful, tone made Osimo raise his eyes and peer closely at her before he dropped his gaze again.

'I understand,' he whispered.

'For our record,' Eadulf intervened, 'when did you last see Brother Ronan?'

'On the day of Wighard's murder, Brother Ronan worked until the sounding of the evening Angelus.'

'Did you ever meet Wighard or any of his entourage?'

Osimo shook his head.

Fidelma turned to Eadulf.

'I have no further questions unless . . .?'

Eadulf made a negative grimace.

'Then, Brother Osimo . . . ah, but I nearly forgot.' She reached into her *marsupium* and pushed the torn piece of papyrus towards the *sub-praetor*. 'Can you tell me what that language is?'

Brother Osimo took up the papyrus and glanced momentarily at Fidelma as if surprised. He recovered his composure within a second, almost before his startled look had registered with her.

'The hieroglyphics are in the language of the Arabians,' he replied. 'Aramaic, it is called.'

'Do they mean anything?' she pressed.

'It is part of some writing. Who knows? Perhaps it is even a letter. Only a few words are decipherable.'

'What words?' pressed Fidelma.

'The language is read from right to left. We have words for "library", "sacred disease", and the rendition of a Greek name, something ending in "ophilus" and then the words for "price" and "exchange". It makes little sense.'

After their frugal evening meal, which left Fidelma suddenly feeling very tired in spite of her afternoon nap, Furius Licinius was sent in search of Abbess Wulfrun or Sister Eafa. Fidelma and Eadulf sat in silence for a while. Fidelma was turning over the statement of Brother Osimo in her mind. She was sure that Osimo's relationship with Ronan Ragallach was something more than a working one; more than he had admitted and that he had intimate knowledge of Ronan Ragallach. In fact, she felt that she would go so far as to take an oath that Ronan had escaped from the *custodes* and gone to Osimo Lando for help. But it was intuition and not fact that prompted her conclusions.

She became aware of Eadulf's fingers drumming aimlessly on the table and sniffed in annoyance at the distraction.

'What are you thinking, Eadulf?' she demanded as the drumming continued.

Eadulf blinked, paused and realised his unconscious action.

'I was just thinking about what Osimo said.'

Fidelma raised an eyebrow in surprise.

'So was I. What were you thinking?'

'About the Arabian words which he translated.'

Fidelma was disappointed.

'Oh, that,' she said, with a shrug. She had thought that

Eadulf might have been paralleling her line of thought about Osimo and Ronan. 'Well, that means little enough.'

Eadulf shook his head.

'Perhaps. Perhaps not. It stirred some memories within me. As you know, Fidelma, for some years I studied in Ireland, at the great medical school of Tuaim Brecain.'

'What has that to do with the words of Arabian?'

'Perhaps nothing. Just that I, as you realise, know something about the practise of medicine.'

'I still do not follow you.'

'I made a note of the words Osimo Lando translated, just in case they made sense at some future time.'

'And?'

'The word "library". was one. The message might have been talking about books. "Sacred disease" were two words together. *On the Sacred Disease* was a tract by Hippocrates, which argued the distinction between the sensory nerves and motor nerves.'

'You have lost me, Eadulf.'

Eadulf smiled indulgently.

'The author of a commentary on Hippocrates' work was Herophilus from Chalcedon, one of the great founders of the medical school of Alexandria. Perhaps his was the name "ophilus" which Osimo Lando could not find the first letters of. The message could have been speaking about Herophilus' work *On the Sacred Disease* in a library somewhere.'

Fidelma sat back with a chuckle.

'Tenuously but well worked out, Eadulf. You may be right. But it does not help us much at the moment.'

'But it may at some future time,' Eadulf said smugly, clearly satisfied with his exercise in deduction.

Furius Licinius returned. Before he could say anything he was pushed aside and the austere figure of Abbess Wulfrun swept in. Close up, she was tall, taller even than Fidelma, with a thin, pale face and sharp features. Her nose was prominent giving her an arrogant expression and the thin lips were pinched into a permanent sneer. Her bright eyes sparkled angrily.

'Well?' she demanded without preamble. 'What nonsense is this?'

Fidelma opened her mouth but Eadulf, seeing the dangerous fiery glint in her eye, spoke first, rising awkwardly.

'No nonsense, my lady,' he said, attempting to remind Fidelma, by adopting a more ceremonial form of address, that Wulfrun was the sister of the queen of Kent. 'Has not the *tesserarius* of the palace *custodes* informed you of our authority from Bishop Gelasius?'

Abbess Wulfrun sniffed, an inward inhalation of breath which seemed to threaten damage to her nasal passages.

'I have been told but find nothing in the matter which is of concern to me.'

'It does not concern you, then, that your archbishop-designate has been murdered?' Fidelma's voice was almost a soft purr, threatening in that quiet almost sibilant tone.

Abbess Wulfrun shot her an angry look.

'I mean, and I think I make myself clear, that your questioning does not concern me. I know nothing of the matter.'

Eadulf smiled in an attempt at placation and gestured to the chair.

'Perhaps you would be good enough to spare us some of your valuable time? A few questions so that we may inform Bishop Gelasius that we have done what he has asked of us.'

Fidelma ground her teeth at his obsequiousness but she

decided that it might be better to allow him to question Wulfrun. A minute with this arrogant woman would be enough to make her lose her temper, in spite of her usual self-control. The abbess seated herself, her left hand tugging in a nervous gesture at her headpiece where it was swept scarf-like round her neck.

'When did you last see the archbishop-designate alive?' began Eadulf.

'Just after the evening meal yesterday. We exchanged some words about the audience with the Holy Father which had been due to take place today. We were no more than ten minutes together at the door of the refectory. Then I went straight to my chambers. Sister Eafa came and helped me prepare for bed and I turned in early. Only when we were at the morning meal did I hear the news of Wighard's death.'

'Everyone seems to have gone early to bed that night,' muttered Fidelma. Eadulf ignored her and pressed on.

'Where was your chamber in relation to those occupied by Wighard?'

The Abbess Wulfrun frowned a moment.

'I am given to understand it was on the floor below those occupied by the male members of our party. You yourself should know this, Brother Eadulf.'

'I meant, was it directly below Wighard's chamber? I am merely trying to ascertain if you heard anything,' he explained smoothly.

'It is not and I did not,' grunted the abbess.

'And what of Sister Eafa?'

'She has the room next to me, the easier to be at hand when I want her.'

'Is Sister Eafa your servant?' interposed Fidelma sharply.

Again came the obstreperous sniff.

'She is one of my community of Sheppey. She is my companion on this journey and assists me.'

'Ah,' Fidelma said ingenuously, 'as you assist her when she is in need?'

Eadulf leant forward hastily.

'You were not disturbed during the night? You heard and saw nothing?'

Distracted, Wulfrun turned her head back to Eadulf.

'I have said as much,' she replied shortly.

'I am told that the scuffle when Brother Ronan Ragallach was arrested by the *custodes* was so loud that it awakened Brother Sebbi,' Fidelma observed. 'Yet you heard nothing of this?'

A flush gathered on the thin prominent cheeks of Abbess Wulfrun.

'You doubt my word?' her voice rose threateningly. 'Do you not know, Irish girl, to whom you speak?'

Fidelma's gentle smile broadened dangerously.

'I speak to a fellow sister of the Faith and, as courtesy demands between equals of the Faith, I expect an answer.'

The sniff became a veritable explosion.

'I am Wulfrun, daughter of Anna, King of the East Angles. My sister Seaxburgh reigns as Queen of Kent, wife to Eorcenberht. That is who I am.'

'You are surely the Abbess Wulfrun of the abbey of Sheppey,' corrected Fidelma quietly. 'Once you have taken the cloth then you are one with the church and have no rank other than that which is bestowed upon you by the church.'

Abbess Wulfrun sat bolt upright. For a moment she forgot to fiddle with the scarf-like material around her neck and stared at Fidelma with a look of incredulity.

'You dare speak to me like that?' Her voice was no more than a whisper. 'I am a Saxon princess!'

'What you were is of little relevance. What you are is a servant of the Christ.'

Wulfrun's mouth opened and closed several times. Then she exploded.

'How dare you, you foreign . . . foreign peasant! I am a princess of Kent. Do you know who *your* father is?'

Eadulf stared aghast at the tinge of red touching Fidelma's cheeks as she stared back at the contemptuous and insolent woman. For a moment he thought the Irish religieuse was going to erupt in wrath at the insult, then Fidelma managed to control herself and sat back with a tight smile. When she spoke, her voice was softly modulated and even.

'My father, and yours, Abbess Wulfrun, is the God we serve . . .'

Abbess Wulfrun's thin lips accentuated the sneer even more and before she could respond Fidelma continued.

'Nevertheless, if you are so concerned with things temporal, and not with the faith to which you should be committed, let me tell you this. My temporal father was Faílbe Fland mac Aedo, King of Cashel and Munster, and my brother, Colgú, now rules there. That is nothing to boast of. It is who I am that counts. At this moment, I am an advocate of the courts of my land, commissioned by the military governor and *nomenclator* of this palace to investigate a murder.'

Eadulf stared at her in surprise. It was the first time that Fidelma had ever referred to her background or family. The religieuse was continuing to gaze calmly on the features of the arrogant Saxon abbess.

'When I entered the service of the risen Christ I accepted His teaching that we are all equal in His sight. Do you know the epistle of Timothy: "Tell the rich and powerful not to be proud or high minded and not to hope for uncertain riches but to set their hopes in the Living God"?'

Abbess Wulfrun, her face working with anger, sprang up, causing her chair to be flung backwards. In her agitation, her scarf came away revealing part of her neck. Fidelma's eyes narrowed a fraction as she saw a red mark on the neck. It was the weal of an old wound or sore. Wulfrun was spluttering, unaware of the fallen cloth.

'I refuse to sit and be insulted by . . . by . . .'

Words failed her, and she turned and stormed from the room. Furius Licinius looked on helplessly.

Brother Eadulf sat back shaking his head.

'You have made an enemy in that one, Fidelma,' he said ruefully.

Fidelma seemed outwardly calm but the bright specks of blood remained on her cheeks and her bright eyes glinted and danced with curious fires.

'The person who has never made an enemy will never make a friend,' she remarked. 'You can judge a person by their enemies and I would prefer to be judged by having such a one as my enemy than as my friend.' She turned to Furius Licinius. 'Try to find Sister Eafa and bring her here without the knowledge of Abbess Wulfrun.'

The bewildered young *tesserarius* raised his hand in salute. It was the first time that he had made the military gesture of courtesy to Fidelma.

'Why the secrecy?' asked Eadulf curiously, after Furius Licinius had left the room.

'This Wulfrun is a very domineering lady. Can she be so stupid or is there some method in her arrogance? Does her insolence exist to conceal something else?'

The Saxon brother grimaced.

'She boasts very powerful relatives, Fidelma. I would have a care.'

'Powerful among the Saxon kingdoms only. I do not intend to return there when I leave here.'

Eadulf wondered why he suddenly felt a tinge of anxiety at the idea of her departure.

'Anyway,' he said, 'Abbess Wulfrun does not seem to add anything to our store of knowledge.'

Fidelma was thoughtful.

'But she does demonstrate that she is not entirely open and prefers to screen herself behind her arrogance. Wasn't it Ovid who said that attack was a good defence?'

Eadulf scowled as he turned the matter over in his mind.

'But what could she be hiding?'

Fidelma grinned.

'Isn't that for us to discover?'

Eadulf half nodded. Then said: 'But of what relevance to our enquiry would anything be that Wulfrun has to say?'

Fidelma reached forward and laid a hand on Eadulf's arm.

'I fear you are simply repeating your question, Eadulf. Let us consider,' she sat back. 'Why would she feel so defensive that she had to attack? Is it her personality, or is it some specific knowledge?'

Eadulf looked helpless.

'I think,' Fidelma continued, after a pause, 'I'd be inclined to believe that it was her personality. I have heard of this King Anna she hails as her father. He was converted from the worship of Woden to the True Faith. I believe that Anna had several daughters and, in his enthusiasm, persuaded them all to serve the church. We know what may happen when fathers force their daughters to follow what the fathers want them to do rather than what daughters desire to achieve for themselves.'

'But daughters have little choice but to obey their fathers,' replied Eadulf. 'Didn't the blessed Paul write: "Children, obey your parents in everything, for this pleases the Lord"?'

Fidelma smiled softly.

'And didn't Paul also write: "Fathers, do not provoke your children, lest they become discouraged"? But I forget, sometimes, that we are separated by a different social and law system. Among the Saxons, daughters seemed to be simply chattels to be bought or sold according to the whims of their fathers.'

'But the law of the Saxons is more in keeping with the teaching of Paul,' Eadulf assured her, knowing from experience how different was the female's role in Ireland. 'Paul says "wives, be subject to your husbands, as is fitting to the Lord. For the husband is the superior to the wife as Christ is the head of the church . . ." We follow that teaching.'

'I would prefer the system of my own land where women have some choice at least,' Fidelma replied irritably. 'One does not have to obey Paul in all his opinions for he was a man of his culture, which is not my culture. Besides, not everyone in Paul's own culture agreed with his teachings. Paul argued for celibacy among the clergy, believing that carnal relationships were an obstruction to the higher aspirations of the soul. Who can believe that is so?'

Eadulf was embarrassed.

'It must be so for it was the cause of the fall of Adam and Eve.'

'Yet how can be it the cause of sin when reproduction is necessary to the survival of humankind? Are we to believe that God would then have us cast into oblivion by making reproduction a sin? If it is a sin, why give us the means to reproduce?'

'Paul told Corinthians that marriage and procreation was no sin,' Eadulf observed mildly.

'But added that it was not so Godly as celibacy. I think Rome's call on its clergy to become celibate holds great dangers.'

'It is a suggestion only,' countered Eadulf. 'From the Council of Nicea until now the Roman church has only advised clerics under the rank of bishop not to sleep with their wives and, indeed, not to marry. But it does not forbid them to do so.'

'They will in time,' replied Fidelma. 'John Chrysostom declared against cohabitation between religious at Antioch.'

'You believe that celibacy is wrong then?'

Fidelma grimaced.

'Let those who want to be celibate, be celibate. But do not force everyone to be the same whether they are willing or not. Is it not a blasphemy to God to argue, in his name, that we can only serve him by rejecting him? Rejecting one of the greatest works of his creation. Does not Genesis say ". . . male and female created he them, and God blessed them and God said unto them, Be fruitful and multiply . . ." Are we to deny that?'

She paused as there came a knock on the door and the anxious-looking Sister Eafa entered, glancing firstly at Fidelma and then at Eadulf.

'I am here, but I do not understand why I should be called,' she said. As she spoke she tried to keep her calloused, sinewy hands held quietly before her but the nervous twisting betrayed an agitation.

Fidelma smiled reassuringly and gestured for her to be seated. Eadulf saw that Fidelma's anger at Abbess Wulfrun had now evaporated. He realised that the argument on celibacy was no more than a means of draining her incensed emotions at the insults of the abbess.

'No more than a formality, Eafa,' she said reassuringly. 'I just wanted to know when you last saw Wighard alive?'

The girl blinked uncertainly.

'I do not understand, sister.'

'Has the *tesserarius* informed you of our commission to investigate Wighard's death?'

'Yes, but . . .'

'You doubtless saw Wighard at the evening meal which you attended with Abbess Wulfrun?'

The girl nodded.

'And after that?' encouraged Fidelma.

'No, not after that. I left Abbess Wulfrun talking with him at the refectory door. They were . . . were arguing about something. I retired to my room. I did not see him afterwards.'

Eadulf leant forward with sudden interest.

'Abbess Wulfrun was actually arguing with Wighard?'

Eafa nodded her agreement again.

'What were they arguing about?'

Eafa shrugged.

'I am not sure. I did not listen.'

Fidelma smiled reassuringly at the girl again.

'So you returned to your room, which was next to Abbess Wulfrun's room?'

'I did,' Eafa replied quietly.

'Did you venture out of your room again that night?'

'Oh no!'

Fidelma raised an eyebrow.

'No?'

The girl frowned, hesitated and then corrected herself: 'I was summoned sometime later to the room of Abbess Wulfrun.'

'For what purpose?'

'Why?' Eafa looked astonished at such a question being asked. 'To help her to prepare for bed.'

'Is that usual?'

The girl looked uncertain.

'I am not sure what you mean, sister.'

'You are Abbess Wulfrun's companion, is this not so?'

A jerk of the head confirmed this question.

'Then why do you have to do so many menial tasks which can be done by Abbess Wulfrun.'

'Because . . .' Eafa paused to consider, 'she is a great lady.'

'She is now simply of the sisterhood. Not even an abbess expects another of her house to wait upon her.'

Eafa did not reply.

'Come, do you feel that you have to be servant to the Abbess Wulfrun?'

The light brown eyes of the girl came up and stared at Fidelma's face. She seemed about to reply then she dropped her head. There was a faint nod.

'Why?' pressed Fidelma. 'Great lady or abbess or lowly sister of the faith, Wulfrun does not have that right. You are servant only to God.'

'I can say no more.' The girl's voice was tight. 'I can only say that I waited on Abbess Wulfrun that night and when she had prepared for bed, I returned to my own room and went to sleep.'

Fidelma was about to press further but she suddenly relented. Bludgeoning the girl would not achieve anything.

'At what time was this, Eafa?'

'I am not sure. It was well before midnight.'

'How did you know?'

'I came awake at the tolling of the midnight Angelus bell and then fell asleep again.'

'Did you wake up after this?'

'I don't think so.'

'What do you mean?' Eadulf demanded, coming into the conversation for the first time. 'You don't *think* that you were awakened again?'

'Well,' the girl was frowning, 'I think I came awake some-time later, hearing sounds of some commotion but I was so tired that I turned over and was asleep again within moments. At the breaking of our fast, on the next day, someone said that an Irish religieux had been caught in the gardens below and that he had killed the archbishop-designate. Is that not true?'

She stared from one to another with large rounded eyes.

'To a point,' conceded Fidelma. 'A religieux was arrested but it has yet to be proved whether he was the guilty party or not.'

The girl opened her mouth, paused but a moment and then snapped it shut. Fidelma was not blind to the involuntary motion.

'You were going to say something?' she encouraged.

'It was just that the morning before the murder I saw an Irish brother in the gardens outside the *domus hospitale*. He

was a fat, moon-faced man with his hair cut in that funny
tonsure the Irish wear.'

Eadulf leaned forward in interest.

'You saw this brother?'

'Oh yes. He asked me some questions about Wighard's
entourage. Who was accompanying Wighard during his visit,
but then Abbess Wulfrun came along and I had to go with her.
I heard that this monk that the *custodes* are searching for is a
large, round-faced Irish religieux.'

There was a silence and Fidelma sat back thoughtfully.

'How long have you been at the abbey of Sheppey?' she
asked somewhat abruptly.

The girl looked puzzled at this sudden change of subject.

'Five years, perhaps a little more, sister.'

'How long have you known Abbess Wulfrun?'

'A little longer . . .'

'So you knew Abbess Wulfrun before you went to
Sheppey?'

'Yes,' admitted the girl.

'Where was this? In another religious house?'

'No. Wulfrun befriended me when I was in need.'

'In need?'

The girl did not rise to the bait but simply nodded.

'Where was this?' pressed Fidelma again.

'In the kingdom of Swithhelm.'

'So?' Eadulf said quickly, 'you are from the kingdom of the
East Saxons?'

The girl shook her head.

'I was originally of Kent. I was taken to Swithhelm's kingdom
as a child and brought back to Kent when I went with Abbess
Wulfrun, who invited me to join her community on Sheppey.'

179

'So you have felt under obligation to Abbess Wulfrun ever since?' concluded Eadulf.

Eafa shrugged as if to imply that he could make his own deductions. Fidelma felt compassion for this girl.

'I am sorry, Eafa, for all these questions but we are nearly through. One thing more. You know that you are a free person under the law of the church?'

Eafa frowned slightly.

'Obedience is surely the rule?' she queried defiantly. 'I am merely an anchoress and must obey my mother superior in all things.'

Fidelma had not wanted to be more precise for fear of upsetting the girl.

'So long as you are aware that you do not have to be insulted by any man, no matter what his rank.'

Eafa flushed, her gaze coming up abruptly to meet Fidelma's face, realising the implication of her words.

'I can take care of myself, Sister Fidelma. I grew up on a farm and had a hard schooling before I reached the age of consent.'

Fidelma smiled sadly.

'I thought that you should be aware of this.'

'Anyway,' Eafa drew her chin up defiantly, 'I do not know what these questions have to do with the murder of Wighard.'

The girl obviously did not want to talk about Puttoc and his advances. Fidelma hoped that the girl would understand that there was help available if ever she needed it.

'You have indulged us enough, Eafa. That will be all . . . for the time being.'

The girl gave another jerky motion of her head and stood up to leave. As Furius Licinius opened the door for her, the gaunt, sallow figure of the Bishop Gelasius stood framed there. Sister Eafa sank to one knee in a low Saxon bow, while Eadulf and Fidelma rose to greet the *nomenclator* of the papal household.

Gelasius entered the room, smiling absently at Sister Eafa who rose and scurried away. Furius Licinius snapped to attention as, behind Gelasius, the military governor of the *custodes, Superista* Marinus, followed the bishop into the room.

'I thought I would come to see if you had arrived at any conclusions,' Gelasius informed them, glancing from Fidelma to Eadulf.

'If you mean, have we resolved the affair,' Fidelma replied, 'then the answer is a negative one.'

The bishop looked disappointed. He crossed to the chair and slumped down in it.

'I must tell you that the Holy Father is desirous of a conclusion as soon as possible.'

'No more than I,' Fidelma said.

Gelasius frowned and stared hard as if wondering whether she was being impertinent. Then he remembered just how outspoken these Irish women could be. He responded with a sigh.

'How far are you into your investigation?'

'It is hard to say,' Fidelma shrugged.

'Are you saying that you doubt the guilt of Brother Ronan?' demanded Marinus, with a look of astonishment. 'But my *custodes* were eyewitnesses, they arrested him and he has compounded his guilt by escaping from our cells.'

Gelasius glanced at the military governor and then back to Fidelma.

'Is it true? Do you doubt the guilt of Ronan Ragallach?'

'It is a foolish judge who, before the evidence is presented, makes a judgment.'

'What more evidence is needed?' demanded Marinus.

'The evidence so far presented does not amount to much. When analysed it is so circumstantial that under the law of the *Fenechus*, any self-respecting Brehon, that is – a judge, would not even consider it.'

Gelasius turned to Brother Eadulf.

'Do you concur in this?'

Eadulf gave a hasty and somewhat guilty glance to Fidelma.

'I think that Brother Ronan Ragallach has a case to answer in spite of the circumstantial evidence. I do not believe it is a weak case. We have another witness to Ronan Ragallach taking an interest in Wighard and his entourage as well as your *custodes*.'

Fidelma held back a sigh of annoyance. She had wanted to keep the information which Eafa had supplied to herself for a while.

Gelasius looked depressed. He did not pursue Eadulf's remark about another witness.

'What you are telling me is the thing I fear most of all. You are divided in your opinions. There is an Irishman who has killed a Saxon bishop of Rome. The Saxon judge says there is a case, the Irish judge says there is not. The spectre of war between the Saxon kingdoms and Ireland still looms on the horizon.'

Fidelma shook her head vehemently.

'This is not so, Gelasius. What we are both in accord with is that our investigation is far from complete. There are many things to be considered. Because we have reached no conclusion today, does not mean that we will not reach a conclusion tomorrow.'

'But surely you have questioned everyone with the exception of the culprit himself . . .'

Eadulf coughed hollowly.

'I think, at this point, we would prefer to refer to Brother Ronan Ragallach as merely a suspect rather than . . .'

Marinus gave an angry hiss of breath.

'Semantics. We have no time to play with the niceties of words. I know what you are saying. You have questioned everyone and must surely have some conclusions.'

Fidelma's features had tightened. She disliked attempts to browbeat her into statements she did not want to make.

Gelasius, seeing the tautness of her expression, raised a pacifying hand.

'Are you telling us that you simply require more time? Is that it, sister?'

'Precisely,' Fidelma said firmly.

'Then you shall have it,' agreed Gelasius. 'Above all, we want to resolve this case in the proper way – a way in which the guilt will be apportioned in the right quarter.'

'That is good,' Fidelma accepted, 'for I would not have it any other way. It is the truth that we are after above all things and not merely a scapegoat.'

Gelasius rose with dignity.

'Remember,' he said slowly, 'the Holy Father is much interested in this matter. He is already under some pressure on what to report about the death of the Canterbury archbishop-designate by the envoy of Saxon kings.'

Fidelma raised an eyebrow.

'Are you speaking of Puttoc?'

'The Abbot Puttoc,' corrected Gelasius softly. Then added: 'Inasmuch as the abbot is the direct envoy of Oswy of Northumbria, who appears to be the overlord of all the Saxon kingdoms, then your answer is to be found in the affirmative.'

'And doubtless Abbot Puttoc has his reasons for pressing for a decision?' smiled Fidelma cynically. 'Perhaps he has even suggested his candidacy to fill the role of archbishop?'

Gelasius stared at her a moment and then his face broke into a tired smile.

'Of course, you have undoubtedly spoken to the abbot. I believe he has made a suggestion that he is best fitted to become archbishop. However, his Holiness has other ideas. In truth, Abbot Puttoc has an aura of ambition which does not endear him. He it was, who even raised an objection to Wighard two days ago on the grounds that Wighard had once been married and sired children.'

Eadulf exchanged a glance of surprise with Fidelma.

'Puttoc would have had Wighard debarred from ordination on the grounds that he was once married with children?' he asked astounded.

'Not in so many words but by gentle hints. No member of the church from abbot and above may be married as you know. Indeed, Rome frowns on those below that rank from forming such carnal relations although it is not forbidden. Anyway, rest assured that the matter was discussed and dismissed when it was revealed that Wighard's family had been killed long ago. However, the fact that the subject was raised did put a question mark over Puttoc's own suitability to aspire to the office.'

'Then there is another candidate?' prompted Fidelma.

'His Holiness is considering the matter.'

Eadulf was surprised.

'I thought there were few Saxons here qualified to aspire to the office of Canterbury?'

'Indeed there are,' agreed Gelasius. 'His Holiness is inclined to believe that the time is not propitious for Rome's primacy in the Saxon kingdoms to be in the hands of a Saxon.'

'That will be the cause of some protest from the Saxons,' Eadulf blurted in astonishment.

Gelasius turned to him with a frown.

'Obedience is the first rule of the Faith.' His voice was threatening. 'The Saxon kingdoms must obey the decision of Rome. I can say no more at this stage but between these walls, you may be assured that Abbot Puttoc is not going to be considered. However, this must remain a secret for the time being.'

'Of course,' Eadulf agreed diplomatically. 'I was merely thinking aloud.' Then he paused and added: 'Does Abbot Puttoc know of this decision, I wonder?'

'I have said that this matter should remain private. Puttoc will know when the time comes.'

Fidelma shot Eadulf a warning glance as he opened his mouth to amplify his question. The Saxon snapped his mouth shut abruptly.

'The main thing at the moment is to resolve the matter of Wighard's death,' went on Gelasius. 'And we are counting on you . . . both.'

He emphasised the last word and then, without a further word, he turned and left the room, followed by a surly Marinus.

'Why did you wish me to be silent about Puttoc?' asked Eadulf, when they had left. 'I merely wanted to know whether he still thought he was a candidate for the archbishop's chair?'

'We must keep our counsel to ourselves. If Puttoc is so ambitious . . .'

'And people have killed for less ambition,' interposed Eadulf, finishing her thought.

'If so, then we must allow him some rope so that he may hang himself. We must not warn him of our suspicions.'

Eadulf shrugged. 'Mind you, I have no suspicions of anyone other than Ronan Ragallach, not after the confirmation given by Eafa. We have evidence that Ronan was skulking around the *domus hospitale* on the night before the murder, then he was asking questions about Wighard and his entourage on the very morning of the murder and, finally, he was arrested fleeing from the *domus hospitale* just after Wighard was murdered. Is that not proof enough?'

'No,' Fidelma said firmly. 'I want something more than a few pieces of circumstantial evidence . . .'

Her sentence ended in a sudden yawn of fatigue which she was not able to stifle. The length of the day, with its crowded events, was suddenly catching up with her. She eyed the uneaten snack which Furius Licinius had brought. In spite of the brief siesta of the afternoon, she was exhausted now; too exhausted even to contemplate it.

'A sleep is my next priority, Eadulf.' Fidelma smothered another yawn. 'We shall meet here tomorrow in the forenoon and assess the evidence that we have gathered.'

'Shall I accompany you to your lodgings?' Eadulf asked.

Smiling, she was about to shake her head when the young *custodes*, Furius Licinius, pushed forward.

'I shall accompany you, sister, as my lodging also lies in your direction.' His voice showed he expected no argument. Fidelma was too tired now to form any. And so, bidding a good night's repose to Eadulf, she sleepily followed the young *custodes* from the marble halls of the Lateran Palace and across the now deserted great hall, through the portico and across to the Via Merulana.

She was almost asleep on her feet when she reached the small hostel situated by the oratory of St Prassede.

The deaconess Epiphania, standing at the gate, hurried forward to greet her. Since she had ascertained that Fidelma now fulfilled some important role at the Lateran Palace and was the confidante of the Bishop Gelasius, and could even command a *tesserarius* of the palace *custodes*, there was little which she would not do to see that her honoured guest had no complaints. Seeing Fidelma's exhausted condition, Epiphania began to cluck in motherly concern. She took the girl's arm and, with a dismissive gesture to the young guard commander, led her tired charge within the gate and straight to her *cubiculum*. Fidelma was asleep even before her head dropped to the pillow. It was a deep although not dreamless sleep, but her dreams were necessary to help her mind relax from the information and imagery which she had absorbed during the day.

Chapter Eleven

When Sister Fidelma stirred, with the limpid glare of a Roman morning flooding into her *cubiculum*, she felt totally refreshed and relaxed. She stretched luxuriously and then noticed how bright it was and how warm. With a slight frown, she threw back the covers and swung out of her bed. She knew it was late but was not particularly concerned. She had needed the sleep. She took her time about her toilet and her dressing before leaving her room. Doubtless, the deaconess Epiphania and her husband Arsenius would have served the *jentaculum*, the first meal of the day, and Fidelma would have to break her fast elsewhere, perhaps buying a piece of fruit from one of the stalls as she passed down the Via Merulana on her way to the Lateran Palace. But Fidelma did not care. It was odd how sleep and relaxation made life a pleasant thing.

To her surprise, as she made her way down into the interior courtyard of the hostel, the deaconess Epiphania appeared smiling brightly. It was such a change from the disinterested and expressionless hostel-keeper of two days before.

'Did you sleep well, sister?' she asked cheerfully.

'I did,' replied Fidelma. 'I was extremely fatigued last night.'

The elderly woman nodded briskly.

'That you were. You scarcely noticed me helping you to bed. We thought it best to let you sleep as long as you wanted to. But food has been prepared for you in our little refectory, sister.'

Fidelma had a dim memory of the woman helping her to bed last night. Fidelma was surprised that she should be so indulged.

'But the hour is late. I would not wish to disturb the routine of the hostel.'

'It is no bother at all, sister,' Epiphania was almost ingratiating, ushering her guest into the small now deserted refectory. A single place was still laid and Epiphania continued to fuss over Fidelma's needs. The meal was excellent, with wheat bread and a dish of honey and fruits, mainly figs and grapes. Fidelma had, in her short stay in the city, learnt enough of the custom of Rome to eat lightly at the *jentaculum* but to indulge at the midday *prandium* for this was the main meal of the day. However, when the sun went down a lighter meal was served called the *cena*. It took a while to adjust to this, for in the abbeys of Ireland and even in Northumbria it was the evening *cena* which was the chief meal of the day.

It was only when Fidelma was finishing her meal that she thought to ask if anyone had been inquiring for her. Furius Licinius had promised to escort her to the Lateran.

'The *tesserarius* of the *custodes* did indeed come to inquire after you earlier this morning,' confirmed Epiphania. 'He told me to tell you to rest as much as you want for he and a brother . . .' Epiphania contorted her expression as she tried to recall the name.

'Brother Eadulf?' Fidelma guessed.

'Ah, the same. He and brother Eadulf would be making

another search for that which is missing . . .' Epiphania pulled a face, clearly, she did not like mystifying messages. 'Does that make sense?'

Fidelma indicated that it did. She would be surprised if Furius Licinius or Eadulf would discover the missing valuables anywhere in the Lateran Palace. They would have been removed long ago.

Epiphania suddenly interrupted with a little exclamation of self-reproach.

'I nearly forgot, sister. There was a written message for you.'

'For me?' Fidelma repeated. 'From the Lateran Palace?'

She presumed it would be from Brother Eadulf.

'No, a small boy brought it at first light.'

Epiphania went to a stand to one side of the room and picked up a small folded papyrus.

Puzzled, Fidelma saw her name inscribed on the outside in firm Latin characters. She opened it up and her mouth rounded as she perceived that the message was written in Ogham. Ogham was the ancient form of writing in Ireland, consisting of short lines drawn to, or crossing, a base line. The alphabet had begun to fall out of use with the wider application of the Latin form by Christian usage. It was said the alphabet was given to the ancient Irish by Ogma, the old pagan god of eloquence and literature. Fidelma had learnt the old alphabet as a natural course for, though it was falling into disuse, several religious still used it in their memorials. It was handy to read the ancient texts, such as the rods of the poets – whole sagas inscribed on wands of yew and hazel – which were now being replaced by an Irish written in Latin characters.

Fidelma's eyes ran quickly over the script. Her eyes widened in surprise.

Sister Fidelma,
I did not kill Wighard. I think you must suspect this is the truth. Meet me in the catacomb of Aurelia Restutus in the cemetery beyond the Metronia Gate. Come alone. Come at noon. I will tell you my story but only to you – alone. Ronan Ragallach, your brother in Christ.

Fidelma let out a breath which was more like a sharp whistle.

'Bad news?' came the voice of the anxious Epiphania, hovering at her shoulder.

'No,' Fidelma said hastily, thrusting the note into the folds of her robe. 'What hour is it?'

Epiphania frowned.

'It lacks the hour to noon. You have slept long and well.'

Fidelma stood up hurriedly.

'I must go.'

Epiphania fussed over her until she reached the gate of the hostel. Sister Fidelma swung swiftly down the Via Merulana, taking a short cut by the Campus Martialis which led over the Hill of Caelius to the Gate of Metronia. She was pleased with her growing knowledge of Roman geography. She presumed that the catacomb of Aurelia Restutus was the same catacomb which Eadulf had shown her on the previous day for that was the only Christian cemetery beyond the Metronia gates.

She made her way into the cemetery and peered round at the memorials. There were many people there examining the tombs. She halted for a moment as she caught sight of a familiar face some way off among the crowds. The handsome cruel features of the Abbot Puttoc were peering around as if looking for someone. A pace behind him walked Brother Eanred looking every inch like a typical servant following his master's footsteps.

Fidelma had no wish to meet the vain abbot, nor his servant for that matter, and so lowered her head and pushed her way into a small group of people. She presumed that Puttoc had come to see the grave of Wighard and pay his respects, though surely Puttoc would have as little regard for Wighard dead as he had for Wighard alive. It seemed that Puttoc and Eanred were making for another part of the cemetery and, after a while, she detached herself from the group of pilgrims, who seemed to be Greeks in search of particular tombs in the cemetery, and made her way in the direction Brother Eadulf had shown her on the previous day.

She found herself at the entrance to the catacomb where the solemn-faced child, Antonio, was seated behind his basket of candles. She bent down with a smile. The boy looked up, recognised her and acknowledged her presence only by a widening of his dark eyes.

'Hello, Antonio,' Fidelma greeted. 'I am in need of candles and directions.'

The boy said nothing but waited for her to explain.

'I am looking for the catacomb of Aurelia Restutus.'

The boy cleared his throat and when he spoke it was in the curious throaty mix of a boy whose voice is changing into manhood.

'Are you alone, sister?'

Fidelma nodded.

'There are only a few people in the catacombs at the moment. My grandfather Salvatore is not here to take you. It is dangerous if you don't know the way.'

Fidelma appreciated the boy's concern, especially after the drama of the previous day.

'I have to go on my own. Which way do I go?'

The boy gazed at her a moment and then shrugged.

'Will you remember these directions? At the bottom of the stairs, take the left-hand passage. Keep along it for one hundred yards. Take the right hand and go down the steps to a lower level. Go straight on, passing a great tomb with a large picture of Our Lord painted on it. Two hundred yards on from here you turn to the left and down a short flight of steps. That is the catacomb of Aurelia Restutus.'

Fidelma closed her eyes and repeated the boy's instructions. She opened them and the boy nodded in solemn confirmation.

'This time I will take two candles,' Fidelma grinned.

The boy shook his head and, reaching behind him, brought forth a small pottery lamp, heavy with oil. He lit it expertly.

'Take this as well as a candle, sister. Then all should be well. Do you have tinder and flint in case it goes out?'

Since the earlier incident Fidelma had come prepared with a tinder box in her *marsupium* in case of any emergency and she nodded affirmatively.

She drew forth some coins and dropped them in his basket smiling. 'In my language, Antonio, we say – *cabhair ó Dhia agat*. God's care at you!'

She had started down the steps into the dark vaults when the boy's voice came behind her.

'*Benigne dicis*, sister.'

Fidelma paused and smiled back at him before continuing on into the darkness.

She turned down into the catacombs, glad already, as she reached the bottom of the cold stone steps, of the bright lamp in her hand and reassured with the extra candles she possessed in her *marsupium*.

In her mind she kept running through the boy Antonio's directions, following them carefully through the dark chill corridors and down deeper into the bowels of the dry and porous stonework. Now and then she heard the sound of voices or an unseemly burst of laughter from other visitors to the catacombs, but the paths of these pilgrims did not cross with her own. She remained isolated as she pressed further, taking the stairways further underground and the turns to left and right as the boy instructed.

Eventually, she came to a man-made cavern some ten feet high and some five or six feet broad with a slightly vaulted roof. No masonry had been employed in its construction and the only support was that which the volcanic stone itself produced. On either side of the cavern, excavated in the lithoid tufa, as Fidelma had ascertained the conglomerate of rock was called, were the *loculi* or resting places for the dead. They differed in size and she was pleased to see that those *loculi* which had been used were sealed up with marble slabs or tiles with some inscriptions and Christian emblems incised or painted on them.

She moved forward, holding the lamp high, and her eyes rested on a *loculus* larger and more grandly adorned than all the rest. The inscription was in Latin with its simple Christian phraseology,

> Domus aeternalis
> Aurelia Restutus
> Deus cum spiritum tuum
> Basin Deo

> The eternal home of
> Aurelia Restutus
> God be with thy spirit
> May you live in God.

Fidelma gave a little sigh of relief. At least she was in the right catacomb. She found herself wondering who Aurelia Restutus had been and why she had deserved such a grandiose tomb. The marble was adorned with doves of peace and above it was the Chi-Ro symbol, the initial Greek letters of the name of Christ.

She set down the lamp on the ledge of an empty *loculus* and peered around the chamber wondering where Ronan Ragallach was. She knew it must be sometime after noon, for as she had descended the steps into the catacombs she had heard a far-off bell chiming the noon Angelus. She was sure that Ronan would give her a while to make the appointment before leaving. It was not that long after the noon hour.

She compressed her lips to stifle a sigh of impatience. Fidelma disliked any form of inaction in spite of her training in contemplation. In that aspect she had not been a good noviate.

Time passed. A matter only of minutes but it seemed an eternity to Fidelma in this place.

She was, at first, not sure whether she had really heard the sound. A soft scuffling noise from one of the chambers beyond. Then she heard something heavy fall.

She held her head to one side for a moment.

'Brother Ronan?' she called softly. 'Is that you?'

There was a silence after her voice had ceased echoing down the darkened vaults.

She turned and picked up her lamp and moved cautiously

into the next chamber. It was, in size and configuration, the same as the one she had left. She crossed it slowly and moved into the sequential chamber.

Fidelma saw the crumpled figure immediately. It lay face downwards, hands outstretched, an extinguished candle lying near the left hand. It was clad in brown homespun, the robe rumpled up to the back of the knees, the feet encased in leather sandals. The figure was rotund, heavy. Only from the fact that the head was shaved with the tonsure of Columba, the hair long at the back, the front shaved from ear to ear, did Fidelma realise that this must be Brother Ronan Ragallach.

She laid her lamp aside and bent down swiftly, turning the monk over.

She stifled an exclamation as she realised that he was beyond all earthly assistance. The sightless eyes, the blackened features and the protruding tongue told their own story. Around his neck was twisted a prayer cord, biting into the flesh of the moon-faced monk and almost breaking the folds of the skin.

With a feeling of frustration she realised that Brother Ronan Ragallach would tell her nothing. He was quite dead.

Fidelma gave a swift glance around and shivered slightly, for his murderer must be close by, as she realised the noise she had heard was Ronan Ragallach's death fall. Reassuring herself that she was in no immediate danger, she began to examine the body carefully.

Her eyes were drawn to the right hand, still clenched into a tight fist. In it was a torn piece of cloth, of brown sackcloth. No, not torn; but cut from his grasp with a knife which had almost ripped it. Brother Ronan had been carrying something and had been determined not to give it up even in death.

Equally determined to have it, the murderer had used a knife to cut the sack free.

Fidelma shook her head in bewilderment and, taking up the lamp again, held it up to view the body.

Something glinted a short distance away.

She rose and went to it, bending to pick it up, her eyes widening in astonishment.

It was a silver chalice of moderate craftsmanship, slightly bent and grazed by being roughly handled. She knew without thinking that she was probably holding one of the missing cups from Wighard's hoard. But what did that mean? Thousands of questions came flooding into her mind. Questions but no answers.

If Ronan Ragallach had possession of the missing treasure of Wighard, did it mean that he had stolen it and, if so, was she wrong and was he truly the murderer after all? But no, something was wrong. Why contact her and arrange this meeting, swearing he had nothing to do with Wighard's death? She paused, perplexed.

Bending down again over the body she went swiftly through the clothing. In Brother Ronan's leather *crumena* or purse there were several coins and a piece of papyrus. She peered closely. It was covered in the same strange hieroglyphics as the piece she had picked up from the floor of his lodgings at the hostel of Bieda. The writing of the Arabians.

She gave a sharp intake of breath as she realised that a portion of the papyrus had been torn off. It was a portion similar in size and shape to the one she had found. This, then, was the rest of the document. Swiftly, she stuffed the papyrus into her *marsupium*. Then, taking the silver chalice in one hand and the lamp in the other, she rose and began to retrace her steps into the catacomb of Aurelia Restutus.

She had barely begun to cross it when she heard the sound of voices coming nearer. She hesitated. The voices were low, intense and echoing. A curious-sounding language.

Reason told Fidelma that the owners of the voices could not have been involved in Brother Ronan's death. Anyone who had just killed the Irish monk would not be returning with raised voices and careless footsteps from the opposite direction to which the killer must surely have fled. Yet some instinct made Fidelma pause. It took her a moment or two to make up her mind. She examined the empty *loculi*, finding one that was near ground level and then, stopping only to extinguish the lamp, she clambered into it, lying in the empty tomb on her back as if she were a corpse.

The voices came nearer.

She could discern two men arguing for even with a lack of knowledge of the language they spoke she could hear the passion in the inflections of their speech. She saw a light bobbing and reflecting against the walls of the catacombs. She lay watching with half-narrowed eyelids, praying that the two were not interested in the corpses which lay in the *loculi* on either side of the chambers through which they were passing.

Two dark figures entered the tomb and, to her horror, halted, looking round with raised candles.

She heard one saying something which incorporated the name 'Aurelia Restutus'. One of the men mentioned the word '*kafir*' several times. It seemed as if they were waiting. She bit her lip in thought. Could it be these strangers were waiting for Brother Ronan Ragallach?

One of them, obviously more impatient than his companion, had wandered further on. She lay still knowing, with a feeling of inevitability, what he would find in the chamber beyond. She heard his sharp cry and something which sounded like '*Bismillah*!' Then she heard the second man run forward to join his companion and exclaim, '*Ma'uzbillah*!'

As soon as the catacomb darkened, Fidelma slipped out of the tomb, clutching lamp and chalice and moved swiftly and quietly forward in the opposite entrance. She could hear the alarmed voices behind her. She dared not stop to light the lamp but moved hopefully forward into the darkness. She tried to concentrate on reciting the boy Antonio's directions, this time in reverse, heading up the short stairway, lamp and chalice held in one hand, the other hand now feeling before her. She managed to negotiate the stairs, though grazing a knee against some protruding stone.

At the top of the stairs she paused to catch her breath then made a right turn into the long passageway as she recalled. How long was it? Two hundred yards before it widened out into a large ornate tomb. She paused again, shoulders heaving, and put her head to one side. She could hear no sounds of pursuit behind her.

Fidelma knelt down in the darkness and, in the utter blackness of the catacomb, she placed the lamp and chalice on the floor before her. Then she reached into her *marsupium* for the tinder box. In her nervousness it took a while before she was able to ignite it and light the lamp.

With the warm golden glow spreading through the chamber, she gave a deep sigh of relief and sat back on her heels for a moment. Then, gathering lamp and chalice, she stood up and moved on through the corridor to the next chamber towards the lengthy stairway which led up to the higher level of the catacombs. Quietly she swore to herself that she would never again venture into this dark labyrinth.

She was now in the last long stretch of corridor, a length of some hundred yards or so. She controlled her inward urge to run and forced herself to walk slowly along its twisting length. She began to feel a little ridiculous. After all, it was obvious that the two strangers had not encompassed Brother Ronan Ragallach's death, so why should they menace her? She wished she had been more courageous but she could not deny the strange dread which had gripped her in that dark, brooding sepulchre. She wondered if they had gone to meet with Brother Ronan and, if so, who were they?

A chill thought suddenly struck her for the first time. The method by which Brother Ronan Ragallach had met his end was exactly the same as that by which Wighard had been murdered. He had been garrotted. Therefore Ronan had not murdered Wighard. But, and here was the conundrum, if Ronan had not slain Wighard what was Ronan doing with at least part of the treasure taken from Wighard's chambers?

Ronan had denied his complicity and had called on her to meet him so that he could explain. Explain what?

She remembered the piece of papyrus in her *marsupium* and wondered if that might hold any of the answers. She would have to find the *sub-praetor* of the Foreign Secretariat, Brother Osimo Lando, and ask him to translate it. Here was certainly a mystery indeed.

She came to the juncture of the passageway and turned to the right to ascend the stairs into the brightness of the cemetery.

She was aware of a figure in front of her as she swung the corner. Aware, briefly, that the figure was familiar even though she saw only a momentary glimpse of its outline. Then she felt a pain against the side of her head and plunged into utter blackness.

A voice was calling her name as if it came from a great distance away.

Fidelma blinked and found she felt nauseous and dizzy. She groaned and someone pressed cold water to her mouth. She took a swallow, coughed and gulped and nearly choked. She opened her eyes and found that the light was momentarily blinding. She blinked again and tried to focus. She appeared to be lying on her back with the blue canopy of the sky above and a merciless yellow sun scorching her face. She groaned again and closed her eyes.

'Sister Fidelma, can you hear me?'

It was a familiar voice and she lay a moment or two trying to recognise it.

Droplets of cold water splashed against her face.

She moaned, wishing whoever it was would go away and leave her to her nausea.

'Sister Fidelma!'

The voice was more urgent now.

Reluctantly, she opened her eyes and focused on the dark figure above her.

The sallow features of Cornelius of Alexandria swam into focus. The swarthy physician looked worried.

'Sister Fidelma, do you recognise me?'

Fidelma grimaced.

'I do. Yet how my head throbs.'

'You received a blow on the skull, a sharp contusion above the temple but the skin is not split. It will heal after a while.'

'I feel sick.'

'That is merely the shock. Lie a while and have some more water.'

Fidelma continued to lie back but let her eyes wander around. Behind the shoulder of the Greek doctor stood the young boy, Antonio, looking scared and anxious. She could hear worried voices. Voices! Was that the sharp, penetrating tone of the Abbess Wulfrun in the background? She tried to raise herself up. She was surely not imagining she could hear the abbess instructing Sister Eafa to follow her?

She struggled to sit up but was gently pushed back by the Alexandrian physician.

'Where am I?' she demanded.

'At the entrance to the catacombs,' replied Cornelius. 'You were carried out unconscious.'

Memory came back sharply.

'Someone knocked me out!' she asserted, attempting to sit up again but Cornelius held her down.

'Be careful,' he warned. 'You must take things slowly.' Then he paused, head to one side. 'Why would anyone knock you out?' he asked sceptically. 'Are you sure you did not hit your head on a protruding rock in the dark of the passageway? It has been done before.'

'No!' Fidelma suddenly paused and stared at him. 'What are you doing here?'

The physician shrugged.

'I happened to be passing the gates of the cemetery when I heard cries for a doctor. I was told that someone had been injured inside the catacomb. I found you at the foot of the steps.'

Fidelma was baffled.

'Who raised the alarm?'

Cornelius shrugged and helped her into a sitting position once he had assessed that she was fit enough.

'One of the pilgrims. I have no idea.'

'That is right, sister.' She turned to find that the boy, Antonio, was nodding. 'A person came out of the catacombs and said that someone was badly injured inside. I recognised the physician's *lecticula* at the gates of the cemetery and asked someone to run and get him to come here.'

'I came and found you at the bottom of the stairway,' repeated Cornelius. 'It looked as if you had hit your head on the side of the passageway. We carried you up.'

Antonio, seeing that Fidelma was not so badly injured, gave an urchin grin. 'You do not have much luck in this place, sister.'

Fidelma returned a rueful smile.

'You speak wisdom, young Antonio.'

She was able to stand up now, the dizziness and nausea having abated a little.

'Where is this person to whom I owe my rescue?'

There were several people standing around but, having ascertained that there was no further drama, they were dispersing on their various errands. She wondered whether she had really heard the Abbess Wulfrun in their midst.

The boy shrugged.

'They went some time ago.'

'Who were they? Do you know that I might thank them?'

The boy shook his head.

'It was just another pilgrim. He wore the garb of the east, I think.'

Fidelma's eyes widened. She wondered if it could have been one of the swarthy men whom she had seen in the catacomb of Aurelia Restutus.

'How many foreigners have been in this place, Antonio, since I arrived?'

Again the boy shrugged.

'Including yourself, several. It is only foreigners that come here to see the dead ones. Also, there are three other entrances such as this one.'

She smiled at her naiveté in thinking the boy would differentiate between herself and the two dark-skinned men she had seen in the tomb.

'How many men from . . .'

Cornelius interrupted her with a grunt of disapproval.

'I think you should worry about thanking your rescuers later. My *lecticula* can transport you back to the Lateran Palace where I can dress your wound properly. Then you should rest for the remainder of the day.'

Fidelma expressed her disagreement with his advice but, as she began to walk, another wave of dizziness washed over her and she realised that the physician was probably right. She sat down promptly on a nearby stone and groaned slightly at the ringing in her head.

She was aware that Cornelius had raised his hand in a signal and through the cemetery trotted two burly men bearing a curiously shaped chair which they carried, one at the back and one at the front, on long poles. Fidelma had seen several of these about the streets of Rome and ascertained they were called *lecticula*. Of the modes of transport used in her own country, Fidelma had never seen anything to compare with these strange chair-like contraptions in which people had themselves carried on the shoulders of slaves or servants.

She was about to protest but realised that, as she felt at the moment, she would be unable to walk back to the Lateran

Palace. So she accepted the transport with a small sigh of resignation. It was when she was clambering into the chair that she realised what she had forgotten.

'Your lamp must still be down at the foot of the stairs where I fell, Antonio,' she called to the boy.

The boy simply grinned and shook his head, picking up the lamp from his side and showing her.

'When we carried you up here, I brought it with me,' he assured her.

'And the silver chalice that I was carrying?'

Antonio looked at her in genuine bewilderment.

'I saw no silver chalice, sister. Nor did you take one down there, that I saw.'

In a sudden panic Fidelma grabbed at her *marsupium*. Her tinder box and coinage were still there but there was no sign of the papyrus she had taken from Brother Ronan. However, the severed piece of sackcloth remained.

She saw Cornelius gazing at her in suspicion.

'One moment,' she said, climbing out of the *lecticula* and walking unsteadily towards the boy. She knelt down by his side and lowered her voice. 'Antonio, in the catacomb of Aurelia Restutus is a body. No,' she saw him start to smile at the idea of a body being found in a tomb. 'I mean someone who has just been slain. I discovered the body. As soon as I return to the Lateran Palace, I shall send the authorities to recover it . . .'

Antonio stared at her with wide, solemn eyes.

'The matter should be reported to the office of the *praetor urbanis*,' he advised.

Fidelma nodded agreement.

'Don't worry. The proper authorities will be notified. But I want you to keep an eye on whoever comes and goes. You see, I did find a silver chalice and a papyrus which, when I was knocked unconscious, I believe were taken from me. So if you see anyone behaving in a suspicious manner, in particular, two men, eastern in appearance and speaking a strange language, I want you to take a careful note of them and where they go.'

'I will, sister,' the boy vowed. 'But there are many other entrances and exits to these catacombs.'

Fidelma groaned inwardly at the news. However, she reached in her *marsupium* and dropped some coins into the boy's basket.

She turned back to where Cornelius was standing fretting at the delay and clambered back into the *lecticula*. The two men gave a heave and a grunt as they lifted it up and began to trot forward along the path to the gate, with Cornelius pacing rapidly alongside.

It was an odd sensation to be carried in such a manner but Fidelma was thankful for the mode of transport. Her head was aching and her forehead was throbbing and tender. She closed her eyes, oblivious of the stares of curiosity that passers-by gave her, for while the *lecticula* were common enough in Rome it was uncommon to see a religieuse being transported.

Fidelma sat back and relaxed her mind, turning over the events of the last hour.

It was only after they had re-entered the city through the Metronia Gate and turned under the shadow of the Caelius Hill that the thought struck her. In her dizziness she had not realised it. She had been convinced that one or other of the two strangers must have followed her, struck her and taken the chalice and papyrus from her. But she had left them behind her in the catacombs. The memory flashed back. It was only when she had turned the corner at the foot of the stairs leading out of the catacomb that she had seen the figure, the familiar figure, obviously waiting for her. A single person had struck her down. A person she knew. But who?

Chapter Twelve

Fidelma sat in the *officium* set aside for the use of Brother Eadulf and herself in the Lateran Palace still nursing her throbbing head. The dizziness and nausea had left her but the soreness remained. It was Eadulf, with his knowledge of medicines, who had insisted on taking over from Cornelius of Alexandria. Cornelius did not seem troubled that the Saxon monk wished to encroach on his role as physician. In fact, he seemed grateful to be able to hurry away on his own business. Brother Eadulf, since his training at Tuaim Brecain, always carried a *pera*, or *lés* as the Irish physicians called their medical bags, full of medicinal herbs. He dressed her wound and prepared a drink made from an infusion of dried flower heads of red clover which, he assured her, would gradually ease her aching head.

Fidelma had absolute faith in Eadulf as she sipped his noxious potion, for he had similarly come to her aid twice before at Hilda's abbey at Witebia in Northumbria. In fact, he had cured her of a throbbing headache with a similar mixture when she had fallen and knocked herself unconscious at the abbey.

As he fussed about her, she explained to him and to Furius

Licinius about her morning's adventure. On learning the basic facts, the young *tesserarius* summoned a *decuria* of the *custodes* and set off for the Christian cemetery at Metrona. Fidelma put up with Eadulf's chiding for a little longer as she sat casting her mind over the events and trying to establish some pattern to them but she realised that for as much information as she had there was still no framework for it. Without a framework none of it seemed to make any sense.

'We must send for Brother Osimo Lando,' she said, suddenly interrupting Eadulf in mid-stream. He had been gently chastising her for going to the catacombs alone without first warning him or letting anyone know where she was going. He blinked.

'Osimo Lando?' he frowned.

'He admitted that he knew Ronan well. I feel he knows much more than he is telling us. With Ronan dead he may now find himself able to tell more.'

The door abruptly opened and Marinus, the military governor, entered with a worried look on his features. He addressed himself directly to Fidelma.

'Is it true? Is it true what I hear . . . that Brother Ronan Ragallach is dead?'

Fidelma gave an affirmative nod.

The expression of the *Superista* of the *custodes* abruptly softened into a smile and he made a sound of emphatic satisfaction: 'Then the matter of the death of Wighard is finally brought to an end.'

Fidelma exchanged a bemused glance with Eadulf.

'I do not follow your logic,' she said coldly.

Marinus spread his hands as if the reason were plain to see.

'The murderer has been caught and killed. No need to spend further time on the matter.'

Fidelma shook her head slowly.

'I can only believe that you are not aware of all the facts, Marinus. Brother Ronan Ragnallach was found garrotted while he was on his way to meet me. He had sent me a message to tell me that he was not the murderer of Wighard and wanted a chance to explain. He was garrotted in the same manner as Wighard. Whoever killed Wighard also killed Ronan Ragallach. The matter, you see, is far from over.'

The military governor blinked rapidly in bewilderment.

'I was simply told that he was dead,' he replied, his face changing to an almost woebegone expression. 'I presumed that he had been killed or killed himself because he realised that he could not escape us forever.'

'Fidelma was right, and we were wrong,' Eadulf entered the conversation. Fidelma stared at him in surprise, somewhat amused by the unexpected respect in his voice, as though he delighted in being proved wrong by her. 'She said all along that she suspected that Ronan Ragalach was not the killer.'

Marinus set his jaw firmly.

'Then we must discover the truth as soon as possible. Only this morning the Holy Father's *scriba aedilicius* contacted me to say that the Holy Father is chiding at the lack of resolution to this matter.'

'He is no more anxious than we are,' replied Fidelma in annoyance at the implication. 'It will be resolved when we have a solution. And now,' she rose, 'we have much work to do. Could you send someone to bring Brother Osimo Lando here? We require his advice.'

Marinus started at being so peremptorily dismissed. He opened his mouth to say something in protest, but snapped it shut again and grimaced his acceptance of the order.

Eadulf grinned slyly at Fidelma.

'I swear you will treat the Holy Father with as much disdain.'

'Disdain?' Fidelma shook her head. 'I do not hold Marinus in contempt. But we are each supposed to be competent in our arts and authority and each should fill his or her office with the qualities we expect in others. Pride in office without competence is as much a sin as competence without confidence.'

Eadulf's eyes grew serious.

'With Ronan Ragallach dead, I can see no leads into this maze, Fidelma.'

She inclined her head slightly.

'Ronan Ragallach, while he denied that he had killed Wighard in his message to me, and which claim I believe to be the truth, nevertheless had some of Wighard's valuables with him when he was killed.' She explained how she had found a chalice and the piece of sack still gripped firmly into his dead hand. She paused and then shrugged. 'Although, of course, I cannot prove that now.'

'Who do you think hit you on the head and stole the chalice and piece of papyrus?'

'I don't know.' Fidelma gave a long sigh. 'I saw his outline for a moment in the darkness, and in that moment thought the figure was familiar, and then ...' She ended with a shrug.

'But it was definitely a male?' pressed Eadulf.

Fidelma frowned again. She had used the masculine form without thinking. Now, as she analysed her memory, she was uncertain.

'I don't even know that for sure.'

Eadulf scratched the end of his nose in thought.

'Well, I cannot see what step forward we can take. Our chief suspect is dead, and, as you say, murdered in the same manner as Wighard . . .'

'Who were the foreigners I saw in the sepulchre?' Fidelma interposed. 'That is surely the next step. Ronan Ragallach had the rest of the papyrus Brother Osimo Lando has identified as written in the tongue of the Arabians. I heard a few words spoken by those foreigners which I think I can imitate. Perhaps Osimo Lando can identify them, for I believe they were Arabians who spoke them.'

'But why would Brother Ronan Ragallach be meeting with Arabians?'

'If I can find the answer to that question, I think we would be very near the answer to this entire mystery,' Fidelma said confidently.

There was a knock on the door and a member of the *custodes* entered. He bore himself stiffly, eyes straight ahead, as he halted and threw up a salute.

'I am ordered to report that Brother Osimo Lando is not in his place of work. He is not in the palace at this time.'

'Can someone be sent to his lodging to see what ails him?'

The young man came smartly to attention so abruptly that Fidelma was startled for a moment.

'It shall be done!' the young guard intoned solemnly and swung on his heel.

Eadulf looked troubled.

'Nothing is ever smooth.'

'Well, there must be someone else in this palace who speaks the language of these Arabians.'

Eadulf rose and started to the door.

'I can soon find out. In the meantime,' he half turned at the door with a concerned expression, 'you rest a while and recover.'

Fidelma gestured absently. In fact her headache was almost gone and only the tender area of bruising remained to irritate her. More than anything, however, she was distracted by the countless swimming questions and thoughts in her mind. After Eadulf departed she stretched comfortably in her chair, hands folded in her lap before her and lowered her eyes. She concentrated on breathing deeply and regularly and, one by one, consciously relaxed her muscles.

When she was young and started her education, her 'fosterage' as it was called, one of the first things she had been taught was the art of the *dercad*, the act of meditation, by which countless generations of Irish mystics had achieved the state of *sitcháin* or peace. Fidelma had regularly practised this art of meditation in times of stress and found it very useful. It was an art that had been practised even before the Faith had reached the shores of Ireland just two centuries earlier by the pagan Druids. The Druid mystics had not disappeared from her homeland entirely. They could still be found as solitary ascetics living in remote fastnesses and wastes. But they were a vanishing people.

When she had been old enough, Fidelma had gone regularly to the *tigh n' alluis*, the sweat house, which was an integral part of the *dercad* ceremony. In a small house of stones, a great fire was lit until the structure became like an oven. Then the person seeking the state of *sitcháin* would enter naked and the door would be sealed. They would sit on a bench perspiring and sweating until an appointed time when the door would be opened and they would come out and plunge into an icy pool. It was merely a step nearer the *dercad* process. Many of the ascetic religious followed this old Druidic practice although, Fidelma knew, several of the younger religious were rejecting many things simply because they were associated with Druids.

Even the Blessed Patrick himself, a Briton who had been prominent in establishing the Faith in Ireland, had expressly forbade the practise of the *teinm laegda* and the *imbas forosnai*, the meditative means of enlightenment. Fidelma felt sad that ancient rituals of self-awareness were being discarded simply because they were ancient and practised long before the Faith arrived in Ireland.

However, the *dercad* was not yet forbidden and she felt that there would be protest among the religious of Ireland if it was. It was a means of relaxing and of calming the riot of thoughts within a troubled mind.

'Sister!'

Fidelma blinked and felt as if she was emerging from a deep, restful sleep.

She was aware of the *tesserarius* Furius Licinius, examining her face with a troubled gaze.

'Sister Fidelma?' His voice was slightly worried. 'Are you all right?'

Fidelma blinked again and allowed a smile to spread over her features.

'Yes, Licinius. I am fine.'

'You did not seem to hear me, I thought you were asleep but your eyes were open.'

'I was merely meditating, Licinius,' smiled Fidelma, standing up and stretching a little.

Furius Licinius took the exact meaning of the Latin word *meditari* rather than the intent of *dercad*.

'Day dreaming more than thinking,' he observed sceptically.

'Though, I grant, that there is much to meditate about in this matter.'

Fidelma did not bother to enlighten him.

'What is your news?' she asked.

Furius Licinius gestured, a brief rise and fall of his shoulder.

'We have recovered the body of Brother Ronan Ragallach from the catacomb. It is now in the *mortuarium* of Cornelius. But there is little else we could find, certainly not a papyrus or chalice.'

Fidelma sighed.

'As I thought. Whoever has done this thing is clever.'

'We searched further on in the catacomb and found another exit or entrance which comes out by the Aurelian Wall. That is where our murderers entered and left. They did not have to follow you into the cemetery.'

Fidelma nodded slowly.

'And there was no sign of anything which might indicate a culprit?'

'Only, as you said, Brother Ronan Ragallach was strangled by a prayer cord in the same manner as Wighard.'

'Well,' Fidelma smiled wanly, 'one thing I realised my attacker didn't make off with is this . . .'

Fidelma reached into her *marsupium* and drew forth the piece of sackcloth which had been clutched in Ronan Ragallach's hand.

Furius Licinius examined it in bewilderment.

'What does it prove? It is only ordinary sackcloth.'

'Indeed,' Fidelma agreed. 'Similar to this piece of ordinary sackcloth.'

She placed on the table the tiny piece which she had detached from the splinter in the door of Brother Eanred's room.

'Are you saying that this is one and the same?'

'The odds are that it is.'

'But supposition is not proof.'

'You are becoming wise in law, Furius Licinius,' agreed Fidelma solemnly. 'But there is enough here to question Eanred again.'

'He seems just a simpleton to me.'

Eadulf abruptly re-entered the room. It was clear from his expression that he had not been successful in his quest.

'Not one person could I find who knows the language of the Arabians,' he reported in disgust.

Furius Licinius frowned.

'What of Brother Osimo Lando?'

Fidelma told Licinius that Osimo could not be found.

'Well, Marcus Narses is on duty, he stands by the portals of the great hall. He would know. He fought the Mahometans at Alexandria three years ago and was taken prisoner for a year until his family paid a ransom for his release. He learnt something of their tongue.'

'Send him to us, Licinius,' ordered Eadulf, sprawling into a chair. 'I am too exhausted to go and find him.'

It did not take long for Furius Licinius to locate Marcus Narses and bring him back to the chamber.

Fidelma came straight to the point.

'I have memorised some words. I think they might be in the language of the Arabians, which I am told you understand. Will you see if you can recognise them?'

The *decurion* inclined his head.

'Very well, sister.'

'The first word is *kafir*.'

The soldier grinned.

'Easy enough. It means "unbeliever". One who does not

believe in the Prophet. As we would say "*infidelis*" to denote a person rejecting the truth of Christ.'

'The Prophet?'

'Mahomet of Mecca who died thirty years ago. His teachings have spread like wildfire among the eastern peoples where they call the new religion Islam, which means a submission to God or Allah.'

Fidelma frowned as she caught his pronunciation.

'So Allah is their name for God. Then what would "*Bismillah*" mean?'

'Easy enough,' replied Marcus Narses. 'That is "In the name of Allah", their God. It is merely an exclamation of surprise which they use.'

Fidelma pursed her lips thoughtfully.

'So, what I suspected is confirmed. Those two were Arabians. And it seems that Brother Ronan was in contact with them. But for what purpose and what bearing does it have on the death of Wighard and on his own?'

Eadulf glanced at Marcus Narses.

'Thank you, *decurion*. You may go now,' he said.

The young *decurion* seemed reluctant to leave but, with a glance at Furius Licinius, he returned to his guard duties in the *atrium*.

'Brother Osimo Lando should be found,' suggested Furius Licinius. 'If anyone would know more of this matter then he, as Brother Ronan's superior, should know if he was engaged in any matter considering the Arabians.'

'I have already despatched someone to see why he is not at his place of work,' Fidelma explained. 'However, I am anxious to speak with Brother Eanred again.'

'We only have Sebbi's word that Eanred is a master of the

garrote,' Eadulf pointed out, guessing what was in her mind.

'We must be accurate in these matters, Eadulf. All Sebbi said was that Eanred was once a slave who killed his master by strangulation and that is a crime for which he has been exonerated by your Saxon law by payment of the *wergild*.'

'Even so . . .' protested Eadulf.

Fidelma was firm.

'Let us go and find him. This room is too stuffy and I fear my headache is returning.'

Eadulf and Licinius followed her as she led the way out of the room and along the corridor to the *atrium*, the main hall of the palace. There were several people standing in groups, as usual, waiting to be summoned to see whoever they had come to solicit and influence. Fidelma was leading the way across the mosaic floor to the *domus hospitale*. They had almost reached the far door when they found Brother Sebbi thrusting his way forward with a grim look of irritation on his features.

He saw Eadulf and halted.

'Are you still secretary and advisor to the Saxon delegation to the Holy Father?' he snapped, without preamble.

They halted and Eadulf frowned at the religious' brusqueness.

'I was so appointed by the archbishop-designate but since his death . . .' he shrugged. 'Is anything the matter?'

'Matter? Matter? Have you seen the Abbot Puttoc?'

'No. Why?'

Sebbi looked closely at Furius Licinius. It was clear that he was not following the conversation for he spoke no Saxon. His gaze sought Fidelma but she merely dropped her eyes and pretended disinterest. Sebbi of Stanggrund brought his gaze back to Eadulf.

'I hear that these Romans are trying to foist a foreign bishop on to Canterbury again.'

Eadulf's mouth quirked into a thin smile.

'I have heard as much. Well, until Deusdedit became the first Saxon to become archbishop of Canterbury ten years ago, all those appointed to Canterbury have been Roman or Greek. If what you say is true, why should this be of great concern? Are we not all one in the eyes of God?'

Sebbi snorted indignantly.

'The people of the Saxon kingdoms want their own bishops, not foreigners. Have they not demonstrated this by ousting the Irish from Northumbria? Didn't we Saxons agree on Wighard of Kent as our next archbishop?'

'But Wighard is dead,' Eadulf pointed out.

'Indeed. And the Holy Father should respect our wishes by appointing Puttoc in his stead. Not some African.'

'African?' Eadulf was bewildered.

'I have just heard that Vitalian has offered Canterbury to Abbot Hadrian of Hiridanum near Naples, who is an African. An African!'

Eadulf's eyes widened with some surprise.

'I have heard of him as a man of great learning and piety.'

'Well, what are we going to do? We Saxons must remain together and protest, demanding that the Holy Father's blessing be given to Puttoc.'

Eadulf's face was a mask.

'Yet you have confessed that you do not like Puttoc, Sebbi. Is it merely that you see your chance to be Abbot of Stanggrund vanishing with Puttoc's lost hopes? Anyway, we Saxons, as you say, can only come together when the mystery of Wighard's death is solved.'

Sebbi opened his mouth, stopped himself and then, with a muttered exclamation, he turned disgustedly away into the crowd.

Eadulf turned to Fidelma.

'Did you understand all that?'

Fidelma nodded thoughtfully.

'It looks as though Puttoc's and Sebbi's ambitions are being brought to an abrupt halt.'

'Brother Sebbi certainly looks as though he can murder someone for . . .' Eadulf suddenly broke off as he realised what he was saying. He looked uneasily at Fidelma.

'We cannot close our minds to any avenue at the moment,' Fidelma read his thoughts. 'I have said as much from the first. Ambition is a powerful motivator.'

'This is true but is it so wrong to be ambitious?'

'Ambition is merely vanity, and from vanity people can be blind to morality. Wasn't it Publius Syrus who said that a man is much to be dreaded who follows his ambition?'

'Not if they are possessed of talent to fulfil ambition,' replied Eadulf. 'The greater evil would be to have men with great ambitions and minor talents.'

Fidelma chuckled appreciatively.

'We must debate philosophy in depth one day, Eadulf of Seaxmund's Ham.'

'Perhaps,' replied Eadulf, with an uneasy grin. 'The best person to talk of philosophy with at this moment is Puttoc. He may need some guidance in this matter of ambition.'

Fidelma led the way forward to the chambers occupied by Wighard's entourage.

They came upon Brother Eanred in the communal *lavantur* or laundry house where he was hard at work washing clothes.

He started nervously at their approach but then continued to beat at the thick woollen robe he was washing.

'Well, Brother Eanred,' Fidelma greeted him. 'You are working hard.'

The religieux hunched his shoulders in an odd gesture of resignation.

'I am washing the clothes of my master.'

'The Abbot Puttoc?' queried Eadulf hastily, lest the reply spark Fidelma into a discourse that those of the Faith had only one master in Christ.

Eanred nodded.

'How long have you been at that job?' queried Fidelma.

'Since . . .' Eanred screwed up his eyes, 'since after the midday Angelus, sister.'

'And before that?'

Eanred looked troubled. Fidelma decided to press him directly.

'Were you in the Christian cemetery at the Metronia Gate?'

'Yes, sister.' There was no guile in Eanred's reply.

'What were you doing there?'

'I went with Abbot Puttoc.'

'And why did he go there?' asked Fidelma patiently, as she tried to draw out the facts from Eanred.

'I think we went to see the grave of Wighard and to make arrangements for a marker, sister.'

Fidelma compressed her lips thoughtfully. It was reasonable enough. There was certainly nothing to link Puttoc and Eanred with the Arabians who had gone there to meet Ronan Ragallach.

She found the pale brown eyes of Eanred watching her expression curiously. There was a strange blankness there, the vacant expression of a simpleton not someone full of shrewdness and deceit. Yet, she bit her lip, there was something else . . . alarm? apprehension?

She caught herself from pursuing such thoughts.

'Thank you, Eanred. Tell me something else. Have you a bag made of sackcloth?'

'No, sister,' the religieux shook her head.

'Have you used any sackcloth since you have been in this place?'

Eanred shrugged. There was no mistaking the incomprehension on his features. Fidelma decided it was pointless pressing the matter. Perhaps Eanred was lying, if so he was a good liar.

She thanked him and walked out of the *lavantur*, followed by a bewildered Eadulf and Licinius.

'That seemed to achieve little, sister,' observed the Saxon brother, his voice edged in disapproval. 'Why didn't you accuse him outright?'

Fidelma spread her arms.

'To paint a picture, Brother Eadulf, you put a little paint here and a little there. Each brush stroke by itself means little, only when all the brush strokes are made and you stand back from the whole is there an outline and a sense of achievement.'

Eadulf bit his lip. He felt that he had been soundly rebuked but did not understand for what. Sometimes Fidelma had an annoying habit of not speaking directly. He sighed. In fact, he mused, Fidelma's countrymen and women all seemed to have that irritating manner of not speaking in plain, simple language but using symbolism, hyperbole, allusion and exaggerated forms of speech.

They halted in the small courtyard. Fidelma seated herself

on the small stone parapet by the gushing fountain in the centre of the courtyard and trailed her slim hand in the cool water, listening with an appreciative ear to the sound of the water. Furius Licinius and Eadulf stood awkwardly by, waiting for her to speak.

'Ah, Brother Eadulf!'

The imperious tones of the Abbess Wulfrun echoed suddenly across the yard as the tall figure of the woman appeared in the doorway. She bore down on them like a vessel under full sail, eyes fixed ahead.

'My lady,' Eadulf greeted her nervously.

Abbess Wulfrun ignored both Fidelma and Furius Licinius. Her hand played with the scarf at her throat. Fidelma watched the involuntary action trying to recall why she felt it should interest her.

'I wish to inform you that tomorrow I and Sister Eafa will be leaving for Porto to seek a ship and commence our journey back to Kent. There is little to remain here for now. I have arranged for a boatman to take us down the Tiber. As secretary of the delegation, I felt that you should be informed.'

She began to turn away when Fidelma, without standing up, called softly. 'That may not be possible, Abbess Wulfrun.'

The woman halted, swung round and stared at her with an expression of astonishment on her face.

'What did you say?' came her threatening, breathless tone.

Fidelma repeated what she had said.

'Do you dare to challenge my right of movement, girl?'

'No,' replied Fidelma complacently. 'I presume, however, that you have not consulted Bishop Gelasius nor the military governor, the *Superista* Marinus?'

'I am on my way there now to inform them of my intentions.'

'Then let me save you the trouble. Until our investigation into the death of Wighard is ended, then no one in Wighard's party may leave Rome.'

Abbess Wulfrun stood staring at Fidelma, still dangling her hand in the fountain apparently unconcerned at the anger of the abbess of Sheppey's face.

'This is outrageous!' she began.

Eadulf shook his head, gathering courage.

'Abbess Wulfrun, my colleague, Fidelma of Kildare, is absolutely right to inform you of the procedure.'

The belligerent abbess turned on him, regarding him as if he were a species of an unpleasant animal life.

'I will see Bishop Gelasius about this,' she said contentiously.

'That is your prerogative,' acknowledged Eadulf. 'But, as a matter of interest, did you intend to make the journey back to the kingdom of Kent alone?'

'And why should Sister Eafa and I not journey by ourselves?'

'Surely you must know of the dangers of such travel? At Massilia there are gangs who prey on lonely pilgrims, especially on women, and take them into slavery, many to be sold among the brothels of the Germans.'

Abbess Wulfrun grimaced with haughty disdain.

'They would not dare. I am of royal blood and . . .'

'The matter will not arise,' Fidelma said firmly, rising to her feet. 'You and Sister Eafa will have to remain here until the investigation is complete. After that you are free to travel wherever and however you wish. But, when that time comes, you would be wise to take Brother Eadulf's advice.'

If looks could have slain, then Fidelma would have been dead under the abbess' withering glance.

'It is true, lady,' Eadulf added, seeking to placate her. 'Best to wait until a whole band of pilgrims are returning to Kent or the other Saxon lands and go with them.'

Without another word, Abbess Wulfrun turned and walked away with the same scornful bearing as she always displayed.

Fidelma smiled and rubbed her chin.

'I am truly sorry for Sister Eafa to be a companion to such an arrogant mistress as that one,' she said, and not for the first time. 'Still one cannot help but wonder why the Abbess Wulfrun is so eager to leave Rome after being here only a week or so.'

Eadulf chuckled critically.

'Probably for the same good reasons that you suggested to me the other day – you were eager to get back to your own country.'

A sigh of impatience brought both their heads round to Furius Licinius, whom they had almost forgotten. The young *tesserarius* of the palace *custodes* had been silent for a long time.

Furius Licinius was clearly bored.

'Surely, if we find these Arabians we will solve this puzzle?' he offered.

'How would we set about finding them?' Fidelma asked.

'There are many trading ships that put in at our ports. Many merchants from the lands of the Arabians live in Rome. In fact, there is a quarter among the *emporia*, the storehouses and markets, along the Tiber. It is a slum area of the city. That is where many of them are to be found. We call it Marmorata.'

'The place of marble?' queried Fidelma.

Furius Licinius nodded.

'In ancient times it was where the stonemasons worked in

226

preparing the marble to build the city.'

'I did not know this,' Eadulf grumbled, slightly annoyed. He had prided himself on his knowledge of the city since his years of study in Rome.

'It is not a place where people go now without an escort,' Licinius explained. 'It is full of sailors from many lands, particularly from Spain and North Africa and Judea. One part of the area is given over to a large rubbish dump where broken and useless *amphora* and *testae* have been dumped in a huge mound. Ships offload their cargoes and the city merchants just dump the containers. They only care for their profits and not for the pollution they create.'

'Is it worth a visit?' demanded Eadulf eagerly. 'Perhaps you can spot your Arabians there?'

Fidelma shook her head.

'It is useful to know that the area exists, that these Arabians might have come from there. But without further information, I fail to see what purpose the knowledge could serve. I certainly would not recognise the two men again. Indeed, I do not even know why I am looking for them. The key must surely lie with Brother Osimo Lando, perhaps he can tell us why Ronan Ragallach would be in contact with them. Which reminds me, it is time that the young *custos* returned with news about him.'

They retraced their footsteps back through the corridors of the Lateran buildings and into the *atrium* of the palace. It was still as busy as ever, still full of waiting dignitaries, impassive *custodes*, and priests and religious of all ages, sexes, nations and manners. Furius Licinius left them to see if there was any news of Brother Osimo Lando while they continued on to the office near the military governor's chambers.

As Fidelma and Eadulf were crossing the hall, the mournful Brother Ine was pushing his way in an opposite direction. A broad smile crossed Fidelma's face and she reached forward a hand to stay the Saxon religieux.

'You are the very person that I was about to seek out,' she told him.

Ine stood frowning with suspicion.

'What do you wish of me?' he asked cautiously.

'You have been among the religious of Kent for many years, have you not?'

Ine acknowledged that he had, looking from Fidelma to Eadulf with a puzzled expression.

'I told you that I was given to the church at the age of ten by my father.'

'Indeed you did. You must know a lot about the church in your kingdom of Kent?'

Ine smirked with pride.

'There is little I do not know, sister.'

Fidelma's smile was even more encouraging.

'I am told that Seaxburgh, the queen of Kent, established the monastery on Sheppey. Is this so?'

'It is. She raised the house there nearly twenty years ago soon after she came from the land of the East Anglians to marry Eorcenberht our king.'

'She was a daughter of Anna, I am told.'

Ine confirmed it at once.

'Anna had several daughters. Seaxburgh was very interested in the Faith. She is a saintly woman and much loved in Kent.'

Fidelma leant closer in confidence.

'Tell me this, Ine, is Abbess Wulfrun equally as loved as her sister?'

'*Sister*!' The word shot out of Ine like an oath. Then he

smiled knowingly. 'When Seaxburgh brought Wulfrun to Kent their relationship was not *that* close. Many think that Seaxburgh made a mistake in placing Wulfrun as abbess in Sheppey.'

'What do you mean by saying that their relationship was not close?' demanded Fidelma.

Ine grimaced shrewdly.

'Have you heard of the pagan Roman feast of Saturnalia, sister? Ask what is the custom at that feast and solve the puzzle yourself.'

With an intensification of his melancholy expression, Ine turned away into the crowd leaving Fidelma bewildered.

'Well?' she demanded of Eadulf, 'what happened at the feast of Saturnalia?'

Eadulf looked scandalised at the idea that he should have knowledge about an ancient pagan Roman festival.

Fidelma sighed and resumed her journey across the *atrium* with Eadulf following her.

'So far as I can see,' Eadulf remarked, as they pushed their way across the hall towards the offices of the military governor, 'our only hope lies in finding these Arabians. Only they will be able to reveal what is behind this mystery. It was surely one of the Arabians or their confederates who attacked you and took the papyrus and chalice.'

'How do you make that out?' queried Fidelma as they reached the room which had become their *officium*.

'Why else would they want the papyrus written in their language?'

'And why take the chalice?'

'Maybe Ronan Ragallach was selling the treasures of Wighard to them.'

Fidelma stood still and blinked rapidly.

'Sometimes, Eadulf,' she whispered in surprise, 'sometimes you make intuitive leaps that make sense where others must struggle with logic.'

Eadulf was unsure whether he was being flattered or insulted. He was about to demand an explanation when the door opened hurriedly and Furius Licinius came blundering in with an excited expression on his features.

Before Fidelma could ask him the meaning of his animation, Licinius blurted: 'I was at the main gate just a moment ago and Abbot Puttoc came hurrying out. He did not see me.' He pulled a face for a moment. 'I suppose one *custos* may look much like another to a foreigner.'

'What is it?' demanded Fidelma impatiently.

The young man swallowed hastily.

'The Abbot Puttoc hired a *lecticula*. I thought you might be interested to hear where he asked the bearers to take him.'

'It is not the time to play games, Licinius,' snapped Fidelma. 'Speak plainly.'

'Abbot Puttoc asked to be taken to the very place that I was speaking of. To Marmorata. The area where the Arabian merchants are to be found.'

Chapter Thirteen

Sister Fidelma clung to one side of the small one-horse carriage which Furius Licinius drove at a rapid pace along the narrow roadway. He seemed impervious to the people flying this way and that before it, leaving them shouting after the vehicle with shaking fists and a variety of curses which Fidelma was thankful she could not translate. On the opposite side of the carriage, pale-faced, and hanging on for dear life was a very unhappy Brother Eadulf. His knuckles showed white as he held tightly to the wickerwork of the carriage as it bucked and swayed over the cobbled paving.

It had been Fidelma's idea. Some instinct drove her to decide that the information must be acted upon at once. As soon as Furius Licinius had reported the departure of the Abbot Puttoc for Marmorata of all places, her intuition told her that they should immediately follow him for there was no valid reason why Puttoc should be going to such an area. But if this was, as Furius Licinius had reported, the area where the Arabian merchants were to be found, then it looked highly suspicious.

Neither Licinius nor Eadulf could argue with her as she almost ran from the palace to the main gate. She had noticed that the *lecticula* carriers travelled at a fast pace through the ancient narrow streets and that it would be difficult to catch up with Puttoc's *lecticula* on foot. Licinius, somewhat unwillingly, was prompted into asking the loan of a single horse carriage from a fellow officer of the palace guards. It was almost a chariot. But Licinius offered to drive them in pursuit of Puttoc to Marmorata.

It was a breathtaking drive and on a few occasions Fidelma thought the bucking vehicle would overturn but Licinius held it firmly to the road, balancing with his legs firmly astride, both hands holding tightly to the reins, while they clung on behind.

They had followed the base of the Hill of Caelius and crossed the Valle Murcia, with its magnificent circus, to the south west and started up a hill which Licinius informed them was the hill of Aventinus, the southernmost of the seven hills. The road ascended quickly through beautiful villas, the palatial homes of the Roman aristocracy.

Fidelma found time to gaze at the grand buildings and gardens with some surprise.

'Is this the way to the slum area you spoke of?' she called to Licinius, for the idea of slums seemed miles away from this incredibly elegant area.

The *tesserarius* grunted in acknowledgment as he continued to flick the reins to urge the horse to greater effort.

'If my guess is right,' he called over his shoulder, 'then Puttoc's *lecticula* will be carried along the Valle Murcia by the Circus Maximus.' He indicated down the northern slope of the hill, which they were ascending. 'The bearers will skirt the hill and then turn south along the bank of the Tiber for it is easier than the way we are going, over the hill itself. Then it is straight south into Marmorata which lies over there along the banks of the Tiber where the ships anchor.'

The carriage continued its rapid progress upwards but moving across the northern shoulder of the hill of Aventinus towards a small exquisite basilica. Here Licinius halted, for the basilica overlooked the broad tawny stretch which was the ancient river Tiber, sedately pushing its way through the north of the city along its western border and south to empty into the Mediterranean between the twin ports of Ostia and Porto.

Licinius climbed down and went to a low wall beyond which the ground fell rapidly down to the stretch of land which separated the base of the hill from the river itself.

'Any sign?' called Eadulf, moving gingerly from his position and stretching his cramped limbs.

Furius Licinius shook his head.

'Can we have missed them?' Fidelma asked anxiously, also taking the opportunity to stretch herself.

'Not unless Puttoc has changed his mind about his destination,' Licinius replied confidently. Fidelma stood and peered around the small square in which they had halted. Her gaze turned to the little basilica with appreciative eyes. She had to admit that there were many beautiful little churches in Rome. She never ceased to admire the embellishments of nature that surrounded the Roman houses, and budding blossom, scented flowers and shrubberies, with streets twisting through deep evergreen groves of the ilex, laurel and cypress whose tall spiral forms rose above all other trees and contrasted with the drooping, pale weeping willows. This hill of Aventinus seem to excel more than the other areas of Rome, bathing in the bright gold rays of the sun which blazed from the deep blue skies. Nothing, she felt, could be more in harmony than the grandeur of the buildings and memorials with the luxuriant motionless beauty of sunbaked nature.

Furius Licinius gave an abrupt cry.

'There is Puttoc's *lecticula* now! Come on, we can cut them off before they enter Marmorata.'

'No!' Fidelma halted him, as he clambered back into the carriage. 'I do not want Puttoc to know we are following him.'

Licinius paused and looked bewildered.

'What then, sister?'

'Keep him in sight and see where he goes,' Fidelma replied. 'If he makes contact with the Arabians then we may be able to spring a trap.'

The young *tesserarius*' eyes lightened as he saw Fidelma's plan and he grinned.

'Get up then, we will follow them along the hillside here and then fall in behind as they enter the *emporia* area.'

'*Emporia*?' queried Eadulf, reluctantly scrambling back into the carriage and gripping the side.

'Yes. We call it the place of trade, it is a market around which Marmorata has spread, but only slaves are sent there to conduct business for it is not an area that people of good quality go willingly to,' explained Licinius.

He urged the horse forward and the beast trotted gently down the southern slopes of the hill. They could see below them the two burly *lecticula* bearers carrying the ornate chair in which the recognisable form of the Abbot Puttoc was slouched. The bearers seemed untired by their long trek across the city.

Fidelma could see now how the buildings were changing character. The stucco opulence was now giving way to shacks of rotting wood with the occasional stone-built construction. Gradually, the grandeur vanished and she realised with some surprise that the colours of the city had become dowdy and dull. A moment ago she was basking in the beauty of the city but now . . .

The day appeared to grow abruptly dark, grey and brooding.

Licinius suddenly halted the carriage at a cross road.

Fidelma was about to ask him why when the *lecticula* came into sight, the bearers trotting at right angles to them across the road.

After a moment or two Licinius flicked his whip over the head of his horse, setting the beast into motion, turning the carriage after the *lecticula.*

Fidelma was aware of a tang in the air which scent informed her of the nearness of a river. It was soon mixed with putrid odours which caused her to wrinkle her nose in distaste.

'This is Marmorata,' grunted Furius Licinius unnecessarily.

They were in an area of dark, narrow streets. People pushed this way and that in all manner of costumes which marked them as strangers from every corner of the world, even if their voices had not proclaimed their foreign origins.

Eadulf grinned across at Fidelma and gestured at the noise of the many languages about them.

' "Go to, let us go down, and there confound their language, that they may not understand one another's speech," ' he quoted unctuously.

'Indeed,' replied Fidelma seriously, 'as Genesis relates, it was God who created all the languages of the world by scattering the people of Shem and languages have become the pedigrees of our nations.'

The smells were pretty vile as they followed the narrow slum roads into a large covered market area which was hot and noisy and oppressive. Dirty stalls and houses peopled by brawling men and women and screaming children lined the road which was now no more than an alleyway. Women and men mauled each other in half-drunken caresses as they spilled from taverns; caresses which brought the blood to tinge Fidelma's cheeks. From the sewer-like gutters, a murky torrent of animal and vegetable offal in every state of putrefaction spread itself with loathsome vapours.

Furius Licinius halted his carriage. Through the stalls and make-shift shelters they could see the *lecticula* had halted and the tall figure of the Abbot Puttoc had descended. He tossed a coin to the bearers and said something. He then turned and made his way into a nearby building.

Fidelma saw the bearers grin at one another and go into a nearby enclosure, leaving their *lecticula* outside. There were chairs and tables in front of this building and it was obvious that the place was a *caupona*, a cheap tavern of sorts. The bearers, free from their labours, sprawled in chairs and called for drinks.

'Look!' whispered Eadulf.

A short man in flowing robes which almost covered his head and a bushy black beard was walking rapidly through the crowd towards the building into which Puttoc had disappeared. He paused outside and peered suspiciously around. Then, seeming to assure himself that he was not being observed by anyone in particular, he pushed swiftly into the building.

'Is he an Arabian?' Fidelma asked Furius Licinius.

The *tesserarius* grimly affirmed it.

'If there is war between you people, why are they allowed to come to Rome?' demanded Eadulf.

'The war is only with those that follow the new prophet,

Mahomet,' replied Licinius. 'There are many Arabians who have not been converted by the new faith. We have traded with these eastern merchants for many years and the practice continues.'

Fidelma was examining the rambling building into which Puttoc and now the Arabian had disappeared. One of the few stone structures in the area, it rose two storeys in height and all its windows were shuttered, each shutter drawn so that no one could peer inside. It had probably been a wealthy villa before the shanty town had grown up around it, a once attractive building on the banks of the winding Tiber.

'Do you know this building, Licinius?'

The young *custos* shook his head vigorously.

'I do not frequent this area of the city, sister,' he said, a little irritated by the implication which he saw in her question.

'I did not ask that,' Fidelma responded firmly. 'I asked whether you had any idea what the building is – whether it is owned by the merchants?'

Furius Licinius answered negatively.

'Look!' hissed Eadulf abruptly.

He pointed to the second floor of the building, to a window at the extreme right of the frontage.

Fidelma sucked in her breath.

The Abbot Puttoc, for clearly it was he, was leaning out to open the shutter a little. It was a momentary appearance.

'Well, at least we know which room Puttoc is in,' she muttered.

'What do we do now?' asked Licinius.

'Knowing Puttoc is there and the Arabian has gone in, I suggest we simply go in and confront our friend, the Abbot of Stanggrund.'

Furius Licinius grinned broadly and dropped his hand to his

gladius, easing it in its scabbard. This was the sort of action he liked, he could understand this, not all that questioning and intellectualising.

They clambered out of the carriage.

Licinius looked around and chose an evil-looking, pock-marked individual who was passing by. He was a burly man, the sort few people would think of starting an argument with.

'You, what is your name?'

The heavy man halted and blinked at being so addressed by a youth, albeit a youth dressed as an officer of the *custodes*.

'I am called Nabor,' he replied in a growling voice.

'Well, Nabor,' relied Licinius, unperturbed by the man's threatening appearance, 'I need you to stand guard over this horse and carriage. If I return and it is here with you still guarding it, then you will receive a *sestertius*. If I return and it is gone, then I will come looking for you with my *gladius*.'

The man named Nabor stared at the youthful officer and his twisted features slowly broke into a grin.

'A *sestertius* will be more welcome than your *gladius*, young one. I'll be here.'

They left him standing by the carriage chuckling to himself at the idea of earning such easy money.

Fidelma cast an appraising glance at Licinius. The young man could be quick-witted at times. She had not considered the fact that leaving the carriage unattended in this quarter would immediately lead to its disappearance. Horses and carriages were valuable commodities in Rome and this was certainly not the place to leave one without a guard.

Fidelma led the way through the market area, pushing through the disinterested crowds, followed by Eadulf and

Licinius. She paused on the steps of the building to gather herself.

'We will head straight to the room in which we saw the abbot. With luck we might find ourselves solving this mystery now.'

She turned and pushed into the building. For a moment she paused to cough in the musty, stygian gloom. With the windows shuttered, the large hall in which they found themselves was dark and only a solitary candle burning on a centre table gave a flickering light. Around the room incense burners smoked, giving an overpowering smell of some fragrance which she could not identify. The odour was quite overwhelming.

There came a squeak of a floorboard and Fidelma turned quickly as through a doorway a large, round-faced woman emerged, rubbing her hands on her short apron. The woman wore a coarse dress and her hair was awry and clearly not combed or dressed. She halted and her eyes widened in momentary astonishment as she saw them and recognised their calling. Her tone when she spoke was belligerent.

'What the devil do you want?' she demanded in a high-pitched voice full of the slang of the Roman streets. 'We do not welcome people of your cloth in here.'

'We want to come in,' replied Fidelma calmly moving forward.

To her surprise, the woman let out a raucous screech and, with hands flailing before her, she launched herself at Fidelma. Fidelma's surprise only lasted a moment. Ignoring Licinius' warning cry to stand aside, she balanced herself on her feet and reached out to meet the woman's tearing claws. Licinius and Eadulf stared in amazement as, without seeming to move at all, Fidelma pulled the woman past her, using her assailant's own momentum, and threw her stumbling against the wall behind.

The collision was a resounding noise of flesh and bone meeting wood at a high velocity.

Even so, the big woman kept her balance and turned with a puzzled expression on her fleshy features. Then she shook her head and snarled.

'Bitch!' she swore with deep vehemence.

Licinius again went to move forward, his *gladius* now drawn, but Fidelma waved him aside and stood ready to meet the charging woman. Again it seemed as if she merely reached out, caught the flailing arms and heaved her assailant into the air, over her hip and sent her cannoning into the wall on the other side of the room. This time the head met a thick wooden post and, with a grunt, the woman slid to the floor unconscious.

Fidelma turned and bent over her, her slender fingers feeling for the pulse and checking the woman's wound.

She stood up without expression.

'She'll be all right,' she announced in relief.

Furius Licinius was gazing at her with open admiration.

'Truly, I have never seen Roman soldiers do better in combat,' he said. 'How could you do such a thing?'

'It is of no importance,' Fidelma was dismissive of her prowess. 'In my country there were once learned men who taught the ancient philosophies of our people. They journeyed far and wide and were subject to attack by thieves and bandits. But, as they believed it was wrong to carry arms to protect themselves, they were forced to develop a technique called *troid-sciathaigid* – battle through defence. I was taught the method of defending myself without the use of weapons when I was young as, indeed, many of our religious missionaries are so taught.'

She pushed through the door leaving them to follow her.

There was a staircase beyond. She paused on the bottom step and listened. She could hear voices; oddly, she thought that she heard the sound of young girls' laughter. But there were no sounds of an alarm being raised. No one had heard the commotion of their entry. She turned and whispered: 'The end room to the right of the building. Come.'

She ascended the stairs rapidly. At the top was a long corridor. There were no difficulties in identifying the door which would give entrance on to the room they sought.

Outside she paused again and listened. Again she thought she heard young girls' laughter from beyond. She glanced at her companions, they nodded that they were ready and she let her hand drop to the handle of the door, turning it slowly and silently pushing the door open.

The scene beyond startled even her.

The room was light for, as they had seen from below, Abbot Puttoc had opened one of the shutters causing the light of the day to stream in. In one corner there was a bed on which were stretched stained but freshly laundered linen sheets. There were a few chairs but the only other piece of furniture was a large wooden tub alongside which were several empty pails. The hot water they had once held was now steaming in the tub.

In the tub sat a surprised Abbot Puttoc, naked so far as she could tell. Seated crossways, on his lap, was an equally surprised and naked girl of no more than sixteen years. They were frozen in an embrace which left nothing to the imagination. Behind them, pail of steaming water in her hand, frozen in the action of pouring it over the occupants of the large tub, was another naked young girl.

Fidelma surveyed the scene with a grim countenance. She took a step forward into the chamber and glanced about to assure herself that the sight which met her eyes was not encumbered by any other interpretation. The abbot's robes lay stretched on the chair at the end of the bed. Other robes, which obviously belonged to the young girls, lay nearby.

She turned back to the still startled abbot with a sarcastic raised eyebrow.

'Well, Abbot Puttoc?' She could not keep the bleak humour out of her voice.

The girl seated in the tub moved first. She clambered out letting water cascade all over the place. Not that she acted with modesty for she now stood, hands on hips, letting forth a voluble stream of abuse at Fidelma. Her companion, dropping her bucket, joined in, moving forward threateningly.

It was Furius Licinius, finally, who silenced them by shouting over them and reinforcing his argument with the jabbing point of his sword. Muttering under their breath the girls backed off gazing at the newcomers with hatred.

Puttoc sat still, with taut, whitened features, his ice-blue eyes staring with an incredible malignancy from Fidelma to Eadulf.

Furius Licinius continued to exchange a few words with the girls in the harsh accents of the Roman streets. Then he turned to Fidelma with a look of embarrassment.

'This place is a *bordellum*, sister, a place where . . .'

Fidelma decided to put the young man out of his confusion.

'I am perfectly aware of what happens in a brothel, Licinius,' she said solemnly. 'What I want to know is what an abbot of the holy church is doing here?'

Abbot Puttoc sat in the tub with an almost resigned expression on his handsome features.

'I doubt that I have to explain it in detail, Fidelma of Kildare,' he replied sourly.

She grimaced.

'Perhaps you are right.'

'I presume that you will report this matter to Bishop Gelasius, Eadulf of Canterbury?' Puttoc directed his next question to the Saxon brother.

Eadulf was totally disapproving.

'I would not have expected you to have raised such a question,' he replied dryly. 'You know the rules by which we live. You will doubtless be expected to resign your office. Penance must follow.'

Puttoc took a deep, noisy breath through his nostrils. He gazed speculatively from Licinius to Fidelma and then to Eadulf.

'Can't we discuss this matter in more conducive surroundings?'

'Conducive to what end, Puttoc?' queried Fidelma. 'No, I think there is little we can discuss about this matter that might alter our attitudes and intentions. But you could tell me this, did you come here merely to pursue your carnal inclinations or to meet someone as well?'

Puttoc did not understand.

'Meet someone? Whom do you mean?'

'You have no liaison with any Arabian merchants?'

She could not doubt the genuine look of bewilderment that came into his face.

'I do not understand you, sister?'

Fidelma did not attempt to explain further. Her shoulders slumped a little as she realised that her intuition had failed her and that she had led her companions on a wild goose chase. Puttoc was guilty, but not, apparently, of anything more damning to his soul than attempting to satiate his lascivious passions.

'We'll leave you to your desires, Puttoc,' she said. 'And to the price which you must pay for them.'

The abbot reached forward a hand as if he would stay her.

Eadulf gave him a withering glance before he followed Fidelma out of the room while Furius Licinius, sheathing his *gladius*, allowed himself to grin lewdly at the prelate before he trailed after them.

In the hallway below the big, fleshy woman was groaning and coming to.

Fidelma paused and sighed. She fished into her *marsupium* and extracted a small coin which she placed on the table.

'I am sorry for your injury,' she said simply to the still stupefied woman.

Outside Nabor, the ugly-faced man, stood by the carriage and watched their approach with interest.

'A *sestertius*, young *custos*,' he grunted, and then with a lecherous grin, he added: 'If I'd known it was that building which you wanted to visit, I could have recommended several better establishments . . .'

Colouring, Furius Licinius threw him the coin, which Nabor caught deftly. Without a word the young officer climbed into the carriage.

No one said anything as Licinius drove them back alongside the Tiber, turning through the Valle Murcia and eastward towards the Lateran Palace.

The *decurion* Marcus Narses was waiting on the steps of the palace as Licinius halted. He came running down to the carriage.

'Sister, I have news of the Brother Osimo Lando,' he gasped.

'Good,' Fidelma replied as she climbed out. At least she could now pursue a more positive lead about Ronan Ragallach's connections. 'Why was Osimo Lando absent from his work this afternoon? Is he ill?'

Marcus Narses shook his head, his expression serious. She knew what he was going to say even before he uttered the words.

'I regret, sister, Brother Osimo is dead.'

'Dead?' The word shot from Eadulf's mouth in a sharp exclamation of surprise.

'Garrotted?' Fidelma inquired calmly.

'No, sister. A short while ago he leapt from the aqueduct, the Aqua Claudia, and fell into the stone street below. He was killed outright.'

Chapter Fourteen

'Suicide?' Fidelma was gazing with a dubious expression at the young Furius Licinius. 'Are you sure?'

'There is no doubt,' affirmed Licinius. 'Osimo Lando was seen by several people as he climbed along the aqueduct and was then seen to cast himself down into the street below.'

Fidelma sat for a moment, her head bowed in thought. Rather than clarify anything, Brother Osimo Lando's death only obscured it.

She and Eadulf were seated in the offices of the *Munera Peregrinitatis* of the Lateran Palace where Osimo and Ronan had worked. Licinius had been despatched to gather details of Osimo's death while Fidelma and Eadulf had searched the office. There was nothing that gave any indication of Ronan Ragallach's links to Arabians. In fact, at his desk, there were only some odd notes and an ancient Greek book which was a medical tract. The work was obviously valuable for Ronan had carefully wrapped it in sacking and placed it at the bottom of a stack of papers so that it would not be disturbed. But apart from that there was little else except ledgers of correspondence from the many churches among the North Africans which looked to Rome for guidance.

Eadulf looked gloomy.

'Could Osimo Lando have killed himself in a fit of remorse for slaying Ronan?' There was no conviction in his voice as he put forward the proposal.

Fidelma did not even bother to answer. 'We should examine Brother Osimo Lando's lodgings. Did he live within the palace?'

Licinius shook his head.

'He stayed in the same lodging house as Ronan Ragallach. In the hostel of the deacon Bieda.'

'Ah, of course,' Fidelma sighed. 'I should have guessed. Let us go then. Perhaps we may find some clue to this mystery there.'

Furius Licinius took them by a short cut through the Lateran buildings this time. The offices of the *Munera Peregrinitatis* were on the top floor of a two-storey building and, instead of making his way down the marble stairs into the courtyard, Licinius led them through a door on to a wooden walkway which led from one building to another. The walkway spanned a courtyard to the edifice which Licinius had previously pointed out as the *Scala Santa*, housing the reconstruction of the holy staircase where Christ had descended from the judgment seat of Pilate.

It was Fidelma who found time from her cogitation to pause and ask about it, to the surprise of her companions. Eadulf sometimes found Fidelma's attitude to timekeeping curious. But many of her countrymen seemed to set little store by the urgency of time.

'The actual *Sancta Sanctorum* is in the centre of the building,' replied Licinius, as they paused on the walkway to look at it. 'The way is barred against us by a gate. I am taking you via another walkway from that building into the chapel devoted to the Blessed Helena and from the chapel we can go directly out of the palace grounds near to the Aqueduct of Claudia. It is a quick route to Bieda's hostel.'

Fidelma gazed thoughtfully at the building.

'Why is this holy place barred to us?' she asked.

'It contains a dark room with one iron grating for a window. But no women,' he laid emphasis on the word, 'are ever admitted to it. There is a holy altar there where not even the Holy Father may perform the mass.' Fidelma smiled thinly.

'Indeed? Then such an altar can serve no purpose.'

Furius Licinius looked outraged for a moment. Then he found himself shrugging in agreement. An altar where not even His Holiness could perform a mass was logically useless. He continued to conduct them in silence along the wooden walkway which turned at right angles from the building holding the *Sancta Sanctorum* and crossed another courtyard one storey above the ground into a small chapel.

'Here is the chapel of the Blessed Helena, mother of Constantine, who collected the holy relics which are displayed here for the veneration of pilgrims,' Furius Licinius explained.

The walkway ended at a door which was secured on the outside by a bored-looking member of the palace *custodes*. He respectfully saluted Licinius and bent to unlock the door and let them inside.

They entered the chapel on to a wooden gallery, high above the mosaic floor of the circular building. The sound of whispering echoed around its dark, vault-like interior. It was an intense sound which caused Fidelma to reach forward and grip Furius Licinius' arm to halt him. She gestured him and Eadulf to silence. Frowning, she went to the edge of the wooden gallery rail overlooking the main floor of the chapel and the tables displaying the holy relics for the examination of pilgrims.

Almost immediately below them stood two figures. A slightly stooping religieuse but with the appearance of no great age and the upright figure of a cenobite. They seemed locked in an intense and intimate conversation. The woman was doing most of the talking while the man stood merely nodding. Fidelma did not know what had made her signal to her companions to remain quiet and not reveal their presence in the chapel. There was something familiar in the whispering voices and now that familiarity was endorsed by the figures themselves. She stared down quizzically, trying to pick up the words but the whispering echoes distorted them and rendered them unintelligible.

Then, to her surprise, the religieuse suddenly reached up and embraced the man, kissing him on the cheek before leaving hurriedly.

Fidelma's eyes widened abruptly.

The light now fell on the man. It was the softly spoken and ingenuous Brother Eanred.

After the chapel door had closed on them, Licinius turned to Fidelma. His smile was slightly cynical.

'Liaison between religious, while not encouraged, is still not forbidden here, sister,' he observed.

Fidelma did not say anything. Licinius was already leading the way down a short spiral staircase from the wooden gallery into the main chapel. It was now deserted. Licinius proudly pointed to the relics as they passed by. Most of the items were laid out in reliquary boxes. Some of them were closed. Licinius began a commentary as they passed between the tables containing the boxes.

'In there is a lock of the Virgin Mary's hair and a piece of her petticoat. That is a robe of Jesus sprinkled with his blood. That phial there has drops of his blood in it and in the other is some of the water which flowed from the wound in his side.'

Fidelma cast a distrustful glance at them.

'And that old piece of sponge?' She nodded to an opened reliquary whose only content seemed a disintegrating piece of fibrous material which Fidelma identified as porous aquatic growth used for swabbing liquids.

'The very sponge which was soaked in vinegar and given to Him on the cross,' replied Licinius reverently. 'And here is the table at which our Saviour ate the last supper . . .'

Fidelma smiled cynically.

'Then it was more miracle than I had allowed for only two people could sit at this table let alone twelve apostles and the Christ.'

Licinius was oblivious to her doubt.

'And what are those stones?' inquired Fidelma, pointing to the small altar which was flanked by some rock-hewn pieces.

Encouraged, Licinius said: 'The left one is a piece of stone of the holy sepulchre while the other is the identical porphyry pillar on which the cock was perched when it crowed after Peter had denied Christ.'

'And all these things the blessed Helena collected and brought back to Rome?' asked Fidelma doubtfully.

Licinius nodded, pointing, 'These towels she found here in the city; the very towels with which the angels wiped the face of the blessed martyr Lawrence when he was boiling on the gridiron. And those are the rods of Moses and of Aaron . . .'

'How did Helena know these relics were genuine?' Fidelma interrupted, irritated by the idea that these objections of veneration, which attracted adoring pilgrims from the four corners of the world, were nothing more than a clever confidence trick by an adroit merchant.

Licinius gaped at her. No one had dared to ask such a question before.

'It strikes me,' went on Fidelma, 'that Helena was a pilgrim in a strange land and when the merchants of that land heard that she was looking for holy relics they found things for her, having first ascertained that she was willing to pay, of course.'

'That is a sacrilege!' Licinius protested indignantly. 'Christ was with her to protect the blessed Helena against such charlatans! Are you saying that Helena was tricked and deceived by cunning merchants and these are worthless?'

'I have been in Rome just over a week and I have seen similar relics being sold to credulous pilgrims by the score, all willing to part with money for a piece of the genuine chain worn by St Peter! And all these relics, we are told, are genuine. I tell you, Licinius, if all the wood of the true cross now being sold in Rome were put together it would form the most miraculous and largest cross you ever saw.'

Eadulf caught her by the sleeve and cautioned her with his eyes to be more prudent with her scepticism.

Licinius continued to be outraged.

'All these items were authenticated by the blessed Helena,' he protested.

'I do not doubt it,' replied Fidelma confidently.

'We have little time to dwell on these matters at the moment,' interrupted Eadulf with concern. 'We can return here another time and debate the journey of Helena to the Holy Land.'

The young *tesserarius* bit his lip and then suppressed his annoyance with a single great intake of breath, continuing to lead the way through the chapel to the side gate in the wall surrounding the Lateran Palace. It brought them out directly opposite to the great aqueduct of Claudia.

The same sluttish woman met them at the entrance of the dingy hostel owned by the deacon Bieda, near the Aqua Claudia and, again, a torrent of abuse sprang from her lips.

'How is one to live when you are causing all my lodgers to be killed off and when you then forbid me to let their rooms? Where is my rent, where is my living?'

Furius Licinius replied roughly to her and the woman disappeared with a muttered curse into a side room, having yielded to Licinius' order to point the way to Osimo Lando's room. Fidelma was not surprised to see that it was opposite Ronan's room but kept with more neatness than the Irish brother's dwelling. Though it was as dark and as dingy, Osimo Lando had tried to make the best of it. There was even a vase of dying flowers in a corner of the room and, framed above the bed, were some Greek words which brought a smile to Fidelma's lips. Obviously, Brother Osimo Lando had possessed a sense of humour. The lines were from Psalm 84, verse 4: 'Blessed are they that dwell in thy house: they will be still praising thee.'

She wondered what praise the tenants of this hostel could have for the terrible conditions and the manner of the slatternly woman who ran it.

'What are we looking for?' demanded Licinius, as he stood by the door watching her.

'I am not quite sure,' Fidelma admitted.

'Osimo was well read,' grunted Eadulf, opening a cupboard. 'Look here.'

Fidelma's eyes widened a little as she saw two books on the shelf with some written papers.

'They are old texts,' she said, taking one of the books and peering at its title. 'Look at this, *De Acerba Tuens*. This is a study by Erasistratus of Ceos.'

'I have heard briefly of it,' Eadulf confessed with some surprise. 'But it was supposed to have been lost during the great destruction of the library of Alexandria in the time of Julius Caesar.'

'These books ought to be removed to a place of safekeeping,' Fidelma suggested.

'I will see to it,' Licinius said stiffly. He was obviously still thinking about the slight to the memory of the blessed Helena.

Fidelma continued to shuffle through the papers. It was obvious that Osimo and Ronan had formed a close relationship. The writings were poetry, concerned with love and fealty mostly written by Osimo and dedicated to Ronan. There was little reason to question that Osimo, hearing of Ronan's death, could not bear to be in this world without him. Fidelma felt sad for them both.

'Let everything you do be done in love,' she whispered, gazing at the sheets of poetry.

Eadulf frowned.

'What did you say?'

Fidelma smiled and shook her head. 'I was just thinking of a line from Paul's epistle to the Corinthians.'

Eadulf gazed at her a moment more in bemusement then, understanding, he resumed his examination of the room.

'There is little more here, Fidelma,' he said. 'Nothing to throw any light on our mystery.'

'Could Osimo have been involved in the death of Ronan?' Licinius asked mystified.

'Not as a culprit,' Fidelma assured him. She was about

to say that they could do no more when something caught her eye.

'What is that, Eadulf?' she asked, pointing.

The Saxon looked in the direction to which she indicated. It was an object on the floor half hidden by the rough wooden cot. He bent to retrieve it.

As he examined it, he let out an exclamation of astonishment.

'It's a broken base from a golden chalice. I recognise it. This was the chalice which Cenewealh of the West Saxons gave to Wighard to have blessed by His Holiness. See the inscription on the base?'

' "*Spero meliora*" ', read Fidelma. ' "I hope for better things." '

'Cenewealh asked Wighard to choose a suitable motto to engrave on his chalice. The top part has become broken off by ill use but I recognise it.'

Licinius was looking more perplexed.

'So the valuables of Wighard were kept in this room? Were Osimo and Ronan partners in this crime?'

Fidelma chewed thoughtfully on her lower lip. She was falling into this unconscious habit and it annoyed her every time she realised she was doing it. She stopped and compressed her lips for a moment.

'Ronan and Osimo certainly had access to the stolen treasure of Wighard,' she admitted.

'So they must have been party to the killing,' exclaimed Eadulf, leaping to a conclusion.

'There is something strange . . .' Fidelma seemed still lost in thought. Then she drew herself up. 'We can do no more here. Licinius, bring those books with you. And, Eadulf, take care of that metal base. There is much to be thought over.'

Eadulf exchanged a puzzled look with Licinius and then shrugged.

Downstairs the woman accosted them again.

'When am I able to offer these rooms again to pilgrims? It is not my fault that these guests have died. Am I to be penalised?'

'Another day or two, woman,' Furius Licinius assured her.

The woman grunted in disgust. Then said: 'I see that you are removing belongings that rightfully should come to me in distraint.'

Fidelma stared at the woman's unexpected use of the Latin law term *bonorum veditio*.

'Have you had many guests whose goods you have had to seize for non payment of their rent?' she asked.

The woman strained to understand her carefully articulated but foreigner's Latin.

She pursed her thin lips and shook her head.

'Never. My guests have always paid.'

'So where did you learn this phrase . . . *bonorum veditio*?'

The slatternly woman frowned.

'What's that to do with you? I know my rights in law.'

Licinius scowled. 'You have only the rights that I say you have,' he said threateningly. 'Speak civilly, and answer the question. How did you learn such a technical phrase?'

The woman cowered fearfully before his angry tone.

'It is true,' she whined. 'The Greek said those are my rights and at least he gave me a coin when he removed the sack from the dead brother's room.'

She had Fidelma's full attention now.

'A Greek? Whose room did he remove a sack from?'

The woman blinked realising that she had said more than she should have.

'Out with it, woman,' snapped Licinius. 'Otherwise it will be the cells for you and it will be a long while before you will be able to discuss your rights again.'

The woman trembled slightly.

'Why . . . why, he searched Osimo Lando's room and left with a sack.'

'A Greek, you say?' pressed Licinius. 'The owner of this hostel, you mean? The Greek deacon Bieda? Did you not tell him of the order not to remove anything until he has our permission?'

'No, no,' the woman replied rapidly with a shake of her head. 'I do not mean that bastard Bieda. I mean the Greek physician from the Lateran. Everyone knows him.'

Fidelma felt her body pushed back in involuntary surprise.

'The Greek physician from the Lateran? Do you mean Cornelius? Cornelius of Alexandria?'

'The same,' affirmed the woman with a defensive scowl. 'He told me of my rights.'

'When did he come and search Osimo Lando's room?' Fidelma demanded.

'Scarcely an hour ago.'

'As soon as he heard of Osimo's suicide, I'll warrant,' Eadulf offered.

'And when he left the room, he was carrying a sack?'

The woman nodded unhappily.

'What size sack? Large or small?'

'A medium-sized sack. I'd say there was metal in it, for it clanked as he walked,' offered the woman, anxious now to restore herself to grace in their eyes. 'He told me that he would give me five *sesterius* if I would go to Osimo Lando's room and take the five books that I would find and hide them in my room until he was able to return for them. I had removed three of them when you arrived. You have the other two.'

'Why would he do that?' asked Fidelma.

'Because he could not carry the books as well as the sack,' replied the woman, misunderstanding her question.

Fidelma was about to open her mouth to explain her question when Eadulf broke in triumphantly: 'So Cornelius was part of this murder and theft all along?'

'We shall see,' Fidelma replied. 'Fetch the three books which you took from Osimo Lando's room, woman.'

Reluctantly the woman did as she was bid. They were old books. Greek books. And they were, as Fidelma suspected, easily identifiable as medical texts. She shook her head in bewilderment. The path to Wighard's murderer seemed strewn with ancient Greek medical texts.

'Do you know where Cornelius lives?' Fidelma asked Licinius.

'Yes. He has a small villa near the Arch of Dolabella and Silanus. Shall I alert the *custodes*?'

'No. We are a long way from unravelling this mystery yet, Licinius. After we have stored our finds in a place of safety in our *officium*, we will go to Cornelius' villa and see what he has to say about this matter.'

The woman was gazing from one to the other, trying to follow the meaning of their exchange.

'What of me?' she demanded, a little more assertively now that she knew she was not immediately being marched off to prison as Licinius had asserted.

'You mind your tongue,' Licinius snapped. 'And if I come

back and find anything else disturbed in the rooms of Ronan and Osimo, even so much as a hair missing from a blanket or a cockroach from the wall, I will ensure that you will not have to worry about collecting your rents ever again. You will be living rent free from the rest of your life in the worst prison I can find for you. Is that understood?'

The woman muttered something inaudible and withdrew into her own room.

Outside Fidelma rebuked him gently: 'You were unduly harsh on her.'

Licinius scowled.

'It is the only way to treat such as she. All they want, these peasants, is to get as much money as they can in life.'

'It is surely the only way they can escape from their poverty,' Fidelma pointed out. 'Their rulers have shown them that salvation comes only by the acquisition of wealth. Why criticise them for following this example until a better example is provided?'

Licinius was disapproving.

'I have heard that you Irish hold to such radical notions. Was this the teaching of the heretic Pelagius?'

'I thought we held only to the teachings of our Lord Christ. "And he said unto them, Take heed, and beware of covetousness; for a man's life consisteth not in the abundance of the things which he possesseth." That is the word of our Lord, according to Luke.'

Licinius flushed and Eadulf, sensing his awkwardness, pushed forward.

'Let us hurry and get these books to the *officium*, then we can go in search of Cornelius.'

'Yes. We must keep them safe,' agreed Fidelma, 'for I have

a feeling that they are a considerable part of this mystery.'

They both stared at her for a moment but she did not make any amplification.

The villa of Cornelius of Alexandria was not very far away on the Hill of Caelius where the emperor Nero had once converted the single ancient arch dedicated to Dolabella and Silanus to build an aqueduct to the neighbouring Palatine Hill. The northern slopes of the hill overlooked the spectacular Colosseum and Cornelius's villa looked out across a small valley to the Palatine Hill with all its ancient and spectacular buildings. Eadulf had told Fidelma that this four-sided Palatine hill was where the first city of Rome had arisen. Here was where all the prominent citizens of the republic had lived and, later, where the despotic Caesars had built their gaudy palaces; where the Ostrogoth kings had ruled and where now Christian churches were replacing their pagan temples.

'How do you propose to approach Cornelius?' demanded Eadulf as Furius Licinius, still a little surly, pointed out the villa.

Fidelma hesitated. In truth she had no idea. In fact, secretly she was regretting her impulse to rush upon Cornelius' villa without a *decuria* of the palace guards as suggested by Licinius. Dusk was creeping westward over the city. She should have simply sent the *custodes* to bring Cornelius to her at the *officium* for questioning. But there were still many things which she could not understand. Each step forward seemed to raise half-a-dozen new questions.

'Well?' prompted Eadulf.

The matter resolved itself even before she opened her mouth in response.

They were standing at a corner on the opposite side of the

street to the villa walls. About ten metres beyond them were the wooden gates leading into the villa's gardens. Clearly, Cornelius of Alexandria lived well. Now these were suddenly thrown open and two bearers carrying a *lecticula* trotted through. Fidelma, Eadulf and Licinius automatically pressed back into the shadows. Cornelius himself was reclining in the chair and, conspicuously on his lap, there was a sack.

The bearers trotted westward from the villa down the hill towards a beautifully built church standing at its foot.

'He's taking the sack somewhere,' Fidelma observed unnecessarily. 'We will follow.'

They had to walk rapidly to keep up with the trotting *lecticula* bearers. Now and again they even had to break into an undignified trot themselves in order to keep up. For all the hair-raising manoeuvring of the carriage, Fidelma wished they still had the single horse cart to pursue their quarry. They crossed the small square in front of the church and came to the bottom of the Palatine Hill.

Cornelius' bearers were now moving rapidly along the roadway running along the valley floor which went on the eastern side of a spectacular building which seemed to go on forever.

'What is this place?' demanded Fidelma, as they breathlessly sought to keep pace.

'The Circus Maximus,' grunted Licinius. 'A site of much martyrdom in the days of the imperial Caesars.'

They confined their breath now to keeping up with the *lecticula* ahead. It moved along the apparently endless wall, skirted the disused circus and headed north towards the River Tiber. Then it made an abrupt turn, round the bottom of the Hill of Aventinus and turning south-west. Fidelma could not believe that two men carrying a third man in a weighty wooden vehicle, however strong, could move so rapidly and with such ease. It was exhausting to keep up with the trained chair bearers. Fidelma observed that they would walk rapidly for a while and then, at the instruction of the man at the rear of the chair, they would begin to trot. In such a manner they followed the bank of the river with its shanty houses, quays and store houses.

Furius Licinius suddenly stumbled in the darkness and swore.

Eadulf reached forward to help the young *tesserarius* back to his feet.

'You may halt a moment,' gasped Fidelma. 'Look, the *lecticula* has stopped.'

Licinius bit his lip and looked around in the gloom. He eased his sword in its scabbard.

'And in the worst place. We've come back to Marmorata.'

Fidelma had seen enough to realise that Cornelius' journey had indeed returned them to the same area of the city to which they had followed Puttoc only a few hours before. Dusk was rapidly spreading itself over the slum area.

Fidelma sucked in a disgusted breath as the loathsome smells of the slum and its festering sewerage assailed her nostrils. They were in a dark and threatening area of decaying buildings. Dogs and cats were roaming the streets searching for food in the form of offal and other discarded matter.

Cornelius' *lecticula* had halted outside what seemed to be an ancient storehouse backing on to the rough wooden quays that ran alongside the river. The bearers had put down the chair and were lounging against it, though Fidelma noticed that they were not so oblivious to their surroundings to remove their hands from the knives they wore in their belts.

Fidelma, Eadulf and Licinius were watching them for many minutes before Fidelma suddenly exclaimed softly. Cornelius had already left the *lecticula* and disappeared.

'He must have gone into the storehouse,' Eadulf suggested when Fidelma pointed out that he had vanished.

'It is obvious that his bearers are waiting to pick him up again,' Licinius observed optimistically.

Fidelma found herself chewing her lip.

'Whoever he is meeting, he is meeting them in that storehouse.' She made up her mind quickly. 'Licinius, you go to the front of the storehouse and wait. Will the *lecticula* bearers be a problem?'

Licinius shook his head.

'They will have respect for my uniform.'

'Very well. If you hear me call for help, come immediately. If they try to prevent you, you must use your weapon. Eadulf, you will come with me now.'

Eadulf was puzzled.

'Where to?' he demanded.

'The storehouse backs on to the river. There is a wooden quay just there. You can see it in the moonlight through that passage along the side of the building. We will make our way down and enter the storehouse from that direction. My aim is to see what Cornelius is involved in.'

Fidelma began to put her instructions into action and moved quickly down the alley with Eadulf trailing behind. Licinius watched them go with some surprise at Eadulf's meekness in taking orders from a woman. Then he loosened his *gladius* and sauntered towards the *lecticula*.

The bearers stiffened at his approach. One of them had lit a lantern in preparation for the journey back. But when they saw his uniform they seemed to relax. Obviously, thought Licinius, they did not appear aware of any wrong doing on the part of their master.

Meanwhile, Fidelma and Eadulf crept cautiously along the side of the wooden storehouse and on to the quay.

They could already hear voices, tense and argumentative.

Fidelma eased her way over the wooden boards of the quay, thankful for the noisy slap of river against the wooden supports of the quay which seemed to deaden the sound of their approach.

She paused at the door which, to her surprise, was ajar. From inside the voices rose and fell in apparent altercation. The language was totally strange to her and she looked through the gloom to Eadulf and gave an exaggerated shrug. He raised a shoulder and let it fall in return, to indicate that he, too, had no understanding of the language.

Fidelma was aware of a dim light inside and she risked widening the aperture of the storehouse door a fraction.

The storehouse was large and almost empty.

At the far side were three men seated around a table on which a lamp was spluttering and giving an eerie low light. An *amphora*, obviously filled with wine, stood on the table with some vessels of pottery. Cornelius was sipping nervously at the vessel he held in his hand. The other two men were not drinking. In the gloom of the flickering light there appeared to be something familiar about them.

It took Fidelma but a moment to recognise the Arabians by their loose costumes and dark features.

It was clear that they were arguing in their own language which Cornelius also understood and spoke with fluency.

Suddenly one of them put something wrapped in a cloth

down on the table. He motioned Cornelius to examine it. The Greek physician bent forward and unwrapped it. Fidelma saw that it was a book. From the side of his chair, Cornelius brought forth a sack, reached in and pulled out a single chalice.

Fidelma smiled grimly.

It was obvious that some exchange was taking place and the puzzle suddenly began to clear in her mind.

While Cornelius was examining the volume, one of the Arabians was examining the chalice.

Eadulf, crouching behind Fidelma and unable to see precisely what was going on, was stirred into an exclamation of protest when Fidelma suddenly rose to her feet and pulled the door fully open, striding into the storeroom.

'Stay still!' she shouted.

Eadulf quickly stumbled into the room behind her, blinking as he took in the scene.

Cornelius of Alexandria was sitting transfixed, his face ghastly pale as he realised that he had been discovered.

'*Tauba*!' exclaimed one of the Arabians, starting up, a hand going to a large curved knife at his belt.

'Stop!' cried Fidelma again. 'This place is surrounded. Licinius!'

Licinius had given an answering cry from outside.

The two Arabians exchanged a glance and, as if on a signal, one of them swept the lamp from the table while the other grabbed towards the sack. Fidelma heard the table turn over in the sudden darkness. She could see the dull light outside as the door opened and she heard Furius Licinius yell in pain.

'Eadulf, a light! Swiftly as you can!'

She heard the scraping of flint and Eadulf emerged in the gloom with a candle held high.

The Arabians were gone but Cornelius still sat on his chair, his shoulders slumped. He was still clutching at the book. The table had indeed been overturned but there was no sign of the sack.

Fidelma went forward and bent to take up the book from Cornelius' shaky hands. As she expected, it was a medical tract written in Greek which appeared ancient.

'Find out if Furius Licinius is hurt, Eadulf,' Fidelma said, setting the table upright.

Eadulf glanced anxiously at Cornelius.

'I have nothing to fear from Cornelius,' she told him. 'But I'm afraid young Licinius may be in trouble.'

Eadulf moved hurriedly to the door.

She heard him exchanging words with, she imagined, the two bearers who were uncertain and confused at what was happening. She stood silently, watching the dejected Cornelius. Eadulf ordered the bearers to wait where they were.

'He can't be hurt badly for he has gone up the road chasing the two that left here,' Eadulf explained when he returned a moment later.

'Well, Cornelius of Alexandria,' Fidelma said quietly, 'you have some explaining to do, don't you?'

The physician's shoulders slumped further and he sunk his chin into his chest with a deep sigh.

Licinius returned a second later with an annoyed shake of his head.

'They are gone like rabbits into a warren,' he said disgustedly.

'Are you hurt?'

'No,' Licinius replied ruefully. 'They bruised and winded me a little when they burst out of the door. I was nearly knocked over. We will not catch them now unless this one talks.'

He prodded the Greek with the tip of his *gladius.*

'No need for that, *tesserarius,*' muttered Cornelius. 'In truth, I do not know where they have gone. You must believe me!'

'Why should we believe you?' Furius Licinius demanded, digging his sharply again.

'By the Holy Cross, I do not know why you should except that I am telling you the truth. They contacted me to arrange places of meeting. I do not know where they come from.'

Fidelma saw that the man was not lying. He was too shocked at the discovery. The brashness had gone from him.

Eadulf had picked up the fallen lamp, discovered that not all the oil had been spilt and relit it from his candle.

'Eadulf, give the good physician some wine to revive his spirits,' Fidelma instructed.

Wordlessly, Eadulf poured some wine from the amphora which, luckily, had not been broken during its tumble from the table and handed it to the Greek. The physician raised it in mock salute. '*Bene vobis!*' he toasted sarcastically, as if recovering something of his old spirit, before gulping it almost in a single mouthful.

Fidelma suddenly bent to the floor and recovered a chalice which had obviously fallen from the sack which one of the Arabians had seized when he had leapt to his feet. It was apparent that the Arabians had made sure of their loot as they fled. Fidelma took a seat opposite Cornelius while Eadulf stood at her side.

Furius Licinius, his sword still held in his hand, placed himself by the door.

Fidelma sat for some moments in silence, turning the chalice around in her hand as she examined it thoughtfully.

267

'You will not deny that this is from the treasure of Wighard? I am sure Eadulf can easily identify it.'

Cornelius shook his head in a quick, nervous motion.

'No need. It is one of the chalices brought by Wighard to be blessed by His Holiness,' he confirmed.

Fidelma said nothing for a moment, allowing the tension to build in the physician.

'I see. You were using this stolen treasure in order to buy books offered to you for sale by these Arabians?'

'So you knew? Yes; books from the Alexandrian Library,' agreed Cornelius, readily enough. A slight tone of defiance rose in his voice. 'Rare and priceless medical texts which would otherwise be lost to the civilised world.'

Fidelma reached forward and placed the chalice on the table between them.

'I know some of your story,' she said, bringing forth looks of surprise from both Eadulf and Licinius. 'Now you had best tell me all of it.'

'I suppose it matters little now,' agreed Cornelius dolefully. 'Young Osimo and his friend Ronan are dead. I am caught but at least I have saved several books.'

'Indeed you have,' agreed Fidelma. 'You left several in Osimo Lando's lodging while Ronan had another hid at his place of work. And here is yet another. And the priceless possessions that belonged to Wighard? What remains of them?'

Cornelius shrugged.

'The remaining pieces were in that sack which the Arabians took.'

'And, in return, the only treasure that you have received is old books?' Furius Licinius was incredulous.

A brightness came into Cornelius's eyes.

'I don't expect a soldier to understand. The books are far more valuable than base metal. I have Erasistratus of Ceos' work on the origin of diseases; Galen's *Physiology*, and several works by Hippocrates such as his *On the Sacred Disease*, on *Epidemics* and his *Aphorisms* as well as Herophilus' commentaries on Hippocrates.' There was a total satisfaction in his voice. 'These are the great treasures of medical literature. How can I expect you to understand what value they represent? Value beyond the mere gold and jewels that I have exchanged for them.'

Fidelma smiled gently.

'But the gold and jewels you exchanged were not yours to do so. They belonged to Wighard the archbishop-designate of Canterbury. Tell us how this came about?'

Cornelius gazed back at her, glancing slowly from Eadulf to Licinius. Then he said simply: 'I did not kill Wighard.'

Chapter Fifteen

'Let me tell you that I, Cornelius, am an Alexandrian first and foremost.' The physician swelled with pride as if this statement would explain all. 'The city was founded nine centuries ago by the great Alexander of Macedon. Ptolemy the First founded the famous library which, according to Callimachus, once possessed seven hundred thousand volumes. But when Julius Caesar was in Alexandria the main library was burnt and many of its books were destroyed. It could never be proved, but rumour had it that the destruction was caused by petty Roman spite for that great treasure. However, the library has been rebuilt and restored and during these last six centuries continues to be regarded as the greatest library in the world.'

'What has this to do with Wighard's death . . .?' interrupted Eadulf impatiently, speaking more to Fidelma than Cornelius, for she seemed to be following his discourse as if it were totally relevant.

Fidelma raised a hand to silence him and motioned for Cornelius to continue.

The physician grimaced in annoyance at the interruption but made no reference to it.

'The library at Alexandria was the greatest in the world,' he repeated stubbornly. 'I was a student in Alexandria many years ago; a student at the great school of medicine which was founded by Herophilus and Erasistratus almost at the same time that the library was founded. In that library were countless literary treasures. I had finished my initial studies and was practising in Alexandria, having been appointed as a professor in the school of medicine, when the terrible disaster overtook us and the world went mad.'

'What disaster was this, Cornelius?' demanded Fidelma.

'The Arabian followers of the new religion of Islam, founded by the Prophet Mahomet but a few decades ago, began to spread westward in a war of conquest out of the eastern peninsular where they had dwelt. Their leaders had raised a cry of *jihad*, a holy war, against all those who would not turn to the new faith, those they called *kafirs*. Twenty years ago they swept into Egypt, came down upon the city of Alexandria and burnt it. Many of us fled, seeking refuge elsewhere in the world. I managed to get a berth on a ship bound for Rome and the last sight of my homeland was of the great white walls of the Library of Alexandria being devoured in flames and smoke together with the vast treasures of man's intellectual endeavours it had once safeguarded.'

Cornelius paused and held out his goblet to Eadulf in silent instruction.

Reluctantly the Saxon cenobite poured him another drink from the *amphora* and Cornelius took it eagerly, swallowing it back in large mouthfuls. Having satisfied his thirst he continue: 'Not long ago I was contacted by a merchant, an Arabian merchant, who told me that he had heard that I had once been a physician in Alexandria and knew its library well. He had something to show me. It was the book of Erasistratus, written in the physician's own hand. I could not believe it. The merchant said that he would sell me the work, plus twelve others which he had. The sum he named was ridiculous; a sum beyond my dreams, although I am considered wealthy by Roman standards. The merchant said he would wait a while and when I could meet his price we would make the exchange.

'What could I do? I spent an entire night in sleepless thought. Finally, I confided in Brother Osimo Lando, who, like me was an Alexandrian. He had no hesitation. If we could not raise the money by fair means, then we must use foul means. We both swore that those great treasures of Greek intellect must be saved for posterity.'

'For posterity . . . or for yourself?' Fidelma asked coldly.

Cornelius was not abashed. His voice was proud.

'Who else but I, I as an Alexandrian physician, could really appreciate the wealth contained in those books? Even Osimo Lando could only see it intellectual terms while I . . . I could commune with the ages, with the great minds that inscribed their words.'

'So you killed Wighard for his treasure to provide you with the money?' sneered Eadulf.

Cornelius shook his head vehemently.

'That is not so.' His voice immediately dropped almost to a whisper.

'How was it, then?' demanded Furius Licinius.

'It is true that we stole Wighard's valuables but we did not kill him,' Cornelius protested, the sweat standing out on his brow as he stared from one to another of them, willing them to believe him.

'Take your time,' Fidelma said coolly. 'How did it come about?'

'Osimo was a close friend of Ronan Ragallach...'
Cornelius gave her a hard look. 'Do you know what I mean?
A close friend.' He repeated it with emphasis.

Fidelma understood. The relationship had been obvious
to her.

'Well, Osimo decided that we should draw Ronan into the
affair. We heard that Wighard had arrived to be ordained as
the archbishop of Canterbury by His Holiness. More impor-
tantly, we knew that Wighard had brought considerable
wealth from the Saxon kingdoms. It was exactly what we
needed. In fact, Ronan Ragallach had encountered this
Wighard before and had no liking for the man. It appealed to
his sense of humour that we should deprive him of this wealth.'

Fidelma made to speak but changed her mind.

'Go on,' she instructed.

'Everything was fairly simple. Ronan first made a survey of
Wighard's chambers, that was the night he was nearly caught
by a *tesserarius*. Ronan told the man his name was "No one",
but in his own language. Which the guard believed.'

Licinius sucked the air between his teeth in an expression
of embarrassment.

'I was the *tesserarius*,' he curtly confessed. 'I did not appreciate your friend's sense of humour.'

Cornelius' glance was expressionless.

'Poor Brother Ronan was a bad conspirator for he shouldn't
have been caught at all.'

'No crime had been committed then,' Licinius said.
'Wighard was murdered the next night.'

'Just so,' Cornelius agreed. 'Osimo and Ronan decided that
they would carry out the robbery between them for I am
well known about the palace. They decided to enter by the

chamber next to the one occupied by the Abbot Puttoc . . .'

'The room where Brother Eanred was sleeping?' Fidelma asked.

'It was the only chamber by which to gain easy entrance to the building. You see, a broad ledge runs around the courtyard from the building of the *Munera Peregrinitatis* to the *domus hospitale*.'

'I have seen this broad ledge. It leads only to the room where Eanred slept.'

Cornelius stared thoughtfully at Fidelma for a moment before confirming it.

'You have a keen eye, sister. Truly, the ledge was a means of entering the *domus hositale* unobserved. The problem was how to ensure that Saxon servant was out of the way when Osimo and Ronan committed the robbery.'

'That was where you came in,' smiled Fidelma confidently, 'and why you invited the simple-minded Eanred to your villa and plied him with drink until you thought that the theft had been committed by your confederates.'

Cornelius nodded slowly, his eyes wide with surprise at Fidelma's knowledge.

'While I kept Eanred out of the way – believe me, it was a hard task to occupy that simpleton – Osimo and Ronan made their way along the ledge to the *domus hospitale*. Osimo remained on watch while Ronan went to Wighard's chambers to see if he was asleep.'

'And Wighard was awakened by Ronan who killed him?' concluded Eadulf sharply.

'No!' snapped Cornelius. 'I have told you as much. Neither Ronan nor Osimo killed Wighard.'

Fidelma gave a warning frown in Eadulf's direction. 'Let

Cornelius tell this story in his own way,' she instructed a little sharply.

Cornelius paused to collect his thoughts before continuing: 'There was no sound in the chambers and so Ronan entered. He went softly to the bedroom and there he saw Wighard, already slain. Unnerved, he was about to leave when it occurred to him that if Wighard was dead then, the valuables were his for the taking. Ronan screwed up his courage and returned from Wighard's chambers with the sack, which he had brought in order to carry away the hoard, now filled with the precious metal cups. The valuables were heavy and cumbersome and so Ronan took one sack to Osimo, waiting in Eanred's chamber, and then had to return for the second.

'Osimo set off back along the ledge to take it to their room in the *Munera Pereginitatis* while Ronan gathered the second sackful. He brought this back to Eanred's room . . .'

'Tearing the sack on a splinter in the door frame,' Fidelma said thoughtfully, almost to herself.

Cornelius paused a moment, not understanding. Then, as she did not explain further, he continued: 'He was about to follow Osimo back along the ledge when he realised that he had not properly secured Wighard's chamber door. Lest the body be discovered and a hue and cry raised before they were ready, he set down the sack by the window, and returned. It was a foolish action for it was the very thing which caused him to be caught. As he told us the story later, he had just left the room and was starting back along the corridor to Wighard's chamber when a *decurion* of the *custodes* suddenly appeared and called on him to halt.

'Ronan had the sense to turn away from Eanred's room, which would have led the *custodes* to his companion Osimo, and he attempted to leave by the stairway at the other end of the building. But he stumbled straight into the arms of the two guards in the garden below.'

'He stood more chance of escaping through Eanred's chamber and back along the ledge,' observed Eadulf.

Cornelius stared sourly at him.

'As I explained, he realised that if he did so he would lead the *decurion* straight to the second sack of treasure and point the way after his friend Osimo. He therefore tried to escape through the gardens.'

'So what happened to the second sack, the one he had left in Eanred's chamber?' Fidelma asked. 'Where did that disappear to? I presume Osimo returned for it?'

'A correct presumption,' agreed Cornelius, in appreciation at her quick mind. 'Having taken the first sack to their office and waited for Ronan, Osimo became worried when he did not appear. After a short while Osimo made the journey back to Eanred's room. He found the second sack and then heard the commotion. Realising that Ronan had been caught, he grabbed the sack and returned to his office. At that point he decided to hide the treasure in his own lodgings. We did not know what to do but Ronan escaped from the cells the next morning, due to the inattention of a guard . . .'

'Who has now been disciplined,' muttered Furius Licinius grimly.

'And Ronan came directly to you?' Fidelma concluded.

Cornelius made an affirmative gesture.

'And you hid him?'

'The plan was to smuggle him out of the city. We would have smuggled him on a boat. But Ronan was a moral person. Yes, when it came to murder, he was moral,' repeated Cornelius, as if they would disagree with him. 'He learned that you, Fidelma of Kildare, were investigating the murder of Wighard of which he stood accused. To Ronan, theft was one thing but murder was another and he told us that you had a reputation in your own land. He had seen you once at the court of your High King in Tara. And he recognised you in the Via Merulana on the very day of the robbery and followed you for a while to make sure he was not mistaken.'

Eadulf nodded as he recalled the incident.

'So Ronan Ragallach was the Irish cenobite that I observed following us?'

No one answered his rhetorical question.

'He said that you, Fidelma of Kildare, were an advocate of your country's law courts and renowned as a solver of puzzles, a person who sought out the truth,' Cornelius repeated. 'While Osimo and I advised him against it, he decided that he wanted to clear his name with you; to convince you that he was not responsible for Wighard's death.'

Furius Licinius gave a harsh laugh.

'Do you expect us to believe that? You have already admitted your guilt in robbing Wighard. Whoever robbed him also killed him.'

Cornelius turned a pleading look on Fidelma.

'This is not true. We were not responsible for the Saxon's death. We robbed him, yes. And for a purpose of which I am not ashamed. If you are the just advocate Ronan believed you to be, you will know this.'

There was a sincerity in Cornelius' face that Fidelma found herself believing.

'And so Ronan contacted me asking for the meeting in the catacombs in order to tell me this story?'

'That was his intent. Of course, he was not going to reveal that Osimo and myself were connected with the matter. But he wanted you to clear his name.'

'And he was killed for his pains.'

Cornelius nodded.

'I advised against this meeting. Indeed, I did not know about the meeting until Osimo told me and I hastened off to the cemetery to intercept Ronan.'

'So that was why you were so conveniently there?'

'Yes. I was frantic to stop Ronan revealing anything which would incriminate Osimo and myself. I wanted the purchase of the books to go ahead. Imagine my horror when I reached the cemetery and encountered the Arab merchant and his companion hurrying from the catacombs. They told me that Ronan lay dead within.'

'What were they doing there following Ronan, if you were dealing with them by yourself?' demanded Fidelma.

'The night before his death, Ronan had volunteered to go in my place to meet the Arabian merchant here in Marmorata, and make the first exchange for the books. The merchant had sent a note with instructions which I gave to Ronan. But after the meeting Ronan told Osimo that he felt that the Arabians were following him. He thought they were suspicious about him.

'When I encountered them at the cemetery, I naturally thought it was they who had slain Ronan. Before I could question them, I was called upon for assistance for, I was told, someone had been injured in the catacombs.

'I suspected it was Ronan. I believed the Arabians might have killed him. I hurried to the main entrance and descended. You can imagine my surprise when I saw you walking towards me and, to my horror, saw that you were carrying one of the stolen chalices. Something took over in me. I drew back and, forgive me, sister, I struck you on the head and took the chalice. I searched your *marsupium* which was a lucky thing for I found the letter which the Arabian merchant had sent giving Ronan the instructions of how the exchanges were to be effected. I also took this but then I heard someone coming down into the catacombs behind me. I had to pretend that I had just discovered you in your unconscious condition. No one questioned that you had been the person reported injured.'

Fidelma was staring at him with bright eyes.

'So it was you who attacked me?'

'Forgive me,' Cornelius repeated, but without contriteness.

'I thought the figure that I saw before I was hit was a familiar one,' murmured Fidelma reflectively.

'You did not seem to be suspicious when you recovered consciousness.'

'One thing worries me, then. The Arabians were behind me in the catacombs. How were they able to get out before me and tell you of Ronan's death?'

Cornelius shrugged. 'You do not know of the many entrances and exits. A few chambers beyond where Ronan was killed is an exit which leads upwards by the cemetery gates. Had you gone that way you would have been out of the catacombs within minutes. Hence, the unknown pilgrim who raised the alarm after leaving the catacombs by another route.'

Licinius nodded agreement. 'That is so, sister. There are several passageways. Doubtless, as Cornelius says, the pilgrim who raised the alarm about Ronan also used a different passage and by-passed you on your way back to the main entrance.'

'Why didn't you go straight to Ronan?' insisted Fidelma.

'To go by the side entrance along the shorter route would immediately arouse suspicion. In fact, I had wanted to go straight to find Ronan's body but there were too many people around and I could not leave you without first taking you back to the palace. By then, it was too late. Licinius here was dispatched to the catacombs in search of Ronan's body.'

'What did you do with the letter and chalice?' Fidelma asked.

'I took the incriminating material and put it in my medical bag. I raced back to tell Osimo the news. The Arabians were obviously responsible for Ronan's death. But why did they kill him? Did they think that he was betraying them?

'It was not the Arabians,' Fidelma said firmly.

Cornelius's eyes widened in surprise.

'That is precisely what they claimed. But if not they, who, then, is responsible?'

'That we must discover.'

'Well, it was not I nor Osimo. That I can swear by the living God!' declared Cornelius.

Fidelma sat back and gazed thoughtfully at the nervous features of the Greek physician.

'One thing puzzles me . . .' she began.

Eadulf guffawed softly in annoyance.

'Only one thing?' he jested. 'This mystery gets no clearer at all to me.'

Furius Licinius was nodding in agreement. Fidelma ignored them.

'You said that Brother Ronan had encountered Wighard before and did not like him. Can you expand on that?'

'I can only give you hearsay, sister,' Cornelius said, 'I can only repeat the story as Ronan told it to Osimo and then as Osimo told me.'

He paused a moment and gathered his thoughts before continuing: 'Ronan Ragallach left his own country many years ago and travelled to preach the word among the Saxons, firstly in the kingdom of the West Saxons and then to the kingdom of Kent. For a time he preached at the church dedicated to the blessed Martin of Tours within the city walls of Canterbury. It is a tiny church, I am told.'

Eadulf inclined his head in agreement.

'I know the place.'

'One night, seven years ago, there came a dying man to that little church. The man was broken in body and spirit, dying of a sickness which took the breath from him. He knew that he was dying and wanted to confess his sins.

'By chance there was only one person at the church that night available to administer to him. It was a visiting monk from Ireland.'

'Ronan Ragallach!' The *tesserarius* Licinius blurted, impatiently following the story.

'Just so,' Cornelius confirmed evenly. 'Brother Ronan. He took the man's confession and great were the sins. The worst was that the man had been a hired assassin. What troubled him was a great sin, greater than any other, which lay on a prominent member of the church. He told the story of his crime in great detail to Ronan. How he was paid by a deacon of the church to kill his family because the deacon had no use for them. Further, the killer confessed that he took the deacon's money, slew his wife, but, seeing a way to increase his store, he took the children into a neighbouring kingdom and sold them to a farmer as slaves. The man was dying. And even as he died he named the deacon who had hired him to slaughter his family. At that time the man was then secretary to Deusdedit, the archbishop . . .'

'Wighard?' Eadulf exclaimed in horror. 'Are you saying that Ronan Ragallach claimed Wighard to have hired an assassin to kill his wife and children?'

Cornelius ignored the question and went on: 'Bound by the rule of confession, Brother Ronan blessed the dead man, for he was not able to absolve such a heinous crime, and later that evening he buried him without the confines of the church. The confession troubled him but he felt unable to confront Wighard nor tell the tale to anyone else. After a few weeks, Ronan decided to leave Canterbury and journey here to Rome and commence a new life. When he saw Wighard in Rome and found he was about to be ordained by His Holiness as archbishop of Canterbury, Ronan was so outraged that he poured out his tale to Osimo and then Osimo later told me.'

'Could Ronan have been so outraged that he killed Wighard?' demanded Licinius.

'And then killed himself by the same method?' replied Fidelma, with a frown. 'That is hardly credible. When did Osimo repeat this story to you, Cornelius?'

'On the day we had discussed the matter of raising the money for the Arabian merchant. The day when Ronan suggested that it would not be a sin to take the valuables from Wighard. I was puzzled by this remark and later, in private, Osimo told me this story by way of explanation as to why Ronan thought that Wighard deserved to be relieved of the treasure.'

There was a silence while Fidelma reflected on the matter.

'I believe you, Cornelius of Alexandria. The story you tell

is too fantastic to be other than the truth for you have admitted much criminal culpability.'

As she gazed thoughtfully at him it occurred to her to ask a question which had nothing to do with what had been discussed.

'You are a knowledgeable man, Cornelius. Do you know anything about the customs concerning the feast of Saturnalia?'

'The feast of Saturnalia?' queried the Alexandrian in surprise. His surprise was mirrored in the faces of Eadulf and Licinius.

Fidelma calmly nodded.

'In the old days it was a religious festival celebrated in late December,' Cornelius explained. 'It was a time of enjoyment, goodwill and present giving. All business ceased and everyone dressed up and had a good time.'

'Were there any special events during that feast?' pressed Fidelma.

Cornelius let the corners of his mouth turn down as if to suggest he had little knowledge.

'The feast began with a sacrifice at the temple and a public banquet was open to everyone. People were even allowed to gamble in public. Oh, and the slaves would don their masters' clothes, being freed from their duties, while the masters would wait upon the slaves.'

Fidelma's eyes shone with green fire and a smile split her face.

'Thank you, Cornelius,' she said, the solemnity of her tone betrayed by the mask of delight at the information. She stood up abruptly.

'What will happen to me?' demanded Cornelius, also rising wearily to his feet.

'That I do not know,' Fidelma admitted. 'I will make my report to the *Superista* and he, undoubtedly, will present the matter to the city magistrates for consideration. I am not skilled in the laws of Rome.'

'In the meantime,' grunted Furius Licinius with satisfaction, 'you will be placed in the cells of the *custodes* and you will not find it so easy to escape from them now as your confederate Ronan Ragallach did. Of that I can assure you.'

Cornelius shrugged. It was a defiant gesture.

'At least I have rescued several great works for posterity when they would otherwise have been lost. That is my compensation.'

Licinius motioned him to the door.

As Cornelius moved a new thought crossed Fidelma's mind. 'One moment!'

Cornelius turned back to her in expectation.

'Did Ronan or Osimo tell anyone else about this strange tale of the alleged murder of Wighard's wife and the selling of his children; of Wighard's responsibility for that terrible deed?'

Cornelius frowned and shook his head slowly.

'No. According to Osimo, Ronan told only him and he in secret. But Osimo told me for the reasons that I have already recounted.'

His expression abruptly changed as a memory stirred. Fidelma was quick to spot it.

'But you passed on that knowledge?' she prompted.

Cornelius was troubled.

'I thought it so ungodly an act, so heinous a crime, if it were true, that I worried over it for several days. Here was a man about to made archbishop, ordained by His Holiness, and yet it had been told by the confession of a dying man that he had paid for his wife and children to be slain. I could not leave it . . . even though I broke the confidence of my friend Osimo. But I told only a churchman of rank and honour.'

Fidelma felt a tingle at the back of her neck.

'You could not remain quiet. That I can understand,' she agreed impatiently. 'So whom did you tell?'

'I thought I should see if one of Wighard's entourage knew anything about the matter and could advise whether the matter could be investigated . . . I sought the advice of someone in authority who could bring the matter to the ear of His Holiness before the ceremony of ordination. In fact, it was the day before Wighard's death that I brought the matter to the attention of one of the Saxons prelates.'

Fidelma closed her eyes and sought for a moment to control her impatience. Eadulf, now realising the importance of what Cornelius was saying, stood white-faced, waiting.

'So who did you tell?' Fidelma repeated sharply.

'Why, the Saxon abbot, of course. The Abbot Puttoc.'

Chapter Sixteen

'Puttoc,' muttered Brother Eadulf, as they hurried through the grounds of the Lateran Palace towards Abbot Puttoc's chamber in the *domus hospitale*. 'It was that lying, lecherous son of a whore the whole time.'

Fidelma gave a critical sideways glance at the vehement expression on her companion's features.

'Your language does not become you, Eadulf,' she reproved softly.

'I am sorry. It is just that my blood runs hot when I think of that lascivious priest who is supposed to instruct others on morality. That he was the murderer . . . ah, but I see that it fits now as I think back.'

'You think so?' she asked.

'In retrospect, of course,' affirmed Eadulf, worried at the slightly amused tone in her voice. Was she mocking him now they had the answer, whereas he had been so blind before? Even at the start of this investigation he would have condemned Ronan Ragallach and not bothered to proceed further. 'Yes, it was obviously Puttoc all along. Although, having learnt the dark secret of Wighard, with his burning ambition to ascend the throne of Augustine of Canterbury,

Puttoc decided to kill Wighard and claim that prize instead. Ambition, naked ambition, is the key to this entire mystery.'

Fidelma gave an inward sigh. Eadulf had a fine mind but, as a fault, he tended to pursue only one path at a time and forget that all the minor detours needed to be checked.

She found herself wondering about Eadulf. Since she had met him at Witebia she had often felt an almost chemical reaction between them. She enjoyed being in his company, enjoyed the banter and the half-serious arguments. Moreover, she was not indifferent to Eadulf's masculinity.

At twenty-eight years old, Fidelma had reached the age when she considered herself long past the age for matrimony in a society where most marriages took place between sixteen and twenty years of age for girls. It was not that Fidelma had ever consciously rejected the idea of marriage, of forsaking the temporal world for the spiritual life. It had simply happened this way. And it was not that she was without experience.

When she was in her second year of studying law at the school of Morann, the Chief Brehon at Tara, she had met a young man. He was a young chieftain of the Fianna, the bodyguard of the High King. The attraction, in retrospect, was no more than physical and the affair was passionate and intense. It ended without drama when the young man, Cian, had left Tara with another young girl; a girl who simply wanted a home and who would not pose any intellectual threat to him. For Fidelma was deep into her studies, always poring over the ancient texts. Cian was purely a physical person whose life was measured in actions and not thoughts.

As Fidelma had reflected, even the *Book of Amos* said: 'Can two walk together, except they be agreed?' Yet in spite of her rationalisation at the ending of the affair, it had left its mark on Fidelma. When she had met Cian, she had been young and carefree. Cian's rejection of her had left her disillusioned and, although she did her best to hide it, she also felt some bitterness at the experience. She had never really recovered from it. She had never forgotten it nor, perhaps, had she ever allowed herself to.

So she had put her zest for life into her studies and the attainment of knowledge and its application. She had never allowed herself to get close to a man again. That was not to say that she had refused all passing affairs. Fidelma was of her culture and did not envy the ascetics of the Faith who denied themselves such natural pleasures. Denial of one's body was unnatural to her. Celibacy was not a concept she believed in as a matter of rule; it was a matter of personal choice and not of religious dogma. But her amours were neither deep nor lasting. Each time she had hoped for more, had almost convinced herself of the sincerity of feeling between herself and her partner but each time the affair ended in disappointment.

She found herself speculatively regarding the Saxon cenobite; trying to work out the feelings of warmth, pleasure and comfort that she always felt in his presence which were strangely at odds with the clash of their personalities and cultures. She remembered that her friend, the Abbess Étain of Kildare, had attempted to explain to her once why she was giving up her office to marry. 'Sometimes you know what is right, instinctively, Fidelma. It happens when a man and woman meet and know that they understand and can be understood. The act of meeting becomes the ultimate intimacy between them, for there is no need for a lengthy friendship and gradual discovery of one another. It is as if two parts have suddenly become as one.' Fidelma frowned. She wished she could be as sure as poor Étain had been.

She suddenly realised that Eadulf had finished speaking and seemed to be expecting an answer.

'Puttoc's ambition? Do you think so?' she finally asked again. She shook her head and brought her mind back to the matter in hand. 'Why didn't Puttoc simply bring his accusations to the Holy Father? How would Wighard have become archbishop once his terrible secret was known?'

Eadulf smiled indulgently.

'But where was Puttoc's proof? He had the word only of Osimo who had it from Ronan, already a condemned thief. Without a credible witness, he would not have been able to prove such an accusation.'

Fidelma conceded the point.

'Then,' continued Eadulf, 'Puttoc also had a dark secret which was certainly known to Brother Sebbi. His own lascivious character. If he made accusations against Wighard, then counter-accusations could easily have been made against himself.'

'This is true,' Fidelma accepted. 'But would Puttoc's ambition take him to the extent of garrotting the archbishop-designate? And why kill Ronan Ragallach, the very source of the story?'

Eadulf shrugged.

'Brother Sebbi confirms that Puttoc was a ruthless man,' he said, a little lamely.

They reached the *domus hospitale* and began to hasten up the stairs.

Eadulf paused abruptly at the head of the stairs with a restraining hand on Fidelma's arm.

'Don't you think we should wait for Furius Licinius and his *custodes* to join us before we confront Puttoc?'

They had left Licinius taking Cornelius to the cells of the *custodes* before joining them at Puttoc's chamber.

Fidelma shook her head impatiently.

'If Puttoc is the guilty one, I doubt whether he will do anything to harm the two of us.'

Eadulf's expression was one of perplexity.

'Do you still doubt Puttoc's involvement after what Cornelius had to say?'

'I do not doubt Puttoc's involvement,' agreed Fidelma. 'But to what extent he was involved has yet to be proven.'

Fidelma led the way along the corridor and paused outside the Abbot of Stanggrund's room.

She leaned forward and tapped gently on the door.

It was only faint, but a sound of movement came from behind the door. Then there was silence.

'Abbot Puttoc! It is I, Fidelma of Kildare.'

There was no reply to her call. Fidelma glanced with raised eyebrows at Eadulf and slowly moved her head in a gesture which Eadulf correctly interpreted.

The Saxon monk reached forward and, gently turning the handle, threw open the door abruptly.

As they crossed the threshold, Fidelma and Eadulf were halted in astonishment at the scene inside the room.

Across the bed lay the figure of the Abbot Puttoc stretched on his back, his ice-blue eyes staring towards the ceiling in the glazed unseeing stare of death. There was little reason to doubt the cause of his death. The prayer cord was still twisted around his sinewy neck, its noose tight, almost cutting through the flesh. A blackened tongue protruded between his lips, adding to the grotesquely comic expression of surprise on his features. The hands were claw-like, grasping at the empty air and, though they had now fallen to rest by his sides, the tension in them had not abated. Abbot Puttoc of Stanggrund had been garrotted in the same manner as Wighard and Brother Ronan Ragallach.

The picture was impressed on the eyes of Fidelma and Eadulf in a fleeting moment of time.

But it was the figure bending over the corpse which caused them both to cry out almost in unison.

As they came into the chamber, Brother Eanred whirled round, his face ghastly as he stared at them. Fidelma had a momentary sensation of facing a cornered animal.

The tableau seemed to remain locked in immobility for an eternity. It was but a split second of time. Then Eanred, with an inarticulate cry, leapt across the room towards the only exit; the window which looked out on the small courtyard three floors below. But, Fidelma realised, it was the small ledge that ran along the side of the building that Eanred was making for.

Eadulf sprang across the room but the tall, ex-slave turned and felled him with one blow. Eadulf went staggering back several paces, collided with a wall and slumped down with a groan of pain.

Fidelma impulsively moved forward.

Eanred, pausing astride the ledge of the window, noticed her movement, reached within the folds of his habit and drew a knife. Fidelma saw its glint and had only a split second to throw herself to one side before it flashed silver-like across the room to embed itself into the door jamb behind her.

While she was thus distracted, Eanred swung over the sill

of the window and balanced on the ledge.

With a grunt of disgust, Eadulf picked himself up, shook his head and realised that his quarry was escaping. He hurled himself across the room but Eanred was moving rapidly along the ledge.

Fidelma joined Eadulf at the window as he was attempting to climb out. She restrained him.

'No. It is too narrow and not safe. I saw as much the other day,' she commanded. 'The plaster is old and insecure.'

'But he'll escape,' protested Eadulf.

'To where?'

Eadulf pointed at the broad ledge which Eanred was trying to reach.

'That leads to the *Munera Peregrinitatis*,' Fidelma replied. 'Eanred will not get far. No need to endanger yourself, Eadulf. We will alert the *custodes*.'

They were turning from the window when they heard the crumbling of masonry and a wild scream.

Eanred, finding the plaster of the ledge crumbling beneath his feet, had attempted to leap from his tiny perch across a space of four feet to the broader ledge. But he was too late, for the dry masonry disintegrated before he could make the jump.

With another piercing shriek the former Saxon slave plunged headlong into the stone courtyard three storeys below.

Fidelma and Eadulf peered downwards.

The head of Eanred was twisted at a peculiar angle. There was a dark stain spreading over the stones. There was no need to ask if he were dead.

Eadulf pushed himself back into the room with a deep exhalation of breath and shook his head in bewilderment.

'Well, that seems to be that. You were right all along,

Fidelma. I did Puttoc an injustice. It was Eanred all the time. The solution seemed too obvious when Sebbi told us that Eanred had garrotted his former master.'

Fidelma said nothing in reply. She drew back into the room and examined it with narrowed eyes.

He paused and scratched his head.

'But would Eanred have done this thing on his own account? He was a simple man. No, perhaps I was not wrong about Puttoc. Perhaps Eanred was acting on the orders of the abbot? That seems more likely,' Eadulf said, with satisfaction. 'And then Eanred, in disgust, turned and slew his master, Puttoc. Indeed, as he had slain his former master when he was a slave. What do you say?'

He turned to gaze at Fidelma but she was not listening. She was still standing seemingly lost in thought. Eadulf sighed audibly.

'Perhaps I'd better go and inform Furius Licinius what has happened here?' Eadulf voiced it as a suggestion.

Fidelma nodded absently. Eadulf could see that she was preoccupied with her own thoughts as she gazed down at the Abbot of Stanggrund's body.

'You'll be all right?' Eadulf asked anxiously. 'I mean, waiting here until I return?'

'Yes, yes,' she replied vaguely, not looking up as she examined the corpse.

Eadulf hesitated and then shrugged, leaving her to go in search of Furius Licinius. Already he could hear the faint cries of concern from outside the building. People had begun to gather in the courtyard below around Eanred's body.

Left alone, Fidelma continued her examination of the body of Puttoc. There was something which she had registered in her first sight of the body which had been pushed to one side by the immediate excitement of Eanred's attempted flight.

She closed her eyes and conjured back the memory. Eanred had been crouched over the body. Crouched over it, trying to prise something out of one of the dead claw-like hands of the abbot. Yes, that was it. She opened her eyes and bent down to examine the hand. Clutched in it was a piece of torn cloth. There was something else. Still pinned to the cloth was a bent piece of copper. It had once been part of a brooch, copper and some red glass.

Fidelma managed to prise it loose after a few minutes. Where had she seen the brooch before? Then she remembered. Slowly a smile of satisfaction crossed her features. At last everything began to fall into place.

She was still standing in the middle of Puttoc's chamber, the object clutched in her hand, when Eadulf returned with Furius Licinius.

'So,' Licinius grunted happily, 'we have finally made a solution to this mystery.'

'Indeed we have,' agreed Fidelma, with firm assurance. 'Has Cornelius of Alexandria been placed in the cells here?'

The *tesserarius* affirmed that he was.

'Then I must see him a moment. In the meantime, Furius Licinius, would you request the military governor, *Superista* Marinus, to request that Bishop Gelasius invite Abbess Wulfrun, Sister Eafa and Brothers Sebbi and Ine to his *officium*? You should tell Marinus that the invitation is mandatory, lest the Abbess start objecting.'

'Very well,' the young officer of the guards agreed.

'Excellent. You go with him, Eadulf. I will see Cornelius and attend shortly. Then, when we have all gathered, I shall explain the mystery in its entirety. And what a tale of evil and vengeance is here, my friend.'

With an abrupt grimace of repugnance, she turned and vanished from the room, leaving Eadulf and Licinius somewhat bewildered.

Chapter Seventeen

As Sister Fidelma had requested, they had all gathered in the chamber used as an *officium* by the military governor of the palace, the *Superista* Marinus. Bishop Gelasius sat dominating the group in a chair before the ornate fireplace, his elbows resting on its arms and his hands fingertip to fingertip, almost resting his chin on them as if in a parody of prayer. His saturnine, hawk-like features gave the impression of a bird of prey, watching and waiting for its quarry from beady black eyes. On the other side of the fireplace sat Marinus, looking distinctly irritable and impatient. He was clearly a man of action, unused to long periods of inactivity. To his side and slightly behind, standing with arms folded and a somewhat bland expression on his features, was the *tesserarius* Furius Licinius.

Chairs had been provided for the Abbess Wulfrun, for Sister Eafa and for Brothers Sebbi and Ine. The Abbess appeared fidgety as if bored with the proceedings. She was continually adjusting the scarf at her neck. At her side sat Sister Eafa with a slightly bewildered expression as if she did not know why she was part of the company.

Brother Ine was even more subdued, his eyes focused

intently on the floor while Brother Sebbi, seated alongside him, was looking his usual smug self. A cynical smile played over his features. Fidelma, on entering, had a momentary picture of Sebbi as a cat about to devour a bowl of cream. Of course, Sebbi undoubtedly believed that he was near to fulfilling his ambition. He had obviously reasoned that there was no one else qualified to step into the shoes of the late, but apparently unlamented, Abbot of Stanggrund.

Eadulf, who had entered the room with Fidelma, took up a position just inside the door of the *officium*. His face carried a slightly tense expression. He was surprised that Fidelma had not discussed matters with him since the death of Brother Eanred earlier that evening. That irritated him. Especially when she refused to accept that the obvious conclusion to the recent events was that Eanred was responsible for the deaths of Wighard, Ronan Ragallach and now the Abbot Puttoc. However, Fidelma had placated him by stating that her idea was just a hypothesis based on the evidence, but conclusive proof could only come about if her summation of the facts forced an admission from the person she suspected. Nevertheless, she had refused to confide in Eadulf the name of the person whom she suspected. She insisted that the same hand that had garrotted Wighard had ended the lives of Ronan and Puttoc, of that she was sure. Yet, she further insisted, that hand had not belonged to the late Brother Eanred.

As she entered the *officium* Gelasius had lifted his head and smiled wanly at her. The bishop-*nomenclator* of the Lateran Palace seemed fatigued.

'Well, sister,' Gelasius raised one hand, as if in a gesture of greeting to her, but let it fall back into position when she halted several paces away from his chair. He had almost grown accustomed to her steadfastly ignoring the Roman custom of kissing his ring of office. 'There is little need for detailed explanations. It seems that all our mysteries have been solved with the death of Eanred. It remains for us to congratulate you and Brother Eadulf on your vigilance.'

There was a mumble of approval from Marinus and the Brothers Sebbi and Ine. Neither Wulfrun nor Eafa registered any emotion.

Fidelma gazed around at the company with a humourless smile.

'It remains, Gelasius,' she said, choosing her words carefully, 'to resolve the matter of Wighard's death by revealing who killed him. For the same person, to cover up that death, has also killed Brother Ronan Ragallach and the Abbot Puttoc.'

There was a sudden tension in the room. She had their close attention now. Everyone wore an expression of shocked surprise, of uncertainty. Their eyes watched her like rabbits observing a snake. Behind one of those masks was a troubled soul, full of guilt. Fidelma hoped that her deductions were accurate but that remained to be seen.

Sister Fidelma took up a position with her back to the fireplace, between Gelasius and Marinus and facing the company with her hands folded demurely before her.

Bishop Gelasius appeared disturbed as he regarded her in silence for a moment. Then he made a rasping noise as he cleared his throat.

'I don't understand, sister? Surely you caught Brother Eanred in the very execution of the deed? I understood from Licinius that Eanred was caught actually standing over the body of his victim, the late abbot, when you and Brother Eadulf burst into the chamber. Isn't this so?'

'I need but a few moments of your time,' Fidelma said, without replying to his question. 'There have been many mysteries in the matter of the death of Wighard. Many things have happened which have obscured the reality. We must now examine them clearly and thereby separate the wheat from the chaff.'

Bishop Gelasius glanced at the military governor as if for approval, but Marinus sat stony-faced, his facial muscles apparently frozen to hide his impatience. Gelasius turned and made a motion with his hand towards Fidelma, half an invitation to continue but also an expression of his utter bewilderment.

'Very well,' Fidelma said, accepting the gesture as approval for her to proceed. 'As you must already know, there were two mysteries to be solved. Two mysteries which caused much confusion when Brother Eadulf and I first began to examine this matter because we, naturally, thought that they were but two aspects of the same single mystery. But they were, in fact, unconnected, co-existing without being part of one another.'

They struggled to follow her but were clearly confused. Fidelma began to elucidate.

'The first mystery was simple. Wighard was murdered. Who murdered him? It was the second mystery which complicated the first. Wighard was robbed of his treasure, the precious items which he had brought with him as gifts to His Holiness and the chalices of the Saxon kingdoms which were to be blessed by the Bishop of Rome. Who robbed Wighard? At first we all thought that the mystery was: Wighard was murdered and robbed. Whoever killed Wighard also robbed him. Or rather, whoever robbed him also killed him.

'But that was not the question nor in it lay the solution. The two actions were separate and unconnected.'

Gelasius inclined his head gravely as he perceived the logic of what she was saying.

'Are you saying that the person who robbed Wighard did not kill him?' His voice was heavy as he strove to emphasise his understanding of her conclusion.

Fidelma glanced at him and smiled agreement.

'Yes. Yet this was not realised at first and this wrong assumption was what held us back. Brother Ronan Ragallach and Brother Osimo Lando were in a plot to take the treasures brought by Wighard of Canterbury to Rome and use them to buy certain valuable books, once held in the great Christian Library of Alexandria. We know that the followers of Mahomet captured that Library of Alexandria some twenty years ago and with it some of the most priceless books of the ancient Greek world.

'A week or so ago an Arabian merchant arrived in Rome with a dozen of the rare medical texts which had been rescued from the destruction at Alexandria. Works by Hippocrates, by Herophilus, Galen of Pergamum and others: several invaluable books which had existed only in Alexandria. This enterprising merchant contacted one of the most distinguished medical men in Rome, a person who had been a student at Alexandria and fled the city when the followers of Mahomet captured it. That man, the merchant knew, would understand the value of the books he offered for sale. It was, of course, Cornelius of Alexandria.'

She paused. No one said anything. The news of Cornelius' arrest had already started to spread through the Lateran Palace.

'Cornelius was well placed as the personal physician to

Vitalian. However, he was not so wealthy that he could raise the ransom demanded by the Arabian. The money which the Arabian trader wanted was far beyond his means. But he coveted those books. He knew the value of these great medical texts, texts that would be lost forever to civilisation if he did not find the means to secure them.'

'Why didn't he come to us that we might raise the money?' demanded Gelasius. 'Heaven knows we have little enough money here to spare but we could have raised it somehow to rescue these works for Christendom.'

It was Eadulf who decided to add to the explanation. He spoke slowly without moving from his position behind the door.

'In a word – greed. Cornelius desired the books for himself. If he owned those texts, he would become wealthy beyond his wildest dreams. But he saw wealth not in terms of pecuniary matter. He saw the books as objects of wealth in themselves. He had to have them. He had to possess them.'

Fidelma nodded appreciatively and continued: 'He therefore took a fellow Alexandrian, Brother Osimo Lando, into his confidence. Cornelius already had a plan to rob the wealthy to ransom the books. Osimo, as *sub-praetor* working in the foreign secretariat, had information about foreign potentates in Rome and their wealth.

'Wighard and his entourage had just arrived and with a treasure which would easily meet the demands of the Arabian merchant. Between them they decided to relieve Wighard of those precious items. Perhaps Osimo was persuaded that it was God's work, rescuing great treasures from the infidels. Perhaps Cornelius did not tell him that he was going to keep the books in his personal possession.'

She paused, smiling as she saw their bewildered expressions.
'Very well,' she went on, after a moment or two in which no one spoke, 'Osimo Lando had a lover in the person of Brother Ronan Ragallach. Osimo persuaded Cornelius that he should be brought into the conspiracy. Three heads were better than one or even two, so Cornelius agreed. The idea was to steal the treasure while Wighard slept. Ronan decided to reconnoitre the *domus hospitale* to form a plan . . .'

'That was the evening before Wighard's murder,' interposed Furius Licinius, confidently speaking for the first time. 'On that occasion I nearly caught him lurking in the courtyard outside the *domus hospitale*.' He shrugged and smiled self-consciously. 'He fooled me on that occasion and escaped.'

'Just so,' agreed Fidelma. 'He was surveying the chambers. Now, at the back of the building there is another, smaller courtyard. Just outside the windows is a small ledge. But where the newer building joins the one in which Wighard was lodged, a broader ledge runs almost directly to what was Brother Eanred's room. In that new building, as luck would have it for the conspirators, was the very *officium* of the *Munera Peregrinitatis*. This was obviously the best way into the *domus hospitale* because there were palace guards stationed in the courtyard and on the stairs.

'To obtain entry, of course, Eanred had to be removed from his room. Cornelius persuaded Eanred to return to his villa on the chosen night and he plied him with drink until after the hour in which Osimo and Ronan would enter the *domus hospitale* and seize the treasure. The plan worked. To an extent . . .'

She paused and examined their expressions carefully.

Marinus was still staring woodenly into the middle distance

but Gelasius was beginning to look interested.

'To an extent?' he repeated. 'How so?'

'The plan was that Ronan Ragallach would enter the chamber of Wighard while Osimo remained in Eanred's *cubiculum*. Ronan would fill a sack and bring it to Osimo. Osimo would then traverse the ledge back to the other building while Ronan would collect a second sack and rejoin him,' Eadulf explained, encouraged by Fidelma's attitude to his first response.

'But when Ronan entered Wighard's chamber he found him dead,' Fidelma continued. 'Ronan was about to flee when it occurred to him that this did not detract from the plan to steal the precious items. There they were in the wooden chest. Ronan filled a sack, hiding the items that were not needed . . . he and his conspirators only wanted items that were of immediate monetary value. He took this sack to Osimo who went back along the ledge while Ronan returned for the rest of the goods.

'He was about to climb from Eanred's *cubiculum* on to the ledge with his second sack when he realised that he had not secured the door of Wighard's chamber. Foolishly, in retrospect for him, he decided to return. Leaving the second sack by the window, he entered the corridor and found the *decurion* Marcus Narses had found the door open. This was the very thing Ronan had feared – Narses had discovered Wighard's body. Ronan was spotted. Quick-witted, he attempted to leave the building by the stairway, leading the trail away from his friend Osimo and the sacks of treasure.'

Fidelma paused and then gave a tired smile.

'Marcus Narses himself unwittingly gave me a clue that Ronan could not have been leaving the scene of the crime directly after the murder. He told me that when he found

Wighard's body, the body was cold. If Ronan had killed Wighard but a moment before, then the body would have been warm still. Wighard had been dead at least an hour or more.'

Gelasius cleared his throat, frowning in thought.

'Why was the second sack of precious items not discovered when the search was made for the missing treasure?'

'Because Osimo, after waiting for Ronan to follow him, became worried and made his way back to Eanred's *cubiculum*. He found the abandoned sack there and heard the sounds of commotion. Realising that Ronan had been spotted he decided to take the second sack and hastened back to his *officium*. Then he removed the sacks to his lodgings and waited for Cornelius to set about the disposal of the silver and gold.'

Fidelma stood regarding them for a moment or two to gauge their reactions.

'The theft of Wighard's treasure was coincidental to his murder and nothing to do with it.'

'Then who murdered Wighard?' demanded Marinus, speaking for the first time. 'You tell us that Ronan Ragallach is not guilty? Now you tell us Brother Eanred is not guilty. Someone must be guilty. Who then?'

Fidelma glanced at the military governor.

'Do you have some water? My throat is dry.'

Furius Licinius moved hastily forward to a table on which a pottery jug stood with some goblets. He poured the water and took the goblet to Fidelma. She smiled her thanks quickly at the young *custos* and sipped slowly at the contents. They waited impatiently.

'It was the late Ronan Ragallach who presented me with an essential clue,' she said at last.

Even Eadulf was leaning forward now, a frown on his features as his mind raced over the information they had gathered, wondering what he had missed.

'Ronan Ragallach, according to Cornelius, had been happy to join the conspiracy to rob Wighard because of Ronan's contempt for the man.' Fidelma put down the goblet on a side table. 'Ronan had told Osimo a story which Osimo had passed on to Cornelius.'

Gelasius gave a sudden intake of breath; a sharp breath which startled several of those in the room.

'Can't we get to the point? Someone tells a story who tells it to someone else who tells it . . .'

Fidelma turned with a raised eyebrow and his voice trailed off.

'I can only get to the point in my own way, Bishop Gelasius.'

The sharpness of her response caused Gelasius to blink rapidly. The bishop hesitated and then raised his hand in a gesture of resignation.

'Very well. But continue as quickly as you can.'

Fidelma turned back to the others.

'Ronan had encountered Wighard's name before. Several years ago he had left Ireland and travelled to the kingdom of Kent where he had served at the church of St Martin's in Canterbury. One night seven years ago, a man came to make his confession; a man who was dying. This man was a thief and hired assassin. But one crime above all others troubled his conscience. Years before, a cleric had come to him and paid him a sum of money if the assassin would slaughter his wife and children.'

Gelasius leant forward with a frown.

'Why would a cleric do this?' he demanded.

'Because,' Fidelma went on, 'this cleric was very ambitious. With a wife and children he could not hope to be appointed in your Church of Rome to the rank of abbot or bishop. Ambition was substituted in this man's mind for morality.'

Abbess Wulfrun's face began to turn bright red.

'I cannot sit here and listen to a cleric of Kent being slighted by a foreigner!' she suddenly exploded, standing up, her hand at her throat, tugging at her head scarf.

Fidelma's eyes held Wulfrun's in a cold grip.

'The assassin carried out the cleric's orders.' She went on evenly, not turning her gaze from Wulfrun. 'The assassin came one night while the cleric was away performing his duties. He slaughtered the cleric's wife, making it appear that a party of Picts had landed nearby to pillage the area. But when it came to the children, the assassin's greed took the better of him. He could sell them for more money – the Saxons have a habit of selling unwanted children into slavery,' she added for the benefit of Gelasius. 'The assassin took the children and rowed them across the great river Tamesis to the kingdom of the East Saxons where he sold them to a farmer, pretending that he was simply a poor man in need of money. There were two children; a boy and a girl.'

She paused for dramatic effect and left them in utter silence. Then she said softly: 'The name of the cleric who paid for his wife and his son and daughter to be slaughtered was none other than Wighard.'

There was a chorus of cries of horror from the assembly.

Abbess Wulfrun's face was a mask of anger.

'How can you let this foreign girl cast such an accusation at a pious bishop of Kent?' she fumed. 'Bishop Gelasius, we are guests in Rome. It is your duty to protect us from such venom.

Moreover, I am not unconnected with the royal family of Kent. Have a heed that these aspersions do not bring the wrath of our people on Rome. I am a princess of the Saxon kingdoms and I demand . . .'

Gelasius was looking worried.

'You must choose your words carefully, Fidelma,' he advised hesitantly.

'Is that enough to rebuke this foreigner?' Wulfrun continued to shout. 'I would have her whipped for such insolence to the memory of the pious archbishop. It is an insult to the royal house . . .'

Fidelma suddenly smiled directly at her.

'*Io Saturnalia!*' she said almost under her breath.

The abbess stopped in mid-flow and looked puzzled.

'What did you say?' she demanded.

Even Eadulf was not sure what Fidelma meant. He tried to remember why Fidelma had been so interested in the pagan Roman feast of Saturnalia.

'There was once a Saxon princess who had a female slave of whom she was fond,' began Fidelma conversationally, as if changing the subject. 'When the princess was betrothed to a neighbouring king, she, naturally, moved her household to that kingdom. The princess was very pious and wanted to involve herself in the good works of Christendom within that kingdom. She founded an abbey on a little island – it was called the island where the sheep are kept – and it occurred to her to free her female slave and appoint her as abbess. She had been very close to this female slave . . . almost as close as a blood sister.'

Wulfrun's face was now the colour of snow. Her hand was clutched around her neck. Her eyes were wide with horror as she gazed at Fidelma. There was no sound; no movement as the abbess stood watching the Irish religieuse.

The spell was broken by Gelasius who, like most of the others in the room, had no understanding of what Fidelma was talking about. Only Brother Ine sat smiling in enjoyment of the abbess' discomfiture.

'This is a laudable tale,' Gelasius said irritably. 'But what has it to do with the matter we are examining? How many freed slaves have made their way to greatness within the church? It is surely not a matter for comment, least of all in the middle of our deliberation about Wighard.'

'Oh,' Fidelma pursed her lips, her sparkling eyes never leaving the unfathomable orbs of the abbess. 'I merely wanted to add that the sin of pride can destroy the best intentions. On the feast of Saturnalia, I am told it was the custom for slaves to dress in the clothes of their masters and mistresses. This freed slave had been generously called "sister" by her mistress and she tried to make that a reality for she felt ashamed of her slave's background. But the result was that she treated everyone around her as slaves, pretending a royal rank, instead of treating everyone with justice and humility.'

Eadulf swallowed with amazement as he slowly realised what the meaning of the curious by-play with Wulfrun meant. He examined the haughty abbess with a new light as the tall woman sat back on her chair abruptly, her eyes bulging with a terrified expression.

So Wulfrun had been a slave? She had always fingered the scarf at her neck nervously. Would the removal of that scarf reveal the scars left by a slave's collar? Then Eadulf turned back to Fidelma wondering how she would follow up this revelation, but it seemed none of the others had understood what Fidelma had meant; certainly not Gelasius.

'I am having difficulty following this,' Bishop Gelasius was saying. 'Can we return to the assassin who told Ronan Ragallach this story?'

Fidelma nodded emphatically.

'By all means. Ronan heard the man's confession before the assassin died. Shortly afterwards Ronan left the kingdom of Kent and came to Rome. He never betrayed that confessional or the name of the cleric who had sought a position in the church by the destruction of his family. That was until he saw Wighard here in Rome and not only as a mere pilgrim, but archbishop-designate of Canterbury, an honoured guest of the Holy Father, lauded and about to be ordained by him. Ronan felt that he could no longer keep the terrible secret to himself. So he told Osimo Lando, who was his *anam chara*, or "soul friend" as you would call it. In our church, you see, we confess our sins and problems to "soul friends" but Osimo Lando was also Ronan's lover. It was that confession which led to a terrible vengeance being visited on Wighard.'

Fidelma paused to take another sip of water.

'The next step was when Cornelius sought Osimo's assistance for his plan. Osimo asked that Ronan should be brought into it for he knew Ronan would not have any scruples about relieving Wighard of his wealth. When Cornelius asked Osimo to explain, Osimo could not keep Ronan's secret and he told Cornelius in order to explain why Ronan would come happily into the conspiracy.'

'And Cornelius felt obliged to tell Puttoc,' interrupted Eadulf, leaping ahead. 'Cornelius felt it was sacrilege that such a man could benefit by high office in the church and he urged Puttoc to protest to the Holy Father . . . as if Puttoc would need to be urged. Puttoc himself coveted the archbishop's throne at Canterbury.'

Gelasius stared at him for a moment and then turned to Fidelma with a look of understanding.

'You see, Gelasius,' Fidelma went on, before he could speak, 'I realised that you had been informed that Wighard had been married because you told us so yourself.'

Gelasius nodded slowly as he remembered. 'Abbot Puttoc told me that Wighard had been married with two children. He presented the information as something which might debar Wighard from the episcopacy of Canterbury. When the matter was taken up with Wighard, he offered me assurances that his wife and children had died many years ago in a Pictish raid on the Kentish kingdom.'

'Doubtless Puttoc would not have let the matter remain there. He would have eventually revealed more of the information Cornelius had supplied him with,' Eadulf said.

'But events overtook him,' Fidelma pointed out. 'And here we have one of those coincidences which happen in life more frequently than they are given credit for.'

Her eyes were resting on Sebbi. The Saxon cenobite suddenly smiled as realisation came to him. He threw back his head and chuckled. His merriment caused the others to stare at him in surprise.

'Surely you don't mean that Puttoc had saved Wighard's son from a hanging?' he chortled, trying to control his humour.

Fidelma regarded him in seriousness.

'The assassin, having sold Wighard's children into slavery in the kingdom of the East Saxons, had departed back to Kent. The children grew up as slaves on the farm to which they had been sold. The assassin confessed to Ronan Ragallach the name of the farmer who had bought them. I shall, at this time, write down that name and give it into the safe keeping of the *Superista*, Marinus.'

She gestured to Eadulf whom she had advised to bring clay tablets and stylus. He handed them to her. She wrote rapidly and handed the tablet to Marinus, telling him not to examine it. Then she turned back to Sebbi.

'Sebbi, I want you to repeat for the company the story you told me about how Puttoc bought the freedom of Brother Eanred. How Eanred had garrotted his master and was about to be hanged.'

Brother Sebbi quickly explained the story in roughly the same words as he had originally told Fidelma.

'So,' concluded Fidelma, 'Eanred had been raised on a farm as a slave with his sister ever since he was four years old. When Eanred's sister came to puberty and their master, the farmer, raped her, Eanred garrotted him. Only Puttoc's intervention freed him from the inevitable consequence under Saxon law. Eadulf will hand you a clay tablet, Sebbi. I want you to write down the name of the farmer who was killed by Eanred. Then give the tablet to Marinus.'

With an air of curiosity, Sebbi did as he was bid.

'Does this charade lead anywhere?' demanded Marinus gruffly as he accepted the second tablet.

'In a moment, we will come to a conclusion,' Fidelma assured him.

'Your conclusion being,' interposed Gelasius, 'that Eanred was the son of Wighard.'

It was Eadulf who responded with positive eagerness to affirm the conclusion.

'That being so,' Gelasius said, 'then surely Eanred was the killer?'

Fidelma looked annoyed.

'It is true that the names written on those tablets will demonstrate that the farmer to whom Wighard's children were sold and the farmer Eanred slew were one and the same. Thus Eanred was Wighard's son. However, it does not mean that Eanred was the slaughterer of his father or of Ronan and Puttoc.'

'Then I don't see . . .' began Gelasius, raising his hands helplessly.

'Patience, bishop,' insisted Fidelma, 'for we are nearly through.'

She turned to the Abbess Wulfrun, standing in front of her and staring down at her pinched, white face.

'Do you think these written names will reveal one and the same person, Abbess of Sheppey?' Fidelma asked innocently.

'How would I know?' grated the woman, but she was somehow deflated, all her pomp and arrogance had vanished.

'How indeed?' wondered Fidelma. 'You were raised in the kingdom of the East Saxons, weren't you?'

All eyes turned on the abbess with curiosity.

'Yes. I am . . . I was . . .'

Eadulf suddenly saw where Fidelma's previous talk about Saturnalia was leading them. He stared at Wulfrun in surprise. Wulfrun, a former slave. Wulfrun . . . the lost sister of Eanred?

'Are you saying that Wulfrun is . . .?' he began.

Wulfrun was about to rise from her chair, her face contorted in consternation when Fidelma abruptly turned away from her.

'As I said earlier, Wighard had two children,' she explained, 'a son and a daughter.'

'I am not . . .' cried Wulfrun, reaching forward as if to catch Fidelma and her headdress fell from her neck, where she had been fondling it. There was a telltale scar around her neck. The mark of a slave collar.

But Fidelma was ignoring Wulfrun. Instead her bright eyes were resting on the dowdy figure of Sister Eafa.

'You were a slave on a farm, weren't you, Eafa?'

The girl blinked but made no reply.

'I will not insist that you remove your headdress, Eafa. Simply confirm what I know we will see there. Like Wulfrun, you bear the scar of a slave collar, don't you?'

The light-brown eyes of the girl were peculiarly animated. They stared at Fidelma with a strange fire.

'If you know, why ask? Yes, I was raised as a slave on a farm in the land of the East Saxons.'

'And it was on that farm that the Abbess Wulfrun found you and bought your freedom, taking you to her abbey on Sheppey to be a servant to her.'

The anchoress simply shrugged.

'Would you like to tell us the name of the owner of that farm and its location?' Fidelma asked. 'Or should we ask Abbess Wulfrun here?'

Sister Eafa bit her lip. Then she said quietly, 'It . . . it was the farm of Fobba, at Fobba's Tun.'

Fidelma's features broadened into a smile.

'Marinus, would you mind reading the name on the two tablets you hold?'

The military governor took up the two tablets and, squinting, read them out, 'Fobba of Fobba's Tun.'

'Because she was raised on the farm of Fobba, it does not necessarily mean anything more than that,' interposed Wulfrun, trying to recover some of her lost authority.

'But it does, for Eafa herself told me during questioning

that she was originally from Kent, taken to the land of the East Saxons as a child. She neglected to say that she was taken there as a slave. She is Eanred's sister and the daughter of Wighard.'

The girl raised her head, her eyes blazing with anger.

'It is no crime to have been Eanred's sister.'

Fidelma smiled sadly.

'No, that was no crime. And if the similarity of the light-brown eyes you share with Eanred were not proof enough, I think I knew that you were brother and sister when I saw you in intimate conversation in the chapel of Helena. The way you embraced . . .'

'Eafa was the woman in the chapel?' cried Furius Licinius, astounded. 'But you did not say you recognised her.'

'It was you, wasn't it, Eafa?' pressed Fidelma.

Eafa shrugged. Her expression admitted the truth of what Fidelma said.

'I suspected as much, but I was not sure,' Fidelma sighed. 'When a brother and sister kiss it is different from a lover's kiss. Eanred was protective of his sister, wasn't he? Kind and anxious to keep you safe. When your mother had been slain and the two of you sold into slavery, he had assumed the role of your protector. He stood near you while you both grew from childhood into young adults. When Fobba raped you, he demanded an eye for an eye. Only Puttoc's intervention saved him from the gallows and he was taken off to Stanggrund. You never saw him again until you arrived in Rome.'

'That is true. I will not hide it,' confessed the girl with quiet dignity. 'But where is the crime?'

'You continued to work on the farm for the heir of Fobba until, as the fates would have it, some months later Abbess

Wulfrun came by looking for an intelligent slave to take to her abbey, someone who would obey her readily. She bought your freedom.'

Fidelma glanced at Abbess Wulfrun who was sitting shaken and bewildered. Her glance demanded verification and Wulfrun gave it with a curt nod.

'I did not know that Eafa was the daughter of Wighard,' she added in a confused tone.

'Of course not. But then neither did Eafa at this time,' agreed Fidelma. 'In fact, both Eanred and Eafa had been raised with such a dim memory of their past that neither knew that they were the children of Wighard nor that their father had ordered them to be killed, together with their mother, simply to enhance his career within the church.'

'Then how . . .?' began Marinus.

'Will you tell us when and from whom you first learnt about your dark secret, Eafa?' asked Fidelma, cutting the *Superista* short.

The young religieuse stuck out her chin defiantly. Fidelma took this to be a negative. She waited a moment more and then went on: 'Abbot Puttoc was a highly intelligent man but he had one fault. He indulged in what Rome would call the sins of the flesh. His greatest sin was forcing his attention on women whether they desired that attention or not.'

Eafa was looking really shaken now as she struggled to keep calm.

'He knew Eanred's story, and how he had killed his master to protect his sister. Puttoc knew that Eanred's master had been Fobba of Fobba's Tun. From something which Wulfrun dropped in conversation he had also placed Eafa at Fobba's Tun and he realised that she was none other than Eanred's sister . . .'

'But how could they be linked to Wighard?' demanded Sebbi, intervening in the conversation.

'Simple,' Fidelma replied. 'Ronan Ragallach knew the name of the man who had bought Wighard's children. He told Osimo, who then told Cornelius and Cornelius . . .'

'Told Puttoc!' ended Eadulf triumphantly.

'And Puttoc told you, didn't he, Eafa?' demanded Fidelma, turning to gaze down at the girl, whose face was working with a strange variety of emotions. 'Shall I tell you why?'

The girl suddenly exploded in anger at Fidelma. Her whole frame and being was transformed into a raging fury.

'No need. He attempted to seduce me and when I rejected him the pig became angry and told me all about . . . all about, my *father*!' The last word was spat out like unpalatable venom.

'So you knew Wighard was your father?' demanded Gelasius in amazement.

'I challenged Wighard that evening after the *cena*. I waited until he was walking in the garden alone and I challenged him to deny it . . .'

'I saw you there,' Brother Sebbi agreed, 'but did not recognise you, only Wighard.'

'What happened?' Fidelma urged the girl. 'Did he deny it?'

'He seemed shocked. But he recovered and told me to come to his chambers later that evening,' Eafa replied. 'He did not deny or confirm it.'

'But you knew,' insisted Fidelma. 'You knew that Wighard was your father and you told Eanred. It was not the first time that Eanred had garrotted someone on your behalf. Eanred kept that appointment, didn't he? He went to Wighard's chamber and killed him before he went on to the Colosseum.'

She turned with assurance to Bishop Gelasius.

'Eanred had garrotted Fobba and now he garrotted his own

father, Wighard, because of what Wighard had done to his mother and to Eafa and himself.'

'And then he killed Ronan Ragallach in the same way,' interposed Eadulf, suddenly seeing the line of thought. 'Puttoc had told Eafa that the information had come from Ronan Ragallach and neglected to mention that it had come by way of Osimo and Cornelius. Therefore, Eafa thought that Ronan was the only other person to know . . . apart from Puttoc. At her behest, both Ronan and Puttoc were also garrotted by her brother!'

He ended with a smile of triumph at the final simplicity of the matter. Then he realised the weakness of the deduction. Eanred had gone to the Colosseum after the evening meal. He had then remained with Cornelius drinking. Ine had seen Wighard much later. Eanred could not have . . .

He saw Fidelma was grinning at him and suddenly knew she was laying a trap.

'No! That is not true!'

Eafa's vehement cry was so strong that they all turned to look at her. She was standing now, her frail body trembling.

'My brother Eanred was a kind person. He was simple and believed in the sacredness of life. He loved animals and would do anything for the people he met. He would do anything for me . . .'

'Even kill?' sneered Licinius. He turned to Gelasius. 'I think you have been presented with the true facts . . .'

'Stop!' It was Abbess Wulfrun whose piercing shriek caused them to start in consternation. Momentarily distracted by her, they now turned back to see Eafa slipping to the floor as if in slow motion. A bright red stain was spreading rapidly across the front of her *stola*.

Fidelma reached forward hurriedly and caught the girl as she reached the floor.

The haft of the knife clutched into Eafa's bosom told its own story.

Wulfrun was moaning softly, completely in shock.

'Why?' demanded Fidelma, as they moved forward in a semicircle around the girl.

Eafa blinked and tried to focus on Fidelma. Her face grimaced in pain.

'Bless me . . . for I have sinned . . .'

'Why did you do this?' urged Fidelma again.

'To save Eanred's soul,' grunted the girl.

'Explain yourself,' Fidelma pressed gently.

Eafa started to cough blood.

'I am not afraid . . .' she whispered. Then her brown eyes suddenly cleared and focused. 'You were wrong, Fidelma. You see, I went to his room that night.'

'So it was the girl he was expecting,' muttered Ine, hovering at the back of the circle. 'That was why he did not want my help that night to prepare for bed.'

It was clear that Eafa had not long before death took her.

'You went there?' Fidelma asked, turning back to Eafa. 'You went to see Wighard?'

The girl had another spasm of coughing.

'I did . . . Again, I told him what I knew. I told him that Eanred and I were his children and that we knew that he had paid to have us and our mother slain.'

'Did he deny it?'

'I . . . I might . . . might have stood it if he had. But he confessed all. He burst into tears and turned and knelt by his bed. Oh . . .' she coughed again. 'Oh, if he had begged my forgiveness, or the forgiveness of Eanred or the shade of my mother. But, no. He started begging God to forgive him. While I stood there, his own daughter whom he denied, he knelt and begged God to forgive him. He had his back to me. He knelt in prayer by the bed. It seems . . .' A racking cough interrupted her speech. 'It seemed that God showed me the way. Quietly I took up his prayer cord and, before he even suspected anything, he was dead.'

Even with her dying breaths there was a grim satisfaction in her voice.

Gelasius gazed in wide-eyed disbelief.

'How could you, a slight girl, garrotte a grown man?'

Eafa's eyes were unable to focus now. The blood was a large pool at her side. Nevertheless, a faintly vicious smile played around her lips.

'I was a slave on a farm. I grew up knowing how to slaughter animals. If you can garrote a pig when you are twelve, there is nothing to killing a man.'

Her body heaved and she coughed again.

Fidelma bent forward quickly.

'Sister, there is not much time. If you killed Wighard, did you also kill Ronan Ragallach?'

The dying girl nodded agreement.

'For the reason you gave earlier. Puttoc made no mention of any others knowing the secret. Only Ronan Ragallach. I killed the Irish monk thinking he alone shared the terrible secret of my father with Puttoc.'

'But how did you know how and where to find Ronan Ragallach when the entire band of *custodes* had been unable to find him?' demanded Licinius. 'Surely you had never even seen Ronan Ragallach?'

Eafa grimaced, half in amusement, mostly in pain.

Fidelma spoke for her.

'You were at the cemetery. You were there with the abbess. I thought I heard her voice when I was recovering consciousness.'

Eafa smiled wryly.

'It was pure chance. The abbess wanted to take flowers to Wighard's grave. I recognised the Irish monk.'

'How could you recognise him?' demanded Licinius.

It was Eadulf who replied.

'She recognised him as the same man who had asked questions about Wighard on the morning of the murder. Eafa had been stopped by Ronan outside the *domus hospitale*. She realised later that he was Ronan Ragallach by the description issued.'

'It was a mistake for Eafa to have told us of her first encounter with Ronan,' Fidelma said. 'When she saw Ronan she slipped away from the abbess and simply followed him into the catacombs and . . .' She shrugged.

'You are right, Fidelma,' Eafa confirmed, her sentence ending in a paroxysm of coughing.

'And Puttoc?' pressed Fidelma.

Eafa's eyes blazed.

'I killed Puttoc, also. Puttoc was a pig. He attempted to rape me as Fobba had done. He deserved to die for that alone but he also shared my father's secret. I think that when I went to his *cubiculum* this afternoon, he was beginning to suspect . . .'

Eadulf, kneeling by the girl's head, was astounded.

'Then what was Eanred doing when we entered Puttoc's chamber? It seemed to us that he had done the deed. If he had not, why did he flee?'

Fidelma glanced up at him.

'When Eafa was killing Puttoc the abbot grasped a piece of her dress, a dress containing a brooch which she had bought here in Rome,' Fidelma explained. 'When she returned to her own chamber, she discovered it missing. Realising that it would link her with the killing, she asked her brother Eanred to go and retrieve it from Puttoc's chamber before his body was discovered. Unfortunately for Eanred we entered and caught him in the act, not of murdering Puttoc but of trying to hide his sister's culpability.'

Eadulf stared at her in horror.

'You *knew*?' he said accusing. 'You knew it was Eafa long before we came here?'

'I began to suspect Eafa entered the story a long time ago. Even from the first meeting with Eanred, when Eanred called Eafa *my* sister. Initially I thought it was a slip of the tongue and he meant sister in the religious sense. Then I realised that he meant that Eafa was his sister in flesh and blood terms and not simply a spiritual one.'

Eadulf grimaced, annoyed that he had been left to follow a false trail.

'Well, it could have been Eanred,' he said in order to justify himself. 'After all, Eanred had killed for his sister before. Don't forget he had garrotted Fobba of Fobba's Tun.'

A low sigh shuddered through the body of the dying girl.

'I . . . not Eanred . . . not Eanred who garrotted Fobba . . . Fobba raped me . . . I killed the pig . . . like a pig . . . There is no blood on Eanred's hands.'

The skin of Eafa was mottled and her lips gave a curious jerk. There was a rattle of breath deep within her throat and then she was still. Even as they watched they saw the strange mottling of blood was clearing and the skin was taking on a yellowing, waxy hue.

Fidelma reached down and closed the girl's eyes and then genuflected.

'*Requiem aeternam dona ea, Domine...*' she began solemnly. And one by one they began to join in the prayer for the dead, their voices rising and falling in cadences but not quite in unison.

Chapter Eighteen

The sun was uncomfortably high in the heavens, blazing down with that curious white light which seemed to reflect even against darker objects as well as the vivid whites of the Roman buildings. Fidelma sat under the shade of a rough canvas awning on the wooden quay near the Bridge of Probi which spanned the muddy waters of the stately Tiber. Behind her, the steeply rising slope of the hill of Aventinus threw a slight shadow but one which failed to reach the exposed banks of the river.

Beside her, though standing and now and again pacing awkwardly in scarcely concealed agitation, was Eadulf.

'At what hour did you say that the boat would arrive?' Eadulf demanded, and not for the first time.

Fidelma did not rebuke him but meekly said, as she had done several times previously: 'At the noon hour, Eadulf. We are the first to arrive. The boatman has to take several people down river to Ostia and Porto.'

Eadulf was obviously worried.

'But is it wise to be travelling alone?'

She shook her head.

'Nothing will happen to me before I reach Ostia. And in

Ostia I shall meet with my compatriots from Columbanus' house of Bobbio who are travelling back to Ireland. We shall all make the journey together to Marsillia and from there continue to Ireland.'

'Are you sure that you will meet them in Ostia?' demanded Eadulf.

She smiled at his fussing. He had insisted on accompanying her from the house of Arsenius and Epiphania, across the city to the quay. There had been a strange awkwardness between them these last few days since the resolution of the mystery of Wighard's death.

'Must you go?' Eadulf suddenly blurted.

Fidelma shrugged expressively.

'Yes,' she replied simply. 'I must go home. Now that the Holy Father has approved and blessed the Rule of my house, I can return to Kildare with my mission complete. Also, I have letters to deliver to Ultan of Armagh.' She paused and examined Eadulf's features reflectively. 'How long do you think that you will remain in Rome now?'

It was Eadulf's turn to spread his arms in a gesture of ignorance.

'It may even be several years before we are ready to commence the journey back to Canterbury. There is much to instruct the new archbishop on.'

Fidelma's eyes widened for she had not heard anything about the appointment.

'So Vitalian has appointed a new archbishop of Canterbury, after all? I wondered why you were locked away in meetings all yesterday afternoon. I thought I would be departing before I saw you again. Is it Abbot Hadrian of Hiridanum who has been appointed?'

Eadulf shifted his weight uncomfortably from one foot to another.

'No one is supposed to know, just yet. But . . .' he punctuated the sentence with his hand. Then he lowered his voice to a confidential tone. 'No, it is not Hadrian. He refused to accept Vitalian's nomination. At first he recommended another abbot called Andrius but he was apparently too ill to accept the office.'

'So? Who has been chosen? Don't tell me that Brother Sebbi . . .?'

Eadulf chuckled warmly.

'No, not Sebbi. It is an elderly Greek monk from Tarsus named Theodore who has been a refugee in Rome these last four years. Tarsus fell to the Arabian followers of Mahomet and he was forced to flee here for safety.'

Fidelma was surprised.

'A Greek? Of the Eastern tonsure?'

Eadulf smiled knowingly.

'I thought you would see the irony of that. But Theodore has promised to convert to Rome after instruction.'

'Your Saxon kings and prelates are not going to like this one bit,' Fidelma pointed out. 'Particularly our friend Wilfrid of Ripon.'

Eadulf agreed.

'And that is why we will be in Rome for some time. Vitalian has appointed Hadrian to instruct Theodore in the ways of Rome. Furthermore, Hadrian has been appointed companion to Theodore when he goes to Canterbury, lest Theodore start to introduce Greek customs into the Saxon kingdoms, customs that will be little different from the observances of the church of Columba.'

Fidelma was grinning mischievously.

'Now that would be something, Eadulf. The decision of Witebia in favour of Rome being overturned by a Roman appointed bishop.'

Eadulf saw her point but was serious.

'As you say, there will be many who will not like this appointment.'

'What of Brothers Sebbi and Ine?'

'Ine has agreed to become Theodore's personal servant and Sebbi will remain here for a while before returning to become Abbot of Stanggrund, as his ambition always desired. He wants for nothing more.'

Fidelma cast a quick glance at Eadulf.

'And you?'

'Me? I have promised Vitalian that I shall remain with Theodore as his *scriptor* and adviser on Saxon law and customs. So this is why it will be a while before we are ready to undertake the return to Canterbury. Not only does Theodore have to be instructed in many things but he is only a monk. He has to go through ordination as priest, deacon and then bishop, formerly rejecting the rites of the Eastern Church for those of Rome.'

Fidelma examined the wood planking on the quay as if she were interested in it. She did not say anything for a moment or two.

'So will you remain here until Theodore is ready before you return to Canterbury?'

'Yes. And will you now go back to Kildare? Will you return there and stay for good?'

Fidelma grimaced but did not answer directly.

'I shall miss you, Eadulf . . .'

There was a movement at the end of the quay and the familiar tall, imperious form of Abbess Wulfrun came striding along. She had two nervous anchoresses in tow, who were struggling with her baggage as she gave them instructions in her usual harsh tones. Wulfrun suddenly caught sight of Fidelma and Eadulf and halted her entourage, deliberately turning her back to them. She took a position standing in the sun rather than moving under the shade of the awning where Fidelma sat.

'Pride goeth before destruction and the haughty spirit before a fall,' muttered Fidelma.

Eadulf grinned knowingly.

'She does not seem to have learnt her lesson,' he agreed. 'She obviously did not like the truth being revealed. Rather would she live in the fantasy that she was a princess and not a former slave.'

'*Veritas odium parit*,' Fidelma replied, quoting a line from Terence. 'Truth begats hatred. Yet I feel sorry for her. It must be sad not to have sufficient faith in oneself that one must invent a background to attract other people's respect. Most of the harm done in this world is due to people who want to feel important and set about trying to impress their importance on others.'

'What were the ironic words of Epictetus?' queried Eadulf, frowning as he tried to remember.

'You mean his question – "What, will the whole world be overturned when you die?" Irony, indeed,' observed Fidelma, smiling. 'Anyway, Abbess Wulfrun seems to have found her-self new acolytes to replace poor, sad Sister Eafa. I can still feel sorrow for her.'

She inclined her head to where Wulfrun was still lecturing

her two new young servants, telling them where to place her baggage and where to stand.

'She will not alter,' Eadulf commented. 'I hope that you do not have to make the entire trip in her company.'

'Ah, her attitude matters not to me, only to her.' Fidelma turned quizzically back to Eadulf, but his eyes were narrowed as he watched another newcomer striding down on to the quay. His expression registered such surprise that Fidelma turned and followed his gaze.

The figure of the *tesserarius* Furius Licinius, carrying a box under his arm, strode past Abbess Wulfrun and her group and came to a halt under the awning before Fidelma.

'I heard that you were leaving Rome only this morning, sister,' he greeted, his expression suddenly embarrassed.

Fidelma smiled up at the awkward young soldier.

'I had not thought the travel arrangements of a poor Irish sister of importance to an officer of the Lateran Palace *custodes*, Furius Licinius,' she said gravely.

'I . . .' Licinius bit his lip and then gave a stiff glance at Eadulf, who pretended to be interested in examining the rushing brown waters of the muddy Tiber. 'I brought you this gift . . . a souvenir of your time in Rome.'

Fidelma saw the young man actually blush as he pushed forward the object which was wrapped in sackcloth. It was obviously a wooden box. Solemnly Fidelma took it and unwrapped the cloth. Indeed; it was a beautifully wrought box of a curious black wood that Fidelma had seen only once before.

'It is called *ebenus*,' explained Licinius.

'It is beautiful,' agreed Fidelma, observing the tiny silver clasp and hinges, shining against the blackness of the box. 'But you should not . . .'

'It is not empty,' Licinius went on eagerly. 'Open it.'

Solemnly, Fidelma did so. Inside were arranged a dozen glass phials in velvet-lined compartments.

'What is it? Herbal cures?' she asked.

Eadulf had turned back now in interest.

Licinius was still colouring furiously as he bent forward and took out a phial, removing its cork stopper.

Fidelma sniffed suspiciously and then her eyes widened in astonishment.

'Perfume!' she breathed.

Licinius swallowed nervously.

'The ladies of Rome make great use of such fragrances. I want you to accept this as a token of my respect, Fidelma of Kildare.'

Fidelma felt suddenly very awkward.

'I don't think . . .' she began.

Licinius reached forward impulsively and caught her slender hand in his.

'You have taught me much about women,' he said earnestly. 'I will not forget. So please accept this token in remembrance of me.'

Fidelma found herself feeling suddenly sad and tears came unbidden to her eyes. She thought of Cian and then of Eadulf and wished she were simply a teenager again facing the *aimsir togu*, the age of choice, with her whole life before her. She tried to smile but it became a wry grimace.

'I will accept this gift, Licinius, for the spirit in which you give it.'

Licinius saw Eadulf staring at him and he abruptly drew himself up, his expression becoming almost wooden.

'Thank you, sister. May I wish you a safe journey back to your homeland? God go with you, Fidelma of Kildare.'

'*Dia ar gach bóthar a rachaidh tú*, Licinius. As we say in my language, God be on every road you travel.'

The young member of the *custodes* of the Lateran Palace drew himself up and saluted, before turning on his heel and striding away.

Eadulf hesitated in discomfort for a moment and then he tried to sound bantering.

'I think that you have made a conquest there, Fidelma.'

He frowned when Fidelma turned abruptly away but not before he had seen the look of anger spread across her features. He wondered what he had said to cause such annoyance. He stood clumsily as she fiddled with the ebony box of perfume before rewrapping it in the sackcloth to put with her baggage.

'Fidelma . . .' Eadulf began awkwardly. Then he stopped and swore in his native tongue.

She was so startled by the unexpected expletive that she jerked her head up in astonishment. Eadulf was staring towards the end of the quay.

A *lecticula* had halted. It was accompanied by a troop of the Lateran Palace *custodes* in their official uniforms which seemed more an echo of Rome's imperial pagan past than her Christian present. The tall figure of Bishop Gelasius climbed out and, waving his attendants aside, began to make his way alone on to the quay.

Abbess Wulfrun went hurrying to meet him. They could hear her harsh, penetrating voice from where Fidelma sat.

'Ah, Bishop; you have heard that I was departing Rome today then?' Wulfrun was greeting him.

Gelasius pulled up, blinking, as if seeing Wulfrun for the first time.

'Oh? No, I had not.' His voice was distant. 'I wish you well on your journey. I have to see someone else now.'

He hurried on by the abbess of Sheppey leaving her with an outraged expression on her arrogant features.

'Pride goeth before a fall,' repeated Eadulf softly.

Bishop Gelasius strode directly to where Fidelma was sitting and she rose hesitantly before him.

'Fidelma of Kildare,' the *nomenclator* of the Bishop of Rome's household smiled a greeting, barely acknowledging Eadulf. 'I could not let you depart from our city without coming to give you my best wishes for a safe journey home.'

'That is most kind of you,' Fidelma replied.

'Kind? No, we owe you much, sister. Had it not been for your diligence ... and Brother Eadulf's help, of course ... Rome might have witnessed the start of a terrible conflict between the Saxon kingdoms and Ireland.'

Fidelma shrugged her shoulders.

'I need no thanks for doing what I have been trained to do, Gelasius,' she said.

'But if even a rumour of Wighard's death at the hands of an Irish cenobite had reached the ears of the Saxons . . .' Gelasius shrugged. He hesitated a moment and then looked quickly at Fidelma. 'I trust that you will respect the wishes of the Holy Father on this matter?'

He seemed astonished when Fidelma chuckled dryly.

'Perhaps that is the true reason for your coming, Gelasius? To ensure that I will not embarrass Rome?'

The bishop blinked, astounded by the effrontery of the woman and then grimaced when he realised that she spoke only the truth. His anxiety had constituted the cause for the greater part of his journey across Rome to see the Irish religieuse before she left. Fidelma was still smiling and he gave her an answering smile.

'Is there no truth that can be hidden from you, Fidelma of Kildare?' he asked wryly.

'There are some,' she confessed, after a pause. Then Fidelma glanced quickly at Eadulf but the Saxon monk was intent on Gelasius.

'Well, since the matter is raised, I think it is best that the official report to the Saxon kings and prelates will be to the effect that Wighard and some of his entourage, Puttoc, Eanred, Eafa . . . that they were stricken by the Yellow Plague. The plague is so viciously prevalent that no one will question the matter.'

'We have already agreed this,' Fidelma said. 'I respect Rome's wish to conceal the truth that churchmen and women are nothing more than men and women, even bishops and abbots can be as great sinners as the meanest of peasants.'

'How else can we cause people to respect the Word of God if they have no respect for those who preach that Word?' Gelasius demanded in justification.

'You need not fear that anyone will learn the truth of Wighard's death from my lips,' affirmed Fidelma. 'But there are others involved . . .'

Fidelma casually inclined to where Abbess Wulfrun was standing, still instructing the two acolytes. Gelasius followed the gesture.

'Wulfrun? As you demonstrated, she is a vain woman. With vanity, Rome can always come to an accommodation. Likewise with ambition; and Sebbi has settled to fulfil that ambition now. Ine is of no account for he has security as servant to the new archbishop. And as for Eadulf . . .'

He swung round and looked thoughtfully at the Saxon monk.

'Eadulf,' interposed Fidelma, 'is a man of intelligence and without ambition, so he can see the efficaciousness of your proposal and needs no bribe other than explanation.'

Gelasius bowed his head to her gravely.

'As do you, Fidelma of Kildare. You have instructed me much about the women of your land. Perhaps we in Rome are wrong to deny our women a place in our public affairs. Such talents as yours are rare indeed.'

'If I may change the subject, Gelasius,' Fidelma said, to hide her embarrassment. 'There was one thing I did need from you, and I would ask whether this has been undertaken?'

Gelasius smiled broadly and nodded.

'You speak of the boy Antonio, son of Nereus, who works at the Christian cemetery selling candles to pilgrims with the old man?'

Fidelma inclined her head.

'It is already done, sister. Young Antonio has been sent north to Lucca, to the monastery of the Blessed Fridian. Fridian is one of your countrymen.'

'I have heard of Fridian,' agreed Fidelma. 'He was the son of an Ulster king who took up the religious life.'

'We thought it a fitting tribute to you, sister, that young Antonio should receive his education in a house established by one of your countrymen.'

'I am pleased for him,' Fidelma said. 'He will bring honour to the Faith. I am glad that I have been able to help that young boy.'

She was disturbed by a sudden shouting across the waters of the Tiber. A large boat was being rowed from its moorings across the river, sweeping in a semicircle from bank to bank towards the quay on which they stood.

'I believe this must be your transport, sister,' Gelasius observed.

A sudden look of panic crossed her face. So soon? So soon, with so much left unsaid?

Gelasius saw the expression and correctly interpreted it. He held out his hand, even smiling when Fidelma took it and simply inclined her head. He had finally grown used to this custom of her church.

'Our thanks go with you, sister, for all that you have done. May you have a safe journey home and a long healthy life. *Deus vobiscum.*'

He turned with a curt nod to Eadulf and strode back down the quay to his waiting *lecticula*, ignoring Abbess Wulfrun entirely, much to her chagrin.

The large boat, rowed by a dozen burly oarsmen, swung closer to the quay.

Fidelma raised her sparkling green eyes to meet Eadulf's warm brown ones.

'Well,' Eadulf said slowly, 'it is time for you to go.'

Fidelma sighed trying to quell her sense of regret.

'*Vestigia . . . nulla retrorsum,*' she said softly, quoting a line from Horace.

Eadulf looked puzzled, not understanding. She did not bother to enlighten him.

She looked slowly at him instead, trying to read the expression in his face but there were no signs that she could interpret.

'I shall miss you, Eadulf of Seaxmund's Ham,' Fidelma said softly.

'And I you, Fidelma of Kildare.'

Then she realised that there was little else to say between them.

She smiled, perhaps her smile was a little forced, and reached forward impulsively to take his hands in both of hers.

'Instruct your new archbishop well in the ways of your land, Eadulf.'

'I will miss our debates, Fidelma. But perhaps we have learnt a little from each other?'

The boat was alongside now. Wulfrun and her two anchoresses had already stored their baggage on board and taken their places in the for'ard seats. One of the boatmen had deposited Fidelma's bags in the boat and now stood waiting impatiently to hand her down.

For a moment or two Fidelma and Eadulf stood face to face and then it was Fidelma who broke the spell with her mischievous, urchin grin. She turned and stepped lightly into the stern of the boat and took a seat, half turning to where Eadulf still stood on the quay.

With a hoarse cry, the oarsmen pushed away from the quay and for a moment the boat drifted with the water and then, with another cry of instruction, the oars dipped into its brown wavelets and the vessel began to be propelled forward downstream at a rapid rate.

Fidelma raised a hand and let it fall as she stared back towards the shrinking figure of Eadulf, standing alone now on the quay. She watched until he disappeared around the bend of the river.

The oarsmen were setting up a chant to help them in their task, made uncomfortable by the hot noon day sun.

> Clouds melt away and the harsh tempest stills,
> effort tames all, great toil is conquered –

Heia ulri! Nostrum reboans echo sonet heia!
Heave men! And let resounding echo sound our heave!

Fidelma sighed gently and sat back in her seat, her eyes watching the passing banks of the great river as they sped southwards. They travelled beyond the hills of Rome and her crowded buildings, beyond the city quays lining the river, and out into the country between banks that were flat and bare, unshaded by wood and ungraced by cultivation. The river was deep and its winding course spoke of none of the beauty Fidelma had once been taught to associate with the great Tiber.

Now and then she saw a height crowned in pines but more often than not the hills were bare. There were only a few scanty patches of corn and these were thinly spread. She had to remind herself that the army of Emperor Constans had recently passed this way and the waste that surrounded the turbidly rolling Tiber was made by man and not by nature.

As she recalled, the river would eventually burst out into the Mediterranean between the twin ports of Ostia and Porto, where the river divided with its reed-veined waters around a central island, the Isola Sacra. It was not a pretty entrance to Rome, surrounded by the low-lying *stagni* or salt marshes. But Ostia and Porto were the twin ancient ports of Rome from which ships came and went to all four corners of the Earth.

The scenery changed a little and now she found herself gazing at the silver-green of the olive trees spreading over the hills as the wasted fields of once cultivated corn gave way to numerous olive groves that had survived Constans' ravages. She noticed that the silver-greens were not the deep greens that she was used to in her own land; not the luxuriant growths and shady trees which grew amidst the temperate climate of Ireland. Ireland with its fuschia-edged lanes leading down to saffron-spotted, grey granite boulders on the stony seaboard. Ireland with its broad green hills and deep, dark marshes, skirted by brambles and heathers and nettle-protected forests replete with yews, hazels and woodbine.

With an abrupt feeling of surprise, Fidelma found that she was homesick. She realised how eager she was to return, to hear her own language being spoken again, to be at ease, to be at home. What was it Homer had written? 'I know of no sweeter sight for the eyes than that of one's own country.' Ah, perhaps he was right.

She stared at the passing scenery and her thoughts went back to Brother Eadulf. She felt uncomfortable at being so sad at the parting. Was she trying to make more of her friendship with Eadulf than there had been or, indeed, than there could be? Was Aristotle right that a friendship is a single soul dwelling in two bodies? Was that why she felt something was lacking in her? She compressed her lips, angry with herself. She often tried to intellectualise her attitudes and thus avoided dealing with emotions. Sometimes she could no longer discern between emotion and rationalisation. It seemed so much easier to analyse other people's attitudes than to sort out her own. Who was it said – physician, heal thyself? She could not recall. There was an old proverb in her own language – every invalid is a physician. That was a truism.

She turned her gaze back to the passing banks of the river and their pallid green vegetation. Again she thought of the sharp contrast with the rich verdure of Ireland. She gazed back to where Rome had disappeared beyond the river's bend and thought briefly of Eadulf again.

She smiled sadly to herself. That which Horace had written was true: *Vestigia . . . nulla retrorsum* – no footsteps back. No, there would be no going back now. She was going home.

If you enjoyed this book here is a selection of other bestselling titles from Headline

CALL THE DEAD AGAIN	Ann Granger	£5.99	☐
A GHOST OF A CHANCE	Peter Guttridge	£5.99	☐
SLAPHEAD	Georgina Wroe	£5.99	☐
THE TRAIN NOW DEPARTING	Martha Grimes	£5.99	☐
A GRAVE DISTURBANCE	D M Greenwood	£5.99	☐
OXFORD BLUE	Veronica Stallwood	£5.99	☐
THE DEVIL'S DOMAIN	Paul Doherty	£5.99	☐
THE ABBOT'S GIBBET	Michael Jecks	£5.99	☐
LISTENING TO VOICES	Sara MacDonald	£5.99	☐
REQUIEM MASS	Elizabeth Corley	£5.99	☐
JANE AND THE WANDERING EYE	Stephanie Barron	£5.99	☐
WHITED SEPULCHRES	Anne Perry	£5.99	☐

Headline books are available at your local bookshop or newsagent. Alternatively, books can be ordered direct from the publisher. Just tick the titles you want and fill in the form below. Prices and availability subject to change without notice.

Buy four books from the selection above and get free postage and packaging and delivery within 48 hours. Just send a cheque or postal order made payable to Bookpoint Ltd to the value of the total cover price of the four books. Alternatively, if you wish to buy fewer than four books the following postage and packaging applies:

UK and BFPO £4.30 for one book; £6.30 for two books; £8.30 for three books.

Overseas and Eire: £4.80 for one book; £7.10 for 2 or 3 books (surface mail).

Please enclose a cheque or postal order made payable to *Bookpoint Limited*, and send to: Headline Publishing Ltd, 39 Milton Park, Abingdon, OXON OX14 4TD, UK.
Email Address: orders@bookpoint.co.uk

If you would prefer to pay by credit card, our call team would be delighted to take your order by telephone. Our direct line is 01235 400 414 (lines open 9.00 am–6.00 pm Monday to Saturday 24 hour message answering service). Alternatively you can send a fax on 01235 400 454.

Name ....

Address ....

....

....

If you would prefer to pay by credit card, please complete:
Please debit my Visa/Access/Diner's Card/American Express (delete as applicable) card number:

Signature .... Expiry Date ....